I0708675

Also by Leslie Lynch

HIJACKED

UNHOLY BONDS

Visit my website at:
www.leslielynch.com

Opal's Jubilee

A Novel of Suspense and Healing

Leslie Lynch

Copyright

Opal's Jubilee
Edited by Pam Berehulke
Cover Art by Marion Sipe
Copyright © 2014 by Leslie Lynch
All Rights Reserved

Dedication

To all who are entangled in abusive relationships:
May you find strength and courage to seek help.
And may you find peace.

A portion of the proceeds from this book will be donated to
education and prevention of domestic abuse, and to the
Women's Prison Association.

Chapter One

OPAL MCBRIDE CLENCHED her hands inside the pockets of her Goodwill prize, a five-dollar coat that probably would have stood up to the cold, but was proving no match for humidity. Bitter wind tugged a strand of her braid loose, and she tucked the errant hair behind her ear. She added another stop at Goodwill for a hat and gloves to her mental list.

Right below *find a job*.

A shiver raced up her arms, triggering a shudder unrelated to the chill.

Traffic roared by on a street barely wide enough to accommodate opposing vehicles. Louisville, Kentucky, wasn't the biggest city around, but it was more than she'd ever encountered before, and it intimidated her.

Unable to avoid a fellow pedestrian, Opal murmured, "Excuse me," as they bumped, but the woman forged on, cell phone to ear, without a glance in her direction. She took a tremulous breath and forced herself to keep walking as if the noise and bustle didn't set her teeth on edge.

She could have borne the cold, even the noise of traffic, but the people—so many of them, so loud, so unpredictable, and worse, heedless of her personal space—well, she'd had enough. She detoured off the main thoroughfare into a residential neighborhood, and ducked her head against a gust.

The farther away from Bardstown Road she got, the easier Opal's breath came. The tension in her shoulders eased and she slowed. She paused and turned in a circle, looking up to examine her new world. Louisville had trees and sky, but its hills couldn't compare to the mountains back home. Nor did sky in the Appalachians hover oppressively, like the perennial low cloud cover here. But she'd had precious few outdoor moments over the past twelve years, and she reveled in the feel of fresh air moving across her skin, no matter how dreary the overcast or biting the temperature.

A pang of homesickness for Jubilee, Kentucky, rolled through her, but it didn't last long. There was nothing left for her in Jubilee, nothing but pain, and she deliberately moved her mind in a different direction.

The wind blew a plastic grocery bag across her path and Opal bent to snag it, concerned that a small animal or bird might become trapped in the suffocating material. She stuffed it in the pocket of her coat for proper disposal later, and her fingers encountered the paper documenting her job search for the day.

She sighed. Nothing like reality to squelch her joy in walking unfettered down a street of her choosing. If she'd gotten a signature at the last place she'd sought an interview, she'd be done and heading back to the house. But no. She'd walked out after the manager leered at her chest, then indicated the back room with piggish, lecherous eyes.

She needed a job, but not that badly.

On the other hand, she really needed a job. The alternative didn't bear contemplation. A shiver of anxiety ran down her spine but Opal straightened, her resolve strengthening. *Not gonna happen.* As long as she could draw a breath of air laced with freedom, she'd keep trying. On the heels of that thought, she glanced up and noticed a worn HIRING sign in the window of a home-based sandwich shop. She stopped, her heart in her throat. Maybe this one.

But a hand appeared above the sign and pulled it out of the window. Opal's hopes sank. She lifted her gaze to the owner of the hand, a young woman who sent her a rueful smile and mouthed *sorry* through the plate glass. Opal managed a that's-the-way-it-goes shrug accompanied by a no-big-deal smile, though worry nipped at her as she turned and began her trek home.

She wondered who was working the evening shift, and whether extra signatures from the past two days would outweigh the one she was short today. Ms. Hannity would take warped pleasure in holding her to the letter of the contract she'd signed upon arrival, but Ms. Millner took a more lenient approach. *Ms. Millner, please…* She steeled herself for getting stuck with Ms. Hannity, though, as Murphy's Law seemed to dog her every step.

Sounds of traffic drifted from Bardstown Road as she approached a strip mall on the back side of the main drag. Her eyes lit on a fabric shop at the end of the line of small businesses. A tidy, hand-lettered sign proclaimed HELP WANTED. She didn't know much about fabric, but then again, she hadn't known anything about dry cleaning or fast food production from her earlier attempts today, either. She veered toward the store, her spirits brightening a little.

Chances were, no men worked here. *That* would be a relief. No "job interview" in the back room.

A little bell over the door tinkled as she entered, and soft, lively instrumental music that promised welcome lilted in the air. She caught a whiff of cinnamon, then another of coffee.

"May I help you?" A diminutive silver-haired woman glanced up from an expansive table, smiled, and set down some tools. She dusted her hands on black slacks and waited expectantly.

Opal bordered on petite, but this woman made her feel tall. For the first time in her weeklong job hunt, she was tongue-tied. She swallowed and said, "I saw the help-wanted sign. Could I apply for the job?"

She crossed her fingers behind her back, and thought *please.* The quiet and homey atmosphere of this place hinted at the promise of acceptance, of belonging. Yearning filled her heart, but Opal squelched it. No use in hoping yet.

The woman's face crinkled into a deep smile, and she extended her hand. "Welcome! My name is May. Of course you can apply."

Opal took her hand and shook it, her lips curving into a return smile.

"What experience do you have?"

At May's question, her smile dimmed. She ended the handshake, and her gaze dropped. She had to force the words out through a throat tight with shame. "None, really. Not a real job, anyway, and nothing like this."

"Oh my." May's voice held no censure, just surprise, and Opal dared glance up through her eyelashes at the woman.

Then she remembered. A few years ago, a group of women had made quilts to present to their victims. Opal had crafted one for Tommy's uncle Obie, which she was certain had been shredded and fed to the hogs upon arrival, but the process of creating beauty from donated scraps of cloth had sparked her imagination.

Afraid May would send her away, she blurted, "But I'm smart. I can learn. And I've made a quilt."

May's blue eyes twinkled with humor. "One?" She took any potential sting out of the word by taking Opal's hand. "Come. Sit. Let's talk."

Hope bloomed in Opal's chest, and she followed May to a sitting area strewn with magazines, all focused on quilts and quilting. Her face heated. "So this is a quilt shop?" At May's amused nod, Opal sighed. "I'm not trying to put one over on you, ma'am. But I do need a job, and I'm a hard worker. Dependable."

Her mind shot to the only jobs she'd ever held. While she was married to Tommy, she cleaned rooms at the local fleabag motel. Then more of the same, but for far less pay. Janitorial, until she graduated to the heat of an industrial kitchen. She'd hated all the jobs, but she could say in full truthfulness she'd worked hard, and she'd never missed a day of work.

Suddenly, this woman's opinion of her mattered, a lot, maybe even too much, and Opal hoped May would offer her the position.

"Well, Miss…" May's brow furrowed slightly.

"Oh! I'm sorry, ma'am." Heat crept into her cheeks. "My name is Opal McBride." She caught herself beginning to fidget, and forced herself to still.

May smiled. "Miss McBride, the position I need to fill is part time and temporary. My assistant is on bed rest while she awaits twins. Therefore, I can guarantee three months"—May leaned forward and whispered—"but I hope she decides to take quite a bit longer once the babies come. They are only small once, and for such a short time." She sat back, a conspiratorial glint in her eyes.

Opal kept her smile in place, though her heart dropped at May's description and definition of temporary. She needed six months, and this would not last long enough. But as Granny McBride always said, the berries within reach are the only ones you need. Opal's spirits lifted at the memory.

Then the reason for the job opening sank in, and her smile faltered. Babies. She hadn't encountered much need to think about babies for years. But a memory of the slight bulge at her waist and butterfly kicks surfaced, and she sucked in a quick breath.

Not now! She stuffed the memory and all the traumatic emotions that accompanied it into the recesses of her mind and swallowed, then nodded. "Uh, yes, ma'am, I've heard that said. Babies do grow fast."

May smiled, and her manner turned more businesslike. "Tell me about yourself, Miss McBride. Or may I call you Opal?" Without waiting for an answer, she added, "And please call me May. 'Ma'am' makes me feel old." She laughed, her eyes twinkling.

Opal's mouth went dry. Then she gave a mental shrug. If May didn't like the truth, there was nothing she could do about it. But she didn't have to start with her record. She cleared her throat. "Well, ma'am—I mean, May—I'm new in town, originally from a little town near the West Virginia border. Like I said, I'm smart and dependable." As she spoke, Opal's confidence faded. Why would anyone hire her? How could she claim to be smart when she hadn't even graduated from high school?

Maybe she wasn't as smart as she thought she was. A GED, as proud as she'd been for the achievement, didn't carry near the weight of pride that a high school diploma conferred. And the long hours of online study in entrepreneurial business hadn't translated to the value she'd expected. Neither qualification had swayed employers during her weeklong search. Nor did she think years of reading the dictionary—a distinctly oddball activity—counted toward a marketable skill.

The bloom of hope she'd felt when she first entered the store withered, and she dropped her gaze to her hands. She hesitated, then added, "I have an associate degree…" Her voice trailed off. Left unsaid was her lack of experience to go with it.

May was silent for several moments, and Opal finally gathered the courage to look at her. The woman regarded her with a gaze that combined both shrewdness and compassion.

"It sounds like you are a bit down on your luck."

Opal grimaced and gave her a slight nod. "You might say that, ma'a—May. But I promise I'll do my very best for you if you hire me."

The bell over the door jingled and Opal glanced toward it, expecting a customer, most likely female. But it was a guy in his midthirties, a shade over six feet tall and dressed in a suit he wore with the ease of a man who'd been born in one. He had nicely cut dark hair that had obviously been combed, then ignored and tousled by the wind. Blue eyes, bright and intelligent. She couldn't help noticing that he was good-looking, if she were in the market. Which she wasn't, even if the rules hadn't forbidden it.

"Hi, Mom. You about ready to close up shop and go to dinner?"

May rose and Opal did the same, feeling extraneous and oddly exposed. May and the man met in the middle of the store and embraced.

"Josh, I'd like to introduce you to my new employee."

Opal blinked. She'd been hired? And she hadn't even told May everything, an oversight she needed to remedy before things got too far along.

Josh turned to her and extended his hand. "Nice to meet you." He smiled, a dimple appearing in his left cheek. His gaze, open and friendly, lingered on her hair for a moment, then settled on her face with directness and curiosity. Well-developed smile lines, pale against tanned skin, fanned out from his eyes.

Opal took his hand, gave it a quick shake, and said, "Likewise."

His grip was strong but not overbearing, and…warm. Discomfited by that small revelation, she nearly snatched her hand from his and hid it in her jacket pocket.

His gaze sharpened and he looked at her more closely. "Do I know you from somewhere? You look familiar."

"No, sir, I'm sure I would remember you if we'd met." Opal could have kicked herself. What a stupid comeback! Nobody talked that way on the outside.

May, oblivious to Opal's unease, turned and led the way through rainbow-hued displays of fabric to a small, well lit, and very tidy office. She opened a file cabinet, retrieved a form, and handed it to Opal. "Fill this out, dear."

"Um, ma'am…" Opal knew she needed to speak up now, but wasn't particularly eager for the woman's son to be in on the conversation.

"*May.*" A hint of steel underlaid the word, but the smile she bestowed on Opal expressed no frustration, just warmth. "Yes, Opal?"

Josh made a strangled sound and Opal glanced at him. His eyes held a mixture of shock and confusion. Then, as she watched, they went hard. A muscle in his jaw worked.

Uh-oh. For the life of her, Opal couldn't figure out what had set the guy off, but his thunderous expression put every cell of her body on high alert.

"Opal McBride?" All the warmth of his earlier mien disappeared. His voice was flat, with a hint of condemnation.

She lifted her chin and stared him down, a patently losing proposition as his narrowed eyes were shooting daggers at her and he stood nearly a foot taller than her.

"That is my name." Opal bit off the part where she asked him what business it was of his. She really needed to work on her sass. It had been counterproductive in the past, and probably wouldn't help much now, either.

"Address 1753 Bonnycastle?"

The address of the halfway house. And if he knew that much, he knew what it was. Her heart plummeted to her toes.

He stepped closer, deliberately intruding into her space, and Opal's nerves started screaming. How did he know she lived there? And her name? She sucked in a breath and straightened, feeling cornered and threatened.

"Children! Stop it right now!" May's voice broke Josh's focus, and he flicked a glance at her. An unrepentant glance.

"You can't hire her, Mom."

A tremor began in Opal's fingers and spread to her hands. If she'd thought her mouth had been dry earlier, it had nothing on the Sahara-like condition of her tongue now. Her heart pounded in her chest as if she'd just sprinted the length of Jubilee's main street.

May crossed her arms. "I can hire whomever I please, Joshua." She tapped one toe, her expression simultaneously appalled, affronted, and confused.

Josh grasped Opal's upper arm and propelled her toward the door. She stumbled, then caught her balance and pulled away, but his grip was like steel.

Why is he doing this?

Panic flooded her and Opal struck out, catching him in the gut, but he anticipated the move and tightened his abs. Her blow didn't slow him down, and now struggling in earnest, she dropped her weight and shot a foot out. He tripped and went down, knocking a table of fabric to the floor. Cursing, he let loose of her arm, and she scrambled away, panting in fear.

"Joshua Braddock Boone! Look what you have done! Stop it this moment!" May's voice cut through her panic, anchoring her in a tenuous place of safety.

He rolled to his feet with the grace of a natural athlete and shrugged his jacket back into place. A blush colored his cheeks and he glanced at May. "Sorry. But you don't know who she is." He turned on Opal and said, "Were you going to tell her?"

He knows. She climbed to her feet, wary in case he took after her again, and nodded. She had to lick her lips three times before she got the words out. "Y-yes. I was trying, before you got physical."

He snorted. "Yeah, right."

Opal recognized a losing battle when she saw one. She forced the tension out of her muscles, and sighed. "I admit to a lot of faults, Mr. Boone, but I don't lie." She turned to May. "Ma'am, I don't think this is going to work out. I'll be on my way, and you can hire someone better suited. Thank you for your time and"—Opal's voice hitched—"hospitality."

She crouched to pick up and replace the fabric onto the table, but Josh stooped and covered her hand with his. Warm and strong, just as before, but not nearly as safe.

She tried to snatch her hand away, but he tightened his grip, then shifted so May couldn't see his face. Opal stilled, not wanting to make more of a scene. She flicked her gaze up to meet Josh Boone's and steeled herself to his censure, covering the roiling, vulnerable—*damn it*—emotions in her gut with the strength she'd earned through the crucible of the past twelve years.

He knelt on one knee, his face only inches from hers. "I'll take care of that. It was my fault, after all." His eyes glittered and his lips were tight, in opposition to the conciliatory tenor of his words. Then he leaned closer and added in a nearly soundless whisper, "Just get out of here and don't come back."

Opal flinched. She stood, and turning a deaf ear to May's objections, walked to the door and pulled it open. Josh's words lashed at her as the bell tinkled merrily above her.

"You can't hire her, Mom, because she's a murderer."

Chapter Two

JOSH TORE HIS GAZE from the woman who'd all but fled the store. Five feet four inches of attitude coupled with almost Victorian courtesy. Nothing she wore was provocative or revealing. In fact, her clothing was notable for being nondescript, worn, and bordering on shapeless—but not loose enough to entirely camouflage her curves. He told himself he'd noticed only because he was male, and far from a saint.

Her hair, curly and a rich, bright chestnut shot through with highlights the color of a new penny, hung in a braid nearly to her waist, and that was what had thrown him.

The mug shot they'd gotten during the briefing last week showed a scrawny, hollow-eyed teenage girl with a really bad haircut. Distracted by his notes for a trial later in the day, he'd glanced at the picture and memorized her description, only coming to full alert when the tension in the room had skyrocketed, and a wave of territorial murmurs filled the room.

Cop killer.

Granted, she'd been married to the guy, but there had been no history of domestic dispute or other extenuating circumstances. Only an unprovoked attack on a fellow cop. His condo in the Highlands wasn't far from the halfway house, and he'd already planned to keep an eye out for her. He just hadn't expected to find her in his mother's shop.

Speaking of whom…

He faced his mother, knowing he was going to get a strip ripped from his hide. Didn't matter that he was thirty-four years old. She glared at him, hands on hips, an uncharacteristic frown marring her normally smooth brow. He almost felt like a ten-year-old again, nailed for throwing rocks at streetlights. Almost.

"You don't know who she is—"

"I am ashamed of you—"

They both spoke at the same time, and Josh shoved a hand through his hair, then took a deep breath. He set the bolts of fabric on the table for his mother to rearrange, and tried to tame his frustration.

She brushed him aside and began straightening the display, her movements brief, efficient, and angry. "I don't care who she is, or what she's done. You behaved abominably toward a client, toward a *woman*—"

Josh winced. She had no clue what it took to subdue a pissed-off suspect, male or female, all of which came with his job. He'd always been able to separate that necessity from the bone-deep respect for women his parents had instilled in him. And he prided himself for never using more force than required, no matter the gender of the suspect.

"—and you did so in my shop!" She skewered him with her gaze. "I am deeply offended, and I expect an apology."

"I already said I was sorry, Mom." And he was. For upsetting her, for trashing her display, and maybe a teensy bit for manhandling Ms. Opal McBride, but only because he'd done it in front of her. Now that his initial flare of protective wrath had subsided, he could see he'd maybe gone overboard.

His mother scoffed, producing a ladylike little *pfft*, and shook her head. "Not to me, Joshua. I am not the one wronged." She paused.

Horror took root as Josh realized the direction of her thinking.

"You owe Opal an apology."

He was shaking his head before she even got the words out. Like hell he owed her an apology. "Not happening. Didn't you hear what I said?"

"What? That she's a murderer?" She waved a hand as if the information were irrelevant. "Yes, I heard, and I expect an explanation from you, but not until we can have a civil conversation."

"Oh, for crying out loud—" Josh clamped his lips over the string of blistering curses he wanted to unleash, then dipped his head while he corralled his exasperation. He looked at her, one of the healthiest and most active sixty-something women he knew, but anyone could see she wouldn't have a chance against Opal if it ever came to a physical confrontation.

He shook his head. "Mom, Opal killed a man. With her own hands. She's bigger than you, and stronger, and younger. I couldn't live with myself if something happened to you because of her."

He couldn't lay it out any plainer than that, and he hoped she would understand and acquiesce, even for the apparently flimsy reason of making him happy. He felt a bit miffed at the notion that he didn't rank higher in her priorities.

She regarded him for a few moments, then said, "I'm sure there's more to her story than you know. And she doesn't look like a harsh woman. Her eyes…she seems so genuine. And respectful." She gave a brief nod, more to herself than to Josh. "I'd still like to hire her."

"Are you out of your mind?" He ground his molars together. "She's not a stray cat, damn it."

"She's out of prison—at least I assume that's how you know her history—and she's seeking gainful employment."

He had to nod. "Yes, but—"

"There is no law against hiring her, correct?" His mother was beginning to look a little smug.

"No law, just a boatload of common sense."

When she got that particular expression, nothing would shake her from the course she'd set. *Damn her soft heart. It's gonna bite her someday.* His head began to throb, and he rubbed his temple.

"Then it's settled." She arranged the fabric to drape the way she wanted it and stepped back to survey the results.

"Over my dead body," he said, knowing full well he'd just declared war. And he'd learned everything he needed to know about being bullheaded from her. He just hadn't absorbed all her lessons on gentility, much to her dismay, and right now he was prepared to use every tactic in his down-and-dirty arsenal to keep Opal McBride away from his mother.

She turned to face him, lifted her chin, and met his gaze without blinking. "What did you say her address was? It was on Bonnycastle."

"Nope." He narrowed his eyes.

She planted her fists on slim hips. "Joshua…"

He snorted. "The full-name business hasn't worked on me since I was a kid and it's not going to work now. The whole point is to keep *you* from being a—" He swallowed the word *corpse* and scrambled for a substitute. "Uh, a case I have to investigate."

The words hung in the air between them. Her expression wavered, then firmed. "I don't believe she is violent, Josh. And I'd want to know more, of course, but she's such a nice young woman, so polite…"

"They teach 'em how to be polite in prison. At least to the authorities. Don't be naive. Opal didn't end up there because she was a victim."

Josh hesitated. The briefing hadn't been long, but the few sentences carried enough detail to demonstrate the utter viciousness of the murder. He wanted to protect his mother from the ugly reality, but she needed to understand what Opal was capable of.

He finally settled on a generic comment. "She was damn violent, Mom."

She shook her head. "I'm sorry, Joshua, I don't see that in her." She looked up at him. "I think it's best if we agree to disagree on this issue."

His molars were in danger of shattering from the pressure, and he purposely unclenched his jaw. Agreeing to disagree was not going to solve their dispute, and he feared she would do an end run around him and hire Opal. But he also realized there was no getting through her thick skull for the moment, and decided to let it go. Or at least give the appearance of it.

He reached in his pocket for his keys. His appetite had taken a dive, and he suspected hers had as well, but they both needed to eat. Dragging a meal out for an hour or so would prevent her from searching for the halfway house tonight.

"Why don't you turn out the lights and I'll warm up the car?"

Traffic was heavy on the short drive to the eclectic café she favored and saved him from further discussion. Thanks to a full restaurant and an atypically slow waitress, it was full dark by the time he dropped her at the house.

"When's Dad getting home?"

Her expression softened. "Tonight."

"Then do me a favor. Please." He was treading on thin ice, and her response could go either way. Spectacularly. But it was getting pretty close to his last-ditch direct effort. If this failed, he'd go for the more underhanded method he'd contemplated during the strained silences at dinner.

She paused, and nodded warily. "I'll consider it."

"Please don't hire Opal until you discuss it with Dad."

"A Stitch in Time is *my* business, not his."

The words popped out without any hesitation, and Josh knew he'd alienated her even further. Her eyes sparked, and she hopped out of the car without waiting for him to come around and open the door. *Uh-oh.* Spitting mad. It didn't happen often, but it was something to behold when it did.

"I would have—and still will—consult with your father, but the final decision is mine."

"Mom—"

"I am not stupid, Joshua. I will research the facts, evaluate the risks, and make the determination based on all available information." She reached back into the car for her purse. "Let it go.

You've made your case, and I will keep your sentiments in mind. But you've overstepped your bounds."

She closed the door a lot more gently than he would have, and marched up to the door. When she got it open, she turned and waved, then blew him a kiss.

He blew one back, feeling a little silly. She'd never stopped doing that, and his teammates had razzed him unmercifully over it back in his teens. But it was an endearing habit and right now, it reaffirmed the strength of their relationship.

She slipped inside, and he waited until a light went on deeper in the house, knowing she'd armed the security system before leaving the foyer.

He sighed and dropped his forehead to the steering wheel. After a moment he lifted his head, checked for traffic, and pulled out. His gaze flicked to the dashboard clock. A few minutes after seven. *Not too late.*

Ten minutes later, he rang the doorbell of the halfway house. Every light in the place was on, and he could hear faint strains of classical music from behind the sturdy door. Seconds stretched into a minute, and he rang the bell again. It chimed over the music, and finally he heard someone working their way up the hallway. He unclipped his badge and held it up to the peephole. After a brief pause, he heard the sounds of the dead bolt being thrown. The door swung open, but only a few inches. An overweight, middle-aged woman peered at him from beneath a frizzy halo of hair.

"Can I help you, Officer?" Her eyes glittered with avid curiosity.

"Are you the supervisor?"

She nodded. "Yes. May I see your badge again, please?" He showed it, and she opened the door all the way. "I'm Sheila Hannity, evening shift. Come in. And tell me why you're here."

The door opened into a foyer, and he noticed Opal's coat hanging with several others on an old-fashioned coat tree.

"I'd like to speak with Opal McBride, please."

Sheila's eyebrows rose, and he could almost hear the gears in her brain churning. She narrowed her eyes. "What's she done? She was awful quiet at dinner—not that she's ever chatty, but definitely more subdued than usual. She oughta know she can't get away with nothin'."

She directed him to a small sitting room off the foyer. "Have a seat. I'll go get 'er."

She bustled off, more eager to be the first in on the news, Josh figured, than actually being helpful. He disliked her on principle.

A few moments later, Sheila's heavy tread creaked on the old house's hardwood floors.

"Here she is, Officer." She put unnecessary emphasis on the word *officer*, and he caught a glimmer of unholy delight in her expression as she ushered her charge into the room. His dislike for the woman deepened.

Opal halted in the wide entry when she saw him, and the blood slid from her face, leaving her skin pale except for a light smattering of freckles across the bridge of her nose. Her lips parted and a tiny, distressed sound escaped, which she quickly extinguished. Then her lips tightened and she crossed her arms over her chest.

"You're a cop?" Her moss-green eyes narrowed.

Josh flipped out his badge yet again, but Opal didn't even bother glancing at it.

"What do you want?" She shot a glance over her shoulder, as though assessing an escape route, then returned her gaze to his. She'd taken her hair out of its earlier braid, and some of it slid over her shoulder to cling to her body.

"Is there somewhere we can speak privately?" He hadn't heard Sheila's footsteps retreat, and guessed the woman was hovering within eavesdropping distance.

Opal's eyes flickered. "Ms. Hannity? Officer Boone would like privacy. Where would you like us to go?" She didn't even raise her voice, confirming Josh's suspicion.

There was a rustle, then Sheila harrumphed and reappeared. "The classroom. Second door on the left." She pointed and this time she left, floorboards creaking all the way to the back of the house.

"After you." Josh gestured for Opal to precede him.

She pivoted, the waterfall of her hair shimmering in concert with her hips as she walked nearly soundlessly. But when she got to the room, she paused, then stopped and faced him.

"I'm not real comfortable with you. Not after this afternoon."

"Yeah, well, I'm not so comfortable with you either, so we're even. Let's just get this over with."

She lifted her chin and hesitated for a heartbeat, then entered the room, but didn't sit.

He pulled the door closed. "Look, Ms. McBride, I only want one thing from you. Stay away from my mother's shop." He blew out a frustrated breath. "I wouldn't put it past her to show up here bent on hiring you. If she does, you decline. Is that clear?"

If anything, her nose went a smidge higher. "What do I get in return, Officer Boone?"

"What?" Was she actually bargaining with him?

"You want something from me. Something that's going to cost me, by the way, but I know you don't care about that." She uncurled her fists and put her hands on the table, leaning toward him, yet staying well out of his reach. "So, what do I get in return for cooperating?" Bitterness, along with something that sounded a lot like desperation and maybe a touch of resignation, rippled in her voice.

His temper flared. "You don't deserve to get anything for staying away from her. Just lie low, stay off of my radar, and you'll be fine. No problems from me."

"That's it? You won't harass me? Doesn't sound like a fair trade." Her expression went mulish. "I'm supposed to give up the one thing that will keep me from going back to prison, and you get to feel like you did a community service."

"No!" She'd put him on the defensive, and he didn't like it. "It's not like that. You can find another job."

"Like you know anything!" She slashed a hand through the air. "That was the first time in ten days anyone offered me anything! A job, a place to sit, a smile…"

Her voice caught and she wheeled, but didn't move to leave the room. She lifted a hand and swiped at her cheeks, trying to hide the motion behind the curtain of her hair.

"You are a fine actress," Josh said. He barely suppressed a sneer, and felt a niggle of guilt for goading her. He fully expected her to either verbally attack him or come on to him.

But instead she shook her head, then slowly turned. She'd missed a tear and it glistened on her cheek, but other than that, she'd gotten her crying under control. Unless, of course, that was all part of her act.

She shrugged one shoulder. "It doesn't matter, Officer Boone. As soon as I show Ms. Hannity my job search documentation for today, I'm out of here. I'll be back at Pee Wee Valley tomorrow." Her lips trembled, but otherwise, she didn't show any emotion.

Josh wondered if he'd pegged her correctly. She didn't seem to be acting at all. No histrionics, no blaming, no more attempts to bargain. Against his better judgment, he asked, "What documentation?"

"I need five signatures a day saying that I've applied for a job somewhere."

Left unsaid was the part about him throwing her out of May's shop. The niggle of guilt became a twinge. "How many did you get today?"

"Four."

He sighed. "So you need one more."

She nodded.

"Give it to me." Josh couldn't believe he was doing this. If any of his colleagues found out, he'd be scorned out of the ranks. On the other hand, guilt now weighed on him like a boulder. While he didn't want her near his mother, she didn't deserve a return to incarceration over this. Fairness compelled him to hold out his hand.

She dug in her jeans pocket and produced a form, then dropped it on the table between them. He picked it up, unfolded it, and saw that, indeed, she had four signatures accompanied by phone numbers and today's date. All were for places along Bardstown Road, and for minimum-wage jobs.

He fished a pen out of his inner jacket pocket and scrawled his name, followed by *for May Boone*. "There. We're even. You get to stay out of prison as long as you stay away from my mom." Josh lifted his gaze to Opal.

Her eyes wide and disbelieving, she stared at him. Hope and relief chased across her face, and suddenly she looked younger than her thirty years, and vulnerable. She nodded, and a sheen of moisture glistened in her eyes. She whispered, "Thank you."

Well, hell, he didn't deserve a thank-you from her. Josh felt like a toad. To cover his uneasiness, he gave her a brisk nod and said, "I'll show myself out."

He stowed the pen, then glanced at her. His next words were cruel, but he meant them from the bottom of his cynical cop's heart.

"I hope I never see you again."

He turned quickly to leave, but not quickly enough to miss seeing the hope in Opal's eyes flicker and her lips flatten.

"Don't worry, Officer. Believe me, the feeling is mutual."

Chapter Three

A WAVE OF RELIEF washed through Opal, so strong she felt light-headed, and she blindly reached for a nearby chair. She sank into it and took a deep breath. A shaky breath. Emotions roiled in her gut, so many that she couldn't sort them out, and she quit trying for the moment.

The door thumped closed behind Josh Boone, and Opal heard Ms. Hannity rush up the hallway on her way to reset the alarm—and probably to ascertain that she hadn't slipped out too.

A *cop*. Finally his behavior at May's shop made sense. No wonder he'd wanted her gone. Not that she blamed him. Much. She supposed if she were in his shoes, she'd do the same. So why did she feel so betrayed? He didn't owe her anything. And he'd only deprived her of one job, not months of lost opportunities had she been incarcerated again.

Ms. Hannity stuck her head in the room, visibly relieved to see Opal still there, and huffed, "Get back to your chores, Finley."

Opal knew it was pointless to argue with her, but she'd changed her name after the conviction. Legally. No way was she going to carry on Tommy's name, but for some obscure reason, Ms. Hannity chose to rub her face in it.

But for as many things she had to ignore and endure, this blatant dig angered Opal. She stood and said, "Ms. Hannity, my name is McBride. I'll thank you kindly for using it." But her words echoed in the empty room, as the supervisor had continued to the front door.

The beeps of the alarm system momentarily clashed with the classical music Ms. Hannity insisted upon playing, and then the heavyset woman reappeared at the entrance to the classroom. She regarded Opal with narrowed eyes and blocked the doorway, planting her fists on ample hips. "You need to stop your back talk, young lady."

Opal sighed. Ms. Hannity was a bully, plain and simple. *Another battle not worth fighting.* The woman outweighed her, plus she wielded all the power—*for now, not forever*—but if push came to shove, Opal could defend herself without much difficulty. And the security camera would record that Opal had not instigated a confrontation.

But she didn't want a confrontation, didn't want to waste precious energy on trying to open this woman's closed mind, so she simply let her head drop forward and her shoulders droop. "Yes, ma'am," she said meekly. *But I'll be out from under your thumb soon.*

Ms. Hannity sniffed. "I'll be ready to meet with you in ten minutes."

Opal nodded, the curtain of her hair concealing her tight-lipped mutiny, and thankfully, the woman trod on down the hall.

Her thoughts returned to Josh Boone. His presence, at first so genuine and, well, *normal* had made her feel like a human being. Of course, his courtesy and obvious affection for his mother fed into that.

Opal hadn't realized until now how badly she'd wanted to be part of what they had, what they represented. All the other people who'd listened to her halting requests for work this week had been polite enough—well, except for the one guy—and with various levels of busyness had projected professional attitudes and not-quite-callous disregard for her situation. She knew they'd forgotten her face, her name before she'd even walked out the door.

But not so at May's Stitches in Time shop. May wouldn't forget her. Her eyes had seen past all of Opal's fears and failures, right to her soul. Even more, May hadn't despised the person Opal knew she really was. A smile softened her face.

Then Josh plowed his way into her memory of the fabric shop. He wouldn't forget her either. Her smile faded. Unfortunately, he was more right about her than May was. Although Opal wasn't nearly as bad as he thought. She refolded the paper and headed to the kitchen to finish the cleanup.

Eight minutes until her meeting with Ms. Hannity. No problem. She'd told May she was a hard worker, and she was. Work and books had gotten her through the last twelve years, and since time for books wouldn't come until after tonight's computer class, she'd focus all her disappointment and confusion—and relief—on physical labor.

Exactly seven minutes later, Opal stowed the bleach under the sink and wiped her hands dry on her jeans. Twenty seconds more put her outside Ms. Hannity's office. The door was closed, so she took a seat in the chair in the hallway. She recognized her roommate's voice blending with Ms. Hannity's in murmured conversation. The supervisor had taken a shine to Aisha, and seemed to bend over backward to help her. Aisha's crime wasn't violent, though, and maybe that was what set Ms. Hannity against Opal. Didn't matter.

Nothing mattered except succeeding here, so she could succeed on her own later.

Opal leaned her head against the wall and closed her eyes. Josh's signature had removed her biggest fear, and she had renewed hope for tomorrow's job hunt. A pang of loss for Stitches in Time rolled through her, but she pushed the emotion away. She'd find something.

She had to.

Aisha's voice rose, overridden by Ms. Hannity's strident tone. Opal opened her eyes and stared at the door. This wasn't a typical outcome of Aisha's usual brownnosing abilities. A scant moment later the door slammed open and her roommate dashed out, one hand over her mouth and struggling to contain tears.

"Hey!" Opal leaped to her feet. "Are you okay?"

It was a truly stupid question, given the shattered expression on Aisha's face, but instead of pointing that out, the taller woman crumpled. Opal ignored her aversion to close physical contact and put her arm around Aisha, who dissolved in noisy sobs.

"I was—" Aisha hiccuped, then moaned. "So close, I was so close."

Baffled, Opal kept up a steady stream of soothing noises, and hoped Ms. Hannity would give Aisha a few moments to collect herself. She patted Aisha's back, an awkward proposition given the difference in their heights, and made infinitely more awkward by Opal's rising anxiety. No one had touched her without intent to either injure or control her since she married at sixteen. Her mind conjured today's memory of May Boone, and Josh's initial handshake. *Except for them.*

Deep yearning for what she would never have and didn't deserve rose within her, and Opal suddenly realized she was thumping Aisha with a rapid staccato rather than the soothing stroke she'd intended.

She extricated herself from Aisha's grasp. "What do you mean?"

Ms. Hannity barked, "She'll get over it. Get in here, Finley."

Opal searched her roommate's eyes, and Aisha jerked her head to indicate the office.

"Better go." Her lips twisted in a parody of a smile, and she added, "She's right. I'll be okay."

Opal didn't believe her, not entirely, but she gave Aisha a quick, encouraging squeeze before she headed into Ms. Hannity's lair. Her heart sank, knowing that the woman was on a rampage, but Ms. Hannity couldn't find fault with anything she'd done or not done, and she lifted her head as she entered.

She pulled her paper from her pocket and placed it on the desk without the tiny flourish of triumph she felt.

Ms. Hannity peered at the entries over imaginary reading glasses, impotent disapproval in her expression. She glanced up at Opal. "Would you like to enlighten me about your visit from one of Louisville's finest?" Her tongue darted out to moisten her lips, and her nostrils flared.

Opal's breath caught. She had nothing to hide, but no matter what she said, Ms. Hannity would twist it. "He came to sign for Mrs. Boone, his mother, at the last shop."

Ms. Hannity's eyes narrowed. "Why didn't you get it yourself while you were there?"

"Because I—because he—"

She felt a blush heat her face, and ducked her head. But then righteous confidence took hold, and she lifted her gaze to the woman's steely censure. She put her hands on the back of the chair Ms. Hannity had not invited her to occupy.

"I didn't get Mrs. Boone's signature because Officer Boone knew who I am and didn't want me to work for his mother." She gripped the chair's rail, then forced herself to relax and let her hands drop to her sides. "I will honor his request."

Ms. Hannity sniffed. "If I find out differently, you'll be in hot water, missy."

Opal lowered her lashes. "Yes, ma'am. I understand." Would she go to the trouble of tracking Officer Boone down and asking? For the life of her, Opal couldn't see a reason for that.

Ms. Hannity waved a pudgy hand bejeweled with too many rings to count. "Go on."

Opal squelched the urge to flee. Her head began to throb. Prison, though its very nature stifled, had a well-ordered sameness that felt safe. Secure. Day in and day out, she knew what to expect. They'd even made her go to what she'd silently dubbed get-out-of-jail classes, full of a plethora of details, expectations, and eventually, her very own customized plan.

Which was going absolutely nowhere. And which, she now suspected, wasn't customized at all. It sure wasn't working. Employers wanted experience she didn't have, or a bachelor's degree. Her associate degree had lost its luster and acquired a hint of tarnish over the last few days. She'd filled out applications with cautious optimism that had degraded into dogged pragmatism. No one had called to arrange an interview. And that was all before she had to explain about her record.

Tears stung the back of her eyelids, but the sun would shine in the hidden crevices of Appalachian coal mines before she'd allow Ms. Hannity the satisfaction of seeing her cry. Opal set her lips and pivoted, leaving the office with measured, even steps.

She'd never expected it to be this hard. She blinked the tears away, angry at her weakness. She'd survived Tommy. She'd survived trial and prison. And she'd survive this, whatever it took.

Opal lifted her chin and entered the classroom. She might be down, but she wasn't out. And no matter what Josh Boone thought of her, it didn't matter. She wouldn't ever see him again.

The pang of loss in her heart came at the knowledge that May's gentle acceptance wouldn't be part of her future.

Unexpected longing for the hills and hollows of her childhood stole her breath, and Opal paused to cover her racing heart with an unsteady hand.

Aisha had told her about a park not far from the halfway house. Cherokee Park, with walking trails, hills. A creek. Opal didn't know exactly where it was, but tomorrow she'd find it, along with her first moments of privacy in years.

Her resolve calmed her, and she drew in a shaky breath.

She'd be okay.

She repeated the words like a mantra during the computer class, trying desperately to believe it. But her secret fear kept growing, the one where freedom was snatched from her grasp once again.

Chapter Four

A YOUNG MAN stormed out of a coffee shop in Opal's path, and she pulled up short in order to stay out of his way. He threw a towel on the ground and ripped off an apron, pitching it next to the towel and then stomped on both. A steady stream of curses rolled off his tongue, and Opal took a step back, regarding him warily.

"I *quit*," he shouted at the closing door. He wheeled and stalked away, pulling a pack of cigarettes and a lighter from the back pocket of his body-hugging, low-waisted jeans. The curses stopped while he lit his smoke, then faded as his footsteps carried him down the sidewalk.

Opal retrieved the towel and apron, intending to return them to the shop, then stared at the objects with dawning realization. She glanced at the sign. Beans & Leaves was in current—and critical—need of an employee.

Well, that was pretty convenient. She was in current—and critical—need of a job. She squared her shoulders, gave her hair a quick pat, and pasted on a smile that she hoped didn't look as desperate as it felt.

Scents laden with rich, strong coffee and laced with cinnamon and vanilla assailed her as she opened the door. She had a brief flashback to May's store, and immediately preferred the softer juxtaposition of aromas there, but she wasn't here to compare ambiences.

She sought out the counter, noting that all the tables were occupied with customers, most of them returning their attention to laptops or reading material now that the show was over. A young woman with spiked hair in shades of purple and pink stood behind the counter with hands on hips, and an expression of exasperation on her face. She'd accessorized her wild hair with black: black turtleneck shirt with the sleeves pushed up to reveal pale, bony forearms, black skull earrings, black apron proclaiming BEANS & LEAVES – PEACE IN THE CITY, and a black nose ring. Her name—Hayley—flowed in calligraphy across a tag affixed to the center of the apron's bib.

Opal took a deep breath. "Hello, Hayley. I'd like to apply for this position." She extended the items and waited, her cheek muscles beginning to ache from the strain of the forced smile.

Hayley snatched the apron and towel from her outstretched hand, and still glaring at the door, muttered, "Asshole." Then she blinked and turned her attention to Opal. Her eyes were hazel, shot through with green, and kinder than the harshness her appearance implied. A smile creased her face, and she said, "Really?"

Tension eased out of Opal's shoulders, and she nodded. "Yes, ma'am." Her smile felt a little more natural as the humor of the situation sank in. "I see you have an opening."

Hayley snorted. "I do—and good riddance." She tossed the towel into a bin in the corner, already overflowing with used linens. She held the apron out to Opal. "Here you go. We'll do the paperwork after the morning rush."

Opal froze. "But—" She had to tell this woman what she was getting into.

"No buts. Get back here." Hayley motioned her behind the counter with impatient gestures, and smiled past her. "Can I help you, sir?"

Opal's pulse picked up, but she did as she was told, with an unsuccessful attempt to brush the footprints from the apron. She gave up and looped the apron over her head, tying it as she rounded the corner. She washed her hands and glanced over her shoulder at her new—boss? Manager? Coworker? She'd barely shaken the moisture off when Hayley's voice rose.

"He wants a large bold." She pointed at the cups, three sizes neatly stacked, then at the labeled urns.

Opal took it in and thought, *I can do this.* Determined to succeed, she filled the order, finding lids and hot sleeves in logical places. She handed the man his drink and stepped back, ready for the next task.

"Minimum wage, but we split the tips at the end of each shift. Do you have barista experience?" Hayley tossed the words over her shoulder as the customer pocketed his change.

Opal shook her head in the negative, and said, "There's something you need to know—"

Hayley ignored her. "I'll show you how to run the register first, and you can learn the drinks over the next couple of days."

Opal couldn't help it. Dollar signs danced in her brain. She already knew how much minimum wage would net her, and the bills stuffed in the tip jar amounted to a good-sized bonus. Once she paid her twenty-dollar-per-week fee for living in the halfway house, she'd be able to save—

"—and once you select any add-ons, like extra espresso shots or flavor, you push here—"

Hayley's voice tugged Opal back to the business at hand, and she shoved her excitement about tips to the side. *Gotta make sure I don't get fired before I get started.*

The next few hours flew by in a blur of so many different variations on coffee and tea that Opal's head began to spin. She caught on to the register fairly quickly, thanks to the evening computer classes, and made only a handful of easily rectified errors.

The shop quieted toward midafternoon, and Hayley brought two scones and cups of tea to a table, along with an application.

"Sit. Thanks for pitching in. It would have been a disaster without you." She pushed a cup and plate toward Opal, and forked a bite of the pastry into her mouth. "It was really cool how you just saw what needed doing and did it. You were more help straight off the street than Jeremy was after eight months of working here."

Jeremy must have been the guy who stalked out.

Opal sank into the chair, and found she was much more tired than she realized. She hesitated before digging into her own scone, but decided she could splurge. She had something to celebrate—a job, and a chance to regroup. The thought slowed her hand and she put the fork down, knowing the sweet biscuit would taste like sawdust under the cloud of her deception.

She couldn't put it off any longer. Opal caught Hayley's gaze and said, "I just got out of prison." She steeled herself for rejection.

Hayley's eyes flickered, but other than that, her expression didn't change and she continued to plow through her scone. "Are you a thief or did you use drugs?"

Opal's tension came out as a short, humorless laugh, but then her throat closed over her answer. She had to take a swallow of tea before she could get the words out.

"No, ma'am." It was the first time she'd gotten this far, and her face heated at what she had to reveal. She hesitated, then shrugged and said, "Second-degree murder."

Hayley's eyebrows rose. "Wow. Who?" She leaned forward, then caught herself and went for a more neutral stance, although her eyes brightened with interest.

Of all the responses Opal expected, this was pretty close to the bottom of the list. "My husband."

Hayley forgot to pose, and waved her fork in the air. "You're kidding." It only took her a nanosecond of searching Opal's eyes to say, "You're not, are you?"

Opal took a bite of her scone to buy a little time, even as she shook her head. For once, the get-out-of-jail classes came in handy, as one of the points stressed came back to her.

Don't discuss details of your crime or incarceration. You have to disclose the fact, but that's all you owe.

She swallowed, then burned her tongue when she took a too-big gulp of tea and winced. "No, ma'am, I'm not kidding." She let the silence grow.

Hayley tapped her fork absently on the table while she regarded Opal. Then she put the silverware down with a decisive clink, and said, "I think I've gotten a pretty good sense of your character today, so I'll give you a chance." Her lips lifted in a slight smile. "Take over Jeremy's shifts, six a.m. until two thirty, starting tomorrow."

A customer entered and Hayley stood, sliding the application to Opal's side of the table. "Fill this out, and I'll split the tips for the day."

As she strode to the counter, Opal thought she heard her mutter something about *being safe enough*, but it didn't make much sense, and she was already counting her share of the tip jar in her mind anyway.

She bussed the tables when she was done with the application, then carried the used dishes to the sink. Before she got started on washing them, Hayley called her over.

"Here." She handed twelve dollars and some change to Opal. "Oh, don't bother with those." She indicated the dishes. "My afternoon shift will do those before closing."

Opal pulled four dollars from her stash and gave it to Hayley, who looked at her blankly. "For my scone and tea," she said.

Hayley rolled her eyes and gently pushed her hand away. "For Pete's sake, that's one of the perks of the job. One pastry and a drink free every shift you work." She glanced at her watch. "You've put in a big first day. I'll see you at six in the morning—sharp—and we'll work on learning the specialty drinks." She made a shooing motion with her hands.

"Thanks," Opal managed. She hid her embarrassment with an extra-bright smile. "I—I'll see you in the morning." Before she made an idiot of herself, she turned and left the store, her heart singing.

A job! She had a job! The breeze kissed her cheeks with a bright touch of freedom, and a grin animated muscles unused for more than a decade. Opal dodged pedestrians with light steps, discovering that they weren't as bothersome today. She got half a block before she remembered she needed Hayley's signature on her form, so she jogged back, and with another quick good-bye, headed home, still walking on air.

She thought about trying to find the park Aisha had told her about, but she only had forty-five minutes before evening check-in. She discarded the idea, aware that she would have a couple of hours after work tomorrow for that. Her spirits lifted even more.

Humming a folk melody, a favorite of Granny McBride's, Opal let herself into the halfway house. Classical music greeted her, so Ms. Hannity was the supervisor again, but even the prospect of dealing with the woman's attitude couldn't deflate her optimism.

Until she rounded the landing on the stairway, and saw her at the door of the room she shared with Aisha.

Opal slowed. Her excitement faded and she continued up the stairs, taking each step with a growing sense of trepidation. The supervisor glowered at her, arms crossed over her ample bosom, one toe tapping on the worn hardwood floor. A uniformed policewoman exited the room and joined Ms. Hannity, whose body language immediately became attentive as she turned to address her.

After a moment's consultation, the officer advanced toward the top of the stairs. "Opal, will you come here, please?" It was an order, not a request.

Opal's mouth went dry. "Yes, ma'am." *What was going on?*

"Can you identify this?" She dangled a baggie from a gloved hand.

Opal's pulse suddenly pounded in her ears, and her vision began to close in. "Yes, ma'am—I mean, no—it's either dope or herbs, but it's not mine." Her fingers went cold.

Aisha! It had to be Aisha's, but if it was, chances were she'd hidden it in Opal's belongings.

No. Opal fought for her breath. Drug possession was an immediate, unequivocal ticket right back to prison. Aisha's words from last night echoed back at her.

So close, so close…

Only to lose it all, to have her freedom snatched from her grasp before she'd had a chance to make it work.

She spotted Aisha, her mocha skin a shade lighter than normal and terror in her eyes, standing in the hallway beyond Ms. Hannity.

Fear squeezed her throat, but anger eclipsed it. Opal glared at her roommate and said, "Tell her, Aisha." She leaned around the cop to jab a finger at her. "Do the right thing for once and *tell the truth.*"

Chapter Five

Josh's cell phone vibrated at his hip. He muttered a mild curse and removed it from the clip on his belt. He set his file down and sighed. This would be the fifth—no, the sixth interruption in the hour that he'd set aside to review for an upcoming trial. Unless it was Charlie or Jenn calling to say his sister had gone into labor, he'd return the call later. But he had to check caller ID.

Dad. A dull pain settled above his eyes, and he rubbed the bridge of his nose. Time to pay the piper for his altercation with his mom's potential employee. *No use in delaying the inevitable.* He connected and said, "Hi, Dad. Have a good trip?"

"Hi, Josh. Yes, I did. Had to divert around some weather, but no delays or reroutes."

He sounded rested and cheerful, so Josh relaxed his guard, but just a little.

"What happened yesterday that got May so upset?" Jacob Boone's voice held an undertone of what-the-hell-were-you-thinking incredulity.

Josh leaned back in his chair, the rise and fall of conversations at other desks in the background filling in his silence as he weighed his words. He decided on the most direct ones. "Well, Mom wants to hire a murderer, and I don't want her to."

"From what she says, the murderer in question is a young woman with—how did she put it? Honest eyes."

The pain behind the bridge of Josh's nose intensified. "Right. Honest." He blew out a heartfelt sigh. "Yeah, Dad, she honestly killed a guy. With her hands and a two-by-four, not with a gun or a vehicle or by accident. She honestly meant to do it, and she didn't even offer up a defense."

Silence. "Is there a chance there's more to the story? Or do you believe she's truly a threat to society, just waiting for the opportunity to kill again?"

Josh flashed to his encounters with Opal. She was an enigma. Could he say, without doubt, that she posed a threat? She exhibited neither the hard edge nor the spineless cowardice that characterized most of the murderers he'd put away. And she wasn't crazy.

His pause was apparently long enough to allow his dad to draw a conclusion. "So she's not an immediate danger. What's her name, by the way? Either May didn't tell me, or I forgot."

Josh snorted. "You probably would've remembered, at least that it's an unusual name. Opal. Opal McBride."

Christian Hasselback at the next desk over paused, his pen hovering over the paperwork he'd been filling out, and stared at Josh.

He held up one finger and mouthed *later*, and Chris nodded before going back to his forms.

"Dad, I'm sorry Mom's upset, but I know what I'm doing. I work with killers all the time. All day, every day." Opal's quiet statement echoed back at him, *I admit to a lot of faults, Mr. Boone, but I don't lie.* Uneasy at the memory, he ignored it. "I'm not sticking my nose in Mom's business. I'm protecting her."

"As long as you're being fair to Opal. I understand your perspective, but your mother and I believe deeply in the capacity for human beings to change. Otherwise, we're all just animals, subject to hormones and instinct." His dad's voice carried all the authority of the retired military man, airline pilot, and father he was.

"I know, Dad. And I'll keep that in mind." Desperate to get off the subject, he asked, "Any word from Jenn?"

The diversion worked, resulting in an exchange about his parents' impending grandparenthood, a favorite topic of late. Hell, he was happy for Jenn and he liked Charlie, and he supposed it would be cool to be an uncle, but he wasn't as tied up in it as the rest of the family. After a few minutes, Josh ended the call, disgruntled at his dad's implication that he couldn't control his bias, or that his judgment was flawed.

The memory of himself in a tuxedo waiting for his bride to float up the aisle toward him flashed in his mind, and he buried it with brutal efficiency. He didn't need to be reminded of that spectacular error of judgment, although no one knew how bad it had been. Just that Lisa had jilted him, not why.

He replaced his phone in its clip and turned to face Chris, who'd assumed a posture of alert expectation. "I ran into Opal McBride yesterday."

Chris's eyes sharpened. "Anything we should know?"

Josh shook his head. "No, she's minding her p's and q's, being a law-abiding citizen and looking for a job." He paused. "In my mom's quilt shop."

"No way," Chris said.

"I warned her off." Josh didn't mention that he'd saved Opal from getting sent back to prison. None of the guys would understand, and he wasn't sure he understood himself. "She's at the halfway house near my condo. I'm going to keep an eye out for her, as it appears she's targeting Bardstown Road businesses."

Chris gave a quick, hard nod. "Good plan. Keep me—us—updated." He swiveled and got back to work just as Lieutenant Morris walked in. Josh began to do the same until he realized Morris was in headed his direction.

"Lieutenant. Can I help you?" Josh rubbed his left eye, as the pain had migrated and coalesced there. He wondered if he had any ibuprofen in his desk.

"Hey, Detective. I'm handing out cold cases for review." He dropped a file—a thick one—on top of Josh's trial prep. "This one's from thirteen years ago, a forty-seven-year-old male named Ezra Johnson. Gunshot wounds to the face. He owned a strip club downtown."

Josh refrained from groaning, barely, and Morris sent him an amused look that conferred temporary levity to his normally dour expression. "Good luck. Send me a weekly report with your progress." He clapped Josh on the back and continued through the office.

As soon as the boss was beyond hearing distance, Chris snorted a laugh through his nose and sent Josh a wry glance. "Better you than me, buddy."

Josh leaned back on his chair, balancing it on two legs. "Screw you, Hasselback." There was no heat to the words, and he yawned, then stretched. He thumped the chair down, pulled his drawer open, and rummaged through it. Nothing.

He lifted his gaze to Chris. "You got any ibuprofen?" After a moment's consideration, he added morosely, "Or antacids? Think I'm going to need some of those too."

"You know, if you'd stop cracking the cold cases, he'd stop dropping them on you." Chris dug in a drawer and tossed him a small bottle of over-the-counter painkillers.

Josh caught them, extracted a couple, and lofted them back. "I suppose." He chased the pills with a slug of hours-old coffee, then grinned at Chris. "But I'd have to give up my rep as the department's most effective secret weapon in the city's war on crime."

Chris made a rude noise. "You bring it on yourself, Boone. Nobody understands how you do it, but your stats on clearing cold cases are way above the norm." He stashed the bottle of pills back in his desk.

Josh made a note of where he stored them. Just in case. "All I do is solid police work. Anybody can do it."

Chris shook his head as if baffled. "Whatever," he said. He picked up his coat and stood. "I've got a ticket for the game." He snickered. "Have a great evening."

"Rub it in, why don't you, Hasselback," Josh said, already refocused on the files overflowing his desk. He muttered another curse, this one not quite so mild. He'd planned on watching the game on television, but he was sliding further behind with every passing moment. On the bright side, barring a massacre, he wasn't on call, so he could catch up on some of it if he worked fast. Or stayed up till one in the morning.

He snorted. The way things were going, a gang war would break out at two a.m., Jenn would go into labor at four, and the trial would actually bypass postponements and get underway at eight.

No matter what else happened between now and morning, though, he had a lot to do. Not so much the files he was stuffing in his laptop pack, but the living up to Lieutenant Morris's expectations, and more important, defending his professional conclusions about Opal to his parents. Their lack of confidence stung.

And there she was again, Opal McBride, her image shimmering in his mind, distracting and provoking him like a piece of sharp gravel inside his running shoe.

Josh ground his molars together, then forced himself to unclench his jaw. His head hurt six ways from Sunday, and that would only make it worse. How in blazes had it all come down to this? A convicted murderer pitting his parents against him and somehow inducing him to keep her out of prison.

He dropped his head into his hands and willed the painkillers to kick in, because his trademark discipline was beginning to wear thin. Right now he wanted nothing more than to kick...something, someone. Even though he had to admit she'd done nothing to deserve it, Opal McBride had earned herself top billing on his current events shit list.

He raised his head and peered at the pile of files on his desk. And sighed.

Time to take his headache home, although he had a niggling suspicion that it wouldn't abate as long as Opal lurked in the recesses of his mind.

Chapter Six

OPAL SLANTED A GLANCE at the clock. Four twenty. Too early. Still. Again.

She'd set the alarm for five a.m., and had watched it creep past most of its hourly digits, listening to the creaks and groans of the old house. Part of her insomnia stemmed from a heady mix of excitement and apprehension over her new job. But most of it came from leftover tension from last night. The muscles in her neck ached and she twisted her head in one direction, then the other, trying to find release.

She sent up a prayer of gratitude that her bed was in the halfway house, and that her immediate future was the same as it had been yesterday when she left Beans & Leaves. Opal clung to the positive thoughts as long as she could, but distress seeped through anyway.

Aisha had tearfully admitted the stash was hers, but only after an hour's knife-edged anxiety on Opal's part. Not to mention the great fun of interrogation, during which Opal had maintained her innocence, and pointed out at least a hundred times that she'd never been implicated with drug use or possession of contraband. Ever.

Left unsaid was Aisha's record—a conviction for prostitution in support of the drug habit that had sent her to prison in the first place, and a laundry list of misdemeanors around the same theme. Not to mention that her random drug test from last week showed traces of marijuana. "I didn't smoke," she'd claimed with wide-eyed innocence. "I was just downwind from some dudes enjoying themselves."

Yeah, right. But Ms. Hannity had bought it hook, line, and sinker.

It didn't matter. Aisha was gone. Opal attempted to dredge up some sympathy for the woman, but anger still burned over Aisha's ill-concealed efforts to pass the infraction off on her.

Ms. Hannity had been even more furious at Aisha's con. Not that it translated to a kinder, gentler attitude toward Opal. Nope. Not hardly. In fact, the supervisor had skewered her with laser eyes after Aisha's departure and said, "Don't think this means I trust you, missy. I'll be watchin' you like a hawk."

She threw the covers aside and got up. So, she'd be early for her first day. Somehow, Hayley didn't seem to be the type to grouse over that, and Opal's spirits lifted. Aisha was old news, and she made a conscious decision to douse the flame of resentment over the woman's actions. Cheered, she set about readying herself for the day, and hoped she didn't have dark circles beneath her eyes. That wouldn't make for a good first impression, although maybe showing up early would offset her hag-like appearance.

An hour and a half later she stood at the darkened door to Beans & Leaves, stomping her feet to keep them warm. Her stomach fluttered, and her fingertips tingled with anticipation—along with a healthy dose of fear she tried to stuff into an inconspicuous corner of her mind.

She hadn't been outside in the dark since, well, since her life with Tommy. The shadows and unfamiliar noises between the halfway house and the coffee shop spooked her. She'd seen a few die-hard joggers, and one homeless guy had scurried out of sight as she rounded a corner, but otherwise the streets were quiet, a welcome relief from the past few days. But the longer she waited, the more exposed and vulnerable she felt.

The headlights of a car briefly lit up the lot behind the store, and a thump of the door announced someone's arrival. Brisk tap-taps on the pavement brought Hayley into view, and Opal released a pent-up breath. She pasted a smile on, and hoped her nervousness didn't show.

"Wow. Hi," Hayley said, digging in her purse for keys. She unlocked the door with efficient movements and ushered Opal in. "I'm used to Jeremy dragging in late."

"Uh, well, you said six sharp." Opal shrugged her coat off and hung it on the rack where Hayley pointed.

"I'll show you how to open, and then talk you through the first few drinks." Hayley turned on the lights and the OPEN sign, then headed for the large coffee urns. She kept up a steady patter of instructions.

Opal snagged a disposable spoon that had fallen between a chair and the half wall behind it, and tossed it in the trash as she went by. A glance assured her that everything else was ready for customers, and she turned her attention to the massive coffee makers and the espresso machine.

An hour later, she'd learned and served up a number of drinks, the biggest challenge being getting the espresso shots right. Opal felt awkward and uncoordinated, and had begun to worry about the number of shots Hayley had told her to dump, as they didn't meet her standards. Granted, they went into a pitcher for use in cold drinks, but as chilly as it was outside, she didn't think demand would be high. "Ma'am, if you have a sec, could you help me with this?"

Hayley wiped her hands and came over behind the machine. "Are you using the scale?"

"Yes, ma'am, and I'm getting more consistent with packing the grounds to thirty pounds, but there are still a lot of them that don't time correctly."

The door thumped open and a rumble of male voices filled the shop. Hayley poked her head around the machine. "Be right with you." She turned to Opal and said, "None of these guys want fancy drinks, just coffee, so we'll work on this later."

Opal nodded, not really expecting that Hayley would pat her on the back and tell her not to worry, that she was doing fine for her first attempts, but disappointment wound through her anyway.

One of the voices broke free of the rest. "The usual, Hayley."

Opal froze. No. *No!* Her heart seized. It couldn't be— What were the chances? She braved a quick peek around the machine, and her heart clanked to the soles of her feet.

Josh Boone.

She drew back, her hands suddenly cold and clammy in spite of the steam from the espresso jets.

"I need a large bold," Hayley called.

Opal ducked to the floor. Hiding, like a pansy. She berated herself over her cowardice even as she processed the implications of the exchange. *The usual, Hayley.* Josh Boone was a regular here! Not only did he have a *usual* drink, he knew the boss by name.

"What are you doing?" Hayley's feet came into Opal's view.

"I—uh, spilled," she said, muffling her voice intentionally.

"Well, I need your help. Clean it up later. That's why we have the rubber mat." Impatience edged Hayley's voice. "A large bold."

Opal's breath caught in her throat and she hesitated.

"Opal—" Hayley's voice faded as she turned to draw the coffee for Josh.

"Opal?" Josh's voice rose, and she peeked over her shoulder. He'd leaned over the counter and stared at her, shock written on his features.

Heat flushed Opal's face and she straightened, firming her spine one vertebra at a time. She had nothing to hide and nothing to fear. Maybe if she told herself that with enough conviction, she'd believe it. She pasted an insincere smile on her face and lifted her chin.

"Good morning, Officer Boone." Her voice came out steady, not weak or shaky as she'd feared it would.

One of the other men said, "Opal McBride?"

Josh broke eye contact with her to nod at him. "Yeah." He sounded like he'd swallowed a tablespoon of ground glass.

The second man loomed behind Josh and said, "That would be *Detective* Boone, Ms. McBride." His voice was hard, and his eyes matched.

Opal shot him a disbelieving look and crossed her arms. *Crap.* Her stomach clenched, and feeling like she was on a slow-motion train wreck, she had to ask, "What kind of detective?"

She was very afraid of what his answer was going to be.

Josh's expression turned to granite, and his eyes, icy. His lips remained nearly motionless as he said, "Homicide."

Double, double crap. A trembling began deep in Opal's gut.

The guy behind him bared his teeth in a humorless sneer. "Me too." He tossed a careless look to the rest of the men in the group. "And the rest of us work in law enforcement in some capacity or another."

Opal wanted to sink into the floor, to disappear. *No wonder Hayley said something yesterday about being "safe enough." Surrounded by cops...*

She shot a glance at her boss, who wore an expression of irritation and had a hand on one outthrust hip. Opal sucked in a fortifying breath, and it ignited a small flame of anger. She turned on Josh Boone and said, "I am not working in your mother's shop. I have a right to this job"—she glanced at Hayley—"as long as she is willing to keep me."

Hayley's eyes flickered and she gave an almost imperceptible nod.

"So, Detective, I'll fill your coffee order, and the orders of all your...your coworkers, and why don't we all just sing 'Kumbaya' and get along." She pointed at the Beans & Leaves tagline. "Peace in the city, just like the apron says."

Opal had blown right through conciliatory into confrontational, and part of her was screaming at her to shut up while she was still ahead. But the other part wanted to goad Josh into coming out from behind that mask of condemnation and show his human face again, the one she'd seen at May's shop.

Where did that come from? She shoved the discomfiting thought to the side, and the next words popped out without the grace of any filter at all. "Besides, I think you can all defend yourselves against me.

Not that I'm going to leap over the counter and—" Her sense finally kicked in and she clamped her lips together.

The other homicide detective let loose a bark of laughter. "We'll keep a sharp eye on you, McBride. Starting with you watching your mouth. Right now." He leaned in, everything about his body language screaming threat and intimidation. His lips twisted and he delivered his knockout punch in a low tone filled with derision. "Cop killer."

Opal forgot about Hayley, forgot about her job, forgot about how badly she needed it, and lost her temper. "I haven't done a damn thing to you." She jabbed a forefinger in his direction. "And you are not my twenty-four-hour-a-day parole officer. If I break the law, we'll have something to talk about, Detective, but not until then." She drew a shaky breath. "Lightning will strike one of us dead before that happens."

Josh interrupted. "Chris, stand down." He stepped between them. "Leave her alone." He sent her an unreadable look, then put his hand on Chris's arm. "Get your coffee, and let's head downtown."

Hayley spun into action, pouring coffee in go cups, and waved off payment. "On the house, guys," she said, handing them out with an overly bright smile.

They left a few minutes later, a mass of grumbling testosterone, and Opal steeled herself for a dressing-down. She deserved it. Her sass had gotten her in more trouble in prison than any infraction of the rules.

"What were you thinking?" Hayley hissed. "I need their business." She grabbed a rag and wiped down the prep area with angry motions. Shooting Opal a furious look, she added, "They're regulars, and there's a bunch of them. The shop's not going under if they go somewhere else, but it matters that they choose to come *here*."

Opal's anger faded, then slid right into misery. "I'm sorry, ma'am." She hadn't thought of Hayley's perspective, only the injustice of Detective Chris's attitude. Heat climbed her neck. "My words were inexcusable. It won't happen again." Too late, Opal wondered if Hayley was leading up to firing her. Stricken, she sought the other woman's gaze.

"*Cop* killer?" Hayley threw the rag down. "Did you not think to mention that little detail to me?"

Opal blinked. Did it matter who she'd killed? Dead at her hands was dead. "My husband was a deputy sheriff." She shrugged. "It was his job, but he wasn't on duty when—" She swallowed, then put her hands out, palms up. "I'm not a threat to anyone."

The moment stretched.

A new customer entered, breaking the silence with the bell above the door. Hayley turned away, a flash of disappointment in her eyes before she replaced it with what Opal was beginning to recognize as her trademark game face.

"Good morning! How can I help you?"

Unsure of her status, Opal began the drink prep as the customer rattled it off, not waiting for Hayley to call it. If she was going to get fired, the boss was going to have to spell it out. Opal wasn't going to run, tail tucked between her legs. Nope. She didn't deserve anything from anybody, but she figured the baptism by fire that she'd just endured had earned her the dignity of fairness. And in spite of Hayley's pique, the woman struck her as evenhanded.

To Opal's surprise, the espresso shot came out perfectly, as did the next one, then every one thereafter.

Well. If she lost her job and went back to prison, at least she'd have one marketable skill to show for her brief foray into society.

Chapter Seven

"DETECTIVE BOONE for the Woodson trial." Josh moved his coffee to his other hand while he flipped his badge out for the court clerk.

"Yes, sir, I have you logged in." The woman pointed down the hall with her pen. "Have a seat in Room B on the right. And remember, no discussion of the case."

"I'm familiar with the requirements," Josh said dryly. "Thank you." He made his way to the small waiting area, files in one hand, coffee in the other, and disbelief still pinging around his brain like a pinball on steroids.

Not disbelief that Opal had found a job, and that he'd run into her, although that had been a surprise. He had to admit her success assuaged the smidgeon of guilt he felt over his tactics the other night. No, his disbelief stemmed from the stunning fact that he'd defended her. Okay, it was backhanded, as in not actively joining the attack that Chris had mounted, but he'd defused the situation, and deflected a much nastier exchange.

Chris's response would have been his, three days ago. The briefing had given the facts, brutal and unforgivable. But Opal McBride in the flesh tilted all his preconceived notions about her. And his parents' reactions, especially his mom's, had sown seeds of doubt about his judgment. *That* rankled.

He found his way to the lounge reserved for witnesses and set his coffee on an end table, sending the paper go cup an annoyed glance. He wouldn't be able to take a sip without remembering Opal's distress, or her moxie. A tendril of reluctant admiration for her spunk curled through him.

Josh shook his head to dislodge thoughts about Opal. He needed to focus on the trial. He picked up the files and shuffled through them. First, he'd run through his report again, never mind that he'd reviewed it so many times he'd committed it to memory. Then, if he didn't get called to testify soon, he'd wade through more of poor old Ezra's cold case.

His mind already spooling up for the tasks at hand, Josh reached for his coffee and brought it to his lips…and nearly spewed the first sip as the unbidden image of Opal formed in his mind. Not her hiding behind the counter. Of course not. Rather, Opal with eyes narrowed, forefinger jabbing at him, color flushing her cheeks, and giving him as much what-for as his mom had the other day. He cursed and set the cup down, brushing at his tie, hoping he hadn't stained his shirt. He glanced down. Nope. Still pristine.

Disgusted, he stood, and holding the coffee nearly an arm's length away, strode to the restroom, where he dumped it. He watched the rich liquid swirl down the drain with regret. Hayley at Beans & Leaves made the best coffee in town, and it had to be a venial sin to waste it. But he'd already proven he was prone to distraction this morning, and that wouldn't help the cause of convicting Hamilton Woodson of capital murder.

He washed his hands and returned to the anteroom, banishing Opal McBride from his thoughts, which ended up being easier than he'd expected. A paper cup of water carried none of the emotional baggage the coffee had, and after one more run-through of the Woodson file, he turned his attention to Lieutenant Morris's cold case.

He combed through most of the material in Ezra's file, making lists of people, events, and documents to delve into more deeply, and formed a decent picture of the victim. The strip club he'd owned was one of the sleazier, not that any of them were classy, but his clientele tended toward a rougher crowd. That in itself provided a fertile pool for suspects. The guy had also been known for his penny-pinching ways, oftentimes cheating both his customers and the dancers. Josh wondered what kept him in business. He filed the thought away, then sighed. This was going to turn into a side investigation of prostitution, drug dealing, gun running, and illegal betting. He knew it to his bones, and he made another note to contact some of the more seasoned veterans in Vice, see what they remembered.

Meanwhile, he could get one of the support folks started on research. He unclipped his phone and hit speed dial. "Hi, Rachel. Do me a favor, please, and see if you can track down…Henry Capshaw, *aka* Hank." He waited for her to write it down. "Then Dante Jones, and Shaniqua Howell, two *l*'s, alias Delilah, no last name." Once she'd confirmed spellings, he thanked her and ended the call.

Josh read through the transcript of Shaniqua's interview again. Something seemed off. He couldn't put his finger on it, because some of the phrasing could be taken different ways depending on tone of voice and inflection. The tape would tell him more, when he had time to listen to it.

"Detective Boone?" The clerk poked her head into the room. "They're ready for you."

Josh looked up at her, then glanced at his watch. Nearly noon. He'd be here until at least two, maybe three, depending on the cross-examination. He rose, adjusted his tie, and went to work.

Good-bye, Hamilton Woodson.

~

It was closing in on four o'clock when Josh strode out of the courtroom, loosening his tie as he walked. He'd done a bang-up job, if he did say so himself, but he knew it would be another few days before the case went to the jury. He'd check back with the prosecutor next week.

Technically, he was free to go home for the day, but on the off chance that Rachel had some information for him, he swung by the office.

Chris, phone to ear, glanced up as he entered and covered the mouthpiece. "How'd it go?"

Josh shrugged. "As well as I could make it." All cops knew too many things were out of their control when it came to the court system, and that nothing was a slam dunk.

Chris grunted, gave him a thumbs-up, and returned his attention to his phone call.

A neat sheet of paper sat on Josh's desk, and he picked it up, scanned it. Bless Rachel's efficient, detail-oriented heart. His eyebrows rose. All three people still had addresses in the Louisville area, the two men near downtown. The woman's address was Pee Wee Valley, just east of Louisville. In the Kentucky Correctional Institution for Women.

Recently vacated by Opal McBride.

She didn't have anything to do with this investigation, and Josh shoved her out of his mind. Refocusing on the list, he whistled. What a stroke of luck. He hadn't held out much hope of finding any of them, never mind all three. He glanced at his watch, then sat and dialed the warden's office of the women's prison.

When Moira, secretary to Warden Phipps, answered, Josh said, "Detective Boone of Louisville Metro Police."

"Detective Boone! It's been a while, quite a while. How are you?" The smile in Moira's voice came across the line with the warmth of a sultry summer day. "Married, with rug rats?"

Josh's mood slipped a notch, and he forced a smile into his voice. "It's been a couple of years, hasn't it?" Then, because he knew he couldn't skip over the subject with any hope of success, he said with as much nonchalance as he could muster, "The wedding got called off, so I'm still footloose and fancy-free." He didn't give her a chance to reply. "Say, you have an inmate there by the name of Shaniqua Howell. I'd like to interview her about a cold-case murder here in Louisville."

"Sure, Detective, no problem." Moira had adopted her professional voice, saving both of them from the depressing details of his personal life, and he was duly grateful.

Josh cleared his throat, then asked, "What is she in for, anyway?" Rachel's notes hadn't said.

A clattering of a keyboard was his answer, then Moira announced, "Armed robbery, assault with a deadly weapon, intent to kill."

He sat up, a thrill of anticipation snaking through his gut. Really? *A violent offender.* Maybe he'd struck pay dirt already.

Moira added, "She's got a long rap sheet of priors, mostly misdemeanor assaults, some drug possession, soliciting. I'll fax it to you."

Huh. Opal might have been housed with her. The thought took hold, then took him aback, and he paused, wondering why.

He pictured Shaniqua, or at least his impression of her based on her record, and came up with a woman who wouldn't hesitate to use all the tools of her body in order to get what she wanted. Then he placed the image of Opal next to her, and his gut twisted.

The likes of Shaniqua were a different breed than Opal, something he'd refused to see until now, forced into visualizing the two in the same unit.

Opal didn't fit. For once, he didn't shove her out of his mind, but turned over each of his encounters with her, examining them. His cynicism wouldn't let him acquit her—not even close—but the seed of doubt that his mom had planted began to crack open.

Josh scowled, then exhaled a long breath that felt almost like a sigh. "Can you provide me with a list of inmates housed with Ms. Howell?"

"Of course. But it will take me a few days to get a full list."

His mind whirled with implications, both for the timing of Shaniqua's incarceration and for what Opal might know. "Thank you, Moira. I'll be in touch."

"Oh, Detective?" Moira's voice warmed. "I'm sorry to hear that things didn't work out for you. It might be that it was a blessing in disguise."

Caught off guard, Josh said the only thing that came to mind. "Oh, it was."

More of a blessing than you can possibly know, and more than I'll ever tell you.

He hesitated, uncomfortable with the turn the conversation had taken, and wanting nothing more than to be out of it.

"Well, we all wish you the best."

"Thanks, Moira." He ended the call, surprised to discover a fine sheen of perspiration had broken out on his forehead.

He took the Woodson file out of his laptop bag and put it away, then paused. Ezra's file had dislodged when he pulled the other paperwork out, and he tucked it back in, regarding it thoughtfully.

Connections, implications, inferences, possibilities—all pointing toward tantalizing questions. The whole mess danced around in his brain, the answers just out of his conscious reach.

He needed to clear his head, give all the bits and pieces a chance to settle where they made some sense. Josh zipped his case closed and headed for the door, for a run, for the fresh air and freedom of Cherokee Park.

Chapter Eight

Opal finally broke the brittle silence between her and Hayley. "Is Beans & Leaves the main hangout for all the cops in the city?" She couldn't believe it, not really, and the prospect depressed her.

Customers had ebbed and flowed all day, a stream of professional folks on their way to work followed by students with laptops and textbooks, then retired couples with newspapers and young mothers with strollers. But there had also been a steady presence of hard-eyed cops, many uniformed and, Opal assumed, some plainclothes.

She knew the guys in suits were cops because they raked her with gazes that assessed and promised…well, whatever they promised, it wasn't good. Not quite retribution. They didn't have cause for that, and all of them knew it, but not one left without making sure she understood they had her in their sights.

Her memory slid to May's quilt shop, the colors and tranquility, the sense of both energy and oasis. A deep yearning for everything May represented struck Opal's heart, but she pushed it aside. Not a dream she could aspire to.

Hayley shot her a sideways look. "There've been a lot more than normal today." She returned her attention to the till, counting receipts for the shift.

Opal rolled her eyes. The law enforcement grapevine had flashed her location to nearly every cop in the city, from what she could see. The first wave this morning had been the worst. Since then, she'd held her head high and served everyone, cop or not, with the same courtesy and smile. Well, okay, she had to admit the smile was a bit tight for the cops, but she was really trying to stay in Hayley's good graces.

"Guess I could keep you on," Hayley muttered.

Opal took her first easy breath since her latest encounter with Josh. "I am truly sorry about this morning, ma'am."

"Yeah, well, just make nice. I won't be so forgiving next time." Hayley finished counting the money and transferred it to a zippered bag. She dipped into the tip jar and split the change. "Here you go."

Opal took her share without looking at it and stuffed it into the pocket of her jeans. "Thank you."

Finally Hayley lifted her gaze and met Opal's. "So, what's your story?"

Opal's throat constricted. No one had ever asked. Not the cops, not her public defender, not the doctor who'd delivered her stillborn baby and stopped the bleeding so she could go back to jail, to trial. To prison.

The image of Tommy lying at her feet, his head bloodied—unconscious, but still breathing, damn it—surged into her mind. Opal shoved the memory away, knowing that if she didn't, mingled terror and horror would steal her breath and her sanity. That was the only way she'd survived living with herself for the past twelve years. How could she explain this to Hayley, or to anyone who hadn't been in her shoes?

Studying her fingernails, Hayley added, "I mean, I guess I pictured a car accident, like maybe you'd been drunk. Or negligent."

Prison had one advantage. Every inmate carried the burden of a sin, some admittedly worse than others, and tacit acceptance of the fact alleviated the need to talk about their crimes. Some did, even bragging about their offenses, but Opal had never spoken about hers. Ever.

And she couldn't find the words now. Nor did she owe Hayley more than the barest of details. She swallowed, then forced air past her paralyzed vocal cords.

"It was self-defense, and he died." Trying to keep the bitterness out of her tone, she added, "And yes, he was a deputy, so every cop in the commonwealth has a chip on their shoulder about it." Her shoulders slumped. "I can't blame them, I suppose. But…"

But all I ask is the chance to make a life for myself, to be normal.

To be accepted, to be free, to be loved. She jerked her thoughts from the direction they were headed. Much of that was out of her reach, and she didn't really deserve any of it. Just freedom. She deserved that.

Hayley's eyes flickered. "So the fact that he was a cop isn't really a factor?"

Opal shook her head. "No." Except that his buddies had conveniently failed to document the beating Tommy had dealt *her*, the bruises—both fresh and in various stages of fading. Nor did they note the bleeding, the hatchet he'd used—

She closed her eyes and clenched her fists to control the trembling that threatened to escalate into full-body shakes. *Do not go there*. She drew in a lungful of air and held it, then released it and opened her eyes.

Hayley shrugged. "Then you can stay."

Opal nearly sagged with relief, but caught herself before she did. The habit of showing no weakness, honed over long years of incarceration, held firm.

"Thank you, ma'am." Opal couldn't contain the smile that took over her face.

"Then get out of here." Hayley gave her a dismissive wave. "I'll see you tomorrow."

She turned, fully intending to take advantage of Hayley's offer of continued, if conditional, employment. But she hesitated, then faced her boss. "Can you tell me how to get to Cherokee Park?"

Hayley slanted Opal a glance. "Yeah." She pointed. "That way a couple of blocks, then left on Eastern Parkway for another four or five." For the first time all day, one side of her mouth quirked up. "Just make sure you pay attention on your way in. It's easy to get lost if you don't retrace your steps."

The clutch of near-constant anxiety in Opal's gut let loose, just a little. "Thanks." She ducked her head and left before Hayley could think too much and change her mind.

A quick jog later, she found a statue in a roundabout that heralded the entrance to the park. Opal's pulse picked up and she glanced around, an irrational sense of guilt shooting through her. She snorted and gave herself a talking-to. Check-in was over two hours away, she'd given Beans & Leaves her full attention and an honest day's work, and no one had a legitimate claim on her time.

And yet, the prospect of two hours without a court-ordered purpose filled her with both exhilaration and an odd mixture of fear, along with the faint sense that she was engaging in an illicit adventure. The realization took her aback, and she stopped. The last time she'd had this much say over her life, she'd been…

Sixteen.

Nearly half her years.

Well. No wonder. If she thought about it that way, it made sense. Opal looked around again, taking her time and letting the details wash over her. The trees, more alive in their dormancy than the inside of any detention facility she'd inhabited. The shrubbery, wild and uncontained. Winter-scented air, crisp and lively, a welcome relief from the stale, processed air she'd become so accustomed to.

A flood of emotion rushed through Opal, opening a Pandora's box of memories so deeply buried that she'd forgotten them, memories so vivid that she'd die of grief if she allowed them to surface.

Mountains, hollows, and ridges, sky so close she could nearly touch it. The hidden caves and cliffs, paths that only Opal and the deer knew. Solitude that was never lonely, not like the bone-deep loneliness she'd known over the past twelve years, constantly surrounded by people.

This was what she'd missed the most.

It lay before her, inviting, waiting only for her to step forward and partake.

Granny McBride's presence wrapped around her, comforting and encouraging and saving her from the harshest bits of her past. Opal clung to the recollection, and savored the notion of Granny's hug for a long moment, then, emboldened, entered the park.

It was probably ordinary. A winding road, open to traffic on one side and reserved for pedestrians on the other, paths leading to secret spaces, and trees arching over all of it. Their branches were bare now, but bore the promise of shade and solitude come spring.

But to Opal, it delivered what everyone else jogging by or walking with strollers or dogs or friends took for granted. Freedom. Surcease from burdens, onerous and borne too long.

Bits and pieces of her childhood came to her, and she stopped to turn her face to the sky. Clouds lay heavy on the treetops, and that wasn't familiar, but the breeze kissing her face was. She remembered when she was six, and came upon baby raccoons in a blackberry bush. They'd been so involved in chattering and bickering with each other that she'd watched them for what seemed like a lifetime to a child.

"Opal," Ma had scolded. "The mama coon is close by, and vicious if she thinks you're a threat."

A spear of betrayal stabbed through Opal's heart. If only Ma had fought for her like a mama coon…

So many losses. She stumbled off the main road onto a dirt path, and followed it blindly. Tears stung at the back of her eyelids, and she sought a tree trunk, slipped around the back side of it, and crouched at its base.

She drew in deep gulps of air and tried to contain the memories, her emotions.

They hadn't gotten to her in prison, because she hadn't let them. And she couldn't afford for them to overwhelm her now, either. She battled them into submission, fiercely clinging to the joy of her freedom. She wouldn't let regrets spoil these few minutes, no matter how poignant, how precious. After a time, the grip of the past eased.

The lure of the earth drew her like a lodestone, and she couldn't resist plunging her fingers into the rich mix of dirt and decaying leaves. She fell to her knees and dug at the chilly ground, grit collecting beneath her fingernails. Oh, how she'd missed this! Her fingers grew cold, and Opal finally rocked back on her heels, surprised to find her cheeks wet with tears. She swiped at them and laughed softly. She probably sported mud smears now.

Voices caught her attention, and she glanced at the paved path. Two women in animated conversation, pushing strollers. One of the kids was kicking his feet and singing a nonsense song, completely tuneless and totally enchanting.

Opal started to avert her gaze like she'd done every time kids came into Beans & Leaves, but she stopped. A defensive tactic on her part, to keep the memories of her babe at bay while she was working, but she didn't have to do that now. For some reason it felt safe to think of Skye, to honor the life cut so short.

She'd be eleven now. The pain that usually knifed through Opal when she thought of her baby didn't sear as deeply this time. The forest held her gentle in its care, and allowed her to do the same with Skye's memory.

More tears tracked down her face but Opal didn't wipe them away, just let them drip onto her coat. No sobs accompanied them, and she surrendered to the silent, tender cascade. The women rounded the corner up the road and disappeared from view as she watched.

It was both catharsis and triumph to be able to look at a child.

Opal sat tailor fashion for a long time, watching people and the occasional car pass by. Bicycles like she'd never seen before, sleek and fast, their riders helmeted and looking like comic book heroes. She absently released her hair from the braid she wore for work, finding it somehow appropriate that even her hair should experience freedom in this moment, and separated the strands with her fingers. There was no wildlife and she missed that, but they'd emerge from their winter haunts once the weather warmed. Cold seeped from the ground into her jeans, but it didn't bother her.

She glanced at her watch. Time to go. She gathered her feet under her to rise, and her hair slid forward. One-handed, she brushed it out of her face, then froze, her attention captured by a man jogging below.

It can't be. Her breathing hitched. But it was. *Josh Boone.* She'd recognize his easy stride anywhere, the angles of his face, the fall of his hair over his forehead, his capable hands.

Opal shrank back, hiding behind the tree and simultaneously gathering her distinctive hair. She should never have unbraided it. She dug the elastic band out of her pocket, secured the tresses into a haphazard half ponytail, half bun, then tugged her coat up to cover what was still visible, praying all the while that he hadn't seen her— and angry that she feared him.

And, if she really wanted to admit it to herself, which she didn't, embarrassed that he might see her with a face dirty from tears. Opal shoved that thought right out of her mind, then cautiously peeked around the tree.

He'd stopped, and was scrutinizing the hillside with narrowed eyes.

Her heart sank. He *had* seen her. But he didn't know for sure, or he would have been plowing his way up the hill already.

Anger spurted through her. Why did he keep showing up, and why now? He'd interrupted her solitude, resurrected the guilt she thought she'd left at the park entrance.

Opal told herself she didn't owe Josh Boone anything, that he had no hold on her. But if that were true, she would stand up right now and walk out of the woods. She'd say *Good afternoon, Detective Boone,* and she'd walk past him like the free woman she was. If it had been any of the other cops she'd seen today, she would have.

But no. She drew her head out of his line of sight, grateful for the olive-drab color of her coat, though she'd really wanted the exuberant coral-and-teal coat two sizes too small to fit. She dared another glance at her watch. *Damn.* If he didn't move on soon, she'd have to run to get home on time.

Her heart thudded to the ground beneath her, now cold and uncomfortable, and anxiety strangled the peace she'd felt only moments before. *Ms. Hannity…*

A shudder racked her, part shiver, part dread, and Opal decided she needed to go whether Josh was there or not. But she didn't have to face him to do it. She eased to her feet, and careful to keep the tree between them, crept up the hill, away from him.

She hadn't done this for years, moving silently through the woods, but the skill came back to her as if she'd never left the hills and hollows of Jubilee.

Until she stepped on a hidden twig and it snapped. To Opal's ears, it sounded like a gunshot. She froze again, and slowly turned her head to see if Josh had heard it too.

Chapter Nine

J OSH QUARTERED THE WOODS above him, searching for the flash of color he'd seen—and he knew he'd seen something. The glimpse of movement he'd caught out of the corner of his eye was definitely copper hued. He must have Opal McBride on the brain, because her hair came immediately to mind. Maybe it was a red fox, rare in the city but not impossible. Especially in the sprawling acreage of the park.

He stood with his hands on his hips, his lungs filling and emptying like a bellows, his pulse pounding in his ears. So what it if had been Opal? Did it matter? This was the fifth time he'd thought about her today, and he had to wonder about that.

There. Another bit of movement, above where he'd been looking, only this one blended into the surroundings. And it went still as soon as his gaze homed in on it. Maybe a deer. He took a few steps to get a different angle, and a shape came into focus. Not a deer. Human.

His protective instincts surfaced. "You, up there. Are you okay?"

Whoever it was, maybe a homeless dude, lit out and headed for the crest of the hill.

Josh shrugged and began to turn away. The guy wasn't injured, not moving like that, and he had no reason to suspect a crime might have been committed. But just as the runner topped the hill, just before disappearing beyond it, the deep shadows of the woods gave way to a patch of almost-sunlight—and another flash of color caught his eye.

Opal. That hair, distinctive with glossy depths and new-penny highlights, was unmistakable. It *had* been her. Josh's muscles tensed to charge after her, every molecule of his body armed for serious hunting…but his logic kicked in. She'd done nothing to warrant his professional attention, a fact that both his parents had taken great pains to point out. He had no right to feel proprietary about the park; he didn't own it and it wasn't off-limits, even to Opal.

Barring her involvement in a crime, he had exactly two reasons for interacting with Opal McBride. To buy coffee from her at Beans & Leaves—and he had given some thought to switching coffee shops for a while—or as a potential interviewee on Ezra's cold case. But only if her name turned up on Moira's list. And he'd face that prospect when it happened, not sooner.

So he had no reason, real or manufactured, to chase her. The urge to follow her faded. But it didn't go away, not entirely, and he quashed it, irritated.

But she'd seen him. *Oh yeah.* She wouldn't have fled through the woods like that if she hadn't. A spurt of satisfaction brought a grim smile to his face, but he didn't want to examine its origin too closely. He told himself it was strictly because of their opposing roles, cop and con. But his habit of brutal self-honesty forced him to admit that her response to him—and vice versa—was more primal in nature. As in his male to her female.

His mood took a nosedive.

Josh deliberately turned his back on Opal, an action performed for his own benefit, not hers, as she was long gone. The sweat he'd worked up began to evaporate, and the light breeze chilled his skin. He started jogging, and the irony of the situation struck him full force. He was running away from her just as surely as she was running away from him. But an extra layer of meaning had just piled on top of the purpose of his run, and it pissed him off.

As soon as his muscles warmed up again, he pushed himself beyond a pleasant jog into a punishing flat-out race, with wind sprints for good measure.

When he got home, he stripped off the sweat-soaked clothes and tossed them on the floor of the bathroom as he waited for the shower to heat. Unfortunately, he couldn't seem to shed the image of Opal as easily.

What really disturbed him was his body's reaction. It had been years since an erection annoyed him. In fact, he couldn't remember being annoyed. Ever. Embarrassed, maybe, but not since his teens. Even his most recent failure in the relationship realm held no candle to this irrational and colossally inappropriate response. He muttered a curse and stepped into the shower, impressed in spite of himself that he needed a cold shower when he was already shivering.

Water sluiced over him, hopefully washing away the vestiges of idiocy along with the remnants of his workout. He lathered up and stuck his head under the spray—and his phone chirped from the other room. It was his work ringtone, the one reserved for emergencies. He debated, sifting through his open cases, looking for critical or open components. Nope. None. Certainly nothing worth an emergency call. He decided to finish his shower. If there were new dead people to investigate, they'd stay that way for another five minutes.

But he did speed up his process, and wrapped a towel around his waist as he padded into the living room, droplets of water clinging to his hair. He placed the call. "Detective Boone."

The dispatcher, trying to sound cool but unable to hide an undercurrent of excitement, said, "We've got five probable homicides off of Dixie Highway, and the lieutenant wants every available asset on the case."

Josh whistled. "Five?" He tucked the phone between his jaw and shoulder and grabbed his notebook. He flipped it open to a blank page. The dispatcher rattled off the address and he verified it after writing it down. "Gangs or drugs?"

"They're pretty close-mouthed at this point."

"Okay, I'll be there in—" He looked at the clock and estimated how long it would take him to get to the location, and added five minutes for a drive-through dinner. "—twenty-five minutes." He ended the call and tossed the towel over the back of a chair to dry. No telling how long it would be before he got back. He slipped a pair of slacks on over clean boxers and shrugged into a button-down collared shirt, but decided to forgo the tie, although he grabbed one and stuffed it in his jacket pocket. He was out the door in minutes, mentally rearranging his schedule as he double-timed down the stairs.

By the time he drove up to the scene—an older neighborhood with small but well-kept houses, now eerily lit with ubiquitous blue-and-red flashing lights—he'd made the necessary phone calls to clear his calendar of nonessential tasks. He knew he'd need to do more, but that was good enough for the moment. He parked, and flipped out his badge to identify himself to the guy manning the entry checkpoint.

"Anything I need to know, Officer?" he asked in a low tone.

The guy removed his hat and scratched his head. "Gunshot wounds. A couple in their fifties or early sixties, a twenty-nine-year-old woman, and a forty-three-year-old man." He replaced his hat. "And a kid, probably six or seven."

Josh took the news about the kid like a kick to the solar plexus. Murder was never fair or right, but it always seemed more obscene when it involved a child. "Motive?"

"Nope." The uniformed cop said, "They found them after someone came upon a toddler, maybe three years old, wandering in the neighborhood and crying. She kept saying, 'There were big, scary noises and Mommy made me run away.'"

Poor kid. She'd survived a bloodbath. If no one else had called already, he'd put in a request for the psychologist to come out and interview the kid. At least as well as anyone could interview a three-year-old. He doubted any substantive information would come from the child, but the specialists could get her started on recovering from the trauma.

"Okay, thanks." He stowed his badge and ducked under the crime scene tape, cataloguing details as he went. A group of neighbors stood in a clump, looking shocked, a few of them crying. No stragglers hanging off to the side or watching from the shadows, at least not that he could see. Full darkness had fallen on his drive over, so it was possible the killer was loitering out of the range of streetlights.

He got to the house and noted that there was no damage to doors or windows, at least at the front. He stepped inside and the smell of death slapped him in the face. The metallic tang of blood, underlaid with the deeper, pervasive odors of body waste.

Chris was already there, looking as grim as Josh felt. He nodded a greeting to the older detective and asked, "How are we going to do this? Task force?"

It only made sense. They were looking at one perpetrator, perhaps with accomplices, but these people had been killed at the same time. There was no use in wasting resources by running five parallel investigations, as if they were awash in resources to begin with.

The woman and boy were closest to the door, facedown, shot in the back as they fled the carnage. They'd almost made it. His gut twisted. Josh couldn't see how the toddler had gotten out alive, and he rotated to take in other details as he processed his impressions.

"Yeah. You, me, and Hoskins." Chris's gravelly voice was lower than usual, almost a growl. "He'll be here shortly."

He gestured for Josh to follow, and circumvented the bodies to get to the kitchen. The older couple had been gunned down as they sat at the kitchen table. The other man was the only one who'd been shot from the front, and he lay sprawled in a posture so clearly protective that Josh could see the whole event play out in his mind's eye.

The shooter had entered from the back porch. The door hung open, squeaking as the breeze moved it. From this angle, he couldn't see any signs of forced entry. Didn't mean there hadn't been coercion of some sort, though. He filed that thought. The forty-six-year-old guy had gotten up, recognized danger, and thrown himself in front of the older couple. They'd most likely been paralyzed with disbelief, not an unusual response from people unaccustomed to violence, and the shooter had popped them before they could break free from their shock.

The coroner looked up from the counter where she was filling out paperwork. "Hi, Chris, Josh."

"Hi, Joanne. We gotta stop meeting like this." Josh sent her a ghost of a smile. He couldn't conjure anything stronger, and it faded as soon as he'd formed it. "You see anything beyond the obvious?"

She smiled back, hers a bit more genuine than his had been. "I'll have to see them at autopsy, but no. It appears pretty straightforward." Waving at the bodies, she said, "Send 'em over when you're done."

Josh's cell phone rang, his mother's ringtone this time, and he excused himself. "Hi, Mom. I can't talk long. What's up?"

"Oh! Are you at work, then?" She didn't give him much opportunity to answer. "I'll make it quick. Jenn's in labor and they're headed for the hospital."

A rush of affection for his kid sister washed through him, and he grinned. "Great! I don't know when I'll be able to get away, but have Charlie text me with updates if he has time."

He ended the call, pocketed his phone, and turned to look at the scene, the angles, the story the bodies had died trying to tell him.

This was an execution. Cold-blooded, calculated, premeditated, and planned. So if the interviews of the next twenty-four hours didn't turn up a clear suspect, he'd ferret out the motive and follow that trail. One way or the other, he'd see that these victims, especially the child, were accorded justice.

It was too bad it took a tragedy of this magnitude to drive Opal McBride out of his mind.

Chapter Ten

OPAL RAN, her feet pounding against the pavement, her breathing hampered by the fact that her heart had lodged in her throat. He'd seen her. *You, up there. Are you okay?*

She'd been fine, or as fine as anyone could expect considering the breach of the dike that normally corralled her emotions. She hazarded a glance backward, tripped, and nearly went down. *"Oof…"* She flung her arms out and scrambled to get her other leg under her.

She caught herself, but the stumble forced her to slow. She hadn't seen him—yet—and hoped that meant he hadn't given chase. Unless he'd been on the tail end of a twenty-mile run, he could outpace her without much trouble. A stitch in her side stopped her and she gave up, bent to try to relieve the pain, and focused on inhaling.

If he caught her now… Why had she fled? The primal response had overridden her logic in the space of a heartbeat—no, even less time than that. More like the snap of static electricity, sort of like how her mind had shorted out at his presence.

Opal couldn't shake the sensation that Josh's hand was going to come down hard on the nape of her neck at any moment, and she straightened, unwilling to be captured in such a passive posture. Still huffing, she pivoted.

No one thundered out of the thicket after her.

Relief stole the strength from her legs. She took a moment to catch her breath, then turned and trudged away from the park. If he really wanted to track her down, he had her address. Her lips flattened. He had no cause to do so. Surely he knew that.

But for some reason, he'd fixated on her.

Opal shook her head, trying to clear her emotions, her thoughts. And once she got past her panic, she realized she'd blown things out of proportion.

He *hadn't* fixated on her, other than running her off from his mother's business. She could grant him that. Beans & Leaves and Cherokee Park were chance encounters. And now that the adrenaline rush had degenerated into generic body shakes, she had to admit both times he'd been nothing less than courteous, even concerned.

Though he didn't know it was her in the woods, he'd stopped to check on a person unknown to him.

Her steps slowed. He'd put himself between her and the asshole cop at the coffee shop this morning. He hadn't looked happy about it, but he'd done it anyway. Detective Boone seemed to have a decent bone or two in his body.

But then again, she'd thought Tommy Finley hung the moon, and he was a cop, a deputy sheriff, and he'd turned on her. It was subtle to begin with, gradually isolating her from Granny McBride and her friends from school. By the time she'd figured out how dangerous he was, she'd been trapped. No haven to run to, no money, no high school diploma—not to mention the degree in nursing she'd planned on pursuing at the local community college. That dream had died soon after she married him.

"You don't need no degree in nothin'," he'd proclaimed, rubbing his belly. "Bring me another beer, will ya, honey?" He'd belched, then added, "I don't got one, and see, I got a good job. Respect. Steady money."

Steady money. Right. He had a point. In a region known for endemic and chronic unemployment, having a job, any job, was a coup.

"But we could have more, even if all I get is a certification in something. The admissions counselor said I can get a scholarship after I get the GED, and it won't cost you anything."

"I said *no!*" Tommy surged out of his recliner and backhanded her before Opal realized she needed to duck. But she was a quick learner, and he'd had to work harder to catch her after that. A lot harder.

Then the whole debacle after she'd killed him. Not one of the county's deputies, not even the sheriff himself, had looked at the evidence in front of their faces. They'd locked her up and thrown away the key, and she'd nearly died as a result. Her mind shied from the memories, memories that had been safe to face in the park, but weren't anymore.

Nope. That sealed it. Cops weren't trustworthy. Not even if they appeared to have hearts and loved their mothers.

With no extra time, Opal kept a brisk pace until she'd climbed the steps of the halfway house. She checked in with minutes to spare and a silent sigh of relief.

"Pushin' it pretty close, aren't you, Finley?" Ms. Hannity sniffed.

Opal glanced at her in surprise. "No, ma'am, I didn't think so."

The door opened behind her and Marya, a mousy, timid woman who probably survived prison only by attaining a cloak of invisibility, blew in with a gust of wind. She struggled to close the door, and Ms. Hannity's beady eyes sought out her new prey.

"Am I on time, Ms. Hannity?" Marya asked breathlessly, shoulders hunched in perpetual submission.

The clock chimed, and a look of frustration crossed Ms. Hannity's features. "Barely. Both of you, get on to your chores. Got no use for lazybones." She pointed at Opal. "I'll meet with you first tonight. Six forty-five." She punctuated the air with a stab of her forefinger. "Sharp."

"Yes, ma'am," Opal said. She waited for the familiar flash of rebellion or resentment to flare in her belly, but it didn't materialize. A smile bloomed as she realized the old biddy was losing her power. Was the woman losing her touch? Or was Opal's skin getting thicker? *Like a rhino.* Her smile broadened at the image.

She really hadn't expected the halfway house to be so much more difficult than prison, and her skin had been plenty thick there. The events of her first year of incarceration were a jumbled mishmash of impressions, leaving her with no template to draw on for this transition. Her only clear memory of that dark time was that she'd no longer wanted to live.

But in those early days, when her days and nights ran together like coal slurry, she nonetheless dredged enough energy to defend herself against the more violent inmates. From there, she'd waged a tortuously slow battle to survive, then to use the resources available to earn her coveted degree.

And now Opal had no doubt that she wanted to do more than survive. She wanted to live. To thrive. As she made her way through her meeting with Ms. Hannity and the evening's activities, she practiced how she would greet Josh Boone tomorrow at the coffee shop. *Good morning, Detective,* she mouthed, then pulled her lips into a smile. She passed a mirror in the hallway, glanced at her attempt, and grimaced. If her face was any tighter, it would crack and fall off her skull.

Marya approached, then stopped, her brows furrowed. "Are you all right, Opal?"

Embarrassed at being seen, Opal wiped the fake smile from her lips. As she caught the other woman's quizzical gaze, she realized how silly the whole situation was, and burst out laughing.

Marya hesitated but joined in, until Ms. Hannity shouted up the stairs for them to "knock off the monkey business." Eyes dancing, they both covered their mouths and quieted.

Marya whispered, "I call her Hateful Hannity."

Opal snorted a guffaw and, afraid she'd draw more attention from Hateful Hannity if she opened her mouth, retreated to her room. She managed a thumbs-up to Marya as she closed her door.

Ms. Hannity huffed her way up the stairs, but all was quiet on the upper floor when she got there, and she had no one to castigate.

By morning, Opal felt confident that she'd be okay, even secretly hoping that Hayley would be impressed and compliment her on her customer service. She got to work early again, and steeled herself for the onslaught of cops.

Each time the bell over the door jangled, she glanced up, her heart in her throat, but Josh didn't show up. Neither did the asshole cop. Plenty of others did, though.

She handed a go cup to one of them and, trying really hard to be sincere, said, "Thanks for stopping at Beans & Leaves. Have a great day."

The guy replied, "Thank you," then immediately turned to his buddy. "Yeah, five of 'em. Shot. All related to each other."

Opal's ears perked up and she tipped her head so she could overhear more, but his voice faded as they walked away. She almost missed the significance of his thank-you as she processed his words.

Five murders. No wonder Josh hadn't stopped for coffee this morning. Tommy had never had a murder to investigate, but some of the other crimes he'd worked on kept him out late. She couldn't imagine the magnitude of this…this carnage.

Relief flooded her, knowing that she wouldn't have to face Josh today. A breath later, shame slid in on its heels. Granted, he was her nemesis at the moment, but murders—even one murder—ranked far higher in importance than momentary discomfort on her part. Opal spun to check the urns, flustered at her conflicted emotions.

People had died, and she shouldn't rejoice about anything related to their misfortune. She hadn't rejoiced at Tommy's death. She hadn't wanted him dead, she'd only wanted him to stop. It took her a long minute, but Opal composed herself and returned to the counter, pasting a smile on her face.

No one seemed to notice her tension. Now that the cops weren't so focused on her, she acquired an air of invisibility, a la Marya. That, combined with her burgeoning sense of confidence, contributed to an uneventful, almost pleasant day.

~

The next day was much the same, and the next. As the days passed, Hayley gradually increased her responsibilities, then said, "You're doing well enough that I'm going to put you on a different shift."

Opal's heart gave a little skip of happiness.

"Oh, and you get a forty-cents-an-hour shift differential."

She couldn't hold back a smile.

"I hired Jeremy back, and you'll be working with him."

Crap. The only time she'd seen the guy was when he'd stormed out the day she'd been hired. She'd seen him throw a temper tantrum, and that made Opal nervous. Unpredictable people were dangerous people. But Hayley liked him enough to rehire him, so Opal straightened, determined to make it work.

"Great." She didn't think her voice sounded as hollow as she felt.

"Unfortunately, though, I'm going to have to cut your hours," Hayley added. "I'm sorry, Opal, but it can't be helped."

Opal's heart thudded in her chest. Her vision narrowed and a buzz of fear raced down her spine. She closed her eyes, then opened them. "Cut—not fired, right?"

Hayley's expression registered surprise. "Oh no. Not fired. I can't afford both of you at full time, so I hired him back at twenty hours a week. You'll essentially share one position."

Her heart sank. It was enough to meet the requirements of the halfway house, but a forty-cent shift differential wasn't going to make up for the lost hours. The imaginary pile of dollars she'd calculated during sleepless nights shimmered and rearranged itself into a much smaller pile. One too small for all the non-imaginary expenses she'd face in a few months.

Opal firmed her lips. She'd faced more daunting obstacles, and she'd meet this challenge. Somehow. But now, instead of enjoying freedom on her first day off, she'd have to spend it looking for another job. She quashed her disappointment and tried to look for a bright side. Maybe she'd have better luck this time, since she didn't need full-time work.

The bell jingled, interrupting them. Opal took a deep breath to regain her composure, put on her hospitable face, and turned to greet the customer.

And froze.

"Good afternoon, Ms. McBride." Josh Boone strode in, looking more purposeful than a cup of coffee warranted. "Hayley." He nodded. "May I borrow Opal for a few minutes?"

"Sure, Josh." Hayley shooed Opal toward the end of the counter, still focused on him. "Have a seat. I've got a fresh pot of bold on. I'll bring you a cup when it's brewed."

Opal's fingers went cold, and it took a not-so-gentle shove from Hayley to move her feet from the quagmire in which they'd suddenly become mired. She moved slowly, her mind in hyperdrive trying to figure out what he wanted.

Get a grip. Easy to think; hard to do. Her vision narrowed and her lips went dry.

"Opal, do you want a latte?" Hayley's voice drew her back from the edge of panic. "You're due a break."

"Uh, sure." She cast a quick glance at her boss. "Maybe a blended chai instead?" That would be the safest drink to order, given how her hands were shaking. The last thing she wanted to do was spill hot coffee on a cop.

Josh held a chair out for her and Opal slid into it, feeling awkward and nervous and trying not to show it. He took the seat opposite her.

"How's it going?" He absently drummed the fingers of one hand on the table, flicked a glance at her, then back toward Hayley.

Opal stared at him. And then words popped out without the benefit of a filter or prior, careful thought. "You came in here to ask how I'm doing?" The incredulity of her tone conveyed her disbelief. Blood rushed to her cheeks, and she snapped her mouth closed, then crossed her arms over her midriff.

His eyes homed in on her. "No, but I thought we could start there." He sounded mellow, affable, and not put off by her attitude. At first glance he appeared relaxed, but lines of fatigue bracketed his mouth, and the creases around his eyes seemed deeper. Even his laugh lines, and Opal had to wonder why she noticed.

"Am I a suspect in something, Detective Boone?" She didn't give him much of a chance to respond, leaning forward to say, "I haven't done one thing illegal, not even close. So why don't we skip the chitchat and get to the reason you're here." She sent him a defiant look.

Hayley showed up with their drinks, defusing the tension, or at least Opal's, because Josh still lounged in his chair with feline grace.

"Thanks, Hayley." He took a sip and closed his eyes. "Ah," he said on a sigh. "Best coffee in the city." The tightness in his face eased and he looked momentarily vulnerable—until he opened his eyes again and pinned Opal in his sights.

"Suit yourself." He shrugged and set his cup down, then pulled a notebook out of his suit jacket. "I'm investigating a cold case, and I hoped you'd be willing to answer a few questions."

Opal's mind went blank. "A murder?" She sagged against the chair.

He nodded, then took another sip.

Her hands went even colder, and she couldn't bear to touch the blended chai Hayley had set in front of her. Condensation began to form on the plastic cup. She dared to look Josh in the eye. "I only killed Tommy. I don't know anything about any other murders."

His lips lifted in a roguish grin. "Oh, but I think you do." He leaned across the table, invading her space and driving the air out of her lungs.

"And you're going to help me, maybe do a little penance for killing Thomas Finley."

Chapter Eleven

J OSH WATCHED OPAL try to worm her way out of the interview. He gave himself extra credit for deciding to approach her here, in her workplace. She didn't dare tell him what she thought of his request, nor did she dare walk away from him, not with her boss watching. Hayley wasn't overt about it, but she definitely had her ears in the best spot for eavesdropping.

But she wouldn't get any tidbits worth her effort.

"Opal?" He nudged her drink toward her, irritated at himself for liking the way her name rolled off his tongue. She had the deer-in-the-headlights look down pat. "Have a sip. You're looking a little green around the gills. This'll help."

She darted a glance at it, then pulled it close and put her lips around the straw.

O-kaaay. Josh shifted in his chair to hide his body's instantaneous response, then dragged his thoughts from the direction she'd sent them. He'd never, never, not ever, had a reaction like this to a suspect or even a witness. He cleared his throat to cover his unease.

She set her drink away, her gaze boring into his, anger simmering in her eyes. "I've paid society's price for what I did, Detective. And I've paid more penance than you can ever know." Her gaze faltered, but she got it back together and straightened her spine. "Besides, I told you I don't know about any other murders."

"Shaniqua Howell."

Moira's list had been waiting for him the other day, but he'd been too busy to work on Ezra's cold case. Truth be told, he didn't have time now, except that Shaniqua was slated for release in the next few weeks, and he expected her to disappear, maybe head south where she had connections and the weather was warmer. His window of opportunity was shrinking. And Shaniqua had already exercised her right to refuse him an interview, which ratcheted her higher on his suspect list.

A flurry of emotions crossed Opal's face. Surprise, awareness, wariness. She was so easy to read, he wondered how she'd survived prison. Then her expression became shuttered, and the door to her thought process slammed shut.

"You know her." It was fact, right there on Moira's list. He hadn't been terribly surprised to see Opal's name. "You were housed together for nearly a year." Violent offenders were placed in the high security section until corrections officials had sufficient grounds to move them. If they did.

A cautious nod from Opal.

"What can you tell me about her?"

"You know I can't act as an informant." Fear flickered across her expression, followed by a flash of triumph. "It's in my parole contract."

"Not without court approval," he countered.

He dug in his suit jacket for the permission he'd requested as soon as he'd seen the list. While he hadn't planned on talking to Opal today, he'd tucked it in his jacket as if it would help him think as he toiled. Maybe his subconscious was working harder than he realized. He opened the sheet of paper, spread it out, turned it, and slid it toward Opal.

"Besides, in agreeing to an interview, you're not technically acting as an informant. But I covered the legal bases anyway."

She inclined her head and studied the paper without touching it. Her brow furrowed and her skin, already porcelain, paled, making the smattering of freckles across her nose stand out. Her lips flattened, and she glanced around at the other patrons before leaning forward.

"Are you crazy?" she hissed. "I'm not telling you anything about her." She hesitated, then added, "If she ever found out—" She clamped her lips together and retreated into herself, arms over her midriff again.

Ah. That's how she'd survived. She slid beneath everyone's radar. Josh made a note to request Opal's history at the women's correctional facility, but he'd put money on finding it to be slim pickings. He was beginning to recognize that her self-preservation instincts were more akin to a rabbit than a mountain lion—blend in and when threatened, run like hell. Then again, he'd better keep in mind that mountain lions did the same, in addition to deadly ambushes when warranted.

He retrieved the paper and stowed it. "If I can guarantee your safety, would you talk about her?" There were no guarantees, not really, but he would cut a deal that would benefit Opal if she could help solve Ezra's murder.

She regarded him suspiciously. "You can't promise that and—" She hesitated. He saw the moment she decided to go for broke before she added, "—lying doesn't flatter you, Detective."

A faint rush of warmth climbed his neck. He sent her a rueful grin. "Busted." He shrugged. "It was worth a try. I *would* do my level best to keep you safe, though." He tapped the pen on his notebook, then dangled the only carrot he had. "If you help me, I can talk with Warden Phipps, see if she'll lean on the parole board to knock off some of your time in the halfway house."

Opal arched an eyebrow and looked down her nose at him. "What makes you think I want out?"

She was all sass and attitude, but he caught the faint tremble of her lips at the question, and he used it. "You want out, Opal." He leaned forward. "You want out so you can go to Cherokee Park whenever you want, day or night, without regard to rules and supervision and check-in times." His encounter with the unpleasant Ms. Hannity flashed into his mind. "And you want to get out from under Ms. Hannity's thumb." He sat back, sure he'd nailed that one, and disturbed at his insight into Opal's life.

He wasn't disappointed. Naked longing crossed her face, and he saw the muscles in her forearms tense, then release. She sighed.

"You're right, Detective Boone." Some of the starch went out of her shoulders. "But there are two holes in your argument." Her gaze, direct and honest, snagged him. "I do want all those things. But I can't give you what you want, because I truly know nothing."

She stood, leaving her froufrou smoothie on the table. "And if Shaniqua *ever* gets even a whiff that I ratted her out, I'll be dead in days. She runs a gang, a strong one with a long reach. Even if I knew something, I wouldn't tell you." She slid her chair back into place. "This interview is over, Detective. Sorry I can't help." She turned her back to him and bussed the tables in the seating area on her way back to the counter.

Josh watched her go, the antennae of his sixth sense perking up. Opal hadn't said it outright, but a persistent and ugly picture of Shaniqua was emerging. Violent, vengeful, and a strong enough personality to influence others to act on her behalf.

Opal had a point. He couldn't protect her, not entirely, and certainly not if she stayed in Louisville. He mulled the problem as he finished his coffee. Maybe she could move to a different halfway house, in Lexington, or Covington. Or heck, south to Bowling Green. West to Paducah.

He stood and stretched, then tossed his cup in the trash on the way out. He kept coming back to the fact that Opal didn't seem to be in the same league as Shaniqua…or any of the women he'd had occasion to arrest over the years.

He pushed his way out the door, a gust of wind nearly yanking it out of his grip. Pellets of sleet slapped his cheek, and he tucked his head against the weather. Frustration tugged at him as he jogged to his car. Several other inmates or ex-cons were on Moira's list, and he'd contacted a couple of them, was waiting for calls back from three others, and couldn't track down the rest.

So far, Opal was the only one whose response rang true. The two he'd spoken with had been too quick with their *I don't know anything* answers, hedging when he'd pressed and going all vague on him. Noncooperation and lies seemed to be the order of the day. In contrast, Opal's honesty was refreshing.

She hadn't been lying when she said she didn't know anything, but Josh suspected she knew more than she realized. It would just take time to tease it out of her. But what rang more true than that was her head-on approach. She didn't hedge or evade or try to wriggle out of responsibility for her own actions.

She'd flat-out told him she wouldn't disclose anything even if she knew.

He hit his key fob to unlock his car, slid in, and turned the heater on as soon as the ignition fired. He blew on his fingers to warm them.

Josh loved nothing more than a good puzzle, a challenge, a problem to be solved. And somehow Opal McBride had insinuated herself into becoming all three.

The defrost finally melted enough of the ice on the windshield that the wipers could work, and as he pulled out of the parking space, Josh contemplated his next step in unraveling the enigma of Opal.

Chapter Twelve

Sleet stung Opal's face as she hurried home—straight home today, since the weather had turned so nasty. She'd left her gloves and hat in her room, and gave herself a dressing-down for her foolishness. She hadn't had to plan her days or her clothing for so long, she'd forgotten that foresight was necessary.

She began to shiver and decided she needed to duck in somewhere to warm up. Or maybe use some of today's tip money on bus fare. Trouble was, she hadn't managed to get much of a grasp of how the system worked. So far it hadn't mattered, and she'd much rather walk, enjoying the freedom of letting her stride lengthen, covering greater distances each day.

Josh Boone's deal hovered at the edges of her mind. Did he really think he could protect her? She snorted. Not from Shaniqua. Unless Opal moved to Idaho or maybe Alaska. Besides, the woman had bragged incessantly, but never about a murder.

Unless you counted her ramblings about the man in the moon. The woman was crazy. Certifiable. Loco. Once in a while, not often, but only when the moon was full, Shaniqua would rant about "getting the moon man," and how she'd gotten away with it. She'd cackle, flashing a conspiratorial smile, and then find someone to beat up so she could go to solitary.

Opal had made certain she wasn't around for the beatings, although she'd gotten trapped in the dayroom a time or two. But she'd been canny enough to stay in range of the cameras, and guards had taken Shaniqua down before she'd taken Opal out.

Opal's eyelashes were freezing over, and she took in the variety of shops available for a moment of shelter, but this block didn't have much to offer. Private offices, for the most part.

But there was a Catholic church, imposing and welcoming at the same time, across the street. If it was unlocked, she could get a break from the cold. With all the stained glass windows, it probably looked pretty neat from the inside. Plus, no one would bother her.

Of course, that thought brought her back to Josh Boone, who was making a career out of bothering her. Would she help him if Shaniqua weren't such a threat? Opal didn't know. On the one hand, she didn't trust cops in general, and for good reason. But on the other hand, integrity seemed to be his hallmark trait. When she'd accused him of lying—she winced at the memory; what had she been thinking?—he'd blushed.

He had to be used to cutting deals, and probably used fairly liberal variations on the truth to pry information out of people all the time. Tommy had told her they'd flat-out lie to suspects as a matter of course in order to trick them into talking. All the more reason to not trust Josh.

And yet…his genuineness seemed authentic, not put on. Opal had the distinct impression that manipulation of people was a tool required by his job, not a facet of his character. His cheerful admission of the attempt only reinforced her perception of his basic nature. She couldn't hold it against him. *Just doing my job, ma'am.* Her lips lifted in a slight smile. She could imagine him saying that with a jaunty little self-deprecating salute.

She checked for traffic, then darted across the street and went to the big double doors at the main entrance. A spurt of nervousness stalled her hand, but she didn't think she'd get thrown out of a church. As long as she stayed quiet and respectful, and left if people began to gather. She'd be extra cautious to not overstep her bounds. A gust of wind made her slip on a patch of ice, and that made her decision for her. She tugged on the door and it opened.

Opal entered, latching the door quickly behind her, and waited, letting her eyes adjust to the dim lighting. A bank of red glass votive candles flickered off to the side, randomly lit and casting soft light on a painting of Mary. She recognized the icon from a tattoo that one of the Hispanic inmates had on her arm. Lourdes had told her it was Our Lady of Guadalupe, and recounted the story of Juan Diego's encounter with the apparition in what had become current-day Mexico City. Opal had found the story engaging, but no more so than Lourdes's bubbly personality.

The ice on her eyelashes began to melt, and Opal wiped them dry with her coat sleeve, then took a seat in the last pew. The wood creaked softly as she sat, but other than that, no sound came to her ears. The utter silence was unnerving and she almost rose to leave, but she contained the urge to flee.

She was tired of running.

Tired of evading Detective Boone, battling to survive on the inside, and struggling to make it on the outside. Tired of living with her memories and tired of trying to either bury or outpace them.

The vaulted roof drew her eyes upward, and she leaned her head back to examine the artwork, painted murals of scenes she recognized as Bible stories. The little clapboard community church that Granny McBride had dragged her to was characterized by weary simplicity, but this—this was like a museum, not that she'd been in one since a sixth-grade trip to Lexington. Or an art gallery, which she'd never experienced. But she'd seen pictures on the computer, and in books she'd checked out of the prison library.

Opal's gaze followed the arches down to the stained glass windows, the colors dark and opaque, thanks to the storm. Even so, she couldn't keep awe from welling up from deep within. A sense of *more* infused the space.

More than the art, more than the artists. More than the visible, more than the known.

Gleaming wood pews marched forward to the altar, the focal point of the entire space. A light, strategically placed on the ceiling, illuminated the spare white cloth covering the polished stone of the altar itself, making it appear to glow.

Tension released its grip on her heart, and peace stole in to replace it. *Sanctuary.* A word she used for the mountains of her childhood, and what she'd had a few precious moments of that day in the park. But not a word she would have used for a building of any kind.

The quality of the silence changed, not an addition of sound, but rather a burgeoning sense of abundance—that was the best word she could come up with to describe it. A flowing, gentle, enveloping embrace. It made no sense to Opal but it beguiled her, and she sank into the sensation, feeling a rare sense of safety.

Her eyes drifted closed. She let go of the ever-present need to watch her back, the need to toil to keep from failing. She got a glimpse of what it might be like to just *be*, and wondered if this was what meditation was all about.

Time passed. Opal reluctantly withdrew from the cocoon of almost pulsating quiet, and checked her watch. She still had time, and relaxed again, curious to see if the impression would recur. For a split second it hovered on the periphery of her awareness, and she held her breath, hoping she could entice it to return. She'd liked the sensation and wanted to experience it again.

But a slight sound, perhaps a distant door closing or a shoe scraping on a wood floor, broke the spell. Opal sat up, casting her gaze around to see who had invaded her solitude. A bolt of guilt shot through her, and she started to her feet.

A man dressed in black with a cleric's collar crossed the front of the church and knelt briefly in front of an ornate cupboard set midway up in the wall. A candle stood sentinel to the side.

A priest. Time for her to depart. A tinge of regret crossed her mind. The peace she'd found here was difficult to leave.

"Wait!" The man's voice rang out, then echoed through the space. "I didn't mean to disturb you."

Opal hesitated. It felt sacrilegious to raise her voice in this place, but she'd have to, in order to reply.

Her pause had given him the opportunity to head down the aisle toward her. She'd missed her chance to escape. Then Granny McBride's voice echoed in her mind. *Mind your elders, child. Especially men of God.*

In a hushed tone, Opal said, "Sir, I was leaving." Still, the acoustics made her words carry.

She had nothing against men of the cloth like some people did. But she had nothing in common with them, either, and though this guy's cheerful countenance did not presage an unpredictable, Bible-thumping, fire-and-brimstone preacher like the ones Granny McBride favored, Opal eyed his approach with trepidation.

He reached her and stopped mere feet away. Her breath eased out in relief that he didn't crowd her. He extended a hand and said, "I'm Father Barnabas, but everyone calls me Father Barney." His pale blue eyes twinkled as he added, "And those who know me best call me Father Blarney." He winked.

Only an inch or so taller than Opal, with fading red hair and fair skin sporting more freckles than a frog, he looked like an overgrown leprechaun. She was enchanted in spite of her wariness.

She took his hand and shook it, a quick pump up and down, then disengaged. "Father Barnabas," she said, tipping her head in acknowledgment. "Uh, I was just going…"

"Splendid, splendid! I'm glad you stopped in." He peered at her and concern crossed his features. "Have you warmed up enough? It's a cold one out there."

Opal found herself nodding. "Yes, sir. I mean, Father." She felt like she was babbling and clamped her lips closed. Heat, not from the heating system, flooded her cheeks.

"And you are—?" he prompted.

She didn't see a way to remain anonymous, and with a sinking heart she said, "Opal McBride."

"'Tis a pleasure to meet you," he said.

Automatically, she responded, "Likewise," and wondered how quickly she could end this encounter.

"Would you care to sit and talk a bit?" He gestured to the pew she'd just vacated.

Opal edged away, then glanced at her watch. "I'm sorry, Father, but I need to be on my way. Thank you for your hospitality."

She guessed he wouldn't invite her to stay if he'd been planning on throwing her out or having her arrested for trespassing, so she relaxed about that a bit. But maybe he wanted to "save" her. There'd been lots of folks like that over the years, doing prison ministry and saving souls. She'd stayed as far from them as possible.

Hellfire and damnation didn't sit well with her. According to Preacher Mac and the good citizens of Pike County, she'd already purchased her eternity in hell—and the bad part about that? Tommy would be there too.

"Well, stop in anytime you like." He smiled beatifically.

Opal regarded him suspiciously, and then some devil inside prodded her to say, "You wouldn't be so nice if you knew me."

Father Barnabas's smile didn't falter. Rather, it broadened. "Oh, but I would. We can discuss it sometime, either the theology or the personal, but I think you'll find they overlap." He patted her shoulder. "I look forward to speaking with you again, Miss Opal McBride."

She mumbled a good-bye, turned, and had to make an effort to not flee. For someone who was tired of running, she still did a bang-up job of it. The doors squealed as she opened them, and wind blasted her as she exited the building. She closed the door quickly, but not soon enough to miss Father Barnabas's jaunty wave.

"I'll see you soon," he called.

No, you won't, Father.

But all the way home, the interlude in the church played through her head, and she had to hand it to him. He'd piqued her curiosity, and that, combined with the odd sense of pregnant silence, of the air *breathing,* had her wondering if he was right.

She'd come back, even if it ran counter to every instinct she owned.

And she found the prospect both frightening and exhilarating.

Chapter Thirteen

"Got anything new for the task force meeting on Monday?"

Chris's question broke Josh's concentration on the reports in front of him. He squinted up at his partner. "When did you get back?" He'd been so absorbed in Shaniqua's file that he hadn't heard the man enter.

"Just now." Chris tossed a fast food sack on his desk, and the odor of French fries permeated the room.

Josh stretched, then shuffled through his pile of documents on the quintuple murder. When he found what he wanted, he pulled it out and handed it to Chris. "Motive."

Chris scanned the report and his face hardened. "Asshole. The kid's only three years old."

Josh grimaced in agreement. "Foster parents took her to the doc for what they thought was a bladder infection. Turned out to be gonorrhea and chlamydia."

Chris swore. "Mom's boyfriend?"

"Yeah, that's what I'm thinking. He's petitioned the courts for custody. He claims the kid is his, but there's no father listed on her birth certificate, so the court is waiting on DNA."

"The kid stays in foster care until it's sorted out?"

Josh nodded. "Thank God for the backlog at the state lab on the DNA, but he's paying for a private lab, so we may not have a lot of time to nail him." Left unspoken was the harsh reality that if they couldn't prove their suspicions, the kid would be turned over—legally—to her rapist and the killer of her family.

Chris dropped his bulk into his chair, which groaned at the burden. "Do we have any proof at all? Anything to go on?"

"Nope. No murder weapon, no record of him ever owning a gun, and he claims he doesn't know how to shoot."

"But if he's the abuser, he's got plenty of motive to kill the mom."

"Yeah, that's the way I see it too." Josh tapped his pen on his knee. "Mom probably figured out what was going on and denied him access, was maybe even planning on turning him in. He decides to take her out so he can have the kid *and* stay out of jail. It goes south from there."

"You think the rest of them just got in his way." Chris's voice was flat.

"Yup. But we've got no proof. I looked at the pings off of cell phone towers to see if they back up his alibi, but it's such a small geographical area that the information is useless." Josh shrugged.

Chris grunted. He rotated in his chair and opened his lunch. "How's your cold case coming along?"

Josh hesitated, loathe to admit what he'd begun to glean about Opal McBride's character. "Leaning toward Shaniqua Howell, up in Pee Wee Valley." He glanced at Chris. "I got good news on the Woodson trial." He grinned for the first time all day. "Jury convicted the bastard."

"Good news, indeed." Chris's expression lightened. "I'll treat you to a beer after work."

Josh shook his head, still grinning. "No, thanks. I've got the weekend off, and I've got plans." He didn't really, just a half-baked idea that had been growing as he studied Shaniqua's and Opal's prison records. He set their files side by side and began reading again.

The emerging picture did not fit his preconceptions about Opal McBride.

His hunch about her had proved right, but that wasn't making him feel any better about himself. Her history at the women's correctional facility included no disciplinary actions, no infractions of the rules, and very few incidents in which she'd been involved. And in every one of those, she'd been cleared of wrongdoing. The worst she'd done was bloody another inmate's nose in self-defense. He shifted in his chair and told himself he wasn't squirming.

He was beginning to wonder if his mom's assessment of Opal was on the mark.

Except that she hadn't offered a defense at the trial. In fact, she'd pled guilty. He wondered about her defense attorney. Court appointed, he was certain. But if those resources in Louisville were stretched thin, it would follow they'd be even scarcer in Appalachia. So she'd gotten a dud. Happened all the time.

Josh told himself he didn't care.

Chris lumbered by on his way to the coffee machine and stopped to peer over Josh's shoulder. "Whatcha got there?"

Josh discreetly slid Opal's file under Shaniqua's. "Cold case files." He pretended to be absorbed in Shaniqua's, and hoped Chris didn't pick up on his confusion about Opal. The guy had a knack for ferreting out tidbits to use for unbridled teasing at Josh's expense.

"Didn't ya say you were going to get McBride's record from Pee Wee Valley?" Chris leaned in and reached around Josh to shuffle through the mess.

"Hey!" Josh shoved his arm away. "You're destroying my filing system." As he'd hoped, the standing joke distracted Chris.

"Yeah, but you deserve it." Chris smirked as he gave the papers an extra swirl with his beefy hand. "You and your fancy suits need to be stirred up once in a while."

Josh made a strangled noise and slammed his hand down to prevent half a dozen sheets from sliding to the floor. "Just because you keep everything color coded, alphabetized, and spreadsheeted doesn't mean anything. I can find everything I need faster than you can, unless you get your grubby paws on my desk."

Chris chortled and walked off, his unpressed khaki slacks and second-day shirt a sharp counterpoint to his immaculate desk. Except for crumbs from doughnuts and fast food.

Josh shuddered, remembering the morning they came to work and found little mouse turds all over Chris's workspace. He smiled. Every once in a while an unsprung mousetrap showed up. The unexpected snaps had made everyone jumpy, especially Chris. Josh wondered if anyone would ever tumble to the fact that he was the culprit who'd been sneaking them in and setting them.

He sniggered and went back to Shaniqua's file. She'd been sent up for lesser crimes, although they were no less violent. *Her* file was thick with appearances before the in-house tribunal for offenses ranging from theft to verbal and physical abuse. She'd spent plenty of time in segregation, and consequently had earned the privilege of serving every day of her sentence, where Opal got out several years early for credit due to model behavior.

Well, not quite model. Opal had refused counseling of any type, group or individual, and had refused to speak to anyone about her crime. She'd stonewalled the psychologists, made few connections with either inmates or staff, yet quietly set about improving herself when opportunities arose.

She'd earned her GED and an associate degree. Josh caught himself mentally congratulating her, and shook his head to dislodge the thought.

In marked contrast, Shaniqua hadn't even tried to obtain her GED, but she'd joined every therapy group possible, then played havoc with the group dynamics until the staff had refused her access.

Of course, she'd contacted the ACLU and claimed her rights had been violated. That lawsuit would go on long after Shaniqua ditched parole and moved on to warmer climes.

And Shaniqua, four inches taller and fifty pounds heavier than Opal, had been the recipient of Opal's nose job.

Josh shuddered, visualizing how that had gone down. He wondered if Opal had ever been injured, and flipped back through her file to check. Treated at the hospital for bleeding after her arrest. No surprise there. Murder by two-by-four was messy business. Treated for bronchitis in the early months of her incarceration. And that was it. No stitches, no broken bones, no head injuries. But having been in his share of fights, both in training and for real, he knew firsthand about the bruises and body aches that resulted.

He tossed her file on his desk, and went back to Shaniqua's. He'd interviewed the other two witnesses, and their stories still matched the original statements. Neither had provided new insights. But when he listened to the tapes of Shaniqua, he was struck by her tone, not to mention her shifting recollection of the night's events. The woman had attitude, a bad one, and without the benefit of a visual record, the audio almost highlighted her cocky, I-dare-you attitude.

She had motive and means, and she sounded like she was gloating. Like she'd popped Ezra and had gotten away with it.

But he couldn't prove it.

And he'd run up against a dead end.

Josh glanced at his watch. Close enough to quitting time for him. He stood and shrugged into his suit jacket, then strode to the coat rack for his overcoat.

"'Bye, Chris. See you on Monday, for the task force meeting with Hoskins."

"Don't do anything I wouldn't do, Boone," Chris muttered, briefly shifting his attention from his computer.

"Fat chance. We're all too exhausted to raise Cain if we wanted to." Josh didn't mention that Chris's preferred methods of dealing with the stress of the job included a revolving door of hard-edged women and a steady supply of Maker's Mark, neither of which appealed to him.

But Josh needed a break. Suddenly, the urge hit him to get out of town, get a change of scenery. A number of options presented themselves, unfortunately all of them solo. Music in Nashville, hockey in Saint Louis, nothing of interest that he could think of in Cincinnati, a Pacers game in Indianapolis. But cities, especially stag, didn't appeal. And it was too cold for his favorite rock-climbing haunts.

Jubilee. That thought broadsided him. Huh. He could kill two birds with one stone. Get out of Dodge and go check out Opal's stomping grounds, get a better sense of who she was.

A reality check bulldozed that notion, and he paused. Exactly why was he interested in learning more about Opal? Other than the obvious—his unwelcome physical response to her. And the inescapable evolution of his perception of her character.

The snapshot of her personality that had emerged from the files Moira had sent him did not fit with a cold-blooded killer, and that *did* intrigue him. Not that he was going to go to Jubilee to clear her name. Not hardly. But the details around her crime, conviction, and incarceration were not adding up to a coherent whole. And he wanted to know why.

Plus, in spite of Opal's assertion that she knew nothing about Shaniqua—and he believed her, not that she was telling the truth, but that she *thought* she was telling the truth—she was still his best shot at unearthing the truth about Ezra's murder.

Sunshine hit him full in the face as he left the building. Yesterday's storm had cleared, leaving just enough clouds to create a stunning sunset. Mind made up, he began to plan tomorrow's road trip.

~

Josh was up before dawn and headed for a Beans & Leaves coffee to go. He wondered if Opal would be there. He'd seen her every time he'd stopped in for the past several weeks. A zing of interest energized him, and his lips lifted when he wondered what she'd say if she knew where he was going.

She wasn't there. Disappointment shot through him. He began to ask about her, but curbed his tongue before the words escaped. It didn't matter. But he wondered if she ever wanted to go back to her roots in Jubilee, and the thought stayed with him as he entered Interstate 64 toward Lexington.

The drive went quickly, at least until Winchester, where he left the interstate. Threads of tension unwound with each passing mile on picturesque back roads. He stopped for a break in a town so small it barely had a diner, then embarked on the last leg of his journey.

Jubilee was even smaller. A bedraggled elementary school was the biggest concern going, with a rusty gas station complete with old-fashioned rotary dial pumps taking halfhearted second place. A run-down church with peeling paint stood sentinel at one end of the short main street, and across from it was a bar with four motorcycles parked out front.

He eyed the chains and gang insignia on the souped-up bikes, and decided to steer clear of the dreary establishment. Josh figured he exuded *city boy* and *outsider* from his pores, because that was what he was. Born and raised in Louisville. The differences between him and Opal couldn't have been more starkly drawn.

Since the ratio of at least four to one didn't appeal to him, he pulled into the gas station. Likely, it was as much of a clearinghouse as the bar for gossip. He got out and stretched, then strolled into the retail area. A layer of dust dulled the colors of candy bar wrappers beneath the counter, although the floor and counter were spotless.

A grizzled mechanic came in from the garage bay. Josh nodded to the man. "Morning."

"Mornin' yerself," the guy said, wiping grease from his hands with a worn red cloth. "How c'n I help you?"

"I'm Detective Boone from Louisville." He extended his hand and the guy took it, gave him a firm shake. "Pleased to meet you, Mr. —?"

"Finley. Obadiah Finley."

Josh's gut tightened as Obadiah regarded him with alert but rheumy eyes. What were the chances? Opal's married name had been Finley. This was a sparsely populated area, and the family name could be a prominent one.

"Well, Mr. Finley, maybe you can fill me in on some history I'm investigating." Okay, he wasn't really investigating Opal, not officially, but he might get further if he phrased it that way. "Did you know a woman named Opal McBride? She hailed from around here."

Finley's face underwent a transformation. The natural curiosity died and revulsion replaced it. He spat on the pristine floor. "That hussy killed my nephew. Ain't nothin' more to know about her."

Josh moved his foot away from the foamy globule, which had landed suspiciously near his shoe. He'd clearly touched a nerve— along with confirming a connection between Opal, Thomas Finley, and Obadiah.

"I'm sorry for your loss, Mr. Finley. I read Ms. McBride's file, so I'm aware of the circumstances. Pretty much, anyway." Josh hesitated. "I'm not investigating Opal herself, but another case, and her name came up. I would appreciate it if you could direct me to where she lived. I'd like to take a look."

"I don't know as how any of that c'n help you, young man, but Tommy had a trailer up Beanblossom Hollow." He pointed to the road leading south out of town. "Take that there road, and turn right at the second opportunity, 'bout six miles. Trailer's about a half mile in, and abandoned. Widow Reese lives up beyond, and she might not take t'yer pokin' around. If you hear her rackin' her shotgun, you'd best be on yer way."

"Appreciate it, Mr. Finley." Josh smiled. "I'll keep your warning about Widow Reese in mind."

Finley's directions were perfect. Less than fifteen minutes later, Josh looked at the sad hulk of the trailer where Opal had killed Tommy. The mountain was claiming it bit by bit, kudzu having covered half of it, rust eating the other half. The door hung open, secured by only one hinge. Wooden steps to the porch were so rotted they wouldn't support a child. He got out of his car, and keeping an ear open for the sound of an angry widow with a shotgun, took a hike around the structure. He peered in a window. Empty. Not only had the furniture been moved out, the cupboards and sinks had been stripped.

But beneath the tangle of weeds and kudzu out front, he discovered rosebushes. Three of them planted at some point, then left to fend for themselves. They'd turned into wild brambles, with no hint to the colors they would display come spring. He wondered if Opal had planted them.

A scuff of sound had him turning around even as he said, "Widow Reese."

"Hmph." The woman's voice was unused and creaky.

Josh straightened. A quick glance catalogued her appearance. Average height, steel-gray hair held back from her face with a bandanna, a faded flannel-lined plaid coat, jeans, leather boots. And a twelve-gauge double-barreled shotgun. The gun lay cradled in her arms with a grace that indicated her competence in its handling, but she hadn't racked it, so he considered that a good sign.

"Good morning, ma'am. I'm Detective Boone from Louisville."

"What business you got up here?"

"Well, ma'am, I'm investigating a case."

"Only thing happened 'round here"—she inclined her head toward the trailer—"was settled a long time ago." Her lips twisted and her expression darkened.

Josh wondered if any other crimes had occurred on this ridge. "Do you mean Thomas Finley's murder?"

"Yes, sir."

He raised an eyebrow. "Then we're talking about the same thing. I'm gathering background information about Opal McBride."

"She's in prison. Why're you investigatin' water under the bridge and long gone?"

"It's actually not her case." Josh cleared his throat. "It's another one, and I think she might be peripherally involved."

Widow Reese shifted the weight of the gun in her arms. "I doubt that." She glanced to the side, but not before Josh caught a flash of pain in her expression.

"Why do you say that, Mrs. Reese?"

"Why would that concern you, Dee-tec-tive?" She drawled his title out, turning it into a derogatory slur. She returned her gaze to him, but the only thing he could read in her eyes now was accusation.

He had to stifle a smile. Opal was so like this woman—direct yet evasive, and so comfortable in her skin that she didn't need outer trappings to enhance the essence of her personality.

He cleared his throat. "I gather you are fond of Ms. McBride."

Her answer was quick. "I am."

"Then maybe you can help me understand her a bit better."

"Why? You's one o' *them*." Distrust oozed from every pore.

Josh's breath came out in a resigned sigh. "A cop? Yup. I can't change what I am. You've apparently had a bad experience in dealing with law enforcement."

Her answer was stony silence.

He decided to backtrack. "Why do you doubt that Opal can be involved in the case I'm investigating?"

"'Cuz she's a good girl, a smart girl, 'n' she don't have it in her to kill nobody."

Josh scratched his head. "Did you attend her trial?"

Widow Reese's face flushed and she broke eye contact, shifting her gaze to follow the flight of a hawk high above. "No, sir." Her lips clamped shut.

Josh softened his tone. "The evidence was overwhelming, Mrs. Reese. Opal did not contradict any of it."

Silence reigned. A host of expressions crossed Widow Reese's face. Finally she returned her gaze to him and said, "Opal is payin' for more than she needs to. I cain't see her gettin' involved in more'n what she got blamed for."

The hair on the back of Josh's neck rose. "What leads you to say that?"

Her face went hard, her eyes flinty, her lips tight.

Josh stooped and pulled some weeds back to expose a rosebush. "What color are these, ma'am?"

She squinted at him. "Why?" A heartbeat passed. Then, as if the words were dragged out of her without her consent, she answered. "That'un's pink."

He crouched and began pulling weeds from around its base. "And the others?"

She took a short step toward him, then halted. "The far one's red, the middle one, white."

"Did Opal plant them?" Josh continued clearing the space around the rosebush. He caught his thumb on a thorn and stifled a curse, shook his hand, then sucked the sting from it.

Two heartbeats, then half a dozen more. He moved from the pink to the white, tugging weeds from the stubborn soil.

"Yes, she did."

Josh heard a half sob catch in her throat. He rotated slowly, letting out a pent-up breath of relief that he hadn't made a mistake in turning his back on an armed and unfriendly woman.

She swiped her free hand at a tear tracking down her weathered cheek. "She was so excited when she got those. Saved for months, got 'em on clearance. Babied 'em until they right flourished." Her voice trailed off. "I tried to take care of them after—"

When it became clear she wasn't going to finish, Josh said in a flat voice, "After she got arrested for killing Thomas Finley."

Her face hardened again, but Josh saw anguish she couldn't conceal in her eyes.

He continued to pull weeds. "What happened, Mrs. Reese?"

"I should've done more for the girl," she whispered, looking beyond him, into the past.

Josh hesitated, then shrugged. "I doubt you could have changed the outcome."

She drew her gaze back to him. "I went to the police station, wantin' to give my statement of what took place that night." Disgust tinged with disgrace colored her features. "They threatened me. I should've stood my ground." She shifted the gun, waving her weapon to indicate the trail leading to the main road. "And yer one of them, so git along now."

The hairs on Josh's forearms came to attention, and he stood. "They threatened you? Who?" His mind raced. The case had been cut and dried, and Opal had refused to defend herself against the accusations. So what was the woman saying? Why would the sheriff's department threaten Widow Reese? Had they suppressed evidence?

Widow Reese bored a hole in him with her gaze, lips clamped shut, hefting the shotgun with more purpose than a few minutes prior.

"Ma'am, if the cops intimidated you out of making a statement, that was wrong." He shoved a hand through his hair. "This throws a whole new light on…" Josh shook his head, trying to make sense of the revelation. "Mrs. Reese, I assure you I do not subscribe to that type of police work. I'm sorry it happened to you." If what Widow Reese said was true…

She dropped her gaze and scuffed at the earth with the toe of her boot. "I let Opal down."

A lead weight settled in Josh's midsection. He couldn't escape the implications of the woman's words. *Opal spent twelve years in prison without the benefit of a fair trial.*

"It wasn't just you who let her down." He hesitated, then said, "We can't change what's done, but I can generate an investigation through the state police. If it still goes on"—he curled his hands into fists—"it has to stop."

Widow Reese regarded him for a long moment, taking his measure, then nodded. "I got nothin' left to lose, and maybe I can get my pride back." She relaxed her grip on the shotgun. "The police threatened to burn down my cabin with me in it if'n I told what I'd heard."

The lead weight in Josh's belly turned sour. Widow Reese kept talking, a flood of words held back for too long, and he struggled to keep up with her.

"They didn't care to look farther'n their own noses to see the truth. They was so mad she killed Tommy that they crucified her. It was self-defense. I heard her screamin'—dear God, it was an awful sound, like an animal—and I tried to get down here to help her, but I couldn't move fast enough. By the time I got here, she was swayin' on her feet with a chunk of lumber in her hands, blood everywhere, and Tommy out cold at her feet."

Her rendition of the event rang true, and fit everything he knew about the trial.

"I found her hair. Lordy, that child did love her hair, and rightly so. It was a glory. But it was all out back at the chopping block. T'weren't nothin' I could do about it, so I buried it in the woods over there." She indicated a copse of hemlock trees with the barrel of the shotgun. "Gave it sort of a funeral. Put it in a plastic bag inside a tin. My atonement for failin' her."

His mind reeled at the implications. "Self-defense?" The words stuck in Josh's craw.

"Ain't you listenin', Detective? He beat her regular, but for some reason, he'd been goin' at it more often and a lot harder the last month or two before it happened. I told her to up 'n' leave the weasel, but she was young. Besotted. In love."

Josh's hands grew cold, and it had nothing to do with the air temperature. "Why didn't she say something, get help?"

But before Widow Reese could answer, he knew, and shame cascaded over his shoulders like a bucket of ice water. *The wall of blue.* He held up a hand to silence her and spoke slowly.

"Finley was a cop, so no one would come to her aid, either before the killing or after."

Widow Reese nodded her head. "Yes, sir. She married Tommy shortly after the county took Granny McBride and put 'er in the old folks' home. Opal'd been doin' a fine job of carin' for Granny, but it got too much. Tore her apart…" The corners of her mouth turned down. "Tommy didn't let her finish high school, kept her up here without a car. And he wouldn't let her go visit her own granny, God rest her soul, when the girl had sacrificed everything for her."

Josh's gut twisted. He'd assumed the evidence that convicted Opal met the same standards to which he held himself. But he'd fallen—hook, line, and sinker—into the cesspool of blind eyes and cover-ups he'd always detested.

He still couldn't acquit Opal in his mind, nor could he label her a victim.

But he couldn't deny that he had lined up with the rest of Louisville's law enforcement community to form a solid blue wall of intimidation aimed at Opal McBride.

Mea culpa. The admission didn't make him feel any better about himself.

"Thanks, Mrs. Reese." He forced a smile. "You've given me exactly what I need."

Mea maxima culpa.

Chapter Fourteen

BLUE SKY AND SUNSHINE greeted Opal as she slipped out of the halfway house. Her spirits lifted, and she took to the sidewalk with a spring in her step. A day of her own, the first in too many years to contemplate. She focused on the novelty of it rather than the depressing lack of autonomy of the past.

It was too early for most of the shops along Bardstown Road to be open, but her innate sense of responsibility obliged her to apply at as many as she could as she made her way toward Cherokee Park.

If she lucked out and found a second job right away, she could spend the day roaming the park's paths. Anticipation fizzed in her veins.

If not… Well, she wouldn't let it drag her down. Not having to provide documentation of her job search stripped it of the desperation that had dogged her a few weeks ago. That, plus her experience at Beans & Leaves, translated to a level of confidence she hadn't possessed then. So whatever the outcome, it was going to be a good day.

An hour and four rejections later, she wound her way through a path in the woods, keeping an eye out for a jogging Detective Boone, and scolded herself at her cowardice.

Sounds of voices and laughter floated in the air, and after a brief battle with herself, Opal's curiosity overrode her concern at meeting up with Josh. She'd never get a good feel for the park if she only skulked around in the shrubbery. Besides, she had just as much right as he did to use it. Emboldened, she made her way down the slope.

Moments later, she emerged on the main road through the park, and joined the diehards who weren't put off by still-cool temperatures. Yesterday's ice storm had melted, except for occasional patches beneath the north faces of the hills. Every so often the road split, and it took Opal a bit to figure out she had to veer left if she wanted to stay within the park.

She retraced her steps from a wrong turn, careful to avoid an icy patch, and looked up.

May Boone was walking directly toward her.

Shock rooted her feet to the pavement, and her heart hammered at her ribs. Should she duck behind a tree? Turn and run? Stay the course and hope May didn't notice her? Indecision paralyzed her.

A flood of emotion washed over her. Longing for the acceptance May represented, resentment at Josh for denying her the opportunity. *Josh!*

Opal whipped her head around, looking for him, but didn't see him. Encountering him on his own would be bad enough, but getting caught talking to May would ignite his ire. The thought galvanized her and she wheeled, already moving toward the cover of the woods.

"Opal!" May's voice rose behind her. "Opal McBride!"

Deep-seated respect for the woman warred with Opal's instinct for self-preservation, but hunger for May's kindness won out. She slowed, then stopped and turned.

May hurried toward her, face alight with pleasure.

"Mrs. Boone." Opal didn't know how to greet her, but she wasn't going to use *ma'am*, not since May had been so insistent about it. And she couldn't bring herself to use her first name. Not yet, anyway. "Hi."

"How *are* you?" May's cheeks were pink in the cool air, and her bright blue eyes as lively as Opal remembered. Her eyes darkened with concern as she reached Opal and grasped her hands in hers. "And it's May, not Mrs. Boone," she added in a slightly admonishing tone.

"I'm fine, thank you"—Opal stumbled over her name—"May."

A man joined them and May looked up at him. She squeezed Opal's hands and said, "This is my husband, Jacob."

Uh-oh. Had Josh gotten his bulldog tenacity from his dad? Opal wanted to tug her hands free, but couldn't bring herself to hurt May's feelings. She tore her gaze from May, meaning to greet him, but her mouth dropped open in stunned recognition.

Of sorts.

An older version of Josh smiled at her, only with brown eyes instead of Josh's blue. Trim build, dark hair going silver at the temples, and with the same innate physical grace Josh possessed.

"Pleased to meet you, Miss McBride."

Opal stared, tongue-tied at the resemblance, and barely noticed when May released her hands. What other characteristics had Josh either inherited or learned from this man?

"I've heard a lot about you." Smile lines deepened at the corners of his eyes, but his words broke the spell he'd cast on her.

"Oh!" Opal could just imagine, between May and Josh. Her face heated. "I—uh, it's a pleasure to meet you too, Mr. Boone."

May beamed. "Josh told me you found a job, but he wouldn't tell me where." A faint scowl marred the smooth skin of her brow. She gave a small shake of her head and replaced the scowl with a smile. And waited expectantly for Opal's answer.

"Um, he is pretty protective of you, ma'a—I mean, May." Opal poked the toe of her shoe against a bit of ice about ready to break away from the edge of the pavement. "I don't mean any disrespect, but it's likely best if I keep that information to myself."

May made an unladylike *pfft* sound. "Best for whom?" She didn't leave any room for debate of the question. "Only for Joshua, and he knows he's overstepped his boundaries on this issue."

Opal took a step backward. She had no interest in getting in Josh's crosshairs again, for any reason. But she wasn't sure she had it in her to stand up to May's will.

Mr. Boone—Jacob—placed a hand on May's shoulder. "You're putting her in an awkward position, love." He glanced at Opal, compassion in the depths of his gaze. "But if I may offer my opinion?"

May smiled up at him. "Of course, dear."

He squeezed her shoulder and said, "What goes on between Josh and Opal is their business, but none of us is bound by his dictate. So"—his gaze sharpened—"if you and Opal would like to walk and talk, there's nothing to stop you." He pulled May into an embrace, her back to his chest, and rested his chin on her head. "I trust your judgment, especially after meeting Miss McBride." His expression sobered and he sent Opal a pointed look over the top of May's head.

His unspoken message snapped in the air between them, and Opal understood. *I'm going to trust you too. But mind your p's and q's, Miss McBride. Don't let me—us—down.*

Opal lifted her chin and sent Jacob a message of her own. *Don't worry, Mr. Boone.* She didn't agree with his assessment that Josh wasn't a factor, but she'd do anything in her power to protect May.

"Thank you, sir. I appreciate your support." She shrugged one shoulder and sent them both a wry smile. "But I don't care to get on Josh's, uh—" *Shit list* almost tumbled off her tongue but she stopped herself in time. "In his bad graces."

May straightened. "Well, he's allowed his opinion, but I make my own decisions."

As long as I don't get caught in the crossfire.

"Now, let's go get a nice cup of hot cocoa and talk." May grasped one of her hands and took off at a brisk pace, tugging Opal in her wake.

Opal threw a glance over her shoulder and couldn't contain a grin. Mr. Boone strode behind them, a resigned expression on his face. It appeared that the Boone men were no match for May. Nor, she realized with chagrin, was she.

May kept a string of chatter going as she led the charge out of the park…on a direct path toward Beans & Leaves.

Opal's grin faded. She'd met everyone on staff, and trepidation crept into her heart. Whoever was working was bound to say something and give away what had suddenly become her secret.

But *she* hadn't sought out an encounter with May. *She* hadn't told May where she worked. So whatever and whenever Josh found out, Opal could say with total truthfulness that she'd kept her part of his devil's bargain. *You get to stay out of prison as long as you stay away from my mom.* He'd meant it in reference to her fabric store, but since this was an unplanned encounter, and Mr. Boone was present as May's bodyguard, Opal didn't think it counted.

She doubted Josh would see the distinction, but the reasoning seemed sound to her.

When they reached the coffee shop, Mr. Boone reached around them to open the door, and all of Opal's worries became moot.

The worst-case scenario awaited her at the counter. Hayley and Jeremy.

Opal wished she could disappear, but there was nothing to do about the situation now, so she firmed her spine and wove her way through the tables behind May. Out of habit and a sudden case of nerves, she bussed one of the tables on the way.

"Welcome to Beans & Leaves," Hayley said, then spotted Opal. "Hey, girl, you like us so much you came back on your time off?" She grabbed a cloth and polished the granite counter. "I'm the only one who's supposed to spend all their time here."

May swiveled and regarded her with a small *O* of surprise. "You work *here?*" She gestured to include the entire space.

Opal gave her a weak smile. "Yes, ma'am. I do."

May didn't miss a beat. "Good." Turning to examine the menu, she asked, "What do you recommend?"

"Uh, do you prefer coffee or tea?"

Opal felt awkward at the sense of role reversal, but a brief give-and-take ended with May ordering a peppermint latte, the Valentine's Day seasonal special. She suspected May knew exactly what she wanted, but found it imperative to showcase Opal's new skills. While the attention added to her discomfort, a tendril of warmth stole through her at the woman's transparent manipulation. Mr. Boone settled on coffee, half-caffeinated, half-decaf, no room for cream. Once she realized Mr. Boone was going to insist on paying, Opal ordered tea, the cheapest item on the menu.

Jeremy placed the coffee drinks on the end of the counter reserved for pickup, and leaned past Jacob Boone so he could see Opal. "Hey, sorry about your hours getting cut."

Her eyes widened in alarm. She gave a tiny shake of her head and ducked so neither of the Boones could see her lips move. *Not now,* she mouthed, and lifted a forefinger to make a shushing gesture.

But to Jeremy, everything was all about Jeremy, and he ignored her frantic body language. "I s'pose it's all my fault, coming back after Hayley got you trained." He grinned, undermining any sense of remorse in his words. "But don't worry, babe, someone else will quit soon enough and you'll pick back up to whatever you want." He winked, confident that his assessment would make her feel warm and fuzzy.

Heat flooded Opal's cheeks. Nothing like letting May know darn near everything about her. *Might as well give her the address of the halfway house.* She let her hair curtain her face as she brought the last mug to the table, but couldn't put off the inevitable and lifted her gaze to meet theirs.

Jacob leaned back in his chair and sipped his coffee in a posture reminiscent of Josh's. May admired the heart Hayley had created in the foam that topped her latte. Opal used the moment to collect her wits, and stirred a bit of honey into her tea. She inhaled the sweet steam while casting about for something to say.

"This is a wonderful shop," May said brightly. "Do you enjoy working here?"

"Yes, ma'a—" Opal winced. She had to get over calling May *ma'am.* "Hayley—she's the owner—is a good boss." Her mind flashed to Hayley's exacting standards, and realized how grateful she was for the woman's firm guidance.

May toyed with her mug. "I couldn't help overhear the young man mention that your hours have been cut."

The warmth that had receded from her face returned. Opal shrugged, her cheeks flaming. Damn her Irish coloring. It broadcast her attempt to stretch the truth with neon intensity, and she tried not to make it worse by squirming. "It's not a big deal."

"I'm still looking for a dependable part-time person, Opal, and I think you'd fill the bill nicely." May pinned her with unflinching and compassionate eyes.

More than a job, May offered acceptance. Belonging. A sense of family that, for Opal, had died with Granny McBride. She gripped her cup, and the pounding of her pulse filled her ears. A rush of longing struck her, weakening her muscles and her resolve. She was glad that she was sitting, because she didn't know if her legs would hold her.

She drew in a breath and became aware of the mug's heat against her palms. She released the cup and glanced at her hands, surprised to see them trembling.

Opal held no illusions about her position at Beans & Leaves. An employee, a team member. Important, to be sure, but ultimately replaceable and forgettable.

Every cell in her body wanted to embrace May's proposition.

She lifted her gaze to May's. She parted her lips to speak, but no words came to mind. Until she exhaled. And the word that whispered on her breath surprised her. "Josh?"

Reality slammed into Opal with the intensity of a landslide, and her heart tumbled.

Josh. *You get to stay out of prison as long as you stay away from my mom.*

A chance meeting was one thing. Accepting May's offer of a job was another.

Even though he'd offered his influence with Warden Phipps in return for any knowledge of Shaniqua Howell—of which she had none—Opal had no doubt regarding the line he'd drawn about his mother. And she'd been foolish to allow herself the luxury of the daydream, because that's all it was. A fantasy, as unlikely and unattainable as escaping from a castle turret and finding her Prince Charming.

Getting out of prison was as good as escaping a fairy-tale castle, but Josh Boone was no Prince Charming.

She shoved to her feet. "I'm sorry, May." Her voice shook, and she swallowed tears that suddenly clogged her throat. "Thank you—" Opal choked out the words, but couldn't say more. She made a helpless motion with her hand, then turned and fled.

But May's stricken expression dogged her all the way back to the halfway house.

Chapter Fifteen

"YOU'VE BEEN AWFULLY QUIET today, Josh," May remarked as she took baby Caleb from Jenn's arms. She walked toward the sunroom and beckoned him to follow. Jenn heaved a sigh and leaned into Charlie, who put his arm around her, then used his free hand to click the remote. The muted sounds of the Boston Celtics and the Miami Heat duking it out on a basketball court drew Josh's interest, but the intimate tableau made his jaw clench.

He'd been headed for marital bliss, a house with a white picket fence, and 2.2 kids of his own three years ago. Right before Lisa stood him up. At the altar, no less. Shame, now familiar and thankfully not quite as knife-edged, rolled through him at the depressing memory.

No way would he begrudge Charlie and Jenn their happiness, but spending time with them highlighted the chasm between his reality and his now-broken dream. He could have manufactured a reason to avoid the weekly dinner at his parents' house, but he'd missed so many due to work that he felt obligated. And he had to admit a growing fascination with Caleb, now that he was getting used to holding the little guy.

Josh reached around his mother to open the door for her, then trailed behind while she settled herself on the cushioned wicker love seat. He chose a single chair off to the side, with a wry recognition of his avoidance tactic and its impending failure.

He scrubbed his hand over his face and glanced at her. "A lot on my mind, Mom. That's all."

"You always have a lot on your mind, son, but you usually tend toward distracted, not withdrawn." She lifted Caleb to her shoulder and patted.

"The quintuple homicide is enough, don't you think?" He leaned back in his chair, tipping it up on its back legs.

She considered his words for a moment, then shook her head. "No. It's more like…" Caleb let loose a belch that rivaled Chris's after too many beers. "Good boy," she said approvingly, then leaned her cheek against the baby's head. "They're so soft, it's like they're not even real."

Josh wondered how he could harbor resentment, even if it wasn't actively directed at his sister and her life. It didn't say much good about his character, which had been taking a beating since he'd met Opal.

He cleared his throat. "Yeah, he is pretty special."

May looked him in the eye. "You are acting like you did after the debacle with Lisa."

Since he'd been ruminating on the same sore subject himself, he wasn't broadsided by her perception, but he put a hand over his heart in mock distress. "Gee, don't pull your punches, Mom."

"Tell me what's going on." She hesitated. "I'm not aware of any romantic interests in your life, and for that matter, I haven't heard of anyone since Lisa." She lifted an eyebrow in question.

Josh let the chair thud to the floor. Caleb twitched, and he moderated his voice to keep from waking him. "Enough, Mom." He thrust a hand through his hair. "You don't need to fish for information. Just ask. But so you don't have to, no, there's been no one since—" His throat closed over Lisa's name, and he stopped to swallow. "—since then, and no one now." He skewered her with a look that should have had her quaking in her shoes—at least it worked that way with suspects—and added, "I'm an adult, and my personal life is my concern."

But of course the look didn't faze her. "I wasn't pumping you for private details." Her expression softened. "I worry about you. All alone, and so busy. Work shouldn't be your whole life. When's the last time you had a day off?"

Feeling like the words were being dragged from his lips, he heard himself say, "Yesterday." He straightened and added a bit defensively, "And today too."

Her face brightened. "Good! What did you do?" She shifted Caleb into a different position and rocked him gently.

Trapped. And she'd done it so skillfully. He'd learned manipulation of reluctant witnesses from the best, but he wasn't ready to share the rawness of his discoveries yesterday. Widow Reese, crooked cops, and the legal lynching of Opal McBride. All on top of the memory of standing at the altar in eager anticipation, followed in quick succession by a niggle of worry, then unease, and finally abject shame. Not only was Lisa's rejection total, but it had been public— and costly. He had attempted to repay both sets of parents, but they'd refused his overtures, leaving him feeling even more inept and irrelevant.

No wonder he'd poured himself into his work, and at the moment, it wasn't the refuge it had been.

He shoved to his feet. "I went for a drive, and I *really* don't want to talk about me. I'm fine. Nothing wrong. Not personally, but if you're talking professionally, then yeah, there's something wrong. I take murders very seriously, and if you define me that way, then my life—my entire life—is cause for occasional moodiness." He snapped his mouth shut before he said anything more. He'd already gone too far.

May rose in a graceful move that didn't disturb the sleeping infant in her arms. "Here."

Before he realized what she was up to, she deposited Caleb in his arms, effectively corralling him and forcing him to tamp down his emotions. It took him a moment to adjust to the weight and warmth of the baby, but once he'd managed, he shot an annoyed look at his mother.

She regarded him with a quizzical look. "No one defines you by your work, Joshua. It's an extension of who you are." She pressed both hands to her chest, then extended them palms up. "Take your Dad. He's a pilot, but he's good at it because he's a good man. As are you."

A lump grew in Josh's throat. He dipped his head to look at Caleb, because the back of his eyelids stung and if he looked at his mother, the tingle might morph into actual tears. Which pissed him off. He swallowed, and the tightness receded a bit.

Her hand settled on his arm. "Be kind to yourself. Just remember that we are here whenever you need us."

He blinked the sting away. "I know, Mom." He lifted his gaze to hers, and his lips tipped in a small smile. "Not much anybody can do about what's on my mind, but I appreciate your vote of confidence."

She gave him a piercing look, then nodded, a quick motion that said she accepted his answer at face value. Her eyes softened. "We saw Opal McBride in the park yesterday."

Heat flooded Josh's neck. He bit back an incredulous *What?* Every muscle in his face tensed and he clenched his jaw, then consciously relaxed it. His pulse pounded in his ears, and he took a breath, waiting for the noise to clear. He took another breath and said, "Really," then realized he'd closed his eyes. He opened them to see May's brow furrowed in confusion.

"Yes," she said cautiously.

The walls of the sunroom closed in on him, incongruous in the extreme as three of them were floor-to-ceiling windows. Why did

Opal matter so much to him? No one—*no one*—had this intense influence on him.

He surrendered to the inevitable. "Tell me about it, Mom."

She sank into her seat again. "Your father and I were walking at Cherokee Park yesterday morning, and she was there."

Yeah, that fits. "I saw her there a couple of weeks ago—from a distance—but she avoided me." He lifted his lips in a wry smile. "I'm not her favorite person."

"I don't know what you've said to her, Joshua, but she's extremely skittish, and her reasons appear to center around you."

May's voice held no censure, for which he was grateful, but he refused to tell her what he'd done. Caleb found his thumb and began sucking noisily in his sleep. Josh nudged the babe's fingers, splayed across his face, to prevent him from scratching an eye.

He caught his mother's gaze. "Not going there, Mom. Not having this discussion again. She's a convicted murderer and I want you to be safe." What he'd learned about Opal yesterday didn't support his original view, but until he nosed around some more, sorted things out, he wasn't backing down.

"I offered her a job again, and she ran away." Pain chased across her face. "That's the only word I can use to describe it. She left her tea and ran out of the coffee shop."

"Whoa." *The coffee shop?* "I thought you said she was in the park." *And you offered her a job?*

"Of course. But we took her to Beans & Leaves for a hot drink." This time she skewered him with her gaze. "You wouldn't tell me where she worked, and it turns out that's where."

If he hadn't developed an immunity to some of his mother's tactics, guilt would be doing a wild Irish clog on his psyche, but he had, and her accusation didn't stand a chance. "Go on."

"The young man behind the counter said he was sorry about her hours getting cut, so I told her the opening at my shop is still unfilled."

Her hours had been cut. *Aw, shit.* He didn't have a defense for the guilt that settled on his shoulders this time. Josh could picture it in his mind, could even see the defiant tilt of Opal's chin…along with her struggle to survive in the face of obstacle after obstacle. His mother's excellent roast beef dinner turned to lead in his stomach.

"Not my problem, Mom." He knew he was being harsh, and he couldn't explain it to her—not yet, anyway. But as bad as he felt about being part and parcel of the wall of blue, he couldn't justify putting his mother at risk.

His dad poked his head around the frame of the door. "There you are." He entered, trim and commanding in his uniform. "I'm leaving." He bent to kiss May, who stood and turned the kiss into a lingering hug.

"'Bye, Dad. Have a good trip, and fly safe."

"Always do. Good to see you today, Josh." He gave May another peck on the cheek and included both of them when he said, "Have a good week."

He left, and Josh used the flurry of activity to divest himself of Caleb and say his own good-byes. It was still light enough for a run, and fifteen minutes later he was pounding his way down the sidewalk toward the park.

The crisp air cleared his head, and a mental list formed. He'd get a transcript of the trial, examine the evidence that had been admitted, and if it supported Widow Reese's take on things—hell, even if all it did was cast doubt on whether Opal had gotten a fair trial, he'd follow up with a phone call to the state police like he'd promised.

But even that was dancing around the issue.

He needed to talk to Opal.

His lips curled in a grim smile at the chance of that happening. She'd done nothing but dodge him at every opportunity. Nor did he relish the prospect of facing her and admitting a very personal failure of the system to which he'd dedicated his life.

It took two circuits of the park's loop and an additional foray into adjoining Seneca Park to plan Opal's interrogation. And an interrogation it would be, although he'd have to frame it as a simple discussion.

He didn't have the normal weight of law on his side. She could refuse to speak to him, which was fully within her rights—yet completely counter to her best interest. He frowned, dislodging several drops of sweat that dripped into his eyes.

Problem was, he didn't know how to approach her in a way that wouldn't send her running. He topped a hill and slowed. His breath made little puffs of mist in the air, and he turned, surveying the hills and hollows below.

The sun, hidden behind a bank of clouds to the west, hung low in the sky. Shadows cast the landscape in mystery, and a pang of regret shot through his heart. While not as vast as the Appalachians Opal had come from, this probably came closer than she'd seen in the last dozen years. No wonder she sought it out.

As the light dimmed and darkness crept up the side of the hills, the similarities between Opal and her roots intertwined until they coalesced into a single, inscrutable entity.

Secrets and mist, obscuring all but the most elemental of each. Strength. Hidden depths.

His lips quirked upward. Hardheadedness. Stubbornness. Well, thanks to his mother, he knew a thing or two about *those* qualities.

He broke into a light jog and headed home. With a detour to Beans & Leaves to find out when Opal was scheduled next.

And if she happened to be at work now? His half smile widened into a wolfish grin. All the better to get started on his interrogation *aka* tête-à-tête.

Chapter Sixteen

Opal pulled the ragged jobs section of the paper out from under the sink where she'd stashed it midway through her shift. She'd gone over it with a fine-toothed comb and circled possibilities during a lull earlier in the afternoon, but a spurt of customers talking about the movie they'd just seen had forced her to abandon the project for a while. They'd cleared out a few minutes ago, so she settled in to scour the ads again.

"Hey, Opal." Denise massaged her temples with the tips of her forefingers.

She frowned. "Are you okay?" Jeremy was off this weekend—*thank you, God*—and her current coworker was a perennially sleep-deprived college student.

"Just a headache." She ruined the disclaimer by scrunching her eyes closed and grimacing. "Do you mind if I go to the office? If it gets busy, call me and I'll be right out."

"No problem." Opal had enough confidence to handle single customers straggling in on her own. She smiled at the revelation and waved Denise toward the darkened room. "If it was up to me, I'd send you home, but Hayley'd have a cow." The boss had an ironclad policy about having at least two employees at the coffee shop when the open sign was lit.

Denise rolled her eyes in agreement, then moaned and disappeared into the office.

Opal returned her attention to the want ads. Her heart sank at the dearth of offerings, at least ones for which she was remotely qualified. She skipped over the health care section, didn't even bother with the professional listings, and put a slash mark through positions requiring experience. That left a customer service position "providing a world-class customer experience," and several housekeeping positions. She doubted she'd get as far as an interview for the first one, and chances were the locations for the others would be problematic.

Not only did she not have a car, the only driving she'd ever done was as an unlicensed teen on Appalachian back roads. Granny McBride's rattletrap pickup truck, complete with bald tires and an unreliable starter, didn't compare to the fancy cars she saw in Louisville. Plus, the thought of taking a test on these busy streets made her heart stutter. Nor had she made sense of the bus system.

Nope. She'd be best off sticking close for a job, somewhere she could get to on foot, but she'd exhausted the possibilities on or near Bardstown Road, May Boone's shop notwithstanding. Her lips turned down at the corners in spite of her determination to keep a positive mindset.

Stupid Josh Boone. She wasn't a threat to anybody, and especially not to May. Her lips softened at the thought of the woman's unwavering goodness. The detective wasn't going to change his mind, though. Opal couldn't influence the situation, and the sooner she accepted the fact and moved on, the better off she'd be.

But if she didn't find another job, her savings wouldn't be enough to support her once the halfway house turned her loose. An invisible fist squeezed her lungs, and she hunched over the newspaper in search of an elusive possibility she might have missed.

A gust of wind blew the door open and set the bell to a mad tinkling. The customer had turned to make sure the latch held by the time Opal glanced up. She stowed the want ads and stood, plastering a smile over the anxiety they had engendered. It wouldn't do to jeopardize the job she *did* have, and she'd made a habit of always acting as though Hayley was watching her every move.

The man, a jogger, turned, and recognition shot through Opal like quicksilver.

Josh. Josh Boone.

It was as if her thoughts had conjured the man. Her smile faltered, but she shored it up with determination born of a mix of resentment and desperation. "Detective." The word came out flat because she couldn't muster enough welcome to support both facial expression and voice.

He swiped an arm across his forehead to rid it of sweat, and grinned. "Josh. I'm off duty." He blew into his cupped hands and approached the counter. "It's wicked out there."

"Your usual?" Opal had already pulled a large to-go cup and halted with it under the spigot of the urn filled with the bold blend. She wished her heart hadn't given a happy little thump at his smile, the one that made him seem like such a nice guy. A smile that had the potential to make her feel special. She quashed the feeling.

He fished his wallet out of his jacket pocket. "Join me?"

Her heart stalled. Encounters with him did not have a good history. "Nope. I'm *on* duty."

He looked around the empty shop, then returned his gaze to hers and lifted an eyebrow.

Opal's cheeks heated. She pressed her lips together and scowled. Lifting the disposable cup, she indicated his normal coffee choice in a silent question.

"Make it half-caf, and put it in a ceramic mug." He slid a couple of ones onto the counter.

She replaced the to-go cup and filled his order, her back prickling under his scrutiny.

He took the cup and sipped, but didn't move away. His posture was casual, his muscles relaxed, but Opal's unease at his proximity escalated. She rang up the sale, handed him the change, then wiped the palms of her hands on her apron.

Without looking away, he dropped the coins in the tip jar and leaned forward. "Hold still."

The words were soft, but the command immobilized Opal as surely as a gun at her temple would have. He lifted his hand, a small furrow between his brows. She watched it, mesmerized and helpless to either stop or evade his touch.

A riot of emotions heaved beneath her motionless exterior. The heightened sense of awareness she felt when he was around. The more logical yet less clear sense of threat, part of which she could attribute to his role as cop and hers as felon, the other deeper, darker, more compelling, more thrilling. Her breath caught and hung suspended as his hand moved closer and closer.

The pupils of his eyes expanded, darkening them. "I've wanted to touch your hair ever since I saw you in Mom's store," he murmured. His fingers plucked something from Opal's crown, and flicked it away. His palm settled on her head, and the urge to turn her face into it struck her, so primal and irresistible that a trembling began deep in her belly. It expanded outward until it encompassed her arms and weakened her knees.

But somehow she refrained from succumbing to the temptation to surrender, to experience a moment's bond to another human being, to know a touch not meant to control or coerce. A touch unmotivated by duty.

The trembling coalesced and traveled to her lips. Opal gazed into his eyes, simultaneously lost and grounded in ways so out of her realm of experience that she felt almost dizzy.

"Did Shaniqua ever say anything that you didn't understand, Opal?" Josh uttered the question in a tone she would have expected to be reserved for a lover, and he stroked her hair in the same manner, tucking a wayward strand behind her ear.

She raised her eyebrows, bemused by what he'd asked and what he was doing. "Only…" Distracted by the warmth of his caress, she sucked in a breath, then tried speaking again, her voice husky and low. "Sometimes she'd act crazy, howling at the moon, attacking people for no reason, and she'd cackle, say she'd offed the man in the moon and got away with it."

Josh's face tightened a bit, but his hand didn't falter in its lazy exploration of her hair. "Mmm?"

Opal's eyes drifted closed. The sensation was so delicious, so lovely, she felt weightless. "She'd point at the moon, draw pictures of it, put dots where a forehead and nose might be, if it was a face. Always in the same place, over and over." She barely stopped herself from letting a hum of pleasure escape. She dragged her eyelids upward to look at him again, but could only get them to about half-mast. "I thought she was nuts, still do. She is. But she always did this on full-moon nights, and I don't think it's anything but the rant of a psychotic."

His fingers slid lower, touching the sensitive skin below her ear. Opal jolted, pulling back, but he slipped his hand around the nape of her neck, and she froze. He kneaded gently, and she melted.

"What did she say she did with the weapon?" His voice was low, hypnotic. Safe.

She managed a shrug against the flow of warmth sliding down her back. "Said it was in plain sight. Something about Swiss cheese." He'd found a knot in the muscles of her neck and settled on it, working it loose. This time she had to bite back a moan.

"What happened to your hair, Opal?"

His tone was still soft, still unthreatening, but with a hint of perplexed curiosity, and the words didn't register for a heartbeat. Then they sank in.

Her eyes flew open and she stiffened under his hand. "What?" The lassitude he'd lulled her into fled, leaving her fingers bloodless, her body suddenly chilled. She jerked away, pushing back from the counter and breaking his admittedly gentle grasp. She stumbled, caught herself, and wrapped her arms around her middle. The trembling returned and doubled in intensity.

He dropped his arm, picked up his still-steaming coffee, took a sip. "Widow Reese said she found your hair out back after you were arrested."

A noise like a howling wind filled Opal's ears, and her breath stalled. Widow Reese? *Widow Reese?* When had he talked to *her?* And why? Her thoughts tangled in an unruly snarl, and her emotions followed.

Memories of that ugly day burbled up, a conglomeration of images, a slide show of chaos and terror. Tommy's drunken aim with the hatchet, her frantic efforts to evade his swings, the sting of her scalp as she fought to escape and he jerked her back. The thunks as he buried the ax in the chopping block. Her screams, a soprano descant to his growling, roaring bass, swirling together to create a macabre opera.

Opal's breath returned and she inhaled great gulps of air, but none of it had any oxygen.

He'd gone to Jubilee. That was the only way he could know about Widow Reese. Anger, white-hot and searing, shot from her core to scorch her skin. Oxygen finally hit her brain and cleared her mind. With a monumental effort, she shoved the memories back where they'd been for twelve years.

"How dare you!" Opal unwrapped one arm from her midriff and pointed an index finger at him. "How *dare* you!" Her voice rose, and she felt incandescent with fury. "You have no right to pry into my life." She noted with almost impassive detachment that her finger was shaking. The trembling traveled up her arm until it looked like a hurricane-force gale was blowing inside the coffee shop.

His eyes widened and he set the cup down with measured care. "Whoa." Holding both hands out, palms up, he said, "Not prying." He stepped back, a cautious movement designed to promote calm.

But Opal was having none of it. "Why? What difference does it make to you?" She fairly spat the words at him.

"Because I think you got a bad deal, Opal." His eyes narrowed and the skin across his cheekbones tightened. "But I can't prove it without your cooperation, and it takes a Mack truck to get past your defenses."

She swayed and grabbed for the counter. "It doesn't matter if I got a bad deal or not, Detective. I deserved what I got, I served my time, and I want it over." Her knees threatened to buckle. "Get out."

"If we can prove it was self-defense, and that evidence was intentionally suppressed, your conviction can be vacated."

"What's this *we?* Since when did you decide to switch sides?" Her vision wavered.

"I haven't switched sides. I've always been on the side of justice." His expression darkened and he scowled. "It just looks like justice may not have been served in your case." He shifted his weight and shrugged one shoulder as if trying to shed an unwelcome truth.

"Too bad." Opal pointed at the door. "Out. Leave me alone."

"I owe you for the information about Shaniqua."

The shift in topic left Opal momentarily adrift.

"I'll get you released from the halfway house." He looked both grim and triumphant.

Opal's heart plummeted. She couldn't afford to live on the outside. Not yet. Her only option would be public housing, and that was almost as bad as prison.

"No," she breathed, but the word emerged soundless.

"Is everything okay out here, Opal?" Denise emerged from the office, a crease in the side of her face from sleeping on the desk. Her gaze darted between the two of them, alarm in her wide-eyed expression.

Josh straightened, and with obvious effort softened the intensity in his muscles. "Yes, ma'am, everything is fine." He glanced at Opal, sending her a silent I'm-not-done-with-you message. "I was just leaving."

Denise turned her questioning gaze to Opal, then to Josh's retreating back. "He left his coffee."

Opal shrugged, the motion stiff. It took her a moment to collect her wits, and she licked her lips before she spoke. "No biggie." She picked up the mug, dumped its contents, and sent Denise a bright, fake smile. "Let's finish the closing chores so we can get out of here on time."

Her coworker looked troubled, but accepted Opal's direction without comment. Which suited her fine, because her thoughts were scattering like a flock of sparrows startled by a hawk.

The halfway house, as much as she hated it, was her stepping-stone to a better life. She'd come from poverty—which honestly hadn't seemed so bad at the time. Everyone had been in the same boat. Granny McBride had been the bulwark holding Opal safe as her family disintegrated around her. It wasn't until the county took Granny away that she realized how tenuous her life really was. So she'd thrown her lot in with Tommy, thinking he'd be like Granny. An ally.

She stopped that line of thought. No, she didn't want to go back to Jubilee, or poverty, or desperation, but Detective Boone seemed bent on forcing her to do exactly that with his misguided charity.

Opal glanced at the clock, went to the front and locked the door, turned the sign to CLOSED, and grabbed the mop. It took her nearly ten minutes of furious cleaning before her panic receded enough for the solution to form.

No part-time job would net enough to support her, but a full-time one would. Ergo, so would two part-time jobs.

And she knew where to find one, Josh Boone be damned.

Chapter Seventeen

WHY IN *HELL* had he given in to the temptation to touch Opal's hair? Some devil in him, or some siren in her, conspired to create a fascination he was helpless to resist.

Of course, she was the most inappropriate object of his wayward hormones, and from now on out, he'd make damn sure he never succumbed to the unconscious allure she presented. *Forewarned is forearmed.* He flattened his lips. Not only did touching Opal represent disaster in his personal life, as in another spectacular lapse in judgment about women, but that touch crossed a line he couldn't afford professionally.

He cursed himself roundly, then did it again for good measure.

Yet, everything about her drew him like a lodestone. Her spirit, her intelligence, the balance she'd achieved between accepting the fairness of her incarceration and her right to build a new life now.

Cold air penetrated his clothes, and his muscles, having tightened in the brief time at Beans & Leaves, protested. Josh broke into an easy jog to loosen and warm them for the short trip home. But he couldn't quiet his mind as easily.

He hadn't meant to ask about her hair. The words had just slipped out, and his mind still reeled at her reaction. *How dare you? You have no right to pry into my life.* Why such an extreme response? Then when he'd laid out his suspicions, she'd as much as told him she didn't care if justice hadn't been served.

Opal was proving to be a mystery with more layers than an onion and more twists than the Cumberland River. He was getting the sense that she was hiding something, which didn't make any sense.

But he needed to put all that aside for now. He had a cold case to solve, and he couldn't believe the wealth of information—prosecutable information—Opal had handed him. She was a gold mine and if he played his cards right, he'd never have to reveal his source. Everything she'd said was verifiable with the prison staff. Even better, if any of the psychologists had saved Shaniqua's drawings…

Sometimes she'd act crazy, howling at the moon, attacking people for no reason, and she'd cackle, say she'd offed the man in the moon and got away with it.

Ezra Johnson's strip club had been called Moonlight Exotic Dancers.

She'd point at the moon, draw pictures of it, put dots where a forehead and nose might be, if it was a face. Always in the same place, over and over.

Opal didn't know Ezra Johnson, didn't know that two shots to the head had taken his life. One in his forehead, the other obliterating his nose. Josh's breath came faster at the uncanny accuracy of Opal's words.

And when he'd asked about the weapon, the hairs at the nape of his neck had come to eerie attention. *Said it was in plain sight. Something about Swiss cheese.* One more detail Opal couldn't know was that a sculpture graced a traffic median not far from Ezra's long-defunct club. A bright yellow sculpture of a wedge of Swiss cheese. Josh had driven by it a thousand times on his way into or out of downtown, someone's idea of drawing attention to the numerous cafés in the area.

Shaniqua might act crazy, but she was crazy like a fox. No one had reason to intentionally nose around that sculpture. It was in the middle of a busy street, and set back a bit even from the pedestrian crosswalk. The only folks likely to get close to it would be the city landscapers, and if he remembered right, the area around the sculpture itself was done in river rock. So they wouldn't even need to get *that* close.

He already had probable cause to interrogate Shaniqua, and the only way she could stonewall him this time would be to invoke legal counsel. Even that wouldn't do her a lot of good, because if Opal's unwitting tip panned out, the commonwealth had a slam-dunk case against Ms. Howell. His blood heated. He didn't even need a warrant to poke around the sculpture.

A grim smile lifted his lips as he let himself into his condo and shed his workout gear. A phone call and a quick shower later, he was out the door, this time dressed for getting dirty.

The drive downtown didn't take long. He parked his car near the cheese sculpture and turned his flashing strobes on.

The forensics van had just pulled up and the tech was pulling klieg lights out. "Hi, Detective. Where do you want these?"

"Light up the cheese." Josh grinned and popped the trunk. "Looking for a gun, a thirty-eight based on the ballistics. Supposedly stashed here twelve years ago." A gust of wind cut through his jeans, chilling his skin.

The tech, whose name tag read DANIELS, shrugged. "Better'n gore, but I'll let you do the honors." He finished setting up the lights and pulled his coat up around his ears. He coughed and swept a hand across his nose, then sniffed. "If you don't mind, I'll wait for you in the van."

"No problem." Daniel's lack of interest didn't deter Josh. "I'll call you when I find it." The tech disappeared into the cab of the van, and Josh hefted the shovel as he eyed the sculpture. His first order of business would be a careful examination of the exterior. *You never know. It could be that obvious.* Stranger things had happened. He left the shovel propped against the car and stowed his flashlight in a pocket.

The initial trip around the statue netted nothing, although there was an access panel that showed no indication of disturbance. His lips quirked up. He fished his cell phone out and hit speed dial.

"Hasselback." Chris sounded like the phone had woken him. Otherwise he would have noticed Josh's caller ID.

"It's too early to be in bed, lazy head. You want in on a little light action?" He kept his voice serious in spite of the irony of his proposal.

A protracted yawn sounded in his ear. Then, "Aren't you off this weekend, Boone?" Without waiting for an answer, Chris added hopefully, "Unless you want to hit the bars...?"

"Dress warm and meet me in front of the Drunken Eggplant." Josh glanced up. "You can't miss me. Got the strobes warning traffic off, and kliegs on the site."

Sounding simultaneously animated and disgruntled, Chris said, "Aw, shit. Did you come up with the murder weapon for the quint-homicide?"

Josh's spirits deflated a bit. "No. Wish I did, though. Naw, this is the cold case."

"Is this really worth getting out of my bed for?"

"Only if you want to. But I'm pretty sure"—he caught himself before Opal's name slipped—"uh, my intelligence is spot-on. Just think, you could be in on the breaking of the latest cold case." Josh crouched and shined his flashlight on the seam of the access panel. With closer inspection, he could see a fine crack in the paint that once sealed the panel to the rest of the structure. He stood to retrieve his camera from his coat pocket.

"Oh hell, there's nothing else going on." Chris sighed, an exhalation far more melodramatic than the situation called for. "I'll be there in twenty."

By the time he showed up, Josh had documented the site and decided that the access panel, besides being the easiest place to search—it involved no digging—was also the most likely. He couldn't see Shaniquah as having enough foresight to bring the large tools required to move river rock and dig, then to replace all of it so as to not draw undue attention. A screwdriver, yeah. Or a table knife, for that matter. A shovel, not so much.

The heavy slam of a car door announced Chris's arrival. Josh glanced up. "I'm about ready to start. Hold the flashlight for me?"

Chris took it without a word, and Josh began on the first screw. They worked in silence for several minutes as screws released their hold one by one. Chris used his bulk to shelter Josh from the wind. The last one proved to be much more stubborn than the others and Josh cursed, hoping the screwdriver wouldn't strip the head.

If it did, he'd have to roust Daniels from the forensics van. A glance showed the tech reclined and likely asleep. Not that it would bother Josh to wake the guy up, but he could identify with being half-sick and wanting to stay somewhere warm.

One more concerted effort popped the screw from its home. Several blister-inducing turns got it out. Josh took the flashlight and illuminated the holes. Nothing obvious, beyond rust that had nearly sealed the final screw in place. Carefully, he placed the flat edge of the screwdriver in the deepest of the cracks between the panel and the body of the sculpture.

The panel squeaked and moved a millimeter or two, but it was enough to open up another lever point. It finally popped off, and Chris caught it in a plastic bag. Josh's pulse sped up, and he dipped his head to see.

Nothing. His heart plummeted. He held his hand out for the flashlight and Chris handed it to him wordlessly. He shone it in the interior and saw nothing but unpainted metal and concrete below, where bolts secured it. He let out a disappointed breath.

Not Opal's fault. He'd been so sure she was right. He sat back on his haunches. "Guess we dig now."

Chris leaned over him and peered inside. "Did you get a good look at the corners nearest you?"

"Thought so, but I'll look again." Careful to not touch the edges of the hole or brush the body of the sculpture, he swept the light into the recesses the best he could—and froze. *There!* He'd been looking for a black gun, a sharp contrast with the light colored concrete, but the damn thing was pink. *Pink, for crying out loud.* He'd seen them in gun catalogs, but he'd never known anyone to actually own one. Faded with age, its contours matched the corner it had landed in and blended perfectly with the neutral background.

"Bingo," he breathed. He shifted to get a better angle, but it didn't help much. "Go wake up the tech. Name's Daniels. I'll need a special camera and tool to document and retrieve this."

"Gotcha." Chris lumbered off.

Opal had come through. A spurt of pride warmed Josh from the inside out. He owed her big-time. Come morning, he'd get on the horn with Warden Phipps and set the process rolling of getting Opal out of the halfway house. She'd still be on parole, but other than the restrictions of staying in Kentucky, drug-free, and off law enforcement's radar, she'd be free.

It was the least he could do.

The tactile memory of her hair surfaced. His jaw tightened, and his hand clutched as if burying itself in the shimmery waves.

He'd screwed up big-time, and she'd let him know it. If he saw her again, he'd run the risk of crossing another line, that of stalker. She'd made it clear she didn't want to see him. Ever.

Josh cringed at the image of Opal's forefinger poking at his chest, high color in her cheeks, the utter fearlessness of her edict. Yeah, he'd respect her boundaries.

He'd told her she could do penance by cooperating with his investigation a couple of weeks ago. It looked like his turn to do some penance.

Chris and Daniels returned with the equipment he'd requested. As he set up the camera, he made a silent promise to Opal, to not only make her life easier in return for this tip, but to investigate the substandard police work that had put her behind bars.

And the bit about what happened to her hair. The hair on his nape lifted. She was hiding something, he knew it.

His mind flashed to that mug shot. Then Widow Reese's voice played in his mind. *I found her hair; it was all out back at the chopping block.* Widow Reese's recounting of Opal's screams. *It was an awful sound, like an animal.*

His blood ran cold as the picture clicked into place in his mind's eye. Thomas Finley, holding Opal to the chopping block with one hand tangled in her hair, swinging an ax with the other. The image made him cringe. It would make anyone scream. And it would explain the really bad haircut in her mug shot.

But that meant Opal's actions had to have been self-defense, which would net involuntary manslaughter at the worst, if the prosecutor even thought the case had merit—which was looking less and less likely. Josh frowned. Why was Opal so ferociously resistant to his interest in a possible miscarriage of justice at her expense?

What *was* Opal McBride hiding? And more important, why?

Chapter Eighteen

"FINLEY!" Ms. Hannity's bellow reverberated up the stairwell.

Opal cringed. *Not yet, please.* She'd been praying for two days that Detective Boone—thinking of him by his title blunted the memory of his touch—had forgotten about his promise to get her out of the halfway house. Her face heated at her gullibility. And her feminine response. She flattened her lips, shoving feelings of embarrassment and anger to the side. It had happened. It was over. Nothing she could do about it now. But she wouldn't repeat the mistake.

For now, duty called, in the form of the frumpy, perennially sour-faced, mean-hearted hag at the foot of the stairs. "Mc*Bride*," Opal muttered, and wrestled into submission her urge to deck Ms. Hannity. She'd never started a fight in her life. Why, when the stakes were so high, were her emotions so unruly?

"Coming, Ms. Hannity," she called, deliberately keeping her voice meek. She smoothed her face into a bland expression totally at odds with the resentment seething beneath the surface.

Marya, who'd been assigned as her roommate, sent her a sympathetic look. "Good luck, Opal." She made a face. "She's been on a tear today."

Opal's breathing hitched. Maybe she'd set the woman off, had gotten in trouble without realizing it. She racked her brain, reviewing the last few days. Nothing. No infractions. A frisson of alarm climbed her spine anyway. She squared her shoulders, determined not to show it. Ms. Hannity fed off weakness.

Whether she'd screwed up or was getting out didn't matter. Both sent bolts of fear through her core. Either way, it was better to face the consequences head-on.

She sent Marya a grateful look and took the stairs at a sedate pace that could be construed as either respectful or dragging her feet.

"Step on it—" Toe tapping, arms crossed over her ample bosom, Ms. Hannity belatedly realized Opal was almost upon her. "Oh." Her expression darkened. "In my office." She jerked her head in the general direction and stalked away.

There'd been no triumph in that look, and Opal relaxed marginally. She hadn't broken one of the myriad rules, or Hateful

Hannity would be gloating. But her spirits sank, because the other option terrified her. Was she up to the challenges of living on her own after years of prison? Her marriage hadn't been much better, although she'd had the freedom to roam her beloved mountains. Of less importance, maybe Ms. Hannity was angry at losing her power to bedevil Opal.

"Yes, ma'am?" Opal pulled the door closed behind her and stood next to the chair she only occupied when Ms. Millner was on duty.

"Your release date has been moved. Effective immediately. You have two weeks to vacate the premises at the current fee." Ms. Hannity shoved a stack of papers across the desk. "You can stay after that, but the fee increases to one hundred dollars a week for the next two weeks, then doubles to eight hundred a month until you move out."

Opal tightened her grip on the chair rail.

It didn't take a rocket scientist to do the math. Ever since Detective Boone had made his charitable promise, she'd been checking apartment prices. Staying here would cost far more than what she could find on the outside. Now she couldn't afford to stay in the only familiar place she knew, even with a second job in May's fabric store. Opal pried her fingers off the chair and reached for the papers, then sifted through them.

"Sign the one on top." Ms. Hannity sounded disgruntled. "The rest is what you need to know about transitioning."

A quick scan revealed nothing more involved than a statement of understanding, so Opal signed and slid the form back across the desk.

"What did you do to rate special treatment?" The woman's tone slipped right into hostile territory.

Opal straightened and frowned. "I don't know, ma'am." She mentally crossed her fingers behind her back at the lie. At least the suspense was over. Josh Boone not only loved his mother, but he was a man of his word. Her lips turned down at the thought. "Believe me, I'm no happier about this than you are."

Surprise chased the hostility off of Ms. Hannity's face.

Her mind churning in concert with her gut, Opal snatched up the how-to-transition handout and wheeled. And tried to tamp down the anxiety that threatened to immobilize her limbs along with her ability to reason.

May's shop was closed on Sundays and Mondays. And she'd lost today, as Hayley had called in a panic asking for coverage for Denise, who'd called in sick. Opal had jumped at the opportunity, even though she ended up unable to get to May's before closing. She couldn't pass up the extra money. The old saw, "a bird in the hand is worth two in the bush," fluttered through her mind.

First thing in the morning, she'd be on the doorstep of Stitches in Time, working on getting possession of that second job.

~

May's shop faced west, so the rising sun's rays hadn't yet penetrated the morning shadows, but at least the temperature had moderated. A gentle breeze hinted at spring. Opal lifted her face and let the air caress her cheeks, her eyelids. Emotion washed through her, and her throat tightened. Intense gratitude at her freedom brought the tingle of tears to her eyes, even in the face of the challenges that weighed on her shoulders like a too-heavy load of firewood. Fierce determination welled up, a promise to herself that she would not only survive, but make it on the outside.

Opal didn't know the exact definition of *make it*, but she knew it didn't include dead-end jobs and no hope. She'd always wanted more, if only to have choices. Poverty didn't scare her; the lack of options did. Prison had reinforced that particular leaning. Although, prison was warm and dependable. *And easy*, whispered a traitorous voice in her head.

She slammed a mental door on the idea before the thought completely formed. *Nope.* Not near enough of a reason to entertain the thought of going back, even short term.

In fact, if she failed now, Opal feared it would trigger an inexorable downward spiral in which she'd be trapped. The soul-killing monotony of incarceration had already leached away precious hallmarks of her personality. Curiosity, willingness to risk. Exercising those characteristics had gotten her the job at Beans & Leaves, so maybe they were just rusty, not obliterated. But Josh Boone had pushed her too far with his crazy sense of integrity. Now that she'd been served notice at the halfway house, the sooner she got out and into her own place, the better off she was.

Now that she was looking for them, FOR RENT signs were everywhere. Her confidence in finding a place in the Highlands, as this area of Louisville was known, soared. If anything ever came of Detective Boone's attempt to pry nonexistent information out of her, then Shaniqua's minions would be far less likely to find her if she frequented non-ex-con venues. Like middle-class jobs and middle-class housing in middle-class neighborhoods.

Rustling of branches in the gloom of the hedges lining the side of the parking lot caught Opal's attention and she whirled, instantly alert. The hairs on the back of her neck stood at attention anyway, and her heart thudded in her chest.

A banshee screech rent the air, and Opal flinched even as she identified the noise—and the movements of the bushes—as a cat. Or maybe two, toms fighting over territory. She forced her shoulder muscles to relax, unclenched her teeth. It took a bit longer for her heart rate to slow. She did a careful analysis of her surroundings as she waited for the effects of the scare to dissipate.

A pedestrian walking along the sidewalk, engrossed in his cell phone. A couple of women chatting with each other as they unlocked the door of a shop at the other end of the mall. A car turned into the lot, its headlights illuminating the bases of the bushes and revealing nothing more sinister than last year's leaves.

Opal shook the sense of imminent danger from her back with an impatient motion. The notion that Shaniqua was already on her tail was an unrealistic one, and irritation tripped across her nerve endings at her inability to shake her past.

The car parked near the middle of the lot, and the door opened. May Boone got out, turned, pulled a bag from the car, then strode toward Stitches in Time, her confident bearing making her petite stature appear taller. "Hello," she called, flipping through her keys to find the one she needed for the door. "Welcome! Let me open the shop, and I'd be glad to help you."

A wave of relief washed through Opal, along with inexplicable shyness. Mingled in the mix was gratitude that Josh had inadvertently pushed her into working for May—and dread for the moment when he discovered that she'd done so. She straightened her spine against the thought and stepped out of the shadows. "Good morning, May," she said, the name rolling off her tongue with more ease this time. "It's me, Opal McBride."

"Opal!" May's expression, already open and generous, lit up. "I'm so glad to see you, dear!"

"May I hold your bag for you?" Opal gestured at the handmade cloth tote in May's hand.

The older woman relinquished it with a smile and turned her attention to the door. "What brings you here on such a beautiful morning?"

Between her own quiet nature and Josh's edict ringing in her mind, Opal's tongue suddenly felt wooden in her mouth. She shoved her worry away and inhaled a gulp of the balmy air. "I—uh, if that job is still available, I'd like to apply." She held her breath, abruptly afraid she'd missed her chance, that May had filled the position since Saturday, that she'd overstepped her bounds or been too forward.

The door gave and swung inward on well-oiled hinges. May held it open and waved Opal in. "Let me get the lights and we'll talk." She strode with sure steps between the displays and disappeared into her office.

Opal trailed behind her, battling the sense of ungainliness that always engulfed her when she encountered May.

Lights flicked on, one bank at a time until colors glowed like jewels on their tables. The hardwood floor gleamed, and the glass storefront sparkled. May reappeared, shedding her handcrafted quilted jacket and hanging it on an antique coat tree.

"Have a seat, Opal. It will take about ten minutes for you to do the required paperwork, and then we'll discuss schedule." A twinkle in her eyes belied the businesslike tone of her words, and a dimple— just like Josh's—deepened in her cheek.

Relief flowed through Opal like a spring stream, sweeping most of her tension away. "Thank you, ma'a—May." She entered the office and set the tote on the desk. The older woman fished the same papers from her file cabinet that she had the first time Opal had been there. The memory of that meeting with Josh flashed through her mind, and warmth flushed her skin, both from his initial kindness and the ensuing emotional tumult he'd caused. Too bad she'd be reminded of him every time she looked at May.

Get over it, she thought, and bent over the form, intent on filling in the answers with her best penmanship.

"Do you have time to stay this morning, Opal?"

She paused in her writing and met May's gaze. "Yes." She calculated the time she'd need to hike over to Beans & Leaves, and added ten minutes for a quick lunch on the way. "I can stay until two thirty."

Satisfaction crossed May's features. "Good. We can get you trained on the basics then."

Opal nodded, then decided she had to bring up the subject neither of them had broached. "What about Josh? I know he doesn't want me here." She straightened, irrationally ready to do battle with him, since he wasn't anywhere near Stitches in Time.

May frowned, two delicate furrows creasing her otherwise smooth forehead. "I've made it clear to him that my business is none of his concern." She hesitated, then added, compassion warming her eyes, "But maybe I haven't been clear enough with you." She leaned forward. "I won't keep a secret from Josh, but I won't go out of my way to let him know, either." She lifted an elegant eyebrow. "Does that sound like a fair solution?"

"Yes. Thank you." Opal relaxed and her lips quirked in a wry smile. "I guess that will buy me—uh, us some time, as long as he doesn't drop in unexpectedly."

Her new employer laughed and her dimple reappeared. A conspiratorial glint sparkled in her eyes. "I'll make sure you're aware if he plans to stop by, but…do we need a code word? So you can duck behind the cutting table if he shows up unannounced?"

The image was as amusing as it was outrageous, and Opal grinned. "No code word, May. I'll avoid him when possible, but I won't hide." She lifted her chin. "Now, show me what I need to know in order to earn my keep."

May took her application, stowed it under a stack of papers in the center of her desk, and stood. "Gladly. First, let's look at the register…"

Opal followed, listening with quiet intensity. In short order she learned how to use the laminated card to translate fractions of yards into correct prices at the computer, then how to measure and cut fabric.

"Be generous on the allowance, about a half inch or so, and watch your fingers. The rotary cutter is dangerous." May bent and pointed at a first aid box hidden discreetly on a shelf beneath the table. "Bandages and tape are here. Try not to bleed on the fabric." She winked. "Plus, the workers' comp documentation is a bear."

"I'll do my best to keep my blood inside my skin," Opal said. Her relief had blossomed into joy humming softly through her heart. She might just be able to pull all this off.

Two jobs, enough money to get by *and* put some back for her future. Little steps to begin with, but big success later. A place to call home, then a business when the time was right. Life, liberty, and the pursuit of happiness.

All of it within tantalizing reach. And Opal planned on grabbing it with both hands, in spite of Josh Boone.

Little did May know that sharp edges weren't the most dangerous aspect of this job. Nope. It was the woman's beloved, well-meaning, bullheaded son. Opal firmed her lips. Just let him try to stand in her way this time.

Her heart gave a little skip. Not of fear, and definitely not of happiness. It took her a moment to identify its origin. Anticipation.

Anticipation?

Shock stole her focus, and she snatched her hand back from the cutting board. The colors of fabrics blurred into a soft swirl and she sucked in a breath.

"—pin the slip with the yardage and unit price to the piece, and—" May's instructions snapped Opal back to the task at hand. She gave a brief shake of her head, and her employer sent her a questioning look.

"Oh—sorry, May. I was… Hair got in my eyes."

The expression on May's face was one of dubious acceptance, but she didn't challenge Opal's explanation, and continued with her instruction.

Opal scowled. Josh Boone wasn't her biggest problem. She'd been so intent on protecting herself from outside attack that she'd failed to appreciate the extent of her own feelings. And all because he'd touched her. She gave a mental snort.

No problem. She'd spent the last twelve years ignoring her emotions. She could handle this stupid, untimely, and totally inconvenient fascination with the guy. An attraction clearly based on long-dormant and unnecessary hormones. An attraction doomed to failure—*no, disaster*—because of its very nature. An attraction she didn't want and would therefore quash without a second thought.

Her scowl deepened into a glower. Trouble was, telling herself to not think about Josh Boone revved up that little zing and sent Opal's blood on a happy gallop through her veins.

Chapter Nineteen

"I'M SORRY, Detective Boone." Genuine regret colored Warden Phipps's voice. "I've delayed to the best of my ability, but Ms. Howell has served her sentence, and we are obligated to release her tomorrow."

Josh gripped the phone more tightly and strove for patience. "You haven't left any technicality untouched, right?" He winced at his question, knowing the warden would move heaven and earth to help him, especially regarding Shaniqua.

"No, but I have put everyone on this request on your behalf. The legal team, social workers, psychologist— Oh! That reminds me." The sound of paper rustling filled the air momentarily. "I *do* have her psych records—it's two inches thick—and I think you may be in luck. One of her original therapists, who has moved on to a private practice, kept some drawings that Shaniqua made." Triumph filled her voice. "You'll be pleased."

"Great." Josh infused his response with as much enthusiasm as he could muster, but the pictures by themselves weren't enough. "Thanks." He needed the prints off the gun. But the lab was busy and a less-than-two-day turnaround from when they had been logged in was asking a lot. He glanced at his watch. "What time will you release her?"

"Normally at noon." Warden Phipps hesitated, then said, "But I'll push that back to four, if that helps."

Thirty-one hours. "It'll have to do. Thank you. I'll see what I can do to speed up the lab."

He ended the call and took a slug of lukewarm coffee, gathering his thoughts. If he wasn't so convinced Shaniqua was going to run, he'd breathe easier, but he could see Ezra Johnson's murderer disappearing as if into a bank of fog the minute she cleared prison property. His gut told him he wouldn't have a chance in hell of finding her.

Josh shoved a hand through his hair—and thought of Opal, then cursed under his breath. The memory of her thick tresses sliding like silk and fire over his fingers morphed into that god-awful mug shot.

The juxtaposition of the two images curdled the coffee in his stomach. He needed to get to the bottom of that fiasco too.

But Opal only drew third place on his to-do list:

Get enough evidence to arrest Shaniqua before she left Pee Wee Valley.

Tie the abuse of the quint-homicide survivor to the mom's boyfriend—and find some evidence, *any* evidence to prove he killed five people so he could continue raping a three-year-old.

And then finally, Opal. Provided not too many people killed each other over the next few days. Josh made a wry face. He wouldn't place any bets on that one. Unfortunately. He would truly prefer a more peaceful world to job security.

First things first. He shrugged into his suit coat and headed for the lab. A face-to-face plea, complete with a suspect already in the system, might bump the gun up from dead last on their list. He'd already e-mailed Lieutenant Morris with an update. If necessary, the guy would go to bat for him with the lab, but Josh had worked hard to cultivate good working relationships with support services and thought they'd be responsive.

He took the stairs, too restless to wait for the elevator, and strode into the foyer of the brightly lit lab. Kayla, the receptionist, smiled as he entered. Josh's mind blanked on her last name; they'd dated briefly several years ago and parted as friends. She'd married since, and it agreed with her, based on her ever-sunny disposition.

"Josh!" Her dimples appeared, then deepened. "What brings you to the dungeon?"

He glanced at the monster-sized, deeply-hued daisies on her desk and the surrounding non-regulation decor. An expressionist oil painting graced one gray wall, and a similar grouping of three smaller canvases broke the monotonous space beneath the government-issue clock. "You've taken the dungeon out of it, haven't you, Kayla?"

She grinned. "I aim to please, Detective."

"I hope you can help me, then." Josh shrugged the tension out of his shoulders. "I need a favor, a big one."

She lifted one eyebrow, and Josh spared a moment of gratitude that their breakup had been amicable. Actually, it had been more of a drift-apart. Either way, he would never again date someone from work.

"Uh, yeah, I logged in a handgun last night." He cleared his throat. "I have a suspect, but I also have a time crunch. Can you prioritize the gun's processing? If her prints are on it, I've got enough for an arrest before she's released from Pee Wee Valley tomorrow."

"That *is* a big favor." Kayla's expression sobered. "Wait here." She rose and pushed through the door into the main lab. Strains of Alison Krauss and Union Station bluegrass music drifted out, then went silent as the door closed.

Several minutes passed, and Josh thought about calling the state police about the Jubilee sheriff's department while he was waiting, but discarded the idea. He needed to do that chore face-to-face too.

The door opened and Stan, the lab's director, strode through, Kayla trailing in his wake. "Detective Boone." His rich bass voice reverberated in the small space. "I can get the gun prints to you in about three hours, provided it's not complicated. I assume you need ballistics too. That should be ready about the same time." He stuck his hand out and Josh automatically shook it. Stan cocked his head to the side. "That work for you?"

"You bet." Josh's tension eased. "If the prints match Shaniqua Howell, we solve a cold case."

Stan's expression hardened. "My favorite hobby. Putting slime buckets behind bars." He gave a wolfish grin and a mock salute. "Got your cell phone number on the requisition?"

"Yeah," Josh said. "I owe you."

"Not really." He rolled his eyes. "I'll have to pull both techs off of your quint-homicide."

A twinge of guilt poked at Josh. "We haven't struck pay dirt on that one since we got it. I doubt a few hours' delay will make much of a difference."

He said his good-byes and headed up the stairs, but detoured out the front door instead of going back to his desk. A quick trip to the state police post would get Opal's process underway, since he was pretty much stymied with the homicide for the moment.

Besides, the weather had turned nice and he'd been itching to get out in it. But before he reached the car, his cell phone rang. He glanced at the caller ID and frowned. "Hey, Chris, what's up? I haven't been gone that long."

"A call just came in. Older couple, possible murder-suicide. You want to ride together?"

"Might as well." Disappointment flashed through him at having to postpone the research into Opal's arrest. On the other hand, there was no deadline associated with her case. Just the guilt weighing on his conscience. He resigned himself to enduring it for another day. "I'm already outside, so we'll take my car."

The next few hours flew by in a flurry of documenting, interviewing, and paperwork. Chris caught a ride back to the office and left Josh to tie up the loose ends, which didn't amount to much. Engrossed in the details, he almost missed the vibration of his cell phone, which he'd set to silent mode on his way to the scene.

The lab. His pulse leaped. A glance at caller ID verified his suspicion. Josh took a moment to switch gears in his mind to Ezra Johnson's case, and tempered his hope that the gun bore Shaniqua's prints. Just in case. "Detective Boone."

Stan's voice filled the speaker. "It's a match. Shaniqua Howell's prints are all over the gun—the grip, the trigger, the barrel." Satisfaction made his voice boom even more than usual. "We're running ballistics on it now, but you'll need to get the evidence from the warehouse for comparison."

Josh grinned. "Great!" He looked at the forms on his makeshift desk and estimated the time needed to finish, then added a trip to the warehouse and back. "I'll get it to the lab by seven."

Energized, he ended the call and applied himself to clearing what was, indeed, the murder-suicide of the elderly couple who'd just been loaded into the coroner's van for the trip to the morgue. He'd be astonished if autopsy showed anything other than the obvious. The wife, known to be terminally ill with cancer, shot in the face through a pillow by the husband, who'd then lain next to her and taken his own life. An aura of despair still pervaded the gloomy house, and Josh paused to offer a silent prayer for their souls, now beyond anyone's temporal aid.

Dusk had arrived by the time he got to the warehouse, and halogen lights lent an otherworldly aura to the deserted parking lot. He signed in and gave the attendant the case number, then sat to wait while the guy searched. Fifteen minutes passed, and an uneasy feeling crept up Josh's spine. He stood and peered through the wire mesh door to the main evidence housing area.

Nothing. The guy had disappeared, but Josh knew the place was a warren, and the warehouse rivaled a city block for size.

"Hey," he called. His voice echoed in the space, but no answering call echoed back. He muttered a curse under his breath and shoved a hand through his hair. Getting Ezra's ballistic report back to the lab was easy, but it looked like finding the report itself might be a tad bit more difficult.

Fifteen minutes stretched into thirty, then forty-five, and his frustration grew. What if the evidence was lost? His case would be doubly hard to make—he *would* make it—but it would take more time. Meanwhile, Shaniqua would disappear. He mulled ideas for tailing her once she was released, but short of having the Forest

Service shoot her with a tranquilizer dart and put a radio collar around her neck, nothing came to mind. He smiled at the thought, but the moment of black humor passed quickly and his smile faded.

He heard a small sound, then faint footsteps that grew louder. Josh's pulse picked up.

The attendant strode around the end of a long aisle between towering stacks of shelving. "Sorry it took so long, Detective." He kept a measured pace all the way to the reception area.

Josh noted a file in the guy's hand, and relaxed. "No problem." If the evidence had been lost, that would have been a problem. He frowned. "That *is* the ballistics report, isn't it?"

The tech grinned. "Yeah. The box was misfiled. Took me a bit to locate it." He unlocked the gate, stepped through, and relocked it. "Sign here for chain-of-evidence purposes." He pointed, Josh signed, and he slid the file across the counter. "Good luck."

A heartfelt thank-you later, Josh was headed back across town to the lab. An hour after that, he had a match. By midnight, he had put together an ironclad case for Shaniqua's arrest warrant. No need to bother a judge in the middle of the night, but he would be first in line come morning.

He drew a deep breath, then released it. *Good job.* He could almost hear his dad saying the words, and a ridiculous spurt of warmth stole through him. Jacob Boone didn't withhold praise, but he held himself—and Josh—to high standards. When he bestowed it, it was well earned.

Heat climbed his neck. He was thirty-four years old, not fourteen, too old to be moved by his father's approval. Still, it soothed the unrelated, yet ever-present sting of Lisa's rejection in a roundabout way. He'd spent the past couple of years burying himself in work in an effort to exorcise her. While he'd excelled at his job, he'd clearly failed at the exorcism.

Josh flattened his lips. He had long since accepted her decision, and though he would never understand the basis for her motivation, he respected the woman's right to live life on her terms.

His tolerance didn't negate the underlying shame that clung to him like a bad odor, though, nor did it fill the lonely hole in his heart. Or warm his bed. Josh shook his head. Sometimes he wished his parents hadn't brought him up with such a strong moral code. He couldn't use women the way Chris did, even if they were willing partners.

Josh shoved the subject aside, although he had a moment of fervent gratitude that Jenn and Charlie had provided his mom with a grandchild. May would deny it to her dying day, but the subtle pressure had been there nonetheless.

His thoughts accompanied him home, and he absently set his alarm to allow for a quick run before heading downtown for the courthouse. Between running and his admittedly unhealthy focus on work, his life had become too narrow for dating.

Opal McBride's eyes, shifting from green to amber with her moods, popped into his mind, and his body stirred with its now-familiar response. Why he had fixated on her was a mystery. Not only did she happen to be the least appropriate romantic interest for him, the situation was compounded by her demand that he stay away from her. Which he would honor, half for her sake, and wholly for his. He uttered a resigned curse and thrust her image away.

But as rain pelted him in the park the next morning, phantom visions of Opal's coppery hair flitted through the bare trees and kept pace with him, then hovered in the back of his awareness as he obtained the warrant for Shaniqua's arrest. Silent and accusing, she haunted him on the dreary drive to Pee Wee Valley, and when he finally met Shaniqua, Opal's censure sat on his shoulder like an angry turkey vulture.

Shaniqua Howell swaggered her way into the conference room where he and Warden Phipps waited. Josh had known the woman had several inches and more than several pounds on Opal, but seeing her in person made guilt congeal in his gut. Neither her physical description nor her mug shot conveyed the sly hatred in her expression or the promise of retribution in her attitude. Solidly built, with muscle comprising the bulk of her weight, she moved with a surprising grace that reminded him of a stalking lion.

"What you want wit' me—" She stopped short of adding a derogatory term, and settled for a smirk instead.

Josh lifted an eyebrow. She'd been an exotic dancer? He'd seen plenty of hookers who were short on looks, but prostitution wasn't about beauty. Shaniqua's feline grace provided the only glimmer of an affinity for dancing, even if it involved a pole.

She turned her sharp gaze on Warden Phipps. "No offense, Warden, but where's my personal belongings? It's time I be getting out of here." Nothing about her mien reflected remorse or conciliation.

Josh stepped forward and held out the warrant. "Ms. Howell, you are under arrest for the murder of Ezra Johnson."

It took a scant second for his words to sink in. Her expression turned thunderous, but rather than the denial Josh expected, she lowered her head and charged him. The warrant flew as she bowled him backward, but the nanosecond between his awareness of her intent and the impact allowed him to tense his body. He staggered with her, twisting to force her to break loose and follow her own momentum. She crashed into the wall, obscenities spewing from her mouth and filling the air like a cloud of toxic waste.

He fell against her, scrabbling to control her wrists before she could start swinging. Warden Phipps and a guard swarmed Shaniqua, and it was over. Shackled and contained, if not subdued, she continued shouting and struggling.

"Police brutality!" She spat at Josh but missed, and he spared a moment's gratitude that he wouldn't have to live with her spittle on his slacks for the next few hours. "Undue force! Racial profiling!"

He had to grin. Still breathing hard, he slanted a glance at Warden Phipps. "You got this all on tape, right?"

The normally unruffled warden smoothed a lock of hair back into place and grinned in return. "Of course, Detective." Then her demeanor and focus shifted. "Ms. Howell, Detective Boone is going to transport you to Louisville Metro Corrections, and should you be convicted, it will be our pleasure—a wry expression crossed her face at the word—"to host you in our facility again."

They helped him load Shaniqua into the cruiser he'd appropriated for the transfer, and started back toward downtown. Josh turned a deaf ear to her imprecations, impressive only in that she never wound down. But near the end of the drive, she quieted.

"Who ratted, Dee-tec-tive?" She stretched out his title, her tone conveying both disdain and disgust. "Ain't too many brave enough to cross me." She caught his gaze in the rearview mirror. "In fact, I can't think of anyone. I know it ain't nobody still in, so it gotta be someone just got out." She spat again, then smirked.

Josh returned his attention to the road.

"Let's see. Only been a coupla sisters get out recently. Was it Sheree Newton?" Shaniqua went silent for a moment, then, with certainty in her voice said, "Sheree's one of mine. She's loyal." Her tone turned thoughtful. "Or maybe that witch Vanessa…what was her last name? She went by Elvira on account of her long black hair and white, white skin."

Time to deflect this line of discussion. "Just good detective work, Ms. Howell," Josh said, keeping his voice neutral. "No informants."

"Or maybe it was Copperhead," she mused.

Copperhead? He'd never asked Opal about her prison nickname. But with hair that color and a conviction for murder, it would fit. He flicked a glance into the mirror.

And wished he hadn't.

Shaniqua was watching him, her gaze crafty. He looked away, but not before he saw her smirk turn into a gloat.

Josh's mouth went dry. He strove for the same bored tone as before, and said, "Who goes by that handle, Ms. Howell? Did you have an accomplice?"

She began to laugh. It quickly turned maniacal and grating. Josh tried to block it out. Then Opal's words came back to him, and he tightened his grip on the steering wheel. *If Shaniqua ever gets even a ghost of a tip that I ratted her out, I'll be dead in days.*

The woman wasn't crazy, no matter how much she acted it. She was crazy like a fox. A manipulator of the highest order.

Surely she hadn't drawn a conclusion based on a single involuntary glance. A fine sweat broke out on Josh's brow, and he restrained himself from reaching up to wipe it away.

How had he ended up in the position of championing a woman for whom nothing added up to a coherent whole? A murderer whose conviction might be based on lies and cover-ups, one who was hell bent on keeping secrets from the only person able to help her, and who outright refused his attempts to find truth, to let justice triumph.

If he was smart, he'd let Opal hoard her secrets and stew in the consequences of miscarried justice.

Yet Josh knew if Shaniqua connected his glance with Opal's prison handle, he'd do everything in his power to keep Opal safe. And never forgive himself if he failed.

Chapter Twenty

"MAYBE YOU SHOULD try the projects, Miss McBride."

The man sitting across from Opal looked at her through rheumy and dispassionate eyes. Sweat stains decorated the armpits of his tired white shirt, and his tie had a splotch of what could only be congealed ketchup on it.

"Isn't there anything…" Her voice died as he stood and moved toward her, a clear message that the meeting was finished.

"No." He indicated the door with his head, dismissing her, and called out, "Next."

She left Acme Apartments's manager with heavy feet and the uncanny sensation that the word *murderer* was floating above her head. Probably in flashing neon pink, since she was forever branded as Lizzie Borden.

Opal snorted. The irony was too rich. Tommy had used the ax on her, not the other way around. She squared her shoulders and let the next prospective tenant pass into the interview room.

Her pool of possible apartments had just shrunk to the size of a puddle. A shallow one. Frustration, a twinge of anger, and barely controlled panic coalesced in her belly.

Sure, she could live in the projects—if she didn't mind hanging out with other ex-cons. Desperation slid like a wisp of smoke under a door, sharpening the edge of her fear.

She had three days until her fee to continue living at the halfway house doubled.

Her only option, outside the projects, was to look for properties leased by individuals, a daunting task since she'd discovered that nearly every APARTMENT FOR RENT sign led back to one of two management companies. Which both did background checks. And both refused tenants with felony criminal records.

Opal's initial optimism for apartment hunting had eroded, and she felt the last of it give a defeated *pop*, fizzing into the atmosphere like a week-old balloon.

Even so, she resolved to stop at every possible place on her way home. But she'd be up front with her record. No use wasting anybody's time. It was likely a self-sabotaging method—after all, how many people would *not* be put off by the information?—but it conserved Opal's spirit for the task. If one more person suggested the projects, she thought she might be driven to do what she'd been sent up for.

She grimaced. Metaphorically speaking, of course. She had no heart for violence, but the approaching deadline stole her breath and made her hands clammy.

Four tries later, her morale hit a new low. Getting a job, even two of them, paled in comparison to finding a place to live. While she hadn't admitted to the details of her conviction, the simple knowledge made people's faces shutter and slam closed faster than their doors. No one wanted a convict living upstairs, downstairs, or next door to them.

They didn't couch their rejections in vague terms or neutral business language, either, and that stung more than it should have. The disdain in their eyes cut deep.

Dragging her feet past the church where she'd sought shelter during the ice storm, Opal slowed. The memory of that strange peacefulness tugged at her, and she veered toward the oversized double doors. This time she didn't hesitate, but pulled one open and slipped in.

Evening sunlight slanted through stained glass windows, bringing life and clarity to what had been shadows and drab colors the last time she'd been there. She saw she wasn't alone in the vast space. Father Barnabas and a man with a shock of white hair held a hushed conversation toward the front of the sanctuary.

She didn't know if it was boldness or despair that gave her permission to slide into the same pew she'd used before, but it no longer mattered. Finding peace did.

Opal's gaze found the bank of votive candles, and she watched them flicker silently. The men's voices rose and fell in a companionable murmur, with an occasional chuckle rising above the soft river of sound. She took in the statues, studied the vibrant scenes in the westernmost windows, and suddenly, it was there. That sense of *more*.

She hadn't imagined it then. She inhaled deeply, wanting to soak it in, maybe take a little of it with her when she left. Her eyelids fluttered closed, and she exhaled.

But rather than peace, an avalanche of emotion rose from deep within, and a wave of tears rose and spilled over before she could blink them back. Her breath seized, and Opal clapped her hands over her face, only dimly noting the warmth of the moisture bathing her cheeks, already dripping off her chin. Wiping furiously, she leaned forward and rested her elbows on her thighs.

She drew in a shuddering breath, suddenly unable to keep her guard or her optimism in place. *It's so hard,* she cried out in the quiet of her mind. *I can't do it.*

Horrified, she muffled the sound of her weeping, afraid it had drawn the attention of the men. She tried to rise and creep out as unobtrusively as she'd crept in, but her legs betrayed her. Trembling, they refused to support her, so Opal ducked her head beneath the level of the pew in hopes that her presence would go unnoticed.

But the soft squeak of a shoe made its rhythmic way up the aisle toward her, its mate nearly soundless. Trapped, Opal shrank even farther into the space between pews.

The footsteps halted instead of walking past. She glimpsed black slacks and worn, yet highly polished black loafers, and then the wooden bench creaked with the priest's weight.

"Och, lassie, tell old Father Blarney what's troubling you." Voice filled with compassion and the promise of patience, he rested a gentle hand on her shoulder.

His kindness was her undoing. Opal couldn't contain or soften the sobs that burst forth, and after a moment of trying, gave in to the wrenching cries. She rocked forward and back, curled in upon her body. She wept until her nose ran and until her throat was raw. Time lost its meaning. Father Barnabas's hand anchored her, imparting wordless comfort and solace.

Slowly the emotional storm abated, and Opal pulled the cuffs of her long-sleeved T-shirt over her hands and used them as a towel, mopping her face dry.

Her hair still hid her face from the priest's view, but that didn't alleviate her sense of her soul having been bared. Maybe that was part of what priests did. Or maybe it was simply a by-product from people who cared. Either way, she couldn't repay him by walking out, but she truly didn't know where to start. Or where to stop.

She ran a hand through her hair and tucked the side closest to him behind her ear. "Sorry, Father." Her voice felt rusty.

He patted her shoulder, then dropped his hand to his lap. "Forgive me, child, but I've misplaced your name. It's a Scots version of our beloved Saint Bride, with reference to a gem, as well…"

Opal stared at him, then realized her mouth was hanging open. She snapped it shut and said, "McBride. Opal."

His eyes twinkled and a dimple appeared in his cheek. "Thank you, dear." His gaze strayed to her hair. "Though I remember thinking topaz or amber might have fit your coloring better."

A flush heated her face, and she was surprised into a smile.

He waited a beat, then inclined his head slightly. "You are carrying a heavy load, Miss McBride. Is there anything I can do to lighten it?"

Her smile faded. "I doubt it, Father." Then, worried that she sounded ungrateful, she added, "But sitting with me helped."

"Not to put too fine a point on it, child, but no one weeps like that without good reason." He regarded her with a disconcerting blend of empathy and challenge, daring her to lay out her secrets.

Opal felt both exposed and trapped, like a worm on a hook. Her gut reaction was to get up and run, but she wasn't sure her legs had recovered from their mutiny. Plus, hadn't she decided a few weeks ago that she was tired of running? It had become such a habit she wasn't sure how to counteract it. Father Barnabas—she couldn't bring herself to call him Father Blarney—radiated bone-deep peace, quiet joy, and an unconscious assurance of emotional sanctuary that echoed the physical space that surrounded them.

"Okay, Father." She felt like she was stepping off a cliff, and took a deep breath to fortify herself. "I got out of prison six, almost seven weeks ago."

The words sprawled between them, naked and graceless. Opal steeled herself against his response. When he didn't reply, she glanced at him.

"Is that all?" His tone carried neither sarcasm nor derision, and his brow furrowed, making him look like a perplexed leprechaun. "If that's the best you can do, you'll not be shocking me speechless."

Opal gaped at him. Again. Without conscious thought, she added, "For murder," as if he'd prodded her into upping the ante.

"Ah. Then I'll keep the both of you in my prayers." His expression smoothed. "And...?"

"Isn't that enough?" Opal scrambled mentally to make sense of his bizarre lack of reaction.

"Perhaps you've prejudged me as harshly as you expect me to judge *you*." He lifted an eyebrow.

She winced and sent him an abashed look. "Touché, Father." She gathered her hair, pulled an elastic hair band from her pocket, and secured it. Facing him, she straightened. "Sorry. I'm just so used to it, I assumed." She extended her hand. "Can we start over?"

He took it between his, gave her a gentle squeeze. "Of course." He winked. "Our God is one of second chances."

"I hope he's up for third and fourth chances too." Opal lifted one shoulder in a shrug. "I figure I'm pretty far down the line on those. Maybe close to running out of them." *Too close*, she thought.

Father Barnabas let go of her hand, threw his head back, and laughed. "Getting to know you is going to be an adventure, Miss McBride." He wiped a tear from the corner of his eye. "So what is the straw that broke your back?"

"I can't find a place to live." When Opal said it out loud, the impossibility of it paled, and it sounded less difficult than it had felt mere minutes earlier. "The halfway house is kicking me out—uh, releasing me—several months sooner than I had expected. Which means it'll cost me too much to live there, so I've been looking for an apartment. But no one will rent to me because of my record." She held her hands out, palms up. "The projects are an option, but—"

Father Barnabas waved his hand in a "go on" motion.

Opal dropped her gaze. "I don't want to sound arrogant, but the projects are a dead end. I can't change where I've been, but I can change where I go. My plan is to live where I want to end up." She brought her gaze up to meet his. "In a neighborhood like this."

"Have ye found work then, lass?"

"Two jobs." Opal smiled and lifted her chin. "I work evenings at Beans & Leaves and days at Stitches in Time."

He nodded. "Isn't Stitches in Time May Boone's shop?"

"You know May?" She'd gotten so used to the urban lack of connections that he'd surprised her again. Back home in Jubilee, quick recognition of a name was taken for granted, but not so here.

"Och, yes. She and Jacob are lifelong parishioners." He smiled beatifically. "Wonderful people, very involved."

Opal shook her head in disbelief. "And most likely, the good detective too," she muttered, looking at the floor.

The priest heard and chuckled. "If you know Josh, then I suppose the two of you are not on the best of terms."

"Not to speak of." She turned in the pew, bringing a knee up on the bench. "So how am I to find a place to live, Father?"

"I have some ideas. Let me look into them." He fished in a pocket and withdrew a small notepad and pen. "I can contact you at May's shop, right?"

She nodded, hope flickering to life.

He wrote her name, then *May*, and replaced the items. "Meanwhile, let's pray." He bowed his head and Opal, feeling suddenly awkward, followed suit.

His voice took on an intimacy that almost made her feel superfluous. "Loving Father, Opal needs your help. Would you be so kind as to let her experience your goodness? We give you thanks. Amen."

She murmured amen and lifted her head.

Father Barnabas made the sign of the cross and said, "Peace be with you, Opal McBride." He stood with a groan and stretched his back. "We will speak again soon." Then he glanced at his watch. "Now, it's time for me to get ready for evening Mass. You're welcome to stay."

Opal rose. "You've been very kind. Thank you." Uncomfortable with the prospect of staying for the service, yet simultaneously curious, she added, "I have to get back to the halfway house before curfew." Genuine regret colored her words.

She left the church feeling at peace and more hopeful than when she'd entered. Maybe that was why she noticed the tiny APARTMENT FOR RENT sign nearly buried beneath advertising flyers at the tattoo parlor she'd passed every day for seven weeks.

If anyone was less inclined to worry about her record, this property owner was probably the one. She halted. But if he or she were an ex-con, she couldn't rent from them. Another clause in the parole contract. *No association with other felons.*

On the other hand, the location was perfect. Close to both jobs, not far from a grocery store, and most important, closer to the park.

She wouldn't know until she asked. She squared her shoulders and entered. Her first impression was one of clutter and color. An explosion of hand-drawn tattoo designs papered the walls. Several magazines along with dog-eared binders bulging with photographs lay strewn on a battered coffee table. The open top half of a Dutch door separated the reception area from a hallway leading into the depths of the building. A rack of cleaning supplies and a rainbow of plastic ink containers took up space in the hallway. The floor, done in retro black and red linoleum tiles, harbored dust bunnies in the corners.

But the shop wasn't filthy, and Granny McBride had taught her plenty about making the best of one's situation. Opal could handle cleaning, as long as the apartment was safe.

Movement from behind the counter caught her attention. She'd missed seeing the people, thanks to visual overload. A burly guy with a foot-long goatee stood, and a slender young woman with long blonde hair remained engrossed in a magazine.

The guy looked her up and down. "Need a tat?"

"No, sir. Is the apartment still available?"

"Sure is. Want to see it?" He opened a desk drawer and pulled out a set of keys.

"I have a felony record."

He didn't even blink. "Who doesn't." He waved her toward the back. "Two fifty a month. You pay utilities. No pets. No drugs. No trouble."

"Do you?"

He stopped and looked at her with raised eyebrows. "Do I what?"

Heat rose in Opal's cheeks. "Have a felony record? I'm on parole—"

A grin split his face. "Gotcha. No association and all that crap." He turned and went out the back door. "Nah, all I got are misdemeanors. Me an' Metro Corrections are on a first-name basis, but that don't count for what you're worried over. You're fine."

Opal followed, her mind spinning. He didn't care about her record. And he quoted a cheaper price than anything she'd looked at in the paper. Half fearful that the place would be rat infested or otherwise uninhabitable, she trailed behind as he led her outside and up a staircase in the alley. A small apartment complex backed up to the other side of the alley, and a halogen light stood guard over its small parking lot. If the light worked, it would illuminate enough of the alley for nighttime safety.

"You need a place to park, you're on your own. Don't park on Bardstown when it's posted, 'cause they'll tow you as soon as it's legal to. Sometimes sooner."

The stairs creaked but were sound. At the landing, which was large enough for a chair and small patio table, maybe even some plants, he shoved a key into a shiny dead-bolt lock and twisted. A standard lock, also new, was next. He pushed the door open and ushered her in.

It was clean, cozy, and boasted windows overlooking Bardstown Road. A sense of homecoming blanketed her. "I'll take it."

He turned, suspended in the action of opening the bathroom door. "Don't you want to look at the bath?"

Heat rose in Opal's cheeks. "Of course." She gave the bathroom an obligatory peek, noting vintage tile, sink, and shower/tub combo. The apartment was so much better than prison—and the shop downstairs—that she wouldn't have turned it down at this point if everything leaked. But the pipes weren't rusted, and there were no water stains on the trim or wallboard.

"My name's Mitch. Cash only, in advance. Five days' grace, then you'll be evicted." He pulled a card out of his back pocket. "Cell number for after-hours emergencies." He eyed her again. "Still want it?"

"Yes." A smile bloomed on her face. "I'll bring the money tomorrow."

He grinned. "Your skin is perfect for a mermaid tat. Susannah does great work." He tossed her the keys. "See ya."

With that, he was out and clattering down the stairs.

Opal spent a few more minutes exploring, looking out each of the windows and trying the shades, but she'd been tight on time before stopping, and knew she'd have to run the rest of the way to the halfway house.

With a start, Opal realized she'd already transferred the designation of *home* to this place. Smiling, she locked the door and took the stairs two at a time.

It was only after sprinting two blocks that she wondered if Father Barnabas's prayer had anything to do with her good fortune.

She slowed, her side beginning to ache. *Nah*, she thought. God wouldn't put her into an apartment over a tattoo parlor with a jailbird for a landlord. But if he had, she had to grin at the irony.

Just in case, and not wanting to be struck by lightning for being ungrateful, she whispered "Thank you," then took off running to beat the clock to her last night in the halfway house.

Chapter Twenty-One

"Thanks for making time to see me." Josh settled into the battered chair in Trooper Nelson's office. He'd known the man since taking a class from him at the police academy. The guy exemplified level-headed excellence in law enforcement, and Josh had purposely chosen him as a role model. Now, with just as much deliberation, he'd purposely chosen to entrust him with this particular investigation.

"No problem, Detective. You've got my curiosity piqued. Tell me more." Nelson leaned back, eliciting a creak from his chair, and ran a weather-roughened hand over nappy black hair shot through with gray.

"Opal McBride, aka Finley. Convicted of manslaughter one, twelve years ago. Killed her husband, a deputy sheriff over in Pike County."

"Yeah, I looked her up after you called." Nelson grunted, the sound laced with disgust. "Served twelve years of a twenty-year sentence."

Josh held a hand up. "Not so fast. That's exactly the reaction I had. Hell, the entire force has been breathing down her neck since she was assigned to a halfway house in Louisville." He shook his head. "I was investigating a cold case and interviewed her."

Nelson raised an eyebrow. "She involved in another murder?" His face hardened.

"No, no." Josh hurried to correct his inference. "She's peripheral to the case, was housed with the suspect in Pee Wee Valley." He rolled his shoulders in an attempt to release his tension. "She was reluctant, but cooperated and gave me enough solid evidence to build the case. I got a righteous arrest." He allowed himself a small smile.

"So why is McBride-slash-Finley of interest to us?"

"Because I have reason to believe that the county sheriff's department withheld evidence. In fact, I have a witness who says she was threatened with death if she came forward."

"Threatened by who?" Nelson's eyes narrowed.

"The sheriff's department." Josh met the trooper's gaze. "They told her they'd set fire to her cabin with her in it if she spoke in

Opal's defense." He drummed his fingers on the desk. "Opal was railroaded. I've looked at the evidence and read the transcript. She never offered a defense, and her court-appointed attorney didn't work very hard at his job."

Nelson shrugged. "Bad stuff happens. There's a loser in every case that goes to court."

Josh shook his head. "No," he said. "That's not the point, although I wonder if Opal was cowed too. The point is, a witness was terrorized and silenced." He leaned forward. "From what I can piece together, there was a pattern of domestic abuse, and the witness said it had escalated in the weeks prior to the incident. On the day it happened, she heard Opal screaming, tried to get down there to help, but when she arrived, Tom Finley was out cold and Opal was swaying, shell-shocked and with the murder weapon—a chunk of lumber—in her hands."

"So you're saying it could have been self-defense." Nelson steepled his hands.

"Yes. The witness says she found Opal's hair around the chopping block behind the trailer. You've seen the mug shot?" When Nelson nodded, Josh continued. "I thought she had bad taste or a terrible haircut, but when you apply this bit of information to the case—which wasn't in any report and wasn't brought up at trial— then you get a very different picture."

"Hair decomposes. Without it, it's just the word of a witness. You got anything more substantial? What does Opal have to say?"

Josh frowned. "She flat-out refuses to talk about it. Refused to defend herself at trial, refused counseling in prison, and told me to back off when I questioned her." He rubbed a hand around the nape of his neck. "But the witness said she gathered the hair, put it in a plastic bag, then put that in a tin and buried it. It may have been airtight and watertight enough to resist decomposition." He straightened. "But it's not my jurisdiction. Plus, if the sheriff's department was involved in a cover-up, then they're going to do everything in their power to avoid exposure."

Nelson gave a quick, firm nod. "Good enough. You have time to drive out there now?"

Josh smiled, although it held no humor. "You bet."

They took the trooper's vehicle and reached Jubilee by midafternoon. Josh pointed out the turnoff, then directed Nelson to the murder site. The silence after the powerful engine turned off was absolute, and the sound of their doors closing echoed up in the crisp mountain air. A few moments later birds began to chirp and squirrels chatter.

Josh stretched, stiff from three hours of sitting, then took Nelson on an abbreviated tour. He turned and looked up the mountain. "Widow Reese? You up here? It's Detective Boone from Louisville. I've come to talk to you about Opal McBride." He waited a moment, then when she didn't materialize, called, "It's safe to show yourself, ma'am. The state trooper's here to look into your allegations about the sheriff's department."

"Put yer guns in the car." The woman's rusty voice came from behind a boulder about twenty yards up the slope.

"Yes, ma'am." Josh made a show of removing his service weapon from its shoulder holster and stowing it in the car. He hitched his head at Nelson, and after shooting Josh a disbelieving look, the man removed his weapon with obvious reluctance.

"I'll have your ass if something happens, Detective," he muttered *sotto voce*.

"You got an ankle piece?" Josh muttered in a low voice. "I do, and I'm not telling her that."

The corner of Nelson's mouth twitched up.

They both turned, raising their hands away from their bodies. The barrel of the woman's shotgun emerged from behind the table-sized rock, followed by a cautious Widow Reese. She was dressed much as she had been the first time, minus the coat. Worn hiking boots, sturdy jeans, flannel shirt over a faded T-shirt. Hair tamed beneath a bandanna. All the colors blended with the forest.

"Git a good distance from the car." She punctuated the command with a wave of her gun.

Josh stepped away. Nelson followed, edging his way over the gravel-strewn path and giving his body armor an unconscious pat.

"Ma'am, I've told Trooper Nelson everything you told me. The best evidence in support of your story is Opal's hair." Josh indicated the copse of trees behind the deteriorating hulk of the trailer. "Can you show us where you buried it?"

"How do I know to trust you?"

A spurt of frustration shot through Josh, but he controlled his expression. "You trusted me before. Remember? We're here to do right by Opal."

The gun barrel remained motionless.

Josh sighed and ran a hand behind his neck. "Ma'am, this is your opportunity to say your piece. We can't do a thing to clean up the corruption around here if you don't want to." He dropped his hand to his side. "Your choice."

The barrel wavered, then lowered. "All right. But you lie to me, and I'll run you off this mountain next time you show up." She cradled the gun and picked her way down the hill with mountain-goat sureness.

"Mind if I get a shovel from the trunk?"

"Not now. You c'n dig after I'm gone." Her tone brooked no dissent. Gesturing for them to go ahead of her, she herded them into the trees.

Trickles of sweat made their way down the side of Nelson's face even in the fifty-degree dappled shade. Josh had a moment of empathy for the guy. He'd felt the same during his first encounter with the widow. Though he knew she'd shoot if provoked, he was banking on her need to make amends to Opal being stronger than their potential threat to her safety.

"Stop there."

They did, and turned.

She pointed at the base of an ancient stump. "Buried it on the west side." Pain chased across her face. "I know it's only hair, but it made me feel like I was giving her the gift of sunsets. Lordy, that child loved the colors of the sky."

Josh glanced to the west. The view from the grove encompassed a gentle valley that opened into lowlands ringed by distant mountains. It was a place of beauty and peaceful solitude, and he could almost imagine Opal slipping through the woods like a wraith in order to catch the setting of the sun.

"Thank you—" He swung around, but Widow Reese was already retreating, her clothing creating effective camouflage among the trunks of the birches and alders. He shrugged and faced Nelson. "You want to get the shovel or give me the keys?"

"Aw, hell, I'll go." The trooper let out a pent-up breath. "And I'm bringing our guns too." He lifted an eyebrow. "You don't figure she'll be back, do you?"

Josh shook his head. "Not while you're here."

Muttering imprecations, the other man crashed his way through the underbrush, the sounds gradually fading until silence reigned. He heard the distant thunk of Nelson slamming the trunk closed. A few minutes later, the sounds reversed until the trooper appeared, loaded up with the spade, Josh's weapon, a camera, and a variety of evidence bags. He huffed into the clearing and hefted the shovel at Josh, then placed everything except the camera on a log.

"I'll take some photos, then you dig." He matched words to action, taking several shots of the surroundings, then a close-up of the stump.

Josh picked up his gun and stowed it in its holster. As soon as Nelson finished documenting the visuals, he went to the west side and plunged the shovel into dirt. If it had been disturbed at some point, it had settled over time and become as packed as the rest of the earth around it. The afternoon sun slanted in, illuminating the focus of his work. He shed his suit jacket fairly quickly, hanging it on a nearby branch, and dug steadily, enlarging the hole and going deeper.

"You think the old bat was telling the truth?" Nelson finally broke the relative silence.

"Hope so." Josh paused to wipe sweat from his eyes. He'd gone over a foot and a half down and was beginning to wonder the same thing. "Didn't think it would be so deep, though."

The other man didn't offer to take a turn, so Josh bent to his task again. Three spadefuls later, the blade struck a solid object. Except that a muffled echo belied its solidity. Josh's pulse picked up. Nelson leaned in and took a photo, then began the documentation process. When he'd finished, Josh extricated a metal box, using the shovel like a dental pick. Rust had obliterated a painted design on a decorative metal tin, like Christmas fruitcakes were packaged in. But it wasn't rusted through. It was intact.

"Do we open it now?" Josh could hardly contain his curiosity, but the state lab might prefer to open it themselves.

Nelson shifted his weight. "Your witness is good so far, Detective. Let's see if she's good for the rest of her story, and if there's a sheriff's department in need of housecleaning." He inclined his head toward the box in Josh's gloved hands. "Do the honors."

Josh squatted next to the stump and set the box on it. First, he tried it by hand, but it was corroded shut, so he took a thin-bladed screwdriver to the seam between lid and body. It gave easily. He lifted again. The lid came loose.

And revealed a cloudy plastic freezer bag. Beyond the faded plastic lay a pillow of hair.

Opal's hair.

It was unmistakable. Waves of warm chestnut, although the copper penny highlights had dulled with time.

A shudder ran through Josh and he closed his eyes reflexively.

"Let's get it back to the lab." Nelson's voice was as grim as Josh felt.

Nelson bagged the evidence as Josh refilled the hole. In minutes, they had retraced their steps and loaded everything into the cruiser.

Just as they'd closed the trunk, Josh heard the strain of another powerful engine ascending the track. Nelson glanced at him. He shrugged and pulled his suit jacket on while they waited to see who was coming.

A law enforcement vehicle came around the bend. Pike County Sheriff's Department. It motored on slowly and deliberately, then rocked to a stop behind the commonwealth car. The aggression of boxing in the trooper's car as if it were a routine traffic stop wasn't lost on Nelson, and his face turned to granite.

Josh did a quick check of his clothes. No dirt, the sweat covered by his jacket. The evidence and the tools secure in the trunk and away from prying eyes.

Nelson stood taller and hitched his pants. Folded his arms. Sent a glare at the county officer climbing out of his cruiser.

"Got a reason for blocking me in, son?" His voice boomed and echoed through the trees.

The county man's name tag read BEUHLY. He used one finger to poke his hat an inch higher on his forehead. "Depends on why the commonwealth is nosing around my jurisdiction without so much as a courtesy call." Veiled hostility coiled in his voice, but the guy was smart enough to keep a layer of unctuous—and phony—civility in it, as well.

"No nosing around going on, Sheriff Beuhly," Nelson said smoothly.

"Then why are you here?" Beuhly pulled a tin of chew from his back pocket and made a show of tearing a piece off. He popped it in his mouth and tongued it into place without breaking eye contact with Nelson.

"Had some free time. Detective Boone and I wanted to check out a lead on a cold case. Opal McBride Finley is a person of interest. Thought we'd get the lay of the land here, so to speak. Might help us clear a murder."

Sheriff Beuhly spat expertly, missing the tire of Nelson's cruiser by inches and on purpose. "Anything involving Opal Finley involves me."

How true, Sheriff. Josh kept his expression bland.

"Finley's old news to you." Nelson's eyes were glacial. "Our investigation is peripheral to the case that happened here. No need for you to get testy."

The sheriff flicked a glance at Josh and dismissed him as irrelevant, then moved into Nelson's space. "I'll get testy if I want to, *boy*, and I'll thank you to move on out now."

Nelson expanded, looming over the sheriff. A muscle in his jaw ticked and a fine tremor transmitted across his back. Josh thought a flush might have darkened the trooper's neck and face, except that the man's skin was ebony and it was difficult to be certain.

"You will never address me or anyone of my race as *boy* again, sir." His voice was icy.

A shiver tripped up Josh's spine. He wished he had his voice recorder in his pocket, but he'd left it in his own car.

Nelson continued in the same deadly tone. "You have overstepped your bounds both professionally and personally. I will thank *you* to move your vehicle."

The standoff stretched out, second upon second. The veins at Sheriff Beuhly's temple turned purple, and his face flushed a clashing ruddy color. Finally, he worked up a spit and delivered it precisely next to Nelson's shoe.

Nelson's big frame was trembling, and he clenched, then unclenched his hands several times.

Beuhly lowered himself into his cruiser, slowly drove up the hill, and executed a three-point turn. He halted just far enough back for Nelson to ease out onto the track and head downhill.

The sheriff tailed them to the county line. Nelson drove a good five miles below the speed limit, gritting his teeth the whole way. Once the county vehicle had turned back, Nelson's grip on the wheel gentled. He slanted a glance at Josh. "You live an interesting life, Detective. Not sure I'm all that happy to have shared it today." His lips unbent, resulting in a humorless smile.

Josh shook his head. "Me neither." He smiled ruefully. "Sorry you caught the brunt of Sheriff Beuhly's prejudice."

Nelson's expression lightened. "Not your fault." He glanced in his rearview mirror. "I'm glad he didn't see the evidence, and that Ms. Reese was long gone when he showed up."

"Oh, I suspect the widow would've melted into the woods had she still been with us." Josh grinned. "I bet she saw the whole thing."

"I'm getting quite eager to get on with this investigation, Boone." Nelson bared his teeth in a shark's rictus. "The good sheriff has motivated me to seek truth and justice."

Josh leaned into his seat. The corners of his lips quirked upward. Widow Reese had come through for Opal.

His smile faded. Twelve years too late. Then again, Opal had never had a chance, not with Sheriff Beuhly.

It was time for the bastard to be held accountable.

Chapter Twenty-Two

THE DOOR TO THE quilt shop banged open with a gust of wind from an impending thunderstorm. Opal's heart lurched even as she tore her attention from the paperwork she'd been readying for May's arrival.

Josh Boone. Never far from her mind, dread of his discovering her in his mom's shop bubbled in her gut and sent her pulse racing. She looked past the cutting board to the front of the shop.

But it wasn't Josh. *Thank You, God.* It was May, struggling with a package almost larger than her petite frame. Opal's gut settled and her heart began to decelerate back to normal.

The hydraulics that normally tugged the door closed strained, then failed, leaving a gaping hole vulnerable to the storm. The squall scattered decorative shamrocks from the Saint Patrick's themed closeout display and they littered the floor like confetti.

Opal leaped to get the door and help May. And resigned herself to spending another several minutes crawling on her knees to pick up shiny green tri-leafed clovers. She'd already gathered and replaced them three times, and it was only ten in the morning. Maybe she could find something heavy to block the door so it couldn't swing so wide.

"May!" Opal sprinted to her side. "Let me get that for you." After a brief skirmish, they managed to get the package in and the door shut, just in time. The heavens opened and let loose a torrential rain that obliterated the view.

In spite of her efforts, May's package slipped out of Opal's grasp and made a pillow-soft landing on the floor. She crouched and got her arms around it—by its size and weight, she guessed it might be a quilt—and carried it to the office.

"I've had half a dozen customers already, May," she called over her shoulder. "Busier than most mornings." They had fallen into a pattern of Opal opening the shop, and May coming in a bit later.

"Wonderful, dear!" May shed her jacket and stowed her unused umbrella next to her desk. "Any problems?"

"No." Opal still had to bite her tongue to keep from adding *ma'am.* "Unless you count the little kids." She hesitated, afraid she might overstep her bounds with her next comment. But she and May had a comfortable, and more important, equal relationship, so she decided to dive in.

"Have you ever thought about an activity center for them? A kid-sized table, some safety scissors, fabric scraps, and a glue stick? Or maybe a simple large-gauge needlework project? It would keep them out from underfoot and free up their mothers to make fabric choices without distraction."

May's eyebrows rose. "That's an excellent idea, Opal. The children would look forward to coming here too."

A blush of pleasure warmed Opal's cheeks at the praise. "And I was thinking too—" She broke off, unwilling to imply that May hadn't developed her shop to its potential.

"Yes?" May fixed her with her trademark open gaze. "Go on."

"You have all sorts of classes for adults. What about some classes for school-age kids?" She warmed to the subject, having spent a lot of time thinking about it over the past few weeks. "Something as simple as a two-hour class with a project they can make and take home, like the pillowcases." She gestured toward the display with pre-built kits that May had instructed Opal to assemble with themed scraps one slow afternoon. "You could even price it so they could choose their own fabric."

Warming to the subject, she went on. "Or you could get more involved and host a week-long, or even two-week class for older kids in the summer. Like camp. They could make a small sampler quilt." She stopped, aware of the work required to plan and execute such an ambitious idea. But it was a *good* idea. She took a deep breath, and said, "You'll create a lot of goodwill with parents, and at least some of the kids will catch the quilting bug. They'll turn into customers in coming years."

May's eyes lit up. "I think those are worthy ideas." She furrowed her brow. "We have plenty of time to decide what we want to do. I may need to hire an extra person for the camp." Her voice trailed off as she contemplated.

Then she gave her head a tiny shake and, returning her attention to Opal, beamed. "I have something for you." She picked up the package and handed it to her with a flourish.

"For me?" She stared at May. For a moment she felt nothing, then a riot of emotions rolled through her. Confusion, humility, gratitude, loss...

No one had given her anything since Granny McBride's decline. Opal's eyes filled with tears, and she blinked them back. "Oh, May, I can't accept this." Her curiosity got the best of her, though, and she peeked through a tear in the wrapping at a corner of the quilt. A rainbow of subdued yet vibrant colors greeted her, and she lost the battle with tears.

"Of course you can." May placed a gentle hand on Opal's arm. "And you will. This is my housewarming gift for your new apartment."

Opal drew the quilt out of the bag. Soft to the touch and thick, it conveyed the sense of a visual, tactile hug. The colors—the colors blurred as she recognized fabrics from bolts she had lingered over during rare moments of free time.

Colors of the mountains in springtime. A prism of heathers. Too rich to be pastel, yet not as bold as jewel tones. A meadow of grasses and wildflowers, sun-kissed and content beneath a clear aqua sky.

The quilt design was simple, log cabin blocks with warm golden centers and rows of like shades rippling out in ever-deepening hues. The effect was not unlike a lake ruffled by a breeze, and it was enhanced by a whimsical quilting design of whorls and wave shapes. It was backed with asymmetrical rows of the fabrics that comprised the front. For an uncomplicated design, the quilt had the feeling of movement. Of life.

"When…?" A quilt like this took time to create, and May spent so much time at the shop, Opal couldn't imagine where she'd squeezed out the hours necessary.

May's eyes twinkled. "Mornings. That's why you've been opening for me."

Opal clutched the quilt to her breast, then buried her face in it. It smelled of violets and lilacs. Of love.

That was her undoing. She broke into noisy sobs, nearly unaware of May's arm around her shoulders.

"There, there." May accompanied her words with gentle pats, and pulled the office door closed to provide privacy.

With effort, Opal controlled her weeping and reached for the tissues on May's desk. "Thank you," she said, her voice breaking. "I will treasure this."

May stepped back, her manner returning to her typical businesslike briskness. "I didn't know what size bed you have, so settled on a double."

Heat flooded Opal's face. She cursed her Irish coloring, knowing her skin would not allow her to keep a secret. Not that it was a secret, exactly, but she hadn't wanted to admit to anyone that her apartment remained mostly bare. She especially didn't want May to know.

But May was nothing if not observant. "What's wrong, Opal?"

Shame tied her tongue and stole her breath. She managed an inarticulate sound and a vague wave of her hand.

May propped a hand on her hip and studied her. "What did I just say that upset you?" Her brows came together.

"I…uh, I don't have a bed yet." Opal's face flamed, and she ducked behind her hair.

"Well, where have you been sleeping, young lady?" May sounded shocked by this information. Maybe even appalled.

The affront to May's sensibilities struck Opal as humorous. She smiled and lifted her head to look at her boss and friend. "It's not the end of the world." She shrugged. "I bought a cheap sleeping bag at Goodwill. I can't afford a real bed yet." Her lips quivered in an attempt to keep from breaking out in laughter. "Believe me, sleeping on the floor in my own apartment is better than prison any day."

That brought a full glower from May, and Opal gave up. She snickered and her mirth took on its own life, much as her weeping had. Soon she was whooping and wiping more tears from her cheeks. At least this time they were happy tears.

May, startled at first, joined her with a decidedly unladylike guffaw.

When they finally wound down, May asked, "Have you thought about a futon?"

Opal shook her head and swiped her eyes one last time, then lifted a shoulder. "What's a futon?" The only word she'd ever heard that sounded like that was *crouton*, and she doubted that crunchy bread for salads had anything to do with bedroom furniture.

Enthusiasm lit May from within. "You'll be pleased. Functional, affordable, and dual purpose. Would you like to go shopping together?"

Surprised again, Opal hesitated.

"Do you work at Beans & Leaves today? Because we could make a quick run to the mall after I close."

A band of apprehension gripped Opal's chest. She *did* have the evening off. Getting in a car and going shopping—as long as it was in Louisville—wasn't a violation of the conditions of her parole. And she had no excuse. But the idea of leaving the Highlands, the name of the neighborhood where she'd ended up, frightened her.

Yet how was she going to function in the world if she was afraid to expand her horizons? She'd done pretty well for herself, considering. From the mountains of Appalachia, to prison, to a city.

Two jobs, one that utilized her degree in entrepreneurial business. An apartment.

This was just another step, although the prospect of dealing with masses of people discomfited her. But if not now, when? And if not with May, then with whom?

Reminding herself that she'd survived the simultaneous close quarters and isolation of incarceration granted her a spurt of courage. A small one. But unmistakable.

Opal stood a bit taller and squared her shoulders. "Yes, May. I would appreciate the opportunity."

The sound of voices reached the office, along with the air pressure changes of the door losing its battle with the wind again.

"It's settled, then." May opened the office door and ushered Opal into the retail area. "Be here at six. And don't worry about transporting your quilt in this weather. We'll take it with us, for when I drop you off afterward."

Opal cast a longing glance over her shoulder at the quilt. It already represented home and love and acceptance and refuge. A bit like the church and its windows, and Father Barnabas.

She'd come to understand a lot about the math and techniques of quilting in the weeks she'd been working for May, but she hadn't fathomed the bond between creator and recipient.

Now she did and she vowed, yet again, to repay May's unbounded kindness.

The trouble was, she had no idea how to do that.

~

At precisely six p.m., Opal waited at May's car while she locked the shop. This would be another first. Butterflies fluttered in her belly at the thought of getting in a car of her own volition since Tommy's murder. An irrational sense of losing control snapped at the butterflies and made her edgy.

May approached, her expression open, trusting, and full of anticipation. "This is going to be so much fun! I've taken the liberty of picking a few stores that carry futons in reasonable price ranges." She hit the remote to unlock the car doors. "One of them is in a strip mall nearby."

Opal told her butterflies to settle down, took a deep breath, and opened the passenger door. She settled into the seat with a thrill of unexpected delight.

It was the *front* seat. It had a handle on the inside. No metal grill or safety glass in sight. No metal loops for attaching leg shackles to the frame.

May continued to chatter but Opal tuned out her words, caught up in the wonder of being able to open her door and make the window roll down, then up. Just to prove she could, she opened the door and pulled it shut again.

The ring of May's cell phone interrupted both May's monologue and Opal's exploration of her new freedoms.

"Josh!"

Opal went still. Her muscles tightened involuntarily.

"Oh, that would be lovely, but I have plans tonight."

Relaxing slightly, Opal tried to eavesdrop on Josh's end of the conversation without appearing to do so. She could only hear the distant rumble of his voice, though. She couldn't make out individual words.

May listened for another moment, then said, "But will we see you on Sunday?" Her face bloomed in a smile and she ended the call. She turned to Opal. "That was Josh wanting to meet me for dinner." Her dimple deepened, and she leaned forward as if to share a secret. "Of course, I didn't tell him my plans involve you."

Heat flooded Opal's face for the umpteenth time that day, even as her fingers went cold. "Oh, May, don't let me get between you and Josh. That is so…so *wrong*."

Not to mention disastrous when he found out. Which he would. It was bad enough that May had hired her. It would be far worse if Josh discovered May had pursued more than an employer-employee relationship.

And of course, Josh would assume that it was all Opal's doing. That she'd somehow manipulated his mother, had insinuated herself into the woman's confidence. That she was waiting to take advantage of the situation.

"I can't—" She fumbled for the door latch, her movements clumsy with distress.

May reached across the interior of the car, placing a hand lightly on Opal's forearm. "It's just a shopping trip. I often have other plans in the evenings when Jacob is on a trip."

Opal's alarm receded enough for her to look at May. The woman's face exuded calm. A bit of it transferred to Opal, and she stopped trying to get out of the car.

"That's better, dear." May gave her a no-nonsense pat. "Let's go furnish your apartment." She put the key in the ignition and started the car. "And you, as my star employee with wonderful marketing ideas, can help me shop for a sturdy child's table and chairs for the kid's craft corner."

May had turned the excursion into part of the job. Opal wanted to bless her for it. While it still felt dangerous, in terms of Josh, her boss had taken most of the potential sting from his knowledge of it. She let out a pent-up breath, and let herself melt into the seat.

Three hours later, they'd made arrangements for a futon to be delivered on Opal's next stretch of free hours, and for the table and chairs to be delivered to May's shop. Opal waved good-bye to her employer—no, her friend—as the woman drove away.

She climbed the stairs, careful to keep her precious quilt from touching the wet railing, and entered her apartment.

Rap music seeped in from the tattoo shop below, and though it wasn't what Opal would choose, it reassured her that she wasn't alone. She debated for a few moments as to where she'd put the quilt, at least until the futon came, and settled on hanging it over the drapery rod in the bedroom. She did so, wishing she had a chair to stand on, but managed. Stepping back, she admired the effect, and imagined her new bed in here.

Home. Her heart squeezed. The last time she'd known a home was…*Granny McBride.* A shaft of grief pierced her. An image of the cozy cabin she and Granny had shared flashed into her mind. Overstuffed furniture, knickknacks, and bits of unusual stone or dried flowers gracing the fireplace mantel. Framed lace tatted by Granny's grandmother decorating the walls.

The familiar sense of failure swamped Opal. She'd done her best for Granny, and if the damn county hadn't stepped in, they would have been fine.

Granny wouldn't have died alone.

Opal would never have married Tommy.

She never would have…

Opal slammed her mind on the thoughts. It was done, all of it, and there was nothing she could do about it now. Nothing but focus on the present, the future. She forced herself to keep her mind on the events of the afternoon, which had been fun, thanks to May. She smiled, thinking about her boss's delight in the mall, pulling Opal into shop after shop. May's insistence on buying frozen yogurt doused in candy sprinkles for both of them—and, with a wink, calling it *supper.*

Now, the money she'd saved by not buying a traditional bed would allow her to get the table and two chairs she'd been eyeing at a consignment shop down the street. Then she'd look for a used couch. Or maybe another futon.

She rubbed her head. It was beginning to ache from all the shopping and planning. The mall had been overwhelming as she'd known it would, but with May as her guide, she hadn't felt the need to flee. She counted the experience as a success, but knew in her heart she would never *like* malls.

However, she'd proved to herself she could endure long enough to accomplish her goal. Which she now realized included *making a home for herself.*

A longing for Cherokee Park struck her, and even though it was late, Opal decided to yield to it. She'd used her free hours this afternoon to do laundry, and suddenly restless, needed to be outside, to breathe fresh—not conditioned—air.

Fifteen minutes later, she rested at the top of a hill, lungs heaving from a sprint to its peak. Apparently being outside wasn't enough. She felt compelled to run, and didn't know if she was running away from or toward something. Her thighs burned and she gulped in more air, sensing her heart rate returning to normal.

A few joggers passed as she regained her breath. The park drew people even late at night, and Opal wondered if it ever really emptied. Light poles threw out circles of anemic light beneath still-cloudy skies. Puddles gleamed and shadows loomed.

A woman, not dressed for jogging, panted her way up the hill, her dark skin melding into the surrounding gloom.

Opal glanced at her, like she did everyone. The habits honed over years of self-preservation in prison had softened a bit, but hadn't left her. The woman looked familiar, and Opal gave her a second glance from beneath her lashes. Maybe from the coffee shop… She frowned. Maybe.

Maybe not.

Something about her made the hairs on Opal's forearms stand up. She straightened and turned to keep the woman in front of her as she passed.

But the woman didn't move on. She stopped. Faced Opal. Deliberately made eye contact. Puffed out her chest, stretched tall, although her full height brought her only eye to eye. She raked Opal with her gaze, then whispered a word.

A noisy group of young men jogged by and stole the sound.

Even so, Opal saw the word on her lips as surely as if she'd shouted it.

Copperhead.

Opal stood rooted to the ground as the woman flashed a gang symbol and faded into the woods, as the pieces clicked into place like a puzzle.

Her blood chilled.

One of Shaniqua's gang. Opal hadn't been housed with this woman for long, so that was why she didn't recognize her immediately. That, plus the fact that Cherokee Park was far from the context for remembering her. In fact, she'd never known the woman's name, just her prison handle. And for the life of her, she couldn't bring even that to mind.

Josh Boone! Fury clouded her vision. Josh must have nabbed Shaniqua, and he'd broken his vow to keep Opal out of it. She'd *told* him, but he hadn't listened. Fear fought its way up through her chest, but she squelched it with ruthless efficiency. Then she pushed her anger to the side. As much as she'd like to indulge it, she needed a clear head.

Unfortunately, a clear head allowed logic to lead unerringly to its deadly conclusion. The only way Shaniqua's pawn could have found her in the park was to have followed her from the apartment.

Which meant she had been lying in wait. Had the woman seen May drop her off? Her heart clutched. Opal couldn't discount the possibility, nor could she discount Shaniqua's reach. If they'd seen May's car, her minions potentially knew where she lived and worked. Or would discover soon.

Opal wanted to lay the danger to his mother at Josh's feet, but that part belonged to her. *She'd* brought evil to May's door. The awareness sat in her gut like a lead weight.

She also recognized the danger to herself, but dismissed it. Outside of a gun, Opal could hold her own in a fight, fair or not. She just had to hone her vigilance again, which the relative safety of life on the outside had rendered nearly obsolete.

More important, as much as she never wanted to see his damnably charming hide again, she needed to talk to Josh.

If she didn't throttle him first.

Chapter Twenty-Three

Tʜᴇ ʟɪɢʜᴛ ᴏᴠᴇʀ ᴛʜᴇ confessional door glowed a clear, soft green, shadowed as it was beneath the choir loft. Murmurs of consultation between the organist and cantor, and occasional snatches of music drifted over the rail into the sanctuary. Josh noted all this more as a measure of procrastination than anything else. His lips curved in a wry smile, and he gave himself a mental kick in the butt.

The fact that he was avoiding the rite of reconciliation told him he needed it more than he wanted to admit. His dad's voice echoed in his mind. *Facing your demons is the most important factor in defeating them, son.*

Opal McBride wasn't a demon, but she called up more emotion in him than he wanted, laid him bare with her pointed words, and she did it consistently. Perhaps he'd find enough grace behind the confessional door to deal with the fallout.

He might as well get it over with. He squared his shoulders and entered the small room, bypassing the kneeler in front of the curtain for his preferred seat in the chair facing the priest. A lamp provided the only illumination, and the effect was one of a cocoon, an oasis from the hustle of the world. Quiet. Protected.

Father Barney lifted his gaze from the book he'd been reading, simultaneously pressing the switch that turned the light over the door to red. His eyes lit up and he smiled, deepening the plethora of laugh lines on his face.

"Josh! It's good to see you."

Josh grinned. "Good to see you too." He sat, and they both made the sign of the cross, Father Barney following with a prayer.

The priest settled back in his chair. "Make your confession with confidence in God's mercy."

"Forgive me, Father, for I have sinned. It has been—" Josh's mind went blank as he tried to remember the last time he'd done this. "Crap. Advent. Four months." His neck heated. "Sorry for the language."

Father Barney laughed. "I'm sure that's the least of it. Go on."

"Obviously, first on the list is that I've turned into a Christmas and Easter Catholic," Josh said with a note of disgust.

"Och, I wouldn't be so hard on yourself. You've been to Mass."

"True. Most of the time. I've missed a couple of times because of work."

"But you've remembered your obligation and made the effort on those occasions?" He didn't wait for Josh's nod. "Surely y'have, as I've known you since you were a bairn. Now, tell old Father Blarney what's really eatin' at you."

Josh stared at the man for a moment, struck mute at his bluntness, then shook his head in resignation. How could he have forgotten that quality of Father Barney's? A smile twitched at his lips, but then he thought of why he had come, and it died.

"I fell into—no, that's not right. I take responsibility for prejudging someone, for choosing to follow my fellow police officers rather than think for myself. This person has borne unnecessary burdens due to my actions and attitude." He hesitated, feeling his way through the emotions, trying to sort out the truth of his part.

"Not only did I do that, I failed to stand up for her, to protect her from our…hazing, for lack of a better term." The muscles in his jaw tightened, and he lifted his gaze to meet Father Barney's. "No, the best term is bullying. Intimidation. The wall of blue." Shame engulfed him and he broke eye contact, shifting his gaze to a point just beyond the priest.

"A sin of both commission and omission, then." Father Barney inclined his head. "Is there more?"

"I tried to make it right. She's…well, she has a criminal history, and the more I got to know her as a person, the more I realized she may have been denied a fair trial. But when I went to bat for her, she acted like I'd committed the worst kind of invasion of privacy, and told me to get out of her life." He fell silent.

"Have you honored her boundary?"

Josh sat up, suddenly restless. "Of course." Then he sighed. "Sort of." Lifting one shoulder, he forced himself to be honest. "I've stayed away from her. I even quit going to Beans & Leaves for coffee." He wondered if the offended tone in his voice came across as a whine and winced. "But I'm pursuing her case whether she wants it or not. There's more at stake than her feelings." He couldn't erase an edge of belligerence in the last sentence.

The priest remained silent and let the words hang in the air.

Defensiveness crept up Josh's arms until the nape of his neck tingled. "It sounds like I'm rationalizing, doesn't it." His words were flat.

"What *is* at stake?"

This time Josh let the question reverberate until it faded away. He shifted. Finally answered. "My pride. Whether I've failed as a cop, as a person. As a man. Her record might be expunged if I can prove self-defense and suppression of evidence by the authorities." He sent Father Barney a sardonic look. "Guess I'm hanging way too much on all the words that refer to me, aren't I?"

"You're human, Josh. Do you truly expect more of yourself than you do of others?"

When Josh would have spoken, the priest talked over him. "*That* is the pride you'll be needin' to confess, not the question of failure." He leaned forward. "There's shame in abusing the power of your position, 'tis true, but you've seen it and are correcting it. There's shame in ignoring your conscience, but you've recognized it and returned to your convictions." His voice gentled. "Yet you're clinging to the notion that you must be noble in order to deserve God's mercy, and that's where you've gone most wrong. Once you accept his grace without focusing on your fallibility, you'll be able to offer that same grace to the young woman."

Father Barney's words buried themselves in Josh's heart, a spear of truth so pure that it flashed across his soul, illuminating and cauterizing and healing at the same time. He took a deep breath, and the heaviness that had been dogging him for weeks began to lift. He placed a hand on his chest, imagining the muscle that beat deep within to be irrationally tender. "*Mea culpa.*"

He sat in silence for a few moments, mulling the priest's words. Though they felt right and true for him, inner peace on his part didn't resolve the problem of Opal. He finally said, "That doesn't release me from my obligation of honor, Father."

"Nay, it does not. But acknowledgment of how you've held yourself back will aid you in moving forward." The man chuckled. "And there will still be a penance for the other."

Josh smiled, knowing his atonement would most likely be to spend time with his family, or another not-often-indulged-in pleasure. That much he *did* remember about Father Barney. One Hail Mary, an Our Father, and a Glory Be, of course, but he'd done those on the way into the church, so he was ahead of the game. "I'm finished then, Father." He bowed his head and recited his act of contrition.

"Have you been to Sunday dinner lately, then?"

"Not for a few weeks."

"Then your penance will be to see your family without rushing off to care for those who can no longer thank ye for your attention."

His mild admonition carried amusement that nullified any sting. "And you'll do your best for the new barista at Beans & Leaves."

It took a nanosecond for Josh to process the fact that he had never named Opal during his confession. He jerked his head up and skewered Father Barney with a narrow-eyed gaze. "How did you know?"

Was Opal Catholic? If she'd been attending Mass here, she could easily have flown under his radar. In a parish of two thousand families, an individual could remain anonymous. Although Opal could never remain unnoticed. Not with that hair.

"Och, she's stopped in a time or two. We've talked." He waved a hand in a vague gesture.

Josh wondered what she'd said, then wondered uneasily if Father Barney figured he had more to answer for than what he'd already confessed.

Before he had a chance to formulate a response, his cell phone rang. It was his work ringtone, and sounded unnaturally loud in the hushed room. "Excuse me, Father." He pulled it out and glanced at caller ID, expecting Dispatch, or even Chris. But he didn't recognize the number. He frowned, then answered. "Detective Boone."

"You arrested Shaniqua, didn't you?"

Opal's distinctive voice hammered at him through the speaker, momentarily disorienting him. "Yes, I did."

"Do you have any idea what you have unleashed?" Her voice rose, and he grasped the phone tighter, then stood.

"What do you mean?" He shoved his other hand through his hair. "I promised I wouldn't implicate you, and I didn't."

"I don't even know what I said that helped you, Detective, but one of her gang members followed me tonight."

Alarm flooded Josh, with guilt close on its heels. Shaniqua *had* connected the dots based on his involuntary glance in the rearview mirror. "Shit. I'm sorry, Opal." He looked at Father Barney and mouthed another *I'm sorry* at him, both for the intrusion of the phone call and for his language. "Can you identify her? We'll file a report and be on the lookout. I'll get you to a safe house—"

"No, you won't." Her voice went hard. "I will not allow you or the gang or the cops or anyone else to yank me out of the life I've built for myself. I will not hide, and I will not be a prisoner ever again, even if it's for my own good." Her voice shook on the last few words, but he couldn't tell if it was from disdain or bravado.

Josh could almost feel her forefinger poking him in the chest. Anger born of frustration boiled to the surface. "Then what do you want me to do for you?"

"I don't know!" Her voice rose with each word, until it was almost a shout. Then, softly, her tone defeated, she said, "I don't know."

Josh finally heard the fear beneath Opal's anger. His stomach cramped, and he felt hollow at the realization of what his blunder had cost her. "Can I meet you somewhere so we can talk through this?" She didn't answer right away, and anxiety replaced his surge of ire from moments before.

If she hung up on him, he didn't know where to find her, at least not right away. Her next shift at Beans & Leaves might not occur for days. And it would take time to cajole the information out of Hayley. It was Friday, and her parole officer wasn't available until Monday. But his cell phone held the number she was using now, so he could track her, work from there. Yet even that took time.

She finally spoke, sounding distracted. "Dante's Tattoo Parlor." He heard voices in the background. She covered the receiver for a moment and said something too muffled to make out. The sound cleared and she said, "On Bardstown Road," then named the cross street.

"I'm not far from there." He picked up the jacket he'd removed when he'd entered the confessional. "Be there in five."

"Oh, Detective?"

He paused, shrugging one-handed into his coat, waiting.

"The worst part is that I'm afraid she saw your mom too." This time her voice was small, like she was a little kid who knew she'd just gotten into big trouble. Even so, there was an edge of antagonism in it.

"My *mom*?" His breath left him like he'd taken a blow to his solar plexus. "How in *hell* did that happen?" He gritted his teeth. "Never mind. On my way." He bit the words out and surged toward the door.

Father Barney stood, an expression of dismay on his face. "May?"

Josh sent him a quick look. "Safe. For now." He grabbed the doorknob and twisted, yanking the door open. He shot an apologetic grimace at the priest. "Absolution will have to wait," he said, and took off at a full run.

Chapter Twenty-Four

A SHIVER CHASED up Opal's spine as she waited on the sidewalk in front of Dante's. Mitch had pitched a fit over a detective entering his establishment, and too distraught to wonder what the man was hiding, she didn't argue.

The same breeze that had caressed her face such a short time ago now felt malevolent. She kept glancing up and down the street, searching nooks and shadows for the woman who had destroyed her peace.

She didn't know how Josh would arrive, either. On foot? He must live near Beans & Leaves, because he often showed up in jogging gear. But tonight he was probably in a car, which set her on edge. Opal had never seen his car, so couldn't bolster her courage by recognizing him a half block away.

But identifying his vehicle turned out to be easy. The flash of red and blue strobes lit the buildings and trees beyond the road's curve and grew brighter as an unmarked Lincoln Town Car came into view.

Opal couldn't help the anxiety that clawed its way upward from her gut at the lights. She shrank into Dante's doorway, then gave herself a good talking-to. She hadn't done anything wrong, definitely nothing illegal. Besides, this might not be him. If it was, she hoped with all her heart that Detective Boone's character wouldn't allow him to turn on her.

The car slid to a stop in front of her and rocked as the driver thrust the gearshift into PARK. The strobes died. Her dread increased. The door flew open, eliciting an offended honk from a passing car, and Josh Boone leaped out. His expression was thunderous, his face carved in granite, and his focus unwaveringly intent. On her. He slammed the door and rounded the trunk, never taking his narrow-slitted gaze from her as he advanced like a conquering army.

Opal's heart broke into a gallop, but she lifted her chin and sent him an unblinking stare. She stuffed her shaking hands into the pockets of her jeans, in part to hide their trembling but also in an irrational—or maybe not so irrational—dread that he would slap handcuffs on her wrists if given a chance.

"How. Did. My. Mother. Get involved with *this*?" The even, clipped tone of his voice belied the ice and heat in his eyes. He reached her, blocking the breeze and the light from the streetlamp. In a purely male move, he loomed over her, hands on hips. Opal was forced to tip her head back in order to see his face.

The urge to retreat from his advance swamped her, but Opal quashed it. "Why don't you tell me why Shaniqua's gang is following me instead?" She fought to project an attitude of syrup and steel, but suspected she fell far short.

His lips tightened. Abruptly he stepped back and shoved a hand through his hair. He drew in a deep breath, as though he was striving for patience. "Get in." He pointed at his car.

"Hell, no, Detective. You must think I'm a real idiot." Opal clamped her lips shut before she said anything worse. Her hands curled into fists inside her pockets.

"Then where are we going to talk?" The words exploded from him, and he slashed his arm through the air in punctuation.

Opal nearly stepped back but knew intuitively that if she did, he'd pounce like a lion on a mouse, and she'd lose any negotiating leverage she had. Which was none. But she wasn't going to let him know that any more than she intended to let him know how much he intimidated her.

She tipped her head. "We walk. Or we go to a restaurant or coffee shop. But I'm not getting in that car."

He shoved his hand through his hair again, turned away and paced two strides, then paced back. "Walk." He jabbed a forefinger at her. "Start talking."

The options were away from town toward a less commercial and therefore more dimly lit area of Bardstown Road, or the surrounding neighborhoods, or the busier, brighter section beyond where Josh had planted himself. No way was she willing to venture into the darker environs. Opal gathered her courage and pushed past him.

He grabbed her upper arm in an iron grip, halting her. "You will tell me everything. Understood?"

A sudden longing for his tender touch pierced her heart. The gentle warmth of his hand at the nape of her neck, the barely-there caress of his fingers slipping through her hair. The comfort from his kneading of muscles tight from stress. This…this *cop's* grip was too familiar, too frightening, and she wanted to shake him loose, wanted to push him away. Wanted to pummel him.

Wanted to wrap her arms around him and lean into his strength, his heat.

She did none of those things. Opal nodded once, a businesslike down, then up.

His grip eased and he wheeled, neatly stepping to the outside of the sidewalk.

"There's not much to tell, but part of it you're not going to like," she said.

"No shit," he muttered under his breath.

Opal halted and faced him. "Look, I haven't broken any laws and this isn't my fault." She couldn't maintain eye contact, though, and dropped her gaze. It was her turn to mutter. "Most of it isn't."

"What are you hiding?" Frustration made his voice rough.

She forced herself to look him in the eye, braced herself, and said, "I've been working for May for a month."

The eruption came right on cue.

"*What?*" His normally smooth baritone emerged a strangled tenor.

She hadn't thought he could loom any more than he had a few minutes ago, but she was wrong.

"She never said—" A lock of inky hair fell over his forehead and vibrated with the vehemence of each word.

Opal saw the exact second he realized May had deceived him. He went still. His eyes narrowed. His lips thinned. She couldn't tell in the artificial light of the streetlamps, but his color seemed to deepen.

"I see." A muscle in his jaw ticked.

The moment stretched. Opal's uneasiness grew, and she ruthlessly quashed her urge to flee. She'd known this moment would come. Now she'd pay the price for defying him. She could only hope the cost wasn't too high—and that her refusal to bend to his edict wouldn't damage his relationship with his mother.

Tears sprang to her eyes and she shifted her gaze, blinked them into submission. Crying wouldn't help anything. Her lips trembled anyway.

Unable to contain the wobble in her voice, she said, "Hayley cut my hours. They were kicking me out of the halfway house." Opal strove to keep her tone neutral, to keep bitterness out of it.

His eyelids flickered, but he said nothing.

She wished he'd admit to his role in her struggle, but let go of the notion as futile. "I needed money." Opal shrugged one shoulder, a tiny motion. "I'm sorry. If I could have found anything else, I would not have gone to May."

"Could you not have tried harder?" The toneless words gave no clue to his state of mind.

Opal bristled. "Everybody does background checks. As soon as my record comes up, I can't get a job, can't get a place to live." She pulled her hands out of her pockets, anchored them on her hips, and leaned into his space. "Hayley's safe enough. Hell, the cops start showing up about ten minutes into my shift every time I go to work. A steady stream of them until I leave. That's why she took a chance on me."

"And my mom has a soft, trusting heart." He leaned in until his nose nearly touched hers. "I don't want her hurt."

"She won't be hurt by me, and you know it."

"But because of you—"

"No! Because of Shaniqua Howell, Detective. You will *not* lay her actions on my doorstep." Sweat dampened Opal's palms, and she wiped them on her jeans but did not back down from Josh's accusation. "I have done *nothing* wrong."

His eyes were stony and unreadable. He was so close she could feel his breath on her lips. But inexplicably, instead of the threat he undoubtedly wanted to project, his proximity caused her nerve endings to riot. A tingling began in her belly, and suddenly she wanted more than anything to close the distance, to touch his lips with hers, to explore the corners and dips and hollows of his mouth. Her lips parted—and then she realized what she was on the verge of doing.

Horrified, Opal straightened, increased the distance. Increased the safety. Her mouth went dry and she swallowed. When she could speak without making a fool of herself, she said, "Stalemate, Detective."

He held her gaze for a long moment, then turned away. A long moment passed, then he cursed under his breath. Finally, the tension in his shoulders ebbed and he faced her. "You're right." Lines bracketing his mouth deepened, and his lips turned briefly downward like he'd just swallowed something unpleasant. He looked away and muttered, "Sorry."

Of all the responses she had anticipated, this was not it. Josh's apology was so unexpected, it stole her will to do battle with him. At the same time, the expression that had crossed his face told her how distasteful she was to him. Maybe it bruised his pride to apologize at all, but she hadn't pegged him for that strong an ego. Her breath hitched on a sob, but she buried it, digging her fingernails into her palms for distraction. For control.

His attitude hurt more than it should have, more than she wanted it to.

Suddenly, Opal needed to move. Rather than giving in to the still-strong urge to run—he'd catch her in two strides anyway—she brushed past him and strode down the sidewalk. He caught up and matched her pace, and they walked in silence for a block, then another.

Finally he broke the silence. "So tell me about the gang member who followed you, and why they know about Mom."

She had to give him credit for sounding normal. It gave her courage to be matter of fact. "I'm *afraid* they know about her. I didn't say they do." Opal ducked her head, imagining for a moment that Josh was on her side. A novel concept, and heady. "May wanted to shop for a kids' activity center for her shop and asked me to come along."

"Those were her plans tonight?" Josh halted and scowled.

Opal almost smiled. He sounded like a disgruntled toddler who'd just had his lollipop taken away. Affronted, baffled, and more than a little put out at his displacement from the top of the pecking order.

"She dropped me off at my apartment—the access is in an alley, pretty well lit but still an alley. I didn't notice anyone hanging around." In case he thought she wasn't observant enough, she added, "There's a parking lot for an apartment building across the way, and I always check."

He started walking again, and she fell in step. "I put something in the apartment—" Opal bit off any reference to the quilt, concerned that he might see it as a deeper investment in her friendship with May than he was willing to accept. "Anyway, I was only home for a few minutes, then left for the park. The woman showed up at the top of the first hill. Behind me. The only way anyone could have found me there was to follow me from the apartment." She hesitated. "So if she saw May's car…"

"What did she look like?"

"African American, a little shorter than me, maybe ten pounds heavier, but not fit. Hair corn-rowed. She flashed the gang symbol, mouthed my handle, and disappeared."

"Copperhead?"

Opal drew up short. "How—?" Her face heated with shame. She turned away from him, feeling abruptly vulnerable.

"Just doing my job, Opal," he said dryly. "Who was she?"

She shook her head, emotion clogging her throat.

"You won't tell me, or you don't know?" His voice held a hard edge.

She swallowed the lump, blinked away tears—again—and took a deep breath. Faced him. "I don't know, Detective." The tightness in her throat eased. "She was in the maximum security unit sometime during my first year. I remember very little of that time." She lifted her chin and held his gaze, fighting to hang on to a scrap of dignity. "When I saw her in the park, I thought she was a customer from Beans & Leaves."

"Think you could identify her mug shot?"

"What good will it do?" Her shoulders sagged. "Catch her, another one will come. Besides, she didn't commit a crime." The unspoken *yet* hovered at the end of her sentence.

"No crime," he conceded. "It's too soon to worry about them getting Mom's address off her tags, assuming the gang has a contact inside DMV. You really think they're that organized? That sophisticated?"

The question set Opal back a bit, and she considered it. "You think I overreacted?" she asked without rancor.

"I think you're scared, and you have a right to be. I'm not discounting the gang's reach, at least locally, nor their perceived duty to exact vengeance." A gust of wind blew last year's leaves across their path. "My question is whether you think they'd go so far as to harm people associated with you."

Opal flashed back to overheard stories of retribution against people who'd crossed Shaniqua. "What I witnessed was straightforward. She'd order someone beaten and they'd get beaten. Anyone who came to their aid got the same." A shudder rolled through her. "But on the outside…" She nodded. "Yes. I'd overhear her gloating about a woman's kids getting bloodied up, or a boyfriend hospitalized from injuries she'd called down on him, just to keep the woman in line."

A new thought occurred to her. She stopped, waited for Josh to face her, and searched his eyes. "What if she followed me to Stitches in Time this afternoon?" Fear stabbed at her. "I missed seeing her at my apartment. Maybe I missed her before." Stricken, she whispered, "I've let my guard down…"

"You can't hold yourself responsible—"

"What if she saw you drive up"—Opal gestured back toward the tattoo parlor—"lights flashing?" Panic raced through her. She stepped back. One step. Then another.

Josh tried to grasp her arm, but Opal danced out of his reach. "It would confirm what she thinks, that I ratted on her." Adrenaline flooded her, making the back of her thighs tingle. "This was a mistake. I should've called you, warned you to watch out for May—"

But she never should have agreed to meet him.

Opal wheeled and sprinted, mind churning, arms and legs pumping. Her breath came harsh and shallow and failed to give her enough oxygen. If he gave chase, he'd catch her.

But he might let her go.

She hoped he did, because this time if he caught her, she'd fight him. Fight him hard, dirty, no holds barred.

Because in spite of all her efforts, she'd ended up in a too-familiar place.

Alone, and battling for her life.

Again.

Chapter Twenty-Five

"OPAL!" JOSH CHARGED after her. "Hold up," he shouted. Half a dozen strides later, even though he had been gaining on her, he realized how badly he'd already botched things. Continuing to chase her would only make things worse.

He had no reason to detain her, and in fact, had more reason to protect her. But she'd rejected his offer to do just that. Now she was so spooked, he might be forced to hurt her if he attempted to corral her long enough to talk. He slowed and watched her dart onto a side street, shadows swallowing her until she became a formless blur.

His palms felt empty, his arms emptier. Josh frowned. He had no right to those feelings. He tried to tell himself he felt the same when he'd botched a righteous arrest, but knew he was fooling himself. Then he remembered exactly how she'd felt under his fingers tonight. And winced. He'd probably bruised her arm when they'd first started walking. No wonder she evaded his touch now, when he meant it to convey compassion instead of constraint.

She disappeared from view, maybe turning down an alley, or, for all he knew, melting into somebody's landscaping. If he knew anything about Opal McBride, it was that she could hide very effectively given a bit of vegetation.

If he knew any *more* about Opal McBride, it was that she'd been telling the truth.

The only person he knew to be less guileless than Opal was his mother. Who had turned out to be not all that guileless. He scowled. He was going to read his mom the riot act the next time he saw her—and with any luck, it would be tonight. He glanced at his watch.

Nope. By the time he retrieved his vehicle and drove to the house he'd grown up in, it would be nearing eleven. Too late.

Restless, he started the hike back to his car, processing information as he walked. Was Opal overreacting? She was likely in some danger, but Josh didn't think it was as dire as she feared. Otherwise, crude as the thought was, he'd be investigating her murder instead of wondering where the hell she lived.

Now that he'd calmed down, he didn't think his mother was in danger either, but it wouldn't hurt to ask for extra patrols past her house and the shop. A little law enforcement visibility went a long way.

He rounded the curve and spotted the tattoo shop, and his car. He scanned the area, Opal's comment in his mind. Had her stalker seen him drive up, then leave on foot with Opal? No borderline petite yet stockily built African American women in sight. It had been ten or fifteen minutes, though, and without knowing Opal's address, he couldn't do a drive-by to check on her, to check on her apartment.

If he could only talk her into looking at mug shots.

But what then? He'd have better luck talking to Shaniqua down at Metro Corrections.

He reached the car, unlocked it, and slid in. As he closed the door, his cell phone rang—the work ringtone for the second time in an hour. Josh rested his forehead on the steering wheel for a moment, eyes unseeing.

He was too tired for this tonight. Between Opal in the confessional and Opal in the flesh—he flinched and squeezed his eyes shut against the inevitable image that sprang to mind—his emotions had been through the wringer. That didn't even count his mom. Pain shafted through his head.

The phone rang again, and he sighed. He had his doubts, but it could be Opal. If so, part of his quandary could be resolved. He straightened, on the theory that looking alert would make him feel less drained, and answered. "Detective Boone."

"We have a hostage situation." The dispatcher named the address.

Disbelief stole his ability to think clearly. "I'm not SWAT or on the negotiating team." He rubbed his temple. "Why are you calling me?"

"Because the officer in charge said you'd be interested in the hostage-taker."

He sat up. "And that would be…?"

"George Bishop."

The guy who'd managed to slip through their fingers on the quint-homicide. The mother's boyfriend, the man who insisted he was the only survivor's father. The man who headed the list as the most likely to have given the toddler chlamydia and gonorrhea.

Josh sat up, headache forgotten, Opal relegated to the back burner. "Who is he holding?"

"Nick and Patricia Hollingsworth. Foster parents to a three-year-old girl he claims is his kid."

"I'll be there in twenty." He cranked the ignition and turned on the strobes. "Tell them to be very careful. This guy's already killed five people. Let's not add to that."

It took him the full anxiety-ridden, sweat-filled twenty minutes, but he found the unremarkable two-story house easily thanks to the flashing lights surrounding it, killed the engine, and popped the trunk. He had to dig for his bulletproof vest. Seldom used, it was buried under his other equipment. Josh donned it over his shirt, looks be damned, and shrugged his holster into place. He grabbed his jacket and logged into the site with a patrol officer. The guy pointed him to the command center. A clot of officials surrounded the incident commander, with the perennial media contained a couple of blocks away, not far enough to be out of range of a rifle, but far enough to give the police some breathing room.

"Major Bush." Already edgy, the unpredictability of the situation gave Josh a sense of unfocused urgency. Homicide, while time critical, involved dead people, not folks he was trying to keep from getting that way. "Detective Boone."

Bush slanted a glance at him, then gave him his full attention. "Did you interview this guy?"

"Yes, sir, I did." During the drive, Josh had scoured his brain for everything he could remember about the man, but without his notes, he worried he might forget a crucial detail. "He's our strongest suspect in the murders, but we don't have enough evidence to charge him yet."

"This situation will get him into jail for you." Left unsaid was *if he survives the night.* Major Bush held up a hand, changed his attention to the radio bud in his ear, then turned back to Josh and said, "I want you to get with Doug Rawlins." He inclined his head toward the negotiating team. "He's the lead."

Josh nodded, then trotted to the communication van, feeling an imaginary target on his back the entire distance. He ducked in, the springs giving with his weight, and introduced himself. "How can I help?" The cool air that followed him in dissipated in moments. With an eye toward staying out of the way of the experts, he squeezed into the only corner not occupied by either technicians or equipment.

Rawlins, a wiry man who bordered on hyperactive on calm days, leaned from his position in front of the control panel to give Josh a quick handshake. "Thanks for coming. Tell me about Bishop."

Josh filled him in on the particulars of the case, finishing with, "My strongest impression was that he was obsessed with the only survivor of the murders, the three-year-old girl. He's trying to gain access to her through the courts. He cooperated, seemed sincere, but there was always this underlying sense of manipulation."

"So far his only demand is the kid." Toes tapping, fingers drumming, Rawlins stared off into space. Then he shifted his attention back to Josh. "Is there more?"

Josh nodded. "Bishop insists he's the father, but he's not listed on the birth certificate. No one is. We're waiting on DNA from the state lab. Meanwhile, Child Protective Services placed Alyssa in foster care." He indicated the house. "Here, I guess. I was never privy to their information. But they've been outstanding. Picked up on Alyssa's STDs within a couple of days and alerted us."

"Why would Bishop go off the deep end today? What changed? Any guesses?" Rawlins's entire leg was vibrating now.

Josh began to shake his head in the negative, but stopped. A hunch caught hold, and the more he considered it, the more his gut said it was on the money. He lifted his gaze to Rawlins's. "He had an independent lab do a separate run on the DNA. I wonder if he got the results." Excitement grew in his belly as he reasoned the idea out. "If it was positive, CPS would be forced to release Alyssa to him. No problem—in his mind." Certainty built that he'd lit on Bishop's motivation. "But if the DNA proved he wasn't her father, he'd lose her."

Both men considered the implications.

Rawlins's mouth tightened into a grim line. "Then you follow up on that suspicion. Get a warrant for the lab and the results." He was already turning around and reaching for the radio. He paused and glanced at Josh again. "And see if you can light a fire under our lab."

Nodding, Josh left the van and loped toward his car. He'd have privacy for the phone calls he needed to make, plus his laptop for Internet access. Silently, he thanked the department for implementing the electronic warrant system a year or so ago. Saved him a trip downtown and a lot of time. The fax and printer rounded out his mobile office, allowing him to obtain the information he needed without turning the ignition.

He reached the car, got in, and launched into his task.

Just over an hour later he emerged from his cocoon, triumphant. Papers in hand, he jogged to the communication van, rapped once, and entered.

Deep creases lined Rawlins's face, making him look haggard and drawn. Stereo speakers carrying the sounds of Mrs. Hollingsworth trying to calm Alyssa filled the small space. It took Josh a moment to identify the source as an open phone line.

Josh leaned in and quietly asked one of the techs, "Shots fired?" He'd been far enough away and so engrossed in his work, it was possible he'd missed a single shot.

"No. But the foster mom managed to get the kid into the bathroom and barricaded the door. Bishop's escalated, is threatening the foster dad."

Shit. Josh's heart clutched. He'd never been in the position of witnessing a murder, even if it was over the phone and from a distance. He didn't want to start now. Sweat beaded on his brow.

"Hush, Alyssa, it's going to be okay." Patricia Hollingsworth was holding herself together, but tension hummed beneath the words. The child continued to scream, though, and the sound filled the van. Her repeated shrieks of terror grated on Josh's nerves.

"Mrs. Hollingsworth, I want you to get in the tub and lie down with Alyssa." Rawlins's voice was calm, even mellow, in direct contrast to his physical demeanor. He was waving his free hand and pointing at another monitor. He flipped a switch and spoke into a different mike, his voice changing to one hard and full of authority. "SWAT team, ready but hold for my order."

A muffled pounding began—or perhaps resumed, as Josh had just walked in on the unfolding drama—and he heard George Bishop shouting. He couldn't make out the words over Alyssa's screams, but the man's voice galvanized him, and he leaned in to pass the report to Rawlins. "The DNA proves Bishop is *not* Alyssa's father."

Rawlins took the paper, didn't acknowledge Josh, and switched back to the phone line. He resumed the serene tone. "Do you have hair spray or Lysol in the bathroom, Mrs. Hollingsworth?"

"Yes, yes. I do." Sounds of movement and a cupboard opening followed, then, in a stronger voice, "Okay, I've got the Lysol spray, and we are both in the tub."

"Good. If he breaches the door, spray the Lysol at his eyes. I'm sending the SWAT team in. Be prepared."

"I will." Her voice wobbled. "Do you have an ambulance for Nick?"

"Absolutely, and that's why we are coming in now." Rawlins jumped up and tried to pace, an impossible effort given the lack of space.

Josh glanced at the tech and lifted his eyebrows in question.

"There was a scuffle when she moved, sounded like the mister got clocked, went down." The guy shrugged, but the motion wasn't one of disinterest. Rather, it conveyed helpless frustration.

The tension in the van coiled, thickened.

Rawlins grabbed the radio transmitter and clicked. "Now, Major Bush. *Now.*"

The pounding on the bathroom door took on a more determined tone. Wood splintered and Alyssa's shrieks escalated, which Josh hadn't thought possible.

"Go-go-go-go-go," Major Bush commanded. The night came alive with movement. The team materialized from their concealment and swarmed the house. Two men used a battering ram on the front door, and Josh assumed another two were at the back door.

Over the open phone line, the bathroom door began to give.

The SWAT team entered the house and disappeared from view.

Their shouts and footsteps came over the phone, getting louder. "Drop the weapon! Drop the weapon!"

Sweat dripped down Josh's temple, and he swiped it away.

Rawlins stepped away from the console and bounced on his toes. The entire van swayed with his movements.

Mrs. Hollingsworth said, "Hush, Alyssa, we're going to keep you safe." Then, in a firm voice, "Stop right there."

Bishop cackled.

The *whisssshhh* of a spray can being deployed filled the speaker.

The man howled. There was a thump, a crash.

Then finally, *Thank You, God*, the sounds of the SWAT team controlling Bishop.

And, *finally*, Alyssa went silent.

The men in the communication van erupted in cheers, and began high-fiving each other.

Josh put a hand over his thudding heart. No murders. Relief made him light-headed. Man, he was not cut out for this kind of police work. He had to wonder if *preferring* Homicide made him a twisted soul. But after considering it for a nanosecond, he managed a weak grin. Nope. No more twisted than anyone in law enforcement.

He congratulated the techs and made his way to Rawlins. "I hope I never see you outside the office again, Doug," he said fervently.

Rawlins, his face wreathed in a smile, said, "Back atcha, Boone." They clapped each other on the shoulder.

Aware that he had a golden opportunity, Josh followed the transporting officer to Metro Corrections, then requested an interview with Bishop. The guy was so furious that he'd been denied his goal, he waived his right to an attorney.

That worked for Josh.

He set the recorder in the center of the table, turned it on, and stated his name, the date, and where they were. George Bishop glowered at him from his chair on the opposite side. His eyes were bloodshot and still running from the Lysol Mrs. Hollingsworth had sprayed in his face.

"Mr. Bishop, would you state your full name and date of birth, please?"

The man drew himself up. "George Washington Bishop." The date he gave matched Josh's notes.

"For the record, verify that you have received the Miranda warning and have waived your right to have an attorney present for this interview."

"Damn straight! I don't need no stinkin' lawyer." He slammed a beefy fist on the table, and Josh retrieved the recorder before it bounced onto the floor.

"Has anyone coerced you into this decision, Mr. Bishop?"

"Hell, no. I ain't no pussy what c'n be intimidated."

"I'm not casting aspersions on your character, sir, just making sure we're all on the same page, and what the circumstances are." Josh kept his features bland, though he did a mental eye roll at Bishop's true character. He doubted he could sully it any more than the man had already managed on his own.

"You remember when we met?" He saw the flicker of awareness in Bishop's eyes, and continued without waiting for the man to comment. "I'm looking at what happened tonight and the night of the murders. There are two common factors in both events. You." Josh pointed his pen at the prisoner. "And Alyssa." He paused. "Can you tell me why that might be?"

Bishop's face flushed a deep plum color. "She belongs to *me*. CPS had no right to put her in a foster home. Everybody knows what happens to kids in foster homes." His expression soured.

"What is that, Mr. Bishop? What happens to kids in foster homes?"

He slammed his fist on the table again. "They get neglected, abused. Molested. I had to save her."

"Huh." Josh pulled at his chin. "She had gonorrhea and chlamydia before she got placed. How do you think that came about?"

Bishop erupted, shoving himself upward from the chair, which tipped, then went over with a crash. "She was pure! That's a lie! She was pure!"

"Not a lie, Mr. Bishop. Obviously somebody had already molested her." Josh gave the appearance of calm, although he'd tensed every muscle at the man's show of aggression.

"It wasn't like that! I didn't give her any diseases!" Bishop's face crumpled. "I loved her!" He made to sit down again, apparently forgetting he'd toppled his seat. Josh leaped up, stopped him, then went around the table and righted the chair.

"Sit."

Bishop's legs gave out and he landed heavily. "I love her," he repeated, sounding bewildered.

"Was Monica leaving you?" Josh asked, referring to Alyssa's mother. The man began to weep. It was a noisy, blubbery, hiccupping mess of breath and tears. Josh put a hand on Bishop's shoulder.

"Y-yes." He buried his face in his hands. "She couldn't take Alyssa from me! I had to stop her."

"How did you stop her?"

Bishop looked up at Josh, naked misery in his eyes. "I didn't mean to shoot anybody. I thought if I waved the gun around, Monica would let Alyssa come with me. But…" He returned his gaze to the table. His hands began to tremble.

"What happened, George?" Josh kept his voice quiet. Calm, as though his gut wasn't revolted by the man's admission.

"Some guy was there. He charged me. I had no choice. It was self-defense." His voice took on a whiny tone and he looked at Josh, anxiety radiating from him in waves.

"Mr. Bishop, I'm going to ask you again if you want a lawyer." It was a calculated risk on Josh's part, one he normally wouldn't take— if there was such a thing as a *normal* murder confession. But making it extremely clear that the defendant had relinquished his rights would add weight to his admission.

Bishop shook his head.

"Would you please answer verbally, for the sake of the recorder?"

"No, I don't want a lawyer." He spoke in a low, defeated voice.

"Tell me more about what happened that night."

"I shot the guy first. Her parents were sitting at the table and I shot them next. By then, Monica and Davy were in the front room. I shouted at her, telling her to get Alyssa for me, but she ran away from me instead. I don't know why. I never hurt anybody. I don't know, I kept shooting and shooting. Then I looked for Alyssa, but she must've gotten out the front door, and I couldn't find her in the dark and the cops were coming and I had to go."

Josh let his breath out. He straightened and took his hand off Bishop's shoulder. "How many shots did you fire?"

"Hell, I don't know. Till it quit. Till it clicked instead of shooting." He moved, restless, then stilled. "I threw the gun in the Ohio River, down at Riverfront Park."

Even if Bishop showed Josh exactly where he'd thrown it, the chances of recovering the murder weapon were nil. Too much time had passed, too many currents had disturbed the riverbed. All the more reason to get as much damning evidence into the statement. "Where did you obtain the weapon?"

He shrugged. "It was mine. Got it years ago at a gun show."

"What make?"

"Sig Sauer."

A 9-millimeter semiautomatic. That fit the ballistics report, along with the number of slugs recovered. Josh returned to his side of the table and sat. As many times as he'd dealt with suspects, he never got accustomed to hearing reasons for taking lives. He hadn't heard one yet that held water.

Bishop looked at him, a mixture of resignation and worry on his face. "What's going to happen to me?"

Josh gave a mental head shake at the man's self-absorption. "You'll be charged, held here for trial. The DA will make the determination as to the level of charges."

"Will I get to see Alyssa?" Hope flickered in the man's eyes, and Josh fought a wave of revulsion.

"No." He picked up his pen. "You know she's not your daughter, right?"

Bishop's face hardened. "That bitch told me she was. She deserved to die." Abruptly, all his bravado drained from his face, leaving stark despair. He stood. "I'm finished. I want to go to my cell."

Josh nodded, gathered the recorder, his notes. Called the corrections officer. Watched the man lumber down the hallway.

Fatigue slammed into him like a barge headed downriver on a flood surge. He still had hours of paperwork to do in preparation for Bishop's arraignment in the morning. Visions of his bed beckoned in his head, but it would be daylight before he got home.

Josh yawned and headed out to his office. He had a fleeting thought about the mess with Opal, his mother, and Shaniqua. This would have been a great time to drag Shaniqua from sleep and catch her off guard, but Josh knew he couldn't hold his own with her. *Tomorrow*, he decided. After recharging his brain cells.

Something about the look in George Bishop's eyes before he had turned away tugged at his consciousness. They'd gone flat. Hopeless.

And the way he'd said *I'm finished.* His tone had more finality than *I'm done with this interview* warranted. If Josh had been a bit less tired, he would have picked up on it. He muttered a curse and reversed direction.

It took him three minutes to track down the watch commander. "If you don't already have Bishop on a suicide watch, do it."

This case had been a tragedy from its inception. On one level, justice for the victims would be best served by Bishop facing trial. However, a common reaction by families left behind was *I hope he rots in hell*, which translated, meant *I wish him dead.* Old Testament eye-for-an-eye justice.

But the guy's suicide wouldn't bring either justice or—as unlikely as Josh thought the prospect was—remorse, repentance, and rehabilitation. Nor would it bring satisfaction to the families, not the satisfaction they craved, anyway.

Josh sighed and trudged to his car. He had done his part. Rather than jubilation, though, bone-deep weariness slowed his movements, and he felt filthy by association with the man he'd just put behind bars.

A hot shower, once he got back to his condo, would provide the illusion of rinsing the sense of contamination away. Past experience told him pride in a job well done would edge his fatigue and profound sadness to the side soon enough.

Too bad his professional achievement didn't fill the emptiness of what passed for his home. Or the loneliness of his heart.

Chapter Twenty-Six

OPAL LOOKED UP from folding her meager supply of pre-owned T-shirts at the Laundromat—and saw the woman from the park slide behind a row of washing machines. Her heart launched into a gallop. *How dare she?* Fury flashed through her. "Hey," she called, and abandoned her laundry, bent on confronting the gang member.

But the aisle was empty when Opal rounded the corner. She pressed her lips together, went back to her pile of clothes, and told herself she'd made up the sighting.

She even believed it until she caught a glimpse of a black woman with cornrows at the far end of the grocery store. The hairs on her forearms stood up, but there was no point in trying to chase her down. Too far away. Opal wheeled and left without buying the dried peas and ham hock she'd planned to use for the week's meals.

When she spotted her a third time as she was passing a McDonald's, her temper snapped.

She'd had enough of feeling on edge. Two days of the same level of vigilance from all those years in prison had sucked her reserves dry. Her eyes were grainy and red, and a constant faint trembling beneath her skin made her feel like it was crawling. A dull, unrelenting ache at the juncture of her neck and skull radiated pain into her jaw and upward into her temples. At home, she had unplugged her stove and muscled it across the kitchen to blockade the door. Even so, she hadn't slept well.

How had she ever done this in prison?

Anger fueled her fear, and Opal stormed into the fast food restaurant, intent on facing down her stalker. The more public, the better. She doubted the woman had the gall to try to take her down with an audience.

But the closer she got, the less familiar *this* woman looked. A little taller, a little thinner. Hair in cornrows, but not the same pattern—but their encounter in the park had been at night, and suddenly, Opal doubted her memory. She slowed, then pulled up. It wasn't *her*. Again.

All the fight went out of her like a balloon with a fast leak.

She was losing her mind.

Shaniqua would win on the basis of Opal self-destructing.

She gave a snort of disgust and headed out the door toward the park. Her shift at Beans & Leaves started in an hour, which would afford her a few minutes in the sanctuary of her beloved forest. No one from prison could best her in the woods, and since she'd seen no sign of a tail, she felt secure that she wouldn't be disturbed.

Opal had refused Josh's offer of a safe house because she refused to be a prisoner out of caution. And she refused to creep around in fear. It was time to stop letting Shaniqua play games.

If the woman was serious and had real power, then Opal didn't have a chance. Someone would likely shoot her before she knew they were there. So be it. She would be vigilant, but not hypervigilant. She would exercise a reasonable degree of care, and she'd be ready to defend herself if it came to a physical confrontation.

But she'd never been cowardly, and she didn't plan to start now.

A weight lifted from her shoulders at the thought. She straightened, and with an occasional glance behind her, wound her way into the park. This time she took an interior trail. No one would be able to follow her without her knowledge, nor would they be able to ambush her. She knew this park like the back of her hand now, and it was her ally.

Underbrush was leafing out and the early trees were flowering. Birds had returned and chirped a wild chorus. Spring was making a noisy and exuberant entrance. Tension flowed from Opal's shoulders, and she moved through the woods with silent footsteps. She came to one of her favorite haunts, a rock overlooking the creek that flowed through the heart of the park. She perched on it and drew her knees up to her chin, wrapping her arms around her legs.

She had to decide what to do about May. More specifically, whether she needed to stop working at the quilt shop in order to protect her boss from Shaniqua. Her initial reaction had been yes, but the more she thought about what Josh had said, the more she wondered if she had overreacted.

She certainly was on a roll of overreacting, what with thinking she was seeing her stalker every time she turned around.

So…maybe it was safe.

Opal hated to leave May in the lurch, never mind that it would be without proper notice and without a replacement. She'd do it if she had to, but it would break her heart. And, she suspected, May's. The woman was naturally outgoing and warm, but not as affectionate to all her employees as she was to Opal. Not that she had that many employees. She didn't. Which led Opal back to her circular thinking.

She sighed and rested her chin on her knees.

The bottom line was that she didn't want to quit. She loved working with May, loved working with colors and textures and creative people.

She glanced at her watch. Time to head to work at the coffee shop. She stood and dusted the seat of her jeans with both hands and retraced her steps.

By the time she donned her apron at Beans & Leaves, she'd found a measure of peace, and her headache was only a memory.

"Hey, Opal." Hayley came out of the office.

"Hayley." Opal looked at her boss in surprise. "What are you doing here? You don't usually work evenings."

"Jeremy quit again, so I'm covering his shift." She grabbed an apron. "If it's quiet, I'll work on taxes."

Opal's pulse picked up at the mention of Jeremy. "Wow. That's too bad, for you, I mean. Do you want me to help fill in his hours?" She didn't know how that might work, since they worked the same shift, but she could always use the extra money.

"Yeah, I'm going to move Denise to cover what she can, but she's coming up on finals and she usually wants to cut hours. You can pick up as many extra evenings as you want."

Opal didn't think twice. "I'll work all of them."

"Seven days a week?" Hayley propped a fist on her outthrust hip. "Girlfriend, you need *some* time off."

A flush warmed Opal's cheeks. "If I have to take a day off here and there, I will, but it doesn't bother me to do them all." In fact, it was exhilarating to be allowed to *choose* to work or not work, and to be paid a fair wage.

Relief flickered across Hayley's face before she covered it with her business face. "It's a deal." She pointed an index finger at her and added sternly, "When you start to get burned out, just say so, and you can take a shift or two off."

"Deal." Two months ago, Opal would never have dared say what she said next. "But do me a favor and think twice before you hire Jeremy back. I'm six times as dependable as he is, and twice as productive. I'd appreciate not having my hours cut on his account again." She held Hayley's gaze—and held her breath.

The moment stretched out, Hayley considering her request with her trademark shrewdness. Finally, her boss gave a decisive nod. "You got it." Then a genuine smile cracked her sober demeanor. "You drive a hard bargain, Opal McBride. I like that in a person."

Opal turned, hiding a smile. It was liberating to say what she wanted without fear of retribution. The bell over the door tinkled, and she glanced at the customer. A cop. Of course. And this guy had been in enough times that she knew he preferred a mild blend over the house bold, and he would say *no room for cream*, then proceed to dump an inch of perfectly good coffee in the trash so he could doctor it with cream and a very particular assortment of accoutrements.

She had it ready for him by the time he got to the counter.

He shot a sour look at her. "That's not the bold, is it?"

"No, sir. It's the mild." Opal smiled sweetly, then peered over his shoulder to the next customer in line. "Can I help you?"

The cop grumbled and moved to the counter loaded with condiments, poured out the top inch, then went about his ritual with all the focus of a neurosurgeon.

Business picked up for the next couple of hours, but finally quieted enough for Hayley to ensconce herself in the office. Opal was dry mopping the floor when the door opened again. She glanced up—and her blood ran cold.

It was the woman who had found her in the park, the one Opal had convinced herself she'd seen half a dozen times in the past few days.

Shaniqua's soldier.

Opal straightened. Her mind leaped into warp speed. Three customers at two tables, all studying. Hayley in the back. No cops. *Damn.* Where were they when you needed them? Her lips flattened at the irony.

The woman appeared to be unarmed. Opal had a mop and handle. Good enough. Unless her adversary was carrying concealed, Opal would come out on top of a physical confrontation. She made the snap decision to treat her as a customer, to start out with, anyway. If things escalated, she'd warn the real customers, get them out of harm's way, and yell for Hayley to call 911.

"How may I help you?" Opal forced a phony smile onto her face. And held the mop in front of her, changing her grip so she could use it as a weapon if necessary.

"Just want some coffee." The woman, a little worn around the edges, now that Opal could see her in good light, swaggered a few steps closer.

"Yes, ma'am." Opal sidled to the counter and slid behind it. "Do you need assistance in choosing a drink, or do you have one in mind?"

The woman never broke eye contact. "Plain coffee."

"Mild or bold? Regular or decaf?" The hairs on Opal's forearms stood at attention.

"Bold. Regular." She leaned in close, then spoke in a low tone. "Shaniqua ain't happy with you, Copperhead."

Opal didn't blink. "Hayley," she called. "Would you mind if I take my break?"

There was a rustle from the office and her boss appeared. "No prob, Opal."

"Everything's covered. I'll be outside." She pulled the coffee. "Put this on my account, Hayley," she said, and handed it to the woman. "Cream and sugar are over there." She pointed.

Looking bemused, Shaniqua's lackey shook her head. "Black's fine."

Opal ushered her out the door with pointed courtesy. In fact, she wasn't about to turn her back on the woman. Besides, this gave her an opportunity to determine that her foe wasn't carrying. A big gun, anyway. She could still have a piece on her ankle, but there was no telltale bulge in her clothing, which was mostly spandex. No lines of a knife, either. As an afterthought, Opal traded the mop for a broom on the way, on the pretext of sweeping the patio. Either would serve as a weapon if need be.

The door closed behind them. Opal, ditching any pretension of being mannerly, said, "I haven't seen Shaniqua for years. She's got no bone to pick with me. What's going on?"

"Boss got arrested instead of released. Ain't nobody else stupid enough to sic the cops on her. She figured you was the one that did it." A sneer twisted her face.

"She figured wrong." Opal's voice was flat. "I'm not stupid, and I didn't sic the cops on anybody." She hesitated for a moment, then asked, "What did she get arrested for?"

"Capital murder. If she can't weasel out of this one, she's going to death row."

A chill slid up Opal's spine. She still didn't know what she'd said that Josh had clearly used to arrest Shaniqua, and she didn't care. Shaniqua brought ruin to herself and everyone around her. Single-handedly.

"And this involves me, how?" Anger building, Opal transferred the broom to her other hand.

"You gonna pay, bitch." The woman sneered.

Opal leaned closer. "You send a message back to Shaniqua. I am not afraid of her, or of anyone she sends." She gripped the broom so tightly her hand began to ache in protest. "I don't know anything about her arrest, or any murder. You know as well as I do that she was full of hot air and manipulated everyone." She straightened. "Whatever grudge she's carrying, it's based on fairy dust. I didn't do anything to hurt her."

"Denial ain't gonna save you."

Opal shrugged. "Truth…whoever you are." She laughed, but it was a sound without humor. "Yeah, you're so important, I don't even remember your name. Only that you're Shaniqua's mule."

The woman stiffened at the words and frowned, turning an already threatening expression murderous.

"In fact, you're the one in denial. You are her slave. And if that isn't pathetic, I don't know what is." Opal straightened, started to turn away, but the stalker grabbed her arm.

"Viper." She fairly snarled the word.

Opal laughed out loud, this one amused. "Is that what defines you, Viper? Your prison handle? Don't you see you are still as much a prisoner here, on the outside, as you ever were on the inside?" She pulled away from Viper's grasp.

"I ain't no slave!" She curled one hand into a fist and raised it. "Who do you think you are?"

Opal faced her, tightening her grip on the broom. "Can you think for yourself? Can you do what *you* want to do? Or do you have to plan everything based on whether or not Shaniqua will approve?"

Uncertainty flickered across Viper's face, then disappeared as she hardened her expression. "You don't understand."

"Oh yes, I do." Opal felt a moment's pity for the woman in front of her. "I understand plenty. I've just made different choices. Nobody owns me. I may be invisible and on the edge of poor, but I've got a job—" Opal stopped herself before she said *two jobs*. No way was she going to give Viper a hint that might impact May's welfare. "—and I've got my own apartment." A smile teased at her lips. "And it's not in the projects, or in the west end." She let her smile widen and gestured to encompass the patio, the street, the people passing by. "So why would I do anything to jeopardize my freedom?"

"What you call freedom is nothin' more than kowtowin' to some rich boss. *I* got status, *I* got a bunch of people watchin' my back."

"No, you don't. You're just Shaniqua's pawn. Say anything other than *yes* to her, you're in as much trouble as you think I am." Opal lowered her voice. "But she knows everything about you. She can track *you* down. Me, I don't count. I'm not a threat, and I'm not worth her effort." She turned to go inside, but stopped and leveled a gaze at Viper. "Think about it. You can do better for yourself. But only if you want it bad enough."

She opened the door and went in, leaving the woman fuming and speechless.

The flame of self-reliance flickered a little brighter in Opal's heart, and her confidence took a corresponding hop uphill.

Why had she panicked? And more, why had she called Josh Boone?

She had handled Viper just fine without him. While she'd be very careful to see if anyone continued to follow her, Opal thought she could stay on at May's shop without putting her mentor at risk.

But she'd steer clear of Josh from now on. No more calling him, no matter what. He was too dangerous to her heart. He'd come to represent everything she would never have. In his quixotic, straight-arrow mind, he seemed to believe he needed to protect her.

And precisely because Opal longed to let him, if only for the space of a few heartbeats, she needed to bury her attraction to the man deeper than Granny McBride's grave.

Chapter Twenty-Seven

"Hey, Dad." Josh poked his head into his father's wood workshop. "You have a minute?"

Jacob cut the power on the sander he'd been using, and slid the protective glasses up to rest on his forehead. "Sure, son." He loosened the vise and eyed the slab of hickory as he tugged his face mask down to dangle around his neck. "What's up?"

"I'm concerned about Mom's safety." He inhaled the aroma of cut wood and stepped into the room. Jacob shot a piercing look at him, and Josh lifted a hand to stave off the sharp comment sure to follow. "Opal called me a couple of days ago. Somebody from a prison gang threatened her. I'm not convinced it's as bad as she fears, but I'm losing sleep over the prospect of someone tailing her to Mom's shop."

Jacob set the wood down and faced Josh, his expression grim. "Have you talked to May about this?"

"No." Josh shook his head. "She thinks I don't know that Opal works for her. We were at loggerheads over the issue."

His father's eyes flickered and he glanced away, confirming Josh's suspicion that both his parents had colluded to keep him in the dark.

Jacob cleared his throat. "You must have changed your mind about Opal herself, then."

Josh nodded. "Without going into detail, I've uncovered some information that…puts a different spin on what happened."

"But…?" Jacob made a go-on motion with his hand, impatience apparent in the abrupt movement.

No better time than the present to eat crow. "You—and Mom—were right about Opal. The more I learn about her, the less I see her being any more dangerous than anyone who gets boxed into an untenable situation. But that's no longer the issue."

He ran a hand over boards awaiting stain. Soft and smooth beneath his fingertips, they brought to mind the image of the chopping block behind the trailer in Jubilee, and then, inevitably, the chunk of lumber Opal had used to defend herself from Finley. He gave a brief shake of his head to clear the thoughts, and lifted his gaze to his dad's.

"I've already asked the local precinct to increase their drive-by presence at the strip mall. Mom won't fire Opal, so I won't even bring that up. I can drop in when I'm in the neighborhood"—Josh grimaced to indicate the unpredictability of that option—"but I was wondering if you might hang out at her shop for a while."

Jacob lifted an eyebrow, and a glint of humor showed in his eyes. "I'm willing, but Stitches in Time is as purely her space as the cockpit is mine." His expression sobered. "What kind of trouble do you anticipate?"

Heat crept up Josh's neck. "Most likely nothing, as I can't imagine the gang wants to attract attention in a public place. Beyond that, I don't know."

"What about Opal's safety, outside of May's shop?"

Josh shrugged. "I can't protect her all the time." The warmth at his collar climbed his face. "She's drawn a line, one I respect. A line I won't cross."

"Even if her life is at stake?"

"Dad, I can't put her in protective custody." His exasperation sounded in his voice. "Actually, I offered, but she wouldn't even consider it. Freedom's pretty important to her."

A slight quirk of Jacob's lips softened his expression. He sighed. "When are you going to talk to your mother?"

Josh sent a sheepish glance at his father. "I've been avoiding it as much as she's avoiding telling me about Opal and the shop." That earned a brief grin and an equally sheepish look from Jacob.

"Let's go tackle the job together." He set down his protective gear and laid the board on the pile ready for stain.

Scents of slow-roasted beef brisket and Memphis barbeque rub permeated the house as Josh entered. He filled his lungs and decided Father Barney was right. He needed to spend more time with his parents, even if his motivation was to improve the quality of his diet. His spirits lifted and a slight smile crossed his face. That wasn't the good priest's intention in assigning a Sunday dinner as penance, but if a world class meal was a side benefit, Josh figured it wouldn't hurt to do it more often.

"Hi, Mom." He leaned over to give her a kiss on her flushed cheek. "Should I set the table for three or five?"

"Three." She gave a small shake of her head as he moved toward the hutch that displayed her good china. "Let's use the everyday stoneware today."

He reversed direction and pulled the hand-thrown plates out of the cupboard, intending to ask why Jenn and Charlie weren't making an appearance. She continued before he had the chance.

"Caleb has an ear infection, and they are catching up on sleep this afternoon. They were up most of the night with him." She pulled the foil-lined pan out of the oven and set it on a wooden cutting board.

"Is he going to be okay?" Josh felt a spurt of alarm. Babies were little, and half scared him as it was. The line between healthy and the few he saw in his business seemed frighteningly easy to cross. Of course, the ones he saw didn't have responsible adults watching out for them, or the responsible adults had been unable to keep them safe.

May nodded. "Oh yes." She glanced at him and stilled. Her expression softened. "Kids are resilient, Josh. He'll be fine."

Silverware rattled as he selected the appropriate pieces, and he ducked his head as he set the table. "I don't know, Mom. They're pretty fragile." He suddenly wondered if he would have made a good father. Maybe Lisa's abandonment had turned out to be a blessing in disguise. He grimaced at the thought and thrust it out of his mind.

Jacob appeared from the half bath at the back entryway, wiping his hands on a towel. "Smells good, May." He shot a glance at Josh, lifting his brows in a silent question.

May pulled potato salad and sliced tomatoes from the fridge and handed them to Josh. "Not many kids make it through toddlerhood without ear infections. Sometimes there are complications, but Jenn and Charlie are attentive and intelligent." She dished the brisket into a matching stoneware serving dish and placed it on a trivet on the table. Sitting, she pinned Josh with a pointed look and a smile, almost as if she'd discerned the origin of his comment. "All new parents feel inadequate, but on-the-job training brings them up to speed pretty quickly."

Josh nodded his acceptance of her opinion, and kept his own reservations to himself. The men sat, Jacob said grace, and silence reigned as they dished food onto their plates.

"This is great, Mom." The weight of the conversation he needed to initiate began to leach some of the pleasure from his meal, and Josh decided avoidance would make the meat taste like sawdust if he kept it up. He cleared his throat. "There's something we need to discuss."

She looked at him, her expression so open and full of trust it felt like a kick to his heart.

"First, I know Opal's working in your shop."

She set her fork down and frowned.

Josh raised a hand before she could launch a defense—or more likely, an offense. "That's not what this is about. I'm not happy about it, but I'm not going to say anything more about the fact that you hired her."

Some of the tension left her face, but she remained wary. And to Josh's grim approval, she looked a tad bit guilty. But a zing of guilt cut through *him* when he had to add, "As I get to know her and her case better, the less I believe she will be violent toward you." He took a sip of water so he didn't have to witness the flash of triumph in his mom's eyes. He had to unclench his jaw to add, "You were closer to the truth of her character than I was."

"You said 'first.' Is there more?" She asked the question with the sense of caution normally used for an unpredictable rottweiler. Thankfully, she didn't gloat at his admission.

Josh watched as his father reached over and covered her delicate hand with his. What would it be like to have an ally for facing life's curveballs? He shook that thought away too and said, "Yes." His parents traded a quick look. "Someone from a prison gang followed Opal the other night after you dropped her off and threatened her."

May gasped and Jacob tightened his grip. "Is she hurt?" Concern flooded her features, worry lines replacing the furrow between her brows.

"She's fine, Mom." He leaned forward. "But she's afraid that the gang member might follow her to your shop. She doesn't want to put you in harm's way."

May paled, and Josh felt like a heel for having caused her distress. But a spurt of gratification followed at her quick grasp of the implications of his words.

He chose his next words carefully. "I expect you won't consider asking her to stay away for a while?" The question hung in the air. He could see the gears turning in her mind, and saw the moment she understood what he had asked of her.

She gave a shake of her head in the negative, and straightened. "She has contributed more ideas for the betterment of the business in the month she's been with me than any of my other employees have. Ever."

Josh narrowed his eyes at her reference to *month*, but made a conscious decision to let their three-way conspiracy against him lie. He let his breath out in a half sigh of frustration. "Then will you let Dad hang out at the shop with you for a while?"

Sparks lit her eyes. She sent a horrified glance at Jacob, then turned her gaze back to Josh. "Absolutely not! That is *my* business, my space, my—well, just *mine*." A flush rose up her neck, bringing color back into her pale cheeks, and she shifted, looking at her husband. "I don't mean that in a way that excludes you, Jacob—"

"I told him that's what you'd say, dear." His tone was apologetic, but the glance he sent Josh conveyed more *What do you propose now* than ruefulness.

"Even if it compromises your safety?" Josh couldn't contain the bite of his words, but winced at his tone. Then he thought of what might make more of a difference to May, and in spite of the notion sticking in his craw, he added, "And what about Opal? You're going to let her be defenseless in the one place you have some influence?"

May flinched, opened her mouth as if to answer, then closed it.

"Is there another option, Josh?" His father gave May's hand a supportive squeeze.

"Like what?" Josh tried to dredge up some patience, but his head was beginning to hurt. Sort of like he'd been banging it against a brick wall.

"A security guard?" Jacob leaned forward to offer the idea. May glowered, but he plowed on. "I can't be there all the time anyway, unless I use sick leave." He shrugged. "I will, but at my age, I might need it."

Both May and Josh were shaking their heads before he finished.

"No, Dad—"

"I can't afford to hire one, even if I wanted to," May said at the same time. Her horrified expression returned. "Besides, what would it look like to my customers, with a guard watching over them? Would they think I suspect them of shoplifting?" She shuddered.

"What about a security system?" The words popped out before Josh even thought the idea through. He sat up, suddenly energized. "You have one at home. Why not at work?" Excitement filled him. "There's no extra person hovering over you, Mom, but you could wear one of those emergency call buttons on a lanyard around your neck. Then if you need help, you get it, even without having to get to the phone."

He bit back his comment about help already being close by. He didn't want her to mention the extra patrols to Opal. Neither one of them would appreciate the gesture or the extra layer of safety it represented. No, they'd both see it as intrusive and an impingement on their independence.

But if that's what it took to take care of them, he'd do it without a shred of repentance.

"You mean like a help-I've-fallen-and-can't-get-up button?" Her expression radiated uncertainty.

Josh gave a short nod. "Yeah. But in this case, it would be a help-I-need-a-cop-*now* button."

A smile softened her face and reached her eyes. "Yes, Josh. Let's do that."

"I'll get someone out there in the morning." He managed to keep his tone neutral, even though he just now realized who he'd included in his territorial boundaries of protection.

Opal McBride.

He'd just committed to a much more personal level of involvement in her life, no matter that she had rejected his offers of help so many times that he'd lost track. It seemed that every time he tried to put distance between them, the effort drew them closer instead.

Josh rubbed his temple, where the generalized ache from a few minutes ago had coalesced.

God save him from bullheaded, stubborn, opinionated, *independent* women.

Chapter Twenty-Eight

THE RECEPTIONIST UNLOCKED the door of the parole office promptly at eight a.m., and Opal, by virtue of being the only parolee in sight, pulled it open. The stale air of the drab office clogged her lungs after nearly an hour of walking. She wrinkled her nose at the ingrained odors of unwashed bodies and cigarette smoke, not unlike the few bus stations she'd had the misfortune of experiencing.

But it beat prison, so she camouflaged her response by pretending to be absorbed in writing her name on the sign-in sheet.

Having the first appointment of the day afforded her the freedom of being able to work both of her jobs, but made for a short night after closing Beans & Leaves. The only saving grace was the growing beauty of the mornings, as the sun rose earlier each week. Plus, she'd found a shortcut that took her through Cherokee Park.

"Ms. McBride. My office." Mr. Luckett emerged from what must be the break room with his ubiquitous oversized cup of coffee and indicated the hallway with a tilt of his head. Powdered sugar, presumably from a doughnut, dusted his navy blue tie. If there was more, it didn't show on his white shirt.

She obediently rose from the chair she'd just that moment lowered herself into, and followed him. Her nerves began to dance a jig in her stomach. A wave of nausea rolled through her and then ebbed as quickly as it had come. She spared a moment's gratitude that she hadn't eaten anything yet, or she might have had to make a dash for the restroom. His brusque manner always made her nervous, or maybe it was just correction officers in general.

Mr. Luckett rounded his desk, set the coffee down, and booted up his computer. Opal stood until he realized she was there and made an impatient gesture toward the chair opposite him. She sat, perching on the front few inches of the seat. The computer fan hummed, the program made a few beeps, and he began asking questions without looking at her.

"Working?"

"Yes, sir. Two part-time jobs. Beans & Leaves and Stitches in Time. No changes. Contact information for my employers is in your files."

They'd been through this drill so often that she saved him four additional questions with her answer. Her goal was to get in and out as fast as possible. Opal knew she hadn't done anything illegal or in violation of her parole contract, but it gave her the willies just being here. Like her freedom could be snatched just by association with people like him.

He tapped at keys, pursing his lips in concentration. "Address?" He reached for his coffee without looking, an action that inevitably filled Opal with dread that he would miss, and spill, but he located it without incident and brought it to his mouth.

"Unchanged, sir. Contact information for my landlord is the same too."

He tapped her answer into the computer. "Any contact with felons?"

"No, sir." Opal wondered if anyone was ever stupid enough to answer that question in the affirmative.

He swung around to face her. "The computer has tagged you for a random drug test today." He picked up the phone and called the receptionist, whose duties included supervising the collection of urine samples from female parolees.

Heat rose from Opal's neck and her face flamed. In the months since she'd been released from prison, she'd become accustomed to a normal sense of privacy. What she'd come to understand as an inmate—namely, that her body belonged to the Commonwealth of Kentucky, and they could inspect it at will—no longer seemed just. She wanted to surge to her feet and walk out, but she didn't dare.

Mr. Luckett's gaze, sharp behind his utilitarian glasses, took in her heightened color. "You have something to hide, Ms. McBride?"

She shook her head. "No, sir." The sample would be clean, no trace of any illegal substance, but she couldn't prove that ahead of time. She held his gaze, determined not to falter and give him more reason to take notice.

The receptionist appeared in the doorway. Mr. Luckett turned his attention to her. "Drug test." The woman beckoned for Opal.

"Am I free to leave after this, sir?" It had never been a problem before, but she'd never blushed like a virgin before, either.

He flicked a glance at her. "Yes." His expression hardened. "We know where to find you if we need to." Turning back to his computer, he addressed the receptionist, "Send the next client back, please."

It took the faucet providing a waterfall of background noise for Opal to be able to fill the bottle under the watchful eye of her overseer, but she did it. Then she subjected the receptionist to the same level of scrutiny as the woman labeled and bagged the sample. No way was she going back to prison because of sloppy clerical work.

The sun blazed overhead by the time she got back to May's shop. Sweaty, with strands of hair plastered to her face, Opal wished she'd thought to bring a change of clothes. It wasn't that hot, but the humidity made her jeans damp, and her shirt felt wet under her arms.

She got the shop open with minutes to spare, and spent as much time as she dared in the restroom, trying to get presentable. By the time May showed up, Opal felt like she had a better handle on the day.

"We're getting a security system put in today." May made the announcement in a businesslike tone that was at odds with her normal warm greeting.

Opal's spirits plummeted. Had she done something to offend May, or worse, cause her mentor to be suspicious? She already felt off kilter from her visit to the parole office this morning, not to mention the drug test and how it had almost made her late. The muscles in her abdomen tightened. Her mouth went dry. "It's because of me, isn't it?"

May turned, her brows arched.

"Josh knows I work here." Opal spoke slowly, the words like icicles in her belly. "He's making you get the security system to protect you from me."

The whole intent of her phone call the other night was to protect May. She'd *told* him that, but had he listened? No, he had to taint her relationship with her boss, who had become so much more. Her friend.

"That's not it at all." Alarm, along with what looked a lot like guilt crossed May's face.

Tears stung the back of Opal's eyelids and she blinked, trying to rid her eyes of the tingle. It was harder to dislodge the pain that had taken residence in her heart. She couldn't control the tremble of her lips or her voice as she said, "I'm sorry. You have every right to do what you need to do, and I was out of line in saying anything." She would never hurt May, not for anything, but Josh's lens of distrust distorted Opal's actions.

May closed the distance between them, holding out her hands and taking Opal's in hers. "Oh dear." She looked into Opal's eyes, hers now guileless and full of concern. "It's a step to protect *both* of us. Josh suggested it in response to the threats you received last week."

It took a moment for May's words to register. "Oh." Resentment flowed out of Opal like water through a sieve, and left her feeling foolish. "So he talked to you." Of course he had.

May blushed, the pale pink livening her cheeks. "Yes." She released Opal's hands, and looked about ready to say more, but the door opened and she peered past Opal's shoulder. "Oh! They're here!" She hurried off to meet with the installer.

Left to herself for the moment, Opal huffed out a frustrated breath. Maybe she should give May her resignation, if working here caused that much consternation to her family. She could imagine the fireworks of the conversation with Josh. They were both mule-headed when they wanted to be. A smile softened her face as she thought of her employer, then evaporated when Josh's face came to mind. She scowled, then felt stingy, because he was looking out for both of them.

And the cost of a security system! Guilt flooded her. It wasn't fair that May shoulder the expense, since it was being installed because of the trouble that seemed to follow Opal around. Her heart sank.

Unfortunately, she didn't have anything to contribute. As impressive as her nest egg had grown—in her eyes—she had no illusions regarding how much she could spare. Granny McBride had taught her how to live on a shoestring, and between the reality of her paychecks and anxiety borne of the tenuous nature of her life, Opal had taken the concept to a new level. Not only was she living on beans, she'd planted some of them and was nursing seedlings in her apartment. She had a strong vision of the harvest she could put up come fall, and a hazier thought of selling any excess at one of the myriad farmer's markets in the area.

But five dollars a week... She could scrounge that much. Whether May would accept it was another question, though.

Before she could roll the dilemma around enough to see a glimmer of a solution, customers entered. Two young women, close to her age, with three children. The older two kids had mops of carrot-orange hair, and clearly belonged to the woman with her own unruly curls of the same color. The other woman, taller, slender, and dark-haired, carried an infant in a sling.

"Lannis, if you can fly an airplane, you can sew. Oh, look!" The redhead grabbed her kids and herded them toward the activity corner Opal had set up. "Let's see what you can play with over there!"

The familiar pain at the sight of kids squeezed Opal's heart, but she squared her shoulders and pasted a smile on her face. "Ma'am, there are crafts for the children, as well as toys."

The girl, maybe four or five, broke away from her mother's grip and raced to the table.

"Megan! Use your inside manners!" The mom shot a grateful glance at Opal. "Would you mind watching them while we look at fabric? I promise it won't take long."

Opal's smile froze. Since the activity center had gone in, she'd observed the kids using it from an emotionally safe distance. She hadn't prepared for the prospect of being pressed into service. "Uh, sure." She moved toward the children, her limbs carrying her without conscious thought or her permission.

Twelve years of burying her memories of Skye, of turning a deaf ear to other inmates' anguish at their forced separation from their children, of avoiding contact—all her barriers came crashing down the closer she got to Megan and her little brother.

Her breath came faster and shallower. Would Skye have pitched toys out of the bin with the same abandon as the little boy? Would she have been as focused with a pair of safety scissors and construction paper like the little girl?

Tears clouded her vision.

Of course she would have. The sudden weight of grief threatened to break her spirit more than Viper or Mr. Luckett. Or Josh. She closed her eyes and breathed a prayer for strength, though she didn't know who might listen.

Opal opened her eyes, swallowed, then crouched near the kids. Her hair, which she'd worn loose today, slid over her shoulder and she absently tucked it behind an ear. There was really nothing for her to *do*, so she said the only thing she could think of. "What's your brother's name, Megan?"

"He's Marty." Her face fierce in concentration, the girl made a tiny motion indicating her brother, who ignored everyone as he continued grabbing blocks with chubby hands.

Opal dodged a particularly vigorous throw and snagged the block before it could roll under a display. The tightness in her throat eased. "What are you cutting out?"

"A square." Megan made it sound like the most complicated task on the planet.

The girl's self-assurance surprised a smile onto Opal's face. "Would you like to use the glue stick? Put it on another big piece of paper? It might look like your mama's quilts." Relaxing a bit, Opal flipped the different colors of construction paper for Megan to choose from. Bits of the women's conversation drifted over. The subject strayed from fabric, and Opal's interest was piqued.

"—so glad Ben doesn't do undercover work anymore." The more introverted brunette's voice pitched low, but a trick of acoustics allowed Opal to make out the words.

That must be Lannis.

"—envy you, that he's home every night." And that would be Maggie, not bothering to keep her words from being overheard.

"Any idea when Mike—"

"Nope." Maggie's abrupt answer put a stop to that direction of the conversation. The women wandered on to a display that faced away from Opal and their words faded.

Just what she needed. If it wasn't cops themselves, it was cops' wives. *Or mothers.*

Opal brought her attention back to the children. Her breath left her in a soft sigh. She should have known avoidance wouldn't protect her heart from memories or its shattered dreams. Not eager to open herself to the inevitable pain of letting children into her life, Opal experienced a moment of resistance, but knew it was futile.

There was nothing to do but surrender to her new reality. It turned out to be as simple as leaning in to help Megan uncap the glue stick. Marty remained engrossed in piling blocks on top of each other, then chortling as he swept a chubby hand through them, sending them flying.

The day she'd been released from prison, she'd held no illusions. Life would be hard—and so far, *that* expectation had been fulfilled. But she never would have predicted this.

Surrounded by cops and kids, the two groups she eschewed more than anything on the planet.

Tears blurred her vision again. She blinked, but instead of controlling them, they spilled down her cheeks, and she dashed them away with the back of her hands.

Of the two, she could handle the cops. All they tried to do was deprive her of freedom.

Children, on the other hand, sliced through every protective barrier she could concoct, reaching to the most vulnerable, most deeply hidden wound of her soul.

Marty chose that moment to turn, and with the innocence and trust of a well-loved toddler, met her eyes with his startling blue ones, then launched himself at her.

Opal didn't have time to think, just threw her arms out to catch him, because if she didn't he would hit the floor. He grabbed a handful of her hair and stuffed it into his mouth, melting into her embrace, fully confident that she would hold him.

She did. And couldn't curb the need to draw his warm, wiggling, *living* weight closer, pulling him to her breast in a purely maternal instinct. Opal curled around him, emotion welling up in her chest, tears spilling down her face.

He allowed her to clutch him for a long moment, seeming to somehow understand her need for the simple contact. A wisp of healing crept into Opal's aching heart, and she squelched a sob before it broke through. His tiny fingers wove through her hair, then tugged. She smiled, her lips wobbly, and lowered her face to his head. She closed her eyes and inhaled the scent of *boy*, and brushed a soft kiss across his curls.

It felt illicit, to kiss a child.

Opal took a deep breath, corralling her emotions. Marty arched his back, now insistent upon getting down. She untangled her hair from his grasp and set him near the blocks. Using her sleeves, she dried her face, knowing it would be blotchy for some time, but no longer caring.

Nothing would fill the void Skye's death had left in Opal's very being. But for the first time, a future without the possibility of another child cut almost as deep.

She might have gotten out of a physical prison, but if she needed further proof that her life remained shackled in invisible bonds, this was it.

Surely Maggie and Lannis had finished by now.

Opal stood, the movement fluid and economical. An irrational urge to flee gripped her, but she quashed it. She couldn't outrun her heart's pain.

Drained and unsettled, she wrapped her arms around her middle and took a step back from the children.

And wished Maggie would make her fabric selections quickly.

Chapter Twenty-Nine

JOSH GLANCED AT the address Opal's parole officer had given him, and lifted an eyebrow. She'd pulled one over on him, and he had to give her credit for deceiving him without lying. The night she'd called him, frightened over her encounter with the woman from prison, she'd met him in front of Dante's Tattoo Parlor. What he hadn't realized was that she lived over said shop. He trekked around back, looking for a separate entryway, and found it.

Wooden stairs led to a white door adorned with what he immediately recognized as a fabric wreath handcrafted by his mother, a generous deck for such a small place, and as Opal had told him, a well-lit parking lot for an apartment complex across the alley. He took the stairs two at a time, even as he wondered about his sanity in what he was about to propose. His boots echoed on the wood as he crossed the deck to the door and rapped on it.

Silence.

He knew she had closed Beans & Leaves last night, so couldn't have gotten home until close to midnight. A glance at his watch told him what he already knew: seven thirty a.m. He seriously doubted she was up and gone so early.

He caught a slight movement of the curtain in the window to his right. She *was* home. Satisfaction mingled with an uncomfortable sense of crossing some boundary, whether it was his or hers or their respective roles. A screeching noise on the other side of the door startled him, and he narrowed his eyes as he tried to identify it. The sound ceased, and he heard a chain guard, the doorknob lock, and a dead bolt get thrown. The door jerked open, and Opal glared at him from a tidy kitchen. She propped one hand on a hip, her feet planted perfectly for self-defense, and her other hand on the door, ready to slam it in his face.

She wore a pair of jeans and a plaid shirt open over a tee, much like Widow Reese's favored attire. Opal looked better in it, though. Her feet were bare, and his heart gave a stutter at the sight. Her glorious hair flowed over her shoulders like living honey. His fingers itched to bury themselves in the silky fall, so he slipped his hands into his pockets.

"What do you want?" She regarded him with haughtiness he was beginning to understand had its roots in insecurity.

Rather than answer, he craned his neck and peered past her. "What's all the noise?" Now he was close enough to smell the floral scent of her shampoo. He inhaled. Bad choice. The fragrance made him want to bury his face in her hair.

A flush sprang into her cheeks, and she stepped back. He took that as an invitation and moved forward.

Opal put a hand up and splayed it on his chest, stopping him, then snatched it away as if he'd burned her. She stuffed her hand in the back pocket of her jeans. "Do you have a warrant, Detective?" She infused the question with enough belligerence and sass to earn some time in segregation, had she still been in prison.

The purely male part of him was pleased he wasn't the only one affected by this weird electricity between them. The sane cop part of him was appalled. "No warrant." He smiled, doing his best to project a nonthreatening manner. "No need. May I come in?"

Her lips flattened. An internal battle waged behind smoldering eyes. After a moment she stepped back. "Whatever."

The first thing he noticed as he crossed the threshold was the stove in the middle of the floor. It didn't take his well-honed detective skills to figure out that she'd pushed it in front of the door as protection during the night. The screech he'd heard was her wrestling it out of the way once she'd decided to acknowledge his presence.

Frustration and helplessness coalesced in his gut. He'd never imagined his teasing of information about Shaniqua from Opal would lead to admittedly reasonable paranoia on her part. Maybe his suggestion for the day would be a small atonement for the effects of his actions.

"Would you like me to help you move that back where it belongs?"

She shrugged. "I'll just move it back tonight."

He let it go and took in the rest of the small kitchen. Bright curtains graced the windows, and the faint aroma of home-baked bread proved she had used the oven recently.

"Other than the atypical placement of your appliances, it seems you've settled in." He glanced past her into the living room.

Every surface was covered with seedlings planted in cast-off soup cans. Opal followed his gaze. Josh lifted his eyebrows in question.

"It's not marijuana, Detective," she drawled. She brushed past him and picked up a plastic watering can.

"Uh, that's not what I—" He needed to get back on track here. He cleared his throat. "I'd like to take you to Jubilee today."

"What?" She whipped around, seedlings forgotten. She paled, her freckles standing out in sharp relief. A flurry of expressions—fear, something that looked like despair, hope, pain—chased across her face. Her breaths came quicker, piling on top of themselves as if she couldn't get enough air.

Her legs wobbled, and Josh grabbed her upper arms to keep her from sliding to the floor. He spotted a folding metal chair among the makeshift plant shelves, and guided her to it.

"Slow down. You're going to hyperventilate."

Opal sagged into the chair and made a visible effort to comply with his instructions. Josh crouched in front of her. She brought her gaze to his, her deep green eyes tormented.

"I can't," she whispered.

"Yes, you can."

"I'm not allowed to leave the county." Her voice was stronger, with a husky, almost seductive quality.

Josh couldn't help himself. He shot a quick glance at her lips. As soon as Opal noticed, she clamped them together. But she didn't pull away and he had the crazy notion that she wanted to lean into him.

"I've cleared it with your parole officer." Convinced that she wasn't going to topple, he removed the temptation to draw her into his arms by letting go. He rocked back on his heels. "Besides, you'll be in my custody the whole time."

Her expression, so open and vulnerable until this moment, underwent a transformation. A cool mask of indifference slid over her face. He might as well have slapped her. *Custody.* That wasn't the tone he'd meant to set.

"I suppose you have a good enough reason to coerce me into going." Her voice was flat with an edge of bitterness.

He shook his head. "No. You don't have to go." He lifted one shoulder in a shrug. "Thought you might like to, and I need a change of scenery."

Opal scowled. "No ulterior motive? No cold cases you think I can solve for you?"

Heat climbed his neck, but he didn't break eye contact. "It wouldn't break my heart if you opened up about your own case. That's up to you, though, not me. Other than that, it's just a drive."

Her expression flickered, but she neither agreed nor refused.

"I wondered if…" Josh cleared his throat. "You haven't had an opportunity to pay your respects to your grandmother."

Opal's eyes widened and a sheen of tears sprang into them. Her shoulders slumped as she blinked furiously, trying not to cry in front of him. She nodded, lips trembling, then stood and brushed past him. It took only moments for her to shove her feet into shoes, grab a coat, and secure her apartment.

Josh guided her to his Jeep, handed her in, and hit the freeway within minutes. He shifted through the gears and considered how monumental this outing was for her. As hard as he tried, he couldn't quite imagine what she felt. Coming home after twelve years away would be heartrending enough. Add to that the circumstances of her departure and subsequent incarceration, and it became even more pivotal.

In spite of the heavy sense of the undertaking, silence hung easily between them. Once the city was behind them, Opal glanced in the backseat and examined his climbing and camping gear. She shot him a look of curiosity, then returned her attention to the passing scenery.

The miles spun beneath the tires, and she eventually rested her forehead against the window. Though her breathing remained even, Josh noted tension in her infrequent movements.

The mountains around Pikeville came into view and she straightened. Josh pulled off the highway into the lot of a restaurant that boasted home cooking.

"What are you doing?" Opal's voice shook.

He slanted a look at her. "I'm hungry, figured you are too." Puzzled, he lifted an eyebrow. "I dragged you out pretty early this morning."

"I—" She clenched her hands in her lap. "Do you mind if we do a drive-through instead?" A blush rose in her cheeks. She swallowed. "I don't want to run into anyone I know."

"Ah." Josh pushed the clutch in and shifted into REVERSE. That hadn't occurred to him, but now that she mentioned it, he could understand. However, he needed to get out of the Jeep before his butt grew roots. "How about a picnic, then?"

Opal's expression lit up. "There's a park down by the Levisa Fork." She lifted her hip to dig in a pocket and drew out some money.

Josh reached over, covering both her hands with one of his. "My treat. Since it was my idea." She didn't pull away, which surprised him a little. Her skin was soft and silky under his palm, warming him and evoking a protective instinct.

She brought her gaze up to meet his, and he saw a fleeting glimpse of longing in her eyes. Did she want something from him? He doubted if it was the same as what he finally acknowledged that he wanted from her. More. Friendship, touch, hell, he didn't know. Just *more*. She scrambled his brain and sharpened his focus at the same time. With effort, he withdrew his hand.

The moment of intimacy passed. A wry half smile lifted the corner of Opal's mouth. "Deal." She stuffed her money back into a pocket and sat back in the seat.

It took Josh a moment to process her answer, since his thoughts had gone so far afield.

Deal.

Buy her lunch.

No matter how much it was beginning to feel like one, this was not a date. It would behoove him to remember that pertinent little fact.

He chose the next fast food place he saw, ordered, and followed Opal's directions to the park. A secluded picnic table met with her approval, and Josh spent the next half hour enjoying the sound of the river. Watching the play of colors in her hair as the breeze lifted it. Appreciating her economical yet fluid and graceful movements. A spurt of pure delight rolled through him, that he'd been the one to provide this experience.

He sobered as he wondered how much longer he could hide his attraction to her.

Chapter Thirty

THE SOUND OF the river, high and boisterous with spring runoff, both soothed and disturbed Opal. It evoked memories of other picnics with classmates, with Granny McBride, and even further back to hazy, happy times with her mama, with her papa. When the memories became too uncomfortable, Opal rose and gathered the food wrappers, and chose the farthest trash can for their disposal. On her way back, she steeled herself and stopped a few feet from Josh.

"I'm ready."

He stood with the same unconscious athletic grace she'd noticed the first time they met. "Where to?"

She named a grocery store, and though he lifted his eyebrows in surprise, he didn't ask why, for which Opal was grateful. Once there, she led the way to the floral department, where she debated over carnations in improbable colors versus more natural looking—and therefore more expensive—sunflowers and roses. The significance of the opportunity Josh had handed her settled on her like a cloak, and that awareness made the decision for her. She quickly chose a bouquet of sunflowers for Granny McBride, then hesitated for a fraction of a breath and picked a group of rainbow-hued carnations.

Her back to Josh, to forestall any offer to help pay, she parted with a good chunk of her money at the cash register. Her pulse picked up and her palms went damp as she sneaked a glance at the cashier. It wasn't anyone she knew and she relaxed a little. However, since her picture had probably been plastered all over the local papers those years ago, she hoped no one recognized her.

Then again, she had no idea if it had been a school picture with her hair long, like she wore it now, or the mug shot with the hatchet job Tommy had done on it. She thought about buying a scarf or a hat to cover it for the day, but decided to not waste her meager funds.

"Will you take me to the cemetery, please?" She shot him a glance. "The one in Jubilee."

Thirty minutes later, Opal crouched at the unadorned plot with the simplest of markers. PEARL INA MCBRIDE. Her birth date. The date of her death, a few months into Opal's incarceration. Pain stabbed her heart, and she knelt to touch the earth. "Oh, Granny…"

Josh, who'd helped her locate the grave and then stood back to give her space, touched Opal's shoulder. "I'm sorry you weren't allowed to attend her funeral."

A lump in her throat prevented Opal from speaking, but she nodded her acknowledgment. Tears dripped down her cheeks, some of them finding her nose. A sob broke free and she bent her head. She had too many regrets, and nothing she could have done would have changed anything. Her voice thick, she said, "I just wish she hadn't died alone." She swallowed and rocked back on her heels.

Josh made an indistinct noise that nonetheless expressed sympathy.

Opal swiped at her tears, then placed the sunflowers at the foot of the marker. She said a silent good-bye and stood. As difficult as this had been, she had another stop.

She faced Josh. "Take me to the Pike County landfill."

"What?" Confusion flickered across his features, and he scratched his head.

"Don't bother asking. Just take me there." Her voice wobbled on the last word. She clamped her lips together and scowled to keep from having to argue the point.

But without comment, he respected both her request and her boundary. It was midafternoon when he pulled up outside the gate. "Do you need to go in? Or is this close enough?"

Opal clenched her hands. "In." It was an effort to squeeze the word through her vocal cords. Then, because she didn't want to seem ungrateful, she forced out, "Please."

He turned and pulled up to the gate, negotiated the entry with quiet confidence, and followed the signs to the area in use. Garbage trucks barreled down the grade, their odors wafting in the breeze they generated as they headed away from the dump. When Josh topped the last rise, he pulled off the dirt track and parked.

Opal closed her eyes, which intensified her perception of the stench. Tears stung the back of her eyelids. This time she didn't even try to contain them. She opened her eyes and climbed out of the Jeep, reaching into the back for the carnations. She wondered for a moment exactly where Skye's remains had been discarded. Knowing didn't matter, though. Pain, far worse than what she'd experienced at Granny McBride's grave, nearly took her to her knees.

Somehow she found the strength to stand, then turned in a circle. She noted that Josh had gotten out and rested his crossed arms on the roof of the Jeep, watching her with a gaze that always seemed to see to the depths of her soul. Her own gaze slipped past him, past the massive earth movers, past piles of rubbish that hadn't been covered yet.

There was no good place, so Opal trudged through the soft soil to the edge of the landfill. This edge faced toward Jubilee, and suddenly it felt like the right choice.

Wind whipped her hair, and she automatically turned into it so her hair would fly behind her. It also dried the tears that coated her cheeks, even as new tears fell. Her lips trembled. She whispered into the wind, "I'm so sorry, sweetie."

Opal held vigil for uncounted minutes, clutching the flowers to her breast. The wind eased, then died down. The sun warmed her face. Her grief lost its knife-sharp edge and began to soften. She knelt and laid the flowers on the precipice. "I brought these for you," she murmured. Many moments passed before she could bring herself to let them go.

She rose, wrapping her arms around her midriff.

"What's this about, Opal?" Josh's voice, low and concerned, came from a foot or two behind her.

Fresh tears threatened, and she shook her head even as her throat tightened again. He touched her shoulder and tugged her around to face him. She didn't have the energy to resist. He tipped her head up with a finger beneath her chin. "Talk to me." His touch was as gentle as his voice, and that was her undoing.

She burst into noisy sobs, and in spite of herself, heard words tumbling from her lips. "My baby—she—she— I couldn't save her—and—"

Josh pulled her into an embrace that felt so natural she melted into him. She wrapped her arms around him and held on as if her life depended on it. The heat from his body warmed her fingers but couldn't touch her frozen heart.

"God, Opal, I'm sorry." He nuzzled her hair with his cheek and used one hand to stroke her back. She felt his muscles tense, and he asked, "A miscarriage?"

She nodded into his chest, embarrassed at the mess her tears and runny nose were making on his shirt, but too bereft to pull away. His arms felt so good around her. Strong. Safe.

He rested his chin on the top of her head.

"I named her Skye, with an *e*." Opal hadn't meant to say the words. Horrified, she heard herself continue. "She was so beautiful, perfect except for the bruise where Tommy hit me. I got to hold her until the guard came and then—" She sniffed, then shrugged, unable to continue.

Josh's hand on her back stilled. "Are you saying this happened the day you—the day Tommy died?"

Opal nodded.

He grasped her shoulders and untangled her enough that he could see her face. He didn't conceal his emotions, and she read pain in his eyes, along with something more complex. Gentleness, sorrow, determination.

"He beat you while you were pregnant." His voice was matter of fact with a hint of underlying steel.

She nodded again, too exhausted to be wary.

"He deliberately targeted your belly and the baby." He uttered the blunt words slowly, as though he was putting the pieces together and just now seeing how they fit.

Her lips trembled. She nodded again, bringing her hands to her mouth, trying to contain the wail building deep within.

His voice gentled. "You used the two-by-four in self-defense, didn't you, Opal?"

She gazed up at him, feeling vulnerable and fragile. The trembling of her lips traveled to her limbs like a wave, until the only thing keeping her from collapse was Josh's grip on her arms. Anguish crossed his features. He drew her close again, close enough that her ear rested over his heart. The steady rhythm promised comfort, but it couldn't stop the keening cry that climbed her throat and clawed its way out.

"Hush, sweetheart." His hand began a lazy trip up and down her back. When she would have pulled away, he held her close, murmuring nonsense into her hair.

Opal sobbed until there was nothing left. No tears, no breath, no strength. When the emotional storm finally abated, she surrendered to his embrace.

In the silence, she tipped her head back to look at him. There was nothing but tenderness in his expression. Then his eyes focused on hers with a purpose she recognized with a jolt of sensual awareness. He saw it in her eyes, and giving her plenty of time to turn away, lowered his mouth to hers. He stopped a hairbreadth away and muttered, "This is a bad idea."

Opal lifted herself on her toes to complete the contact, and he followed her as she sank back down. He was warm, soft and hard at the same time, gentle and insistent, safe and dangerous. And she wanted him with a ferocity that stunned her. She brought her hands up to frame his face, then slipped her arms around his neck. His hands roamed her back, her shoulders, her waist, her hips, tugging her tighter against his chest and thighs.

Her heart thudded and her blood heated. She didn't realize her body had found a fresh supply of tears until she tasted them in their kiss. With great reluctance, she slid her hands down and pushed at the flat planes of his chest. He immediately loosened his hold, but it took a few moments for both of them to break the kiss.

Josh was breathing hard, and shoved a hand through his hair. He turned away from Opal in a clear attempt to regain his composure, then looked at the flowers she'd laid on the edge of the landfill for Skye. She followed his gaze. Twelve years of pent-up grief had spent itself, and while she knew she'd always feel sorrow when she thought of her lost daughter, a small measure of healing had occurred here. A stray hiccup caught her by surprise, and she swiped at her face with the heels of her hands.

"Why didn't any of this come out in the trial?" He sounded strained, and maybe a little angry.

Opal could understand strained, but she didn't understand anger. It gave her just enough energy to firm her spine and answer. "Because no one ever asked, Detective."

There was nothing left to do for Skye here, or for herself, and she turned and marched to the Jeep. Even so, tears blurred her vision.

No one ever asked.

Except for an unexpectedly kind, thoroughly confusing, and unfairly sexy detective who was awakening urges best left buried as deeply as Skye's remains.

Chapter Thirty-One

Suspect taken to Pikeville Community Hospital for bleeding at 8:45 p.m. Treated and released. Returned to cell at 11:55 p.m.

Josh wanted to throw up. He'd assumed—*assumed!*—that she'd gotten stitched up for cuts on her hands, that the force required to wield the lumber in a killing arc had done some damage to her too.

The terse entry in Opal's records left out the most important part. Why was she bleeding? What wounds had she sustained in the incident? Domestic abuse often escalated when a woman was pregnant, and he flashed back to Widow Reese's comment. Something about how Tommy had been beating her more in the few months prior to the murder.

He had to stop thinking about it in terms of murder.

Trooper Nelson was going to have a field day with this new information. Not only a miscarriage of justice—he winced at the term—but a flat-out cover-up. His thoughts darted six different directions as he drove Opal away from her baby's final resting place. A wave of nausea rose at the thought, though the pragmatic part of him knew that miscarried fetuses got flushed down the toilet all the time. Which made him wonder, why was she so sure Skye's remains were here?

"How far along were you, Opal?" He dreaded the answer.

She'd been looking out the window, pensive but somehow less burdened, and turned to face him. "Four and a half months." She lifted a shoulder. "Near as I could figure, anyway. Tommy wouldn't let me go to the doctor. Said it cost too much." Sadness slid across her face. "He had good insurance, I know prenatal care was covered. I guess he didn't want to pay…" A shadow darkened her eyes. "And eighteen weeks or so fits with the pictures I looked up in the prison library."

"Why…how do you know she…Skye…is *here?* I mean—" He knew full well what he meant, but he couldn't bring himself to say it.

"Because…" She turned and looked out the window. When she spoke, her voice was thin and tight. "I saw them put her in a biohazard bag."

Josh's stomach rolled. He pulled over to the side of the road and threw the transmission into NEUTRAL, then yanked the parking brake on. He didn't quite make it out the door before he lost his lunch. The bastard had beaten her with the intent of killing his own child, she'd fought back, and lost anyway.

Josh stumbled the rest of the way out, desperate for some space and fresh air. He inhaled, and got nothing but the stench of the landfill. He retched again, perspiration dampening his brow. The wind drove it away and chilled his skin. Hands on knees and breathing through his mouth so he wouldn't have to deal with the odors, he didn't hear Opal approach. But that could only be her hand that landed softly on his shoulder.

"It's okay, Josh." She rubbed a calming rhythm across his shoulders, which were tight from anger and impotence. "I've had twelve years to work through all of it."

True. Maybe Father Barney was right. He'd spent so much time on the dead over the past three years, he'd forgotten about the toll that death ripped from the living.

He straightened. "Did you ever tell *anybody* what happened?" He looked down into her moss-green eyes, and nearly lost himself in their depths.

"No." Her gaze and voice were both steady. She looked...at peace.

"Why not?" In Josh's experience, the only people who didn't shout their innocence all the way to jail and through the trial and on into prison were the sick perverts who got their jollies from glorifying the inhumanity of their deed.

She smiled, although it was crooked. "You know why. The cops weren't inclined to listen to me anyway." The smile faded and she looked haunted for a moment. She shook her head and added, "Besides, it was the most traumatic day of my life. I almost died, more than once, and words were too...insubstantial to save me."

Josh bit back his reply. *Yes, words mattered,* but she hadn't uttered them. She'd done the best she could with a bad situation, though, and he couldn't blame her. "Would you like to make a statement?"

Confusion rippled across her face. "What for?"

He lifted a hand and caught a lock of her hair, sick all over again at the image of Tommy holding her head to the chopping block and hacking the fiery tresses off with an ax.

"Witness, Opal. You didn't have a voice then, but you do now. I'd be honored to bear witness to the injustice you suffered."

The tidbits she'd already divulged both corroborated and blew holes in the police report, and if more damning information came to light, so be it. Sheriff Beuhly and his cronies were on the fast track to accountability.

A garbage truck roared by, stirring up a small dust devil that didn't have enough energy to last. It settled to the earth with a sigh.

Opal searched his eyes and, apparently convinced that he meant what he said, nodded slowly. She still looked a little nonplussed, so he followed his instinct and dropped a kiss on the tip of her freckled nose.

He stepped back before his instincts took him any further. "If you're up to it, let's go to the trailer, and you can walk me through what happened."

The sun was sliding behind the highest peaks by the time the Jeep bounced up the overgrown track that led to the ruins of the trailer. Opal's face became stonier the closer they got, and her knuckles went white as they rounded the last bend.

In an effort to defuse her tension, he said, "It's a lot different, Opal. The trailer's just a rusted shell."

And there it was. Josh tried to see it the way she might, but without the emotional baggage, the abandoned mobile home looked like any other pile of scrap metal. A sharp intake of Opal's breath told him she viewed it quite differently. He parked and turned the engine off. The wind whispered through the trees in the ensuing silence.

"You okay?" he asked, half turning in his seat to look at her.

She met his gaze head-on, her enigmatic green eyes full of resolve. "Yes." She got out and set off for the front door.

Josh grabbed his digital recorder and scrambled to keep up with her. He keyed the RECORD button as he jogged and stated the essentials.

Her voice floated back to him. "It started inside, like it usually did."

He hoped the recorder had picked up her words. "Watch the steps, Opal. They're rotten." She'd already reached them, and tested them with her foot before scaling them with easy grace.

She pushed the door, hanging by one hinge, out of the way and disappeared inside. "That day..." Her voice trailed off, and Josh followed her in. The stripped interior didn't seem to bother her. She pointed at an empty space, likely the living room.

"I told Tommy I needed the truck on his next day off so I could go to the free clinic in Pikeville." Sadness flowed across her features.

"I wanted to hear the baby's heartbeat." She threw her shoulders back, as if she were pushing the emotion away. "He ignored me, ordered me to get him a beer, but I wasn't quick enough and he came out of the recliner swinging." She took a moment to glance at the rest of the interior, then pointed at the door. "I ran out." Her lips twisted. "But he caught up to me out back."

"This happen often?" Josh knew the answer, but needed it on record. He held up the digital instrument so she'd know the conversation was official. Her eyes flickered and she gave him a nearly imperceptible nod of acknowledgment.

"It started about three months after we got married. He was real unpredictable. I never knew what was going to set him off. After the first time—"

Josh interrupted. "The first time, what?"

"The first time he beat me."

The matter-of-factness of her delivery chilled him. He nodded at her to continue.

"I learned how to get out of his way. Wasn't very often that he bothered tracking me once I got to the woods, and if he did bother, he couldn't find me." The floor creaked as she went to the door and negotiated the steps again. "He was furious that I got pregnant, accused me of sleeping around—like I had a steady stream of men coming up here or something." Disgust dripped from the words. "He'd even show up unannounced while he was on shift, to check on me."

Josh worked at keeping his expression neutral. Like most law enforcement personnel, he hated domestic violence. The difference here was that he usually investigated the victim's death, not the perpetrator's.

Opal shook off the morbid thoughts. Her hair shimmered with the slight movement. "That day, being as how I was getting bigger and wasn't quite as nimble, he grabbed my hair and yanked me back." By this time, she'd reached the chopping block. She thrust her hands into the pockets of her jacket, but Josh saw them tremble as she did. "He jerked me down on the ground, kicked my belly a bunch of times, and started with the ax." A shudder rolled through her slender frame.

She turned to face him, and Josh recognized the haunted expression from her mug shot. He wanted to pull her into his arms and protect her from any other asshole men—and her memories— but he restrained himself. *Keep it professional until the recorder is off.*

"I honestly don't remember much after that. I must have screamed, because my throat was raw later. I remember fighting, just trying to get Tommy to stop before he killed me. Widow Reese showed up about the same time as the first sheriff's car. I didn't even realize I had the wood in my hand until they took it away from me."

Opal let her breath out in a sigh. "I didn't mean to kill him, but later that night, when I lost Skye, I was glad." She lifted her gaze to his. "I know that makes me a bad person, the murderer that they said I was." The wind blew a strand of hair across her face, and she hooked a finger around it, sliding it behind her ear. "That I am."

Her words were a sucker punch to Josh's gut. He gaped at her, then gathered his wits and shut the recorder off. "Opal, you're no more a murderer than I am. The law allows for sufficient force to defend your life. For that matter, the church does too."

She wasn't swayed by his argument. "I may not have meant to do it, but I am responsible for his death. Just like he's responsible for Skye's." Her voice shook on her baby's name.

The rumble of a truck coming up the mountain drew his attention, and he narrowed his eyes. It didn't sound like a police cruiser. Sheriff Beuhly would be eager to throw him—and Opal—out of the county, if he could find a pretext for doing so.

Opal tensed and glanced past Josh. A dented pickup with patches of missing paint rolled into the clearing and parked next to the Jeep. A man dressed in worn overalls stepped out.

"Obadiah." Opal's voice was flat.

"What're you doing out of prison?" The man didn't bother to temper the venom in his voice.

"Good behavior." There was no sense of boasting in her toneless answer.

Obadiah spat and reached into his truck. When he reappeared, he had a shotgun in his hands.

Josh's pulse hammered into overdrive. He made to step in front of Opal, but she shot her arm out in front of him. Deciding to risk trusting her judgment, Josh stopped, but he crouched as if tying a shoelace and surreptitiously withdrew his .38 from his ankle holster. It felt as effective as a peashooter in the face of a shotgun, though.

Without taking her eyes off the man, Opal said, "Put it away, Obie. There's been enough bloodshed. No good will come from you shootin' me."

The sound of another shotgun being racked up the hill drew everyone's attention. "I'd think twice, Mr. Finley." Widow Reese appeared from behind a large tree that would serve as cover should she need it. She held the dominant position, her gun pointed at Obadiah and steady in her hands. Josh had no doubt she'd pull the trigger. Sweat trickled down his temple.

"Oh, for pity's sake!" Opal sounded like she was dealing with a roomful of toddlers, not two armed people with revenge on their minds. "What is this—the shootout at the OK Corral?" She sketched a wave at Widow Reese. "Hi, Fiona."

Widow Reese acknowledged her greeting with a smile, but the gun and her attention didn't budge. Neither did Obadiah, although his face darkened with fury and purple veins stood out on his forehead.

"Obie, I know you can't find it in your heart to forgive me, and I won't ask. But for your own sake, you need to let go of the bitterness. It eats at your soul." Her tone was neutral except for a hint of compassion.

The man spat again, his hands trembling with his fury.

Opal sighed. "I won't cast aspersions on Tommy, but there was more to the situation than you know." A crooked smile crossed her face, although pain, not humor, filled her expression. "Always more to the story…" She shrugged.

Obadiah's expression went even more thunderous.

Time to defuse.

Josh cleared his throat. "Opal and I were just leaving, Mr. Finley. I'd appreciate it if you'd let us do that, in peace."

The man's hands clenched and unclenched around the shotgun's grip, but he apparently also believed Widow Reese's willingness to shoot. "Sheriff Beuhly's gonna hear about this." He spat again and tossed the gun back into his truck, then got in. He fired up the engine and over-revved it several times before turning around and roaring back down the track.

Tension slid out of Josh's shoulders once the truck disappeared around the bend. Opal took off at a run up the hill. Widow Reese set her gun down on a boulder and met her halfway. The two women embraced, and Josh couldn't tell who was crying the hardest.

He crouched and replaced his weapon. The sooner they got out of Jubilee, the better. Another showdown, next time with the sheriff, might end poorly. No use pushing their luck.

"Opal. Widow Reese. I'm really sorry, but it would be best if we go. Now."

The women separated but clutched each other's shoulders. They exchanged a few words, too low for Josh to hear, then touched foreheads before Opal turned and descended the hill.

"Thank you, ma'am." Josh saluted Widow Reese, who gave him a curt nod, picked up her weapon, and vanished into the shadows.

Opal, her nose red and eyes still watering, halted in front of him. "Thank *you*." She looked like she wanted to say more, but ran with light steps to the Jeep instead.

It wasn't until they'd left the county that Josh recalled she'd used his first name at the landfill. Warmth curled through him even as he wrestled with the ramifications of the lines they'd crossed today. Seeking justice? No problem. Falling for Opal? Risky.

A risk he discovered he was willing to take.

Chapter Thirty-Two

"I GOTTA SAY, you've led a colorful life."

Josh's voice broke into Opal's swirling thoughts, and she glanced at him. Darkness had fallen during the drive back to Louisville, cocooning them in cozy isolation. The headlights of approaching vehicles slid across his face, providing glimpses of his strong profile. A slight smile softened his expression, and he sounded more bemused than judgmental.

As long as Josh had remained silent, she'd been able to push the memory of his kiss to the back of her mind. With the fresh grief—and peace—of paying tribute to Granny McBride and Skye, and the reliving of the terrible day of Tommy's death, it wasn't hard to ignore what he'd done.

Now, his rumbling baritone slid over her like warm rain. Desire shot through Opal. Her own face heated. Glad he couldn't see, and discomfited by the unfamiliar sensation, she cleared her suddenly dry throat. *I wanted it as badly as he did.* Honesty didn't help curb the craving for more of his touch, or the itch in her fingertips that wanted to test the firmness of his muscles and the smoothness of his skin.

"Uh, I suppose." Opal didn't see why it was so colorful. Fiona and Obie were fixtures of her childhood, as were the ubiquitous shotguns. She'd grown up comfortable with guns, except for the first time she'd fired a shotgun. The kick had knocked her on her butt. Experience was a good teacher and she was a quick learner, and it hadn't happened the next time.

"Most people think my job is exciting." He shook his head. "Dead people don't pull guns on me, though."

Opal felt the irrational need to defend Obie. "They're not always like that. I mean, it's not like the Hatfields and McCoys."

Josh sent her an amused glance. "This was my third time in Jubilee. Seems to be the standard response to my presence."

"I hate stereotypes." Even as the words slipped out, Opal knew she was guilty of prejudging Josh, of assuming he was like Tommy. Maybe even to a deeper degree than his view of her hometown.

"Then tell me about your life there. What was it like, growing up in the mountains?"

She sensed a touch of wistfulness in his tone. "You like the outdoors." Opal tipped her head toward the contents of the backseat. "It's not new to you."

"No, but I'm a city guy. I camp, I hike, I climb, but I've never spent more than a few stolen days in the wilderness."

Definitely wistful. "I suppose it was a whole lot of your stolen days strung together." Opal smiled into the darkness. "Before…" She hesitated, then changed tack. "Granny McBride let me have the run of the mountain as long as I was home by dark. She taught me how to be at home in the woods, how to identify plants and their uses, how to track and understand wildlife."

"Before what?" Josh cocked his head, curious.

Leave it to him to pick up on what she *didn't* want to talk about. But he'd given her such a gift today that Opal felt she owed him that much. She inhaled, and let the words out on the exhale. "Papa died when I was five, coming home from the mine. The driver rolled the truck, killed both of them. There was no settlement since it didn't happen at work. Mama moved us in with Granny, then sort of faded away."

Opal shrugged, the betrayal by her mother still a bafflement to her, and still an arrow to her heart. "Now that I'm an adult, I think she started drinking, maybe doing some drugs. She went to sleep one night and never woke up. I was seven."

Josh reached across the cab of the Jeep and covered her hand with his. His voice was rough with emotion when he spoke. "You've had a lot of loss in your life."

Opal's throat tightened. She rotated her hand under his and curled her fingers around his larger, longer ones. "It was all a long time ago. Each day that passes, the memories get hazier. And sharper, if that makes any sense."

The only sound was tires rolling over the highway for a mile or so. Opal squeezed Josh's hand, then reluctantly let it go. She didn't know what to make of his kindness or his touch, but she both yearned for more and feared it.

She turned in her seat to face him. "I'm tired of talking about my past. Tell me some stories about *you* growing up." Images of May and Jacob and a gangly, dark-haired son formed in her mind, and she had a moment of wistfulness of her own. "It must have been wonderful." She hadn't meant to say that, but it was too late. Lifting her chin a notch higher, she settled against the door so she could watch him.

Comfortable in his own skin, he handled the Jeep with the same easy confidence on the freeway as he did on the track up the mountain, and through the less stable soil at the landfill.

He considered her question gravely, as though it were of great import. "It was wonderful." He glanced at her, the lights of the dash illuminating his face from below. "I take it for granted. Dad's an airline pilot, so he was gone a lot, and Mom was a drill sergeant disguised as a miniature puffball."

His description surprised a laugh from Opal. "I can see that. She hasn't changed, has she?"

"Nope." Josh grinned. "They subscribed to the Greek approach to a well-rounded education. Academics, music, and sports—soccer for me, volleyball for Jenn—"

"Jenn's your sister, right?" May had shown Opal pictures of a female version of Josh, eclipsed by the presence of a baby, May's grandson, which would make Josh an uncle. "And the baby is Caleb."

"Yup." Josh flashed another grin at her. "I figure by the time he's walking, I will have finally adapted to holding a baby."

"You're not married." Opal could kick herself. He'd better not be married if he was hanging out with her, and kissing her. "I mean…"

"No. I came real close once." The muscles in his jaw tightened.

She let the silence lengthen, feeling like she'd stumbled upon forbidden ground.

Then he sighed. "She jilted me at the altar."

Opal gasped. "Ouch. That must've stung."

The corner of his mouth tipped up. "I haven't told a soul, so I'm trusting you with this, Opal." He glanced at her to assess her understanding.

She felt her eyes widen. "You're trusting me with a *secret*?" A surprise visit ending in a trip into her past, a kiss, and now a secret? Her head would swim if it hadn't been treading water all day.

"Yeah. Not sure why." He sent her a wry look. "That wasn't the worst part."

Opal didn't know how it could get worse, but she hazarded a guess. "She ran off with your best man?"

That earned a guffaw from Josh. "I didn't think I'd ever laugh about it." He sobered. "She ran off with her maid of honor."

It took a full minute for that to sink in. "She was…?"

"Yup." His voice was tight.

"Oh."

Opal had seen lesbian relationships in prison, but she'd assumed it was mostly a response to the lack of heterosexual opportunity. Although, in that environment, it had seemed more a dynamic of power, not love. Maybe on the outside, love could be the driver of such relationships, but she was so inexperienced in love-based relationships, whether heterosexual or homosexual, as to consider herself a rube.

"You didn't...?" She couldn't bring herself to say the words, whether it was the romantic *make love*, the pragmatic *have sex*, and certainly not the vulgar terms she'd grown used to in prison.

"Nope." His tone had turned downright grim. "I was sticking to the virtue of chastity that the church teaches, and knew...like I knew anything...figured she'd be as enthusiastic as me once we'd gone past second base."

"Oh." Opal couldn't believe they were having this conversation. "My." She cleared her throat for lack of anything else to say.

Their cocoon turned brittle. Josh gave a short, harsh snort. "So much for my excellent detective skills. Lisa slid that little fact right past me, and me with my eyes wide open, no less."

Heat suffused Opal's face, but suddenly she had to know. "Is that why you kissed me? To prove something? To yourself, or to me?"

"Uh..."

Opal had the keen sense that Josh was blushing, but she couldn't verify it in the uncertain light.

He shifted in his seat, looking, for the first time ever, uncomfortable. "Not trying to prove anything." He slanted a glance at her, his gaze lingering as long as he could without looking at the road. "You fascinate me. Your spirit, your passion, your hair." He turned back to the road, a muscle jumping in his jaw. "I apologize. It never should have happened."

"I liked it." It must have been the intimacy of the dark, the enclosed space, the sense that they were alone in the world that loosened Opal's tongue.

He stiffened, then set his shoulders. "It was an abuse of power. You could report me for it."

Opal shook her head. "If that was an abuse of power, then my whole marriage was...well, I can't think of a vile enough word. I know what it means to be abused by a law enforcement officer, and your kiss doesn't even approach that." She searched for a way to explain what she felt. "It was...solace. Healing. Life."

"The fact remains that I'm an officer of the law and you're…" He trailed off.

"What, Josh? I'm a con? An ex-con?" The warm feelings of a few minutes ago fled, and a small flare of anger took their place. She sat up. "I'm all of those things, but the kiss was you being human to my being human. It had nothing to do with power." She crossed her arms over her midriff and scowled. "I would know."

There was a beat of silence, and then he asked, "How old were you when you got married?"

She sniffed, then swiped at her nose, confused at the direction the conversation had taken and angry that his opinion of her mattered. "We had to wait until my sixteenth birthday, when it was legal."

Josh's voice quieted and turned hard. "How old was Tommy?"

"Twenty-three. So what?" Opal didn't bother hiding her belligerence.

"So, don't take this wrong. I'm going somewhere with this. Maybe. When getting married was legal?" He let the words trail off in a go-on, fill-in-the-blank verbal prompt.

Opal's temper ignited. "The county was trying to force me into foster care. He was my ticket to freedom, except he wasn't, was he? Sex was great until we got married, then everything went sour and I was too young and stupid to figure out what was happening." All the anger left her like a deflating balloon. "By then I was trapped."

"He was having sex with you when you were fifteen?" Josh's tone went from steely to deadly, and he pulled off the highway, deep onto the shoulder.

"We. Not just him." Opal didn't know what the big deal was, but everything about this exchange made her feel defensive.

He stared at her for a moment, then dropped his forehead to the steering wheel. He lifted his head and gently beat it against the wheel two more times.

Finally he lifted his gaze to hers. "That was statutory rape, and he knew it."

"No, it wasn't. I was a willing partner." She narrowed her eyes and glared at him.

"Doesn't matter how willing you were. What matters is that the law says you're not mature enough to make that decision until you're sixteen, and if he's over eighteen, he's taking unfair advantage. End of story."

Opal leaned into his space. "Again I say. So. What?"

He reached up and touched her cheek. The tenderness of the gesture broke through her hastily erected walls. His dark eyes held compassion, and she sensed tightly leashed desire in their depths. Her anger flowed away and she melted into his palm. Tears inexplicably filled her eyes.

"What it means is that you call all the shots. Whatever happens between the two of us is up to you." Cars roared by, their headlights like strobes on his face.

Mesmerized, Opal tried to blink the tears away, but couldn't manage even that small motion. His face swam in the moisture of her eyes. The events of the day swirled in her mind. So much healing. Such a cathartic look into her past. She latched onto the only moment that had brought a spark of life and an ill-defined hope for a future.

She wanted to repeat it. Opal lifted her hands and cupped his face. Pulled him, unresisting, toward her. Settled her lips on his.

He hesitated, and Opal wondered if she'd overstepped his boundary. Then he slid his other arm around her and returned the kiss.

Her eyelids fluttered closed as she lost herself in the sensations of the present.

Not the past.

Not the future.

Just this moment in time, with this generous man who carried too much responsibility on his shoulders.

Chapter Thirty-Three

"Would you stop it?" Chris threw his pen down on his desk and glared at Josh. "You're driving me nuts!"

Josh looked at his friend in surprise and leaned back in his chair. "Stop what?" Truly baffled, he wondered for a moment if Chris had overindulged one time too many.

"Whistling under your breath."

"Oh." Heat crept up Josh's neck. "Sorry."

Half his attention on the paperwork in front of him, he'd been reliving Opal's kiss Saturday night with the other half. It wouldn't do for Chris to divine the cause of his good mood. Besides, he wasn't sure himself of the nature of his relationship with Opal, never mind the minefield said relationship presented on a professional level.

The fact remained that she was a convicted murderer—even if he was convinced the charge had been an error of the greatest magnitude. Until he proved it and the courts vacated her conviction, it was a moot point.

Even thinking about her crossed a line that was clear to him on one level, but it had blurred over the past few days. He'd put a call in to Trooper Nelson with the new information he'd gleaned during Opal's visit to Jubilee, but the man hadn't responded yet.

Chris's glare turned into a knowing look. "You're hiding something from me." One eyebrow rose. He straightened and pointed a beefy forefinger at Josh. "More like some*one*."

Josh shook his head. "Nope. No such luck, Hasselback." In spite of his denial, the skin beneath his collar warmed even more, and he had to resist the impulse to loosen his tie.

Chris chortled. "Can't fool me, Boone. It's about time." He turned back to his work, but couldn't let the subject go without a final shot. "I'll figure out who."

The elation that had carried Josh through the weekend deflated. Bad enough that Chris might deduce Opal's role in Josh's good mood, but if Internal Affairs found out, would they see his relationship with her as compromising?

He tightened his lips. In his mind, no. And once all the evidence came to light, no. In the meantime, he needed to cut Chris off before he got even more curious.

He tamped down his frustration and let loose a sigh, making sure it was exaggerated. "My first full weekend off in a month. Took a road trip, checked out some rock-climbing sites." He affected a wounded expression. "Can't a guy get away without coming under scrutiny?"

"The last time you whistled like that was before the wedding that wasn't." Chris snorted. "You can deny all you want, but…" He left the threat implied but unfinished, and turned back to his work with a lousy attempt at mimicking Josh's whistle.

Josh rolled his eyes. "Cripes, if that's how bad I sound, no wonder." He went back to his own work and told himself to forget about Opal for the moment.

Trouble was, her face swam in his mind, displacing the case in front of him. The texture of her hair in his hands, the sweet warmth of her lips, the sensation of her breasts pressed against his chest—

The more he tried to shove her out of his brain, the more the memories conspired to thwart him. He muttered a curse, glanced at the clock, and decided he could leave early, provided his excuse sounded legitimate.

"Hey, I'm going to stop at the prosecutor's office, see if there's anything they need on the quint-homicide." The case was coming to trial soon, as the perpetrator had stymied every effort on the parts of his court-appointed lawyer to defend him.

"Whatever."

Chris sounded like he'd dropped his interest, but Josh knew better. He wouldn't put it past his partner to follow him. He kept an eye out as he left, and even dropped in to the DA's office to reinforce his ruse. As he'd expected, they didn't need anything from him, so he headed for the parking lot and his car.

No Chris lurking behind the wheel of his own car, or hunkered down between vehicles. No car tailing him as he made his way out of downtown and up Bardstown Road. Anticipation built as he searched for a parking place at Beans & Leaves. The place was surprisingly busy at four thirty.

Opal glanced up as he entered, and a smile ghosted across her face. She put her business mien on as he approached the counter. "Your usual?" A cup already in hand, the other hovered over the spigot for the house dark blend.

"Yeah, thanks." He leaned forward and lowered his voice. "Want to go out for dinner when you get off?"

She sent him an indecipherable look. "You know that's late."

"You still have to eat." He glanced toward the door, half expecting Chris to traipse through it. "And so do I."

Opal shrugged, the motion simultaneously remote and wistful. "You don't have to stay up until ten thirty to do it, though." A blush colored her cheeks pink beneath the smattering of freckles.

Josh returned his full attention to her. "No, I don't have to. I want to."

She slid the cup toward him and rang up the sale. Without being told, she dropped his change into the tip jar as was his habit. Their fingers touched as he reached for the cup, and he wondered if she felt the same zing he did at the contact. She brought her gaze up to meet his, and he got his answer.

Desire, confusion, and more than a hint of vulnerability lurked in her green eyes. "Why are you doing this?" She drew her hand back and wiped it on her apron. "I understand Saturday. Sort of. Are you sure you want to be seen with me? In Louisville?"

His mouth went dry. That was the question, wasn't it? But he knew he was right about her innocence, and the wheels of justice—true justice, in Opal's case—were already turning.

Josh, aware of the implications of his decision, nodded. "Yes."

She hesitated, and the sound of someone clearing their throat behind him broke the spell. He stepped to the side as Opal peered past him and said, "Can I help you?" But she glanced back at him and nodded. She mouthed *later*, then got to work filling the next customer's order.

Josh left, whistling again, and eager for the next six hours to pass. Trooper Nelson finally returned his call, and they discussed the new information. Afterward, Josh went for a run and in a fit of uncharacteristic domestic fussiness, cleaned his condo. When he picked up Opal, he was good and hungry, but not just for food.

It seemed her companionship was what he needed. The twenty-four-hour diner's menu didn't rival the eclectic cafés on Bardstown Road, but still conferred a sense of both homey comfort and anonymity. Opal's direct gaze and smile made the place seem more special than it was.

"So what *is* this about, Josh?" Her gaze wasn't her only direct quality.

He swallowed the bite of hamburger he'd just taken and lifted one shoulder. "I like you. I'd like to get to know you better."

"You know it can't go anywhere, except maybe, uh…" A furious blush made its way across her cheeks, and she developed a sudden interest in her fries.

Josh's mind shot to the intensity of their embrace the other night. Answering heat crept up his neck. "Well, it's not going any further than it did." He cringed at how prim his words sounded. Opal slanted him a look of disbelief, heavy with wariness. He couldn't help feeling a spurt of amusement at their combined discomfort. They were both acting like junior high kids, at least the ones he went to school with. Today's middle school was worlds different.

"You already know you are in total charge of where this goes or doesn't go. Everything about the two of us has been over the top, and yet nothing is as clear as it seemed at the beginning. Maybe if we take it slow and easy, we can figure out what the next step is." At her look of alarm, he added, "Or isn't."

"You know everything about me."

He shook his head. "I know about your *case*, not about you. What's your favorite color?" Josh didn't pause for an answer. "What's mine? What kind of music do you like? Do you really like working at the coffee shop? Or at Mom's? What are your dreams?" Caught up in his questions, he leaned forward and took her hand in his. "Do you want to know me outside of my role?"

Opal didn't resist his admittedly gentle grip, though he wanted more than nonresistance. He wanted her to curl her fingers into his so he could feel the skin of her palm against his.

After a long moment, she said, "Coral and teal, like the moment just before the sun rises or right after it sets. The hundred shades of green you can find in one square foot of the forest. Red on a woodpecker. Black and white feathers that contrast with the red. The thousand hues of brown on a hawk, or in the leaves once they've fallen. All the brilliance of autumn, set against the evergreens. The sparkles on a lake, or the clear blue of the water. White, pure and untouched, like new snow." A sad smile lifted the corners of her lips. "Even no color, like rain." She fell silent.

Josh heard what she didn't say. The loss of all those for twelve years, not only the colors, but the experiences and tactile senses.

His gut clenched and he squeezed her hand. "See? There's so much more to you."

Rather than pull back and build another wall, she met his gaze, then turned her hand beneath his and held it. "What about you?"

"Red." He laughed. "I'm about as simple as they come. No complexity here."

She smiled, her dimple appearing. "I should have guessed, looking at your climbing gear. I thought that was the only color it came in, but I see now it's more likely that you picked it."

"Guilty as charged." As soon as the words were out of his mouth, Josh's smile faded. He couldn't have picked a more inappropriate response if he'd spent ten minutes thinking of one. "Sorry."

Opal shrugged and pulled her hand free. "Don't go getting all careful on my account. If we can't be ourselves around each other, then there's no point. Right?" She popped another fry in her mouth, appearing totally at ease with who and what she believed she was.

If Josh had anything to say about it, which he did, she would readjust her perceptions. Radically. And soon. "Right. No more worrying about hurting your feelings by inserting my foot into my mouth."

She snickered, her expression lightening.

He took her home, knowing that he'd be tired come morning, but not caring. Her hair rippled silver in the light from the lot across the alley and he couldn't resist touching it. She came into his arms as naturally as water flowing down an ancient fall, and when he lowered his mouth to taste hers, she met him with the same enthusiasm as she had on Saturday. Many moments later, he groaned and set her away, though he wanted more than anything to get even closer.

"Tomorrow night?" He tweaked her nose.

Opal nodded, came up on her tiptoes, and planted a kiss on his jaw. She turned and ran up the stairs as he watched, then sketched a wave before disappearing inside.

~

The next night they went to a different all-night diner and talked about dreams. Chagrined, Josh realized he'd reached all his with the exception of the wife, 2.2 children, house with a picket fence, and a dog. She had wanted to be a nurse, a profession now closed to her, given her record. Now she was thinking organic herbs, but doubted she could make a living at it.

"Do you like where you're working now?"

"I'm not a fool. It doesn't matter if I like the jobs. I need both of them, and I like them well enough." Her face softened. "May is a gem. I'd work there forever, just to be around her. Plus, she's teaching me how to quilt, and she says I have a knack for design."

Josh thought about the curtains in her apartment. A light dawned. "Mom made the door wreath and the quilt on the futon at your place, but you made—"

Opal grinned. "The curtains. Out of scraps."

"Huh." He glanced around as though May might materialize and overhear him. "Don't tell Mom, but I've always wondered why people cut fabric apart just to sew it back together, flat." He winked. "Although I recognize that the curtains are more artistic than not."

She laughed outright and gave him a playful punch on the shoulder. "They're just curtains."

But he could tell she was pleased, and a different kind of warmth spread through him. Pleasing Opal could grow on him. In fact, it could become downright addictive. He had a flash of understanding regarding the relationship between his parents.

On its heels came shame. He hadn't mentioned his burgeoning friendship with Opal to them. One weekly Sunday family dinner had come and gone, and he'd used the excuse of Opal's seven-day-a-week job to gloss over the fact that he hadn't invited her. He told himself it was that the whole thing was too new, that he didn't want to share it yet. He hadn't hesitated out of embarrassment, or a sense of her not quite fitting in with his family because of her past.

Except that he did feel that way, in spite of everything he now knew. Until all the evidence came to light and her conviction was overturned or vacated, Opal remained a murderer in the eyes of the commonwealth.

He didn't like the way he felt, or that he had reason to tread carefully. But as Opal captured his gaze and his heart once again, he threw caution to the wind. Again.

Josh kissed her, knowing that he could never get enough of that, either.

And wished the circumstances swirling around them were far different, because he wouldn't hesitate to take her home, or let Chris know who was bringing him back from the dark place his life had become over the past three years.

He thrust the thoughts out of his head and concentrated on Opal, filling his hands with her hair and reveling in her aliveness.

To hell with the consequences.

He needed her—and that realization shook him to the soles of his running shoes. Suddenly, clearing her name became more than righting the wrongs she'd endured. Getting her conviction overturned or vacated became central to his future too.

It was the only means to ensure *their* future...if one was even possible.

Chapter Thirty-Four

OPAL OPENED Stitches in Time, excited for the morning's class, yet with a pang of regret that she had to spend a glorious summer day inside. Maybe she should take one of those days off that Hayley kept bugging her about. Her mind conjured her last day off, two months ago, and she smiled at the memory.

That day had been beautiful, too, though not quite as warm. It sparkled in her mind as a priceless gift. Several gifts, all orchestrated by Josh. She could finally reflect on Granny and Skye without the crushing burden of guilt that had accompanied their memories.

Then her mind turned toward their first kiss, which, of course, reminded her of all the other kisses they'd shared since then. A little thrill raced through her, and she knew she had to be blushing fiercely. Her face felt like it was on fire.

The bell over the door tinkled at the same time May's "Good morning!" floated into the shop. Opal ducked into the bathroom to throw some cold water on her cheeks, then went to greet her employer. She had a fleeting thought about mentioning Josh, but discarded the idea as quickly as it came. She wasn't going to bring up their relationship to his mother until he did, although it felt vaguely illicit, like she was lying by omission in withholding that information.

In any event, the opportunity passed. Seven tweens, including two boys who'd signed up "to meet babes" were set to arrive any moment, and Opal took a quick look at the classroom to make sure it was ready.

Customers followed on May's heels and then the kids showed up, and the shop was a hive of boisterous activity until noon. When the last of the tweens left, May plopped down in a chair in feigned exhaustion.

"Would you like some tea?" Opal indicated the electric teapot, which she'd filled and started several minutes earlier.

"I'd love some." May sank into the cushions. "This has been a great success, and I thank you for the idea. Who knew quilted backpacks would become the next middle-school rage?" She smiled, the skin around her eyes crinkling and making her look like a pleased fairy.

Opal grabbed May's favorite tea and set it to steep, then chose a new variety for herself. The opportunity to choose still delighted her, though she'd been out of prison for six months now. When the mugs were ready, she carried them over and sat across from her employer, who took a sip and sighed in bliss.

May opened her eyes and she regarded Opal. "I've been meaning to ask you, but time gets away. Would you like to come to dinner tomorrow? We can have it early, at one, so you have plenty of time to get to Beans & Leaves by three."

Opal nearly bobbled her tea. Her mind went blank, then filled in with an oversized image of Josh. She couldn't discern his expression, though, and breathed his name. "Josh?"

May flipped a hand as if to brush off the question. "He may or may not be there. It always depends on his work." She slanted a look at Opal. "Besides, he knows you work here, and has, for quite some time. It's not our secret anymore."

"Um…" Opal's mouth went dry and she took a quick gulp of tea, nearly scalding the roof of her mouth in the process. She'd known it wasn't a secret, either, but hadn't mentioned it to May.

More to the point, what would Josh think if she showed up at his parents' home? Did she dare take that step? Yearning for even a sliver of what he took for granted swamped her. Yet she didn't want to take the liberty of invading his domain, so to speak.

"Well?" A line of concern marred May's forehead, and a hint of disappointment lurked in her expression.

Trapped, Opal realized she would hurt May's feelings if she declined the invitation, and risk Josh's…Josh's what? His ire? He hadn't been angry with her for months. His disapproval? Well, he hadn't disapproved of much about her lately, especially not the kisses nor the late-night talks. Her face heated again, a now-standard response to thinking about his lips meeting hers.

She took a deep breath and let it out. "Yes, and thank you, May." She'd talk to him about it tonight.

But he didn't show up at the coffee shop as had become his custom, nor did he call. The later it got, the more Opal worried about showing up unannounced tomorrow. She could call him, but his business card was tucked in a drawer at her apartment. It would be after eleven by the time she got home, and she was loathe to call him so late.

Before she could dredge up the courage to call the general number for the police department, a bevy of customers poured in.

She and Denise were swamped, and she never had another chance to think about calling, much less take the time to do so.

She resigned herself to calling from Dante's, but when she got home, the card wasn't where she had put it. Nor was it on the floor, behind the drawer, or in any other conceivable nook or cranny of the apartment. Heart sinking, she got on her hands and knees and searched a third time. Finally she gave up and trudged down the stairs and around front.

Smoke filled the front room of the tattoo parlor, along with fumes from the alcohol already consumed by the three young men clustered around a pattern book. They were engaged in a lively debate regarding the merits of skulls and roses versus dragons.

Opal had to raise her voice over the hard rock music. "Mitch, can I use the phone?"

Mitch shot her a scowl. "You're not gonna call the cops down here again, are you?"

"Oh no!" Heat rose in Opal's cheeks. She didn't dare tell him she was calling them, though no one was going to show up this time. Nor did she dare let him know Josh had become a regular visitor, albeit to the back door.

His scowl deepened. "Okay. But the next time they show up on your account, I'm evicting you. I don't need no trouble, y'hear?"

"No problem, Mitch." Opal reached for the phone before she lost her nerve. Her palms went damp as she dialed, and she turned to muffle her voice and get at least the illusion of privacy.

A recorded voice answered, and she heaved a sigh of relief. The potential of speaking with a real person had filled her with dread. She followed several prompts, hoping to end up at Josh's voice mail. The last prompt was for Homicide. It rang twice, and she was rehearsing her message when someone picked up the phone.

"Homicide, Detective Hasselback." He fairly barked the words, bringing the image of a territorial bulldog to her mind. His voice was gravelly, impatient, and intimidating.

Opal gripped the receiver. Her throat closed and her mouth went dry. She tried to swallow, but only succeeded in proving her muscles were paralyzed too.

"Can I help you." The words were a question, but his flat tone was a statement. It held more than a hint of challenge.

It was enough to break the spell fear had on her tongue. "I...uh, is Detective Boone available?"

"No. Can I take a message." Again, the question was a statement, and something about his voice began to seem familiar. Paper rustled in the background.

Panic threatened to cut off Opal's air supply. "No!" Realizing how abrupt she sounded, she added, "Thank you." Now thoroughly rattled, she straightened her spine and sucked in a breath. All she wanted was to leave him a message, but not one that anyone at his work would hear. In desperation, she blurted, "Can I have his voice mail, please?"

Detective Hasselback went silent for a long moment. "Sure." His tone changed, the word sounding silky and…knowing. "Here you go."

Something clicked, and Josh's voice came on the line. "Detective Boone. Leave a message. I'll get back to you as soon as possible."

Nearly dizzy with anxiety and relief, Opal said, "Josh, it's me. I lost your cell phone number…" She cleared her throat. "Your mom invited me to dinner tomorrow." She glanced at the clock. "Well, today now. Before I go to work. I just wanted you to know. I'll be at home all morning, in case you stop by."

She hung up, feeling like she'd just wrestled with the devil. It didn't surprise her that it took nearly two hours for her to fall asleep. Then she tossed and turned the rest of the night, never really drifting into more than a doze. Josh didn't knock on her door, and she finally dragged herself out of bed. By noon, she gave up on him.

At that point, whatever happened, happened. Other than repaying May's hospitality with the rudeness of not showing up, and doing so without the courtesy of a phone call, Opal was out of options. She set out for the address May had given her. The warmth of the sun combined with fresh air to dispel the bulk of her nervousness.

Until she arrived.

Opal climbed the steps to the beautiful stone and brick home near Cherokee Park that looked like it had sprouted from the earth. The landscaping was understated and lovely. A majestic elm tree provided shade for a bed of hostas. Bees and butterflies shared the blooms of bee balm plants, and two rosebushes in shades of pink stood sentry at the front of the small yard. A dogwood, its blooms long past, was tucked in near the house.

She lifted her hand to ring the bell, holding the freshly potted rosemary she'd grown from seed. As a hostess gift, it was entirely inadequate, but Opal had nothing more to offer.

Insecurity attacked her, and she nearly turned tail. She would have, if it didn't hurt May. So she rang the bell and stood straighter. Josh's dad, Jacob, answered the door, swinging it wide. "Come in, come in." He smiled, laugh lines crinkling the skin around his eyes. "Welcome."

A young woman, a carbon copy of May except for her dark hair and eyes, peered around the edge of an overstuffed floral couch. "Hey, Opal! I'm Jenn, and the little guy rolling around on the floor is Caleb." She pointed at a lanky man with thick blond hair, slouched on a matching love seat. "The lazy head is my husband, Charlie."

His eyes flickered with amusement. "Says the woman who slept half the day away."

Jenn sat up and flipped her hair over her shoulder, Opal apparently forgotten. "That's because I'm the one who was up until five with *your* progeny." Her tone carried no heat, and her lips quirked up in a smile so reminiscent of Josh's that Opal's breath caught.

Delicious aromas emanated from the kitchen, and Opal excused herself to see if she could help.

May greeted her with a hug. "What a lovely plant! Rosemary is one of my favorites!" She took Opal's offering as though it were a rare and unusual variety of orchid and made a place for it in the bay window over the kitchen sink.

"Thank you for inviting me. Is Josh coming?" Opal couldn't help voicing the anxiety eating at her, though she managed a conversational tone.

May, who ran her kitchen with the same efficiency as she did the quilt shop, turned to transfer roasted chicken from a slow cooker to a serving platter. "I've set a place for him, but he's on call this weekend. It's a disappointment when he can't be here, but a pleasant surprise when he is." She finished, arranged a sprig of fresh parsley on the steaming dish, and handed the platter to Opal. "Here you go, dear. Would you call the rest of the family?"

A flurry of activity got everyone seated, with the empty place setting opposite Opal. More certain of her welcome, Opal was still acutely nervous. She hadn't eaten anywhere that required manners since the etiquette class her sixth-grade teacher had imposed on a roomful of disinterested students. Opal took her lead from May and Jacob, as she stole glances from beneath her lashes. Charlie and Jenn filled in the conversational gaps, so Opal didn't feel like she was on display.

It soon became clear that neither knew of her record or her past. The meal flew by and she began to relax. Topics flowed from parenting and lack of sleep to Jenn's recent decision to be a stay-at-home mom, and Charlie's job. Opal had just fielded a question about her background—she was from a small town in Appalachia—and had deflected it into praise for May's artistic bent when the back door opened.

May's expression lit up. "Josh!" She set down the bite of peach cobbler she'd just lifted from an heirloom dessert dish.

Opal rotated in her chair, her heart in her throat. Questions tumbled over each other in her mind. Had he gotten the voice mail she left for him last night? If so, he'd be aware of her presence. If not, how would he react to her in his parents' house? Her body seized in a combination of dread and yearning. The lack of his company last night highlighted the loss of what she'd come to anticipate.

His touch.

His eyes, seeing far more than she intended to disclose.

His approval, which meant more to Opal than she wanted it to mean.

Josh blew into the room, a force of his own and an open, generous smile on his face. "Sorry I'm late—" His gaze took in everyone around the table, then fell on her. His smile froze.

Her heart dropped.

"Opal!" Astonishment led the emotions that chased across his face, followed in rapid order by shock and confusion. Then horror, quickly masked by neutrality. The moment stretched. He swallowed, then cleared his throat. "Uh…"

He finally settled on polite civility that belied the depth of the relationship she thought they had established. "Hey, how are you?"

Shame flooded her. He sounded pretty normal, but she could hear the tension beneath the words. She dropped her gaze to the remains of her cobbler, the dessert suddenly looking as appetizing as glue.

He didn't want to acknowledge their friendship in front of his family. Part of her could understand. Heck, she had even worried about encroaching on his personal territory, or worse, forcing his hand by coming here today.

A bigger part of her couldn't understand, though, and pain sliced through her shattered heart.

But Granny McBride had been fond of saying Opal was made of sterner stuff than that, and after the past dozen years, Opal was inclined to agree with her. She sat up a little straighter, pulled her shoulders back, and lifted her gaze to meet Josh's.

And gave back as good as he'd given her.

A bright, fake smile, empty words, and an acting job worthy of an Oscar.

She ignored the glimpse of misery in his eyes, the silent plea for understanding that no one else noticed. Opal scooted her chair back and got to her feet.

"This has been wonderful, May"—Opal nearly choked on the word *wonderful*—"but I need to get to work." Jacob and Charlie stood, as well, and she had the absurd notion that she was leading a game of Simon Says. "It was a pleasure meeting you." Opal smiled, wondering if her expression looked as brittle and fragile as she felt.

May put down her napkin. "I'm glad you could come, Opal." She got to her feet and enveloped Opal in a hug, then walked her to the door. "You're welcome anytime."

Opal nodded, her vocal cords strangled by the urge to cry. She blinked away the sting behind her eyelids and embraced the woman who had become a surrogate for both her mother and Granny McBride. She managed a whispered "See you tomorrow" and took the front steps two at a time.

As kind as May was, Opal had deluded herself in pretending that she could be part of a family—especially this particular family. The sooner Opal got that fact firmly where it belonged, front and center in her psyche, the better off all of them were.

She'd never broken up with anyone before, but she told herself she'd get over Josh without fanfare or drama.

But she instinctively knew the pain in her heart would linger for a long time.

Chapter Thirty-Five

Josh had screwed up. Big-time. He knew it the second he failed to greet Opal with a hug.

The sight of her at the table had caused his heart to leap for joy—but then it leaped right into his throat because he had kept their relationship a secret from his family. Why, he wasn't sure. There would have been no censure from that quarter.

They loved Opal.

By the time he'd gotten past the shock of seeing her, she was on her way to the door. He took a step toward her, intending to make it right, but she avoided him and slipped out in a move so smooth she might have been a wraith made of mist.

Then the back door opened and he turned, wondering who had followed him in.

"Any chance I can get a home-cooked meal?" Chris Hasselback's distinctive, whiskey-roughened voice boomed from the kitchen.

Josh's blood turned cold. *Shit!* If his partner saw Opal here, he might connect Josh's good mood of the other day with her, and Josh was not ready for that. He wouldn't hide his relationship with Opal from his family—not anymore—but their relationship put his job at risk until Trooper Nelson completed the case for overturning her conviction. He swung his attention back to the front door, and saw May closing it. Relief rushed through him, but it didn't last long.

Chris came up behind him and clapped him on the back, then leaned in and whispered with a conspiratorial air, "I came to meet your new lady friend."

Josh wheeled and faced him. "What?" He didn't have to manufacture any incredulity. How did his partner know, when he'd been clueless until a few minutes ago? "What are you talking about?"

Chris winked. "You got a call last night, late. Went to voice mail." Without an iota of guilt, he added, "Nice-sounding young woman, said she was coming to dinner today." He waggled his eyebrows, clearly waiting for Josh to divulge a name.

"She told you this?" Opal would never have given that much detail to anyone at the station. In fact, he had a hard time believing she'd called there.

"Well, no." Chris rubbed the side of his purple-veined nose.

Josh's anger flared. Chris only used that body language when he was guilty, or evading the truth. "You listened to my voice mail, didn't you?" His mind reeled at the audacity of Chris's invasion of privacy.

His partner's expression changed from gloating anticipation to wary caution. "Yeah. I did." He stuck his chin out, matching the belligerence in his tone.

Josh grabbed his arm and towed him through the kitchen and out the back door. "What the hell do you think gave you the right?" He drew his hand into a fist and raised it, astonished at how badly he wanted to punch his partner.

Chris's eyes widened and he grabbed Josh's wrist. "Whoa. What's got your dander up? I told you I'd find out who you were mooning over the other day. Didn't mean anything by it."

"Not. Your. Business." Josh forced the words out through gritted teeth, his entire body humming with fury.

The door creaked. He turned to see May peering out at them, questions and alarm in her expression. He dropped his hand and let go of Chris, who scowled and stepped back.

"Sorry, Mom." Josh shot a look at Chris and held his gaze. "We just got a call to go back in to work."

Chris tightened his lips, then looked at May. "*I'm* sorry I don't get to sample some of your delicious cooking today, Mrs. Boone." He sent a frustrated look at Josh. "But we have to go."

"Oh, come in anyway. I'll dish up plates for you to take with you." She waved them in and withdrew into the kitchen.

Left with no alternative, Josh trudged behind Chris, hoping his mom would keep her mouth shut about Opal. He could practically feel the gray hairs forming at his temples with his anxiety.

Luckily, Jenn and Caleb were in the kitchen and Josh was able to steer the conversation to other subjects in the few minutes it took to dish leftovers onto paper plates and cover them with foil.

He and Chris left together but parted ways as soon as they backed out of the driveway. It was going to take a run—or six—before Josh worked the anger out of his system enough to be civil with the man.

First, though, was Opal. Less than five minutes later, with a jaundiced eye glued to his rearview mirror in case Chris had the crazy notion that he could keep up his half-joking surveillance, Josh pulled into a parking spot at Beans & Leaves. A couple of fortifying breaths later, he walked into the shop.

Opal flicked a glance in his direction as he entered. Her lips flattened and she returned her attention to her customer. By the time he'd reached the head of the line, she had his usual poured and slid it across the counter toward him, careful to avoid contact with his fingers. He pulled his wallet out, and she finally lifted her gaze to meet his. Her eyes smoldered with disdain and impatience.

"Don't bother, Detective. It's on the house." She leaned to the side, looking for a customer behind him, her dismissal clear and final.

Josh moved to stay in her line of sight, simultaneously peeved she was ignoring him and aware he'd earned her rejection. He glanced behind him, slightly cheered to see no one in line.

"Opal, I'm sorry." He imbued the words with all the sincerity born of his failure. His neck heated. "I was going to tell them about us, but you left so fast—"

She stared past his head, arms crossed over her midriff and her expression tight.

"I—then Chris, my partner at work, showed up—"

Opal shifted her eyes, meeting his. This time she didn't bother hiding the spark of anger in them. "I can understand work, Detective. I *get* that." She unfolded her arms and poked him in the chest with a pointy forefinger. "But with May, with your family—"

Tears glistened in her eyes. She swallowed, then straightened and folded her arms again. "I have discovered I'm not interested in being anyone's dirty little secret. Least of all, yours." Her voice hitched on the last word, and she swiped at the lone tear that had escaped. Blinking furiously, she wrestled the trembling of her lips into submission. "So it's over between us." She slashed one arm through the air. "Whatever *it* was, and whatever *us* meant."

Heaviness lodged in Josh's gut as Opal turned away from him, her back ramrod stiff. A plea for a chance to redeem himself died on his lips. But he couldn't walk away in silence.

"I deserve all that, Opal. I *am* sorry. Truly. For what it's worth, I *want* there to be an *us*. A public *us*. The time isn't right, and I can't control that." The words solidified the conclusion he'd come to over the past few weeks, and his conviction grew stronger as he spoke. "When it's time, Opal, I'll be back. You can count on it."

The only sign that she heard him was the angry set to her shoulders as she grabbed a rag and scrubbed the spotless prep area.

Leaving his coffee untouched on the counter, Josh strode out, his teeth clenched against the emptiness of his heart. He knew he wasn't going to be able to outrun that.

The punishing eight miles he put in along the river that afternoon did little to assuage his feelings.

~

The next morning, still too angry at Chris to go to the office, Josh took care of a couple of interviews in the field, then spent his lunch break on another run in Cherokee Park.

He made his way up the last hill, pushing himself to a sprint past a pair of young mothers with strollers and an older couple who'd stopped to survey the midsummer flowers. Sweat dripped off his nose in the heat.

At the crest, huffing like a bellows, Josh slowed to a walk. Ten minutes to get home, shower, and then face Chris. Maybe he'd worked off enough of his anger to be polite but distant. As he let himself into his condo, his cell phone trilled, then fell silent. He grabbed a towel and mopped his face, then checked the phone. Seven missed calls, three of them from Chris. Three voice mails.

Dread gathered in his gut. No murders warranted that many calls, not even the quint-homicide from January. Never acknowledged, but always simmering just below the surface, images of airline crashes flashed through his mind. *Dad.* Then he thought of Caleb. Six months old. Though he didn't have risk factors for Sudden Infant Death Syndrome, it was still a possibility.

He sent a wordless prayer heavenward, then stabbed at the numbers on his phone. Ignoring the slight tremor of his hand, he brought the phone to his ear to listen to the messages.

Chris's voice sounded in his ear. "Call me. ASAP." He fairly barked the words, then hung up.

Josh brought up the second message. Chris again. "Where the hell are you? Call me!"

He didn't wait to hear the third one, but hit speed dial as he strode through the living room to grab his wallet and keys.

Chris answered in the middle of the second ring. "You need to get to U of L. The ER. Now."

University of Louisville. Its emergency department was the region's highest-level trauma center. A giant fist squeezed his heart. "Who?"

"Your mom."

Mom! His legs turned to jelly, and he dropped into the nearest chair. Of all the possible scenarios, she hadn't made his list of potential catastrophes.

"What happened?" Stroke? Heart attack? She was healthy as a horse. *Hail Mary…*

"She got knocked on the head—aw, hell, just get down there. I'll meet you and tell you what we know." He hung up, and Josh wanted to howl with frustration.

Why was Chris calling him, anyway? Other than being his friend and partner. *I'll meet you and tell you what we know.* His blood turned to ice.

Had May been attacked? He shot to his feet and tore out of the condo without a shower and without changing. Without knowing how badly his mom had been hurt, or what had happened.

His heart in his throat, he drove dangerously fast, even with siren blaring and the light bar flashing. The security guards eyed him with suspicion when he presented his badge, still clad in running gear, but they let him pass without comment.

When he found her, the sight of his mother shook him to the core. She was pale, somehow much smaller than she should be, with a bruise on her left temple. Unconscious, she looked too much like a corpse, and his gorge rose. His vision narrowed. Josh had the foresight to slide into the room's lone chair and drop his head between his knees. A stern mental talking-to and a few moments later, he sat up.

A nurse came in and he stood. "I'm her son. Tell me everything."

"She has a closed head injury. Just got back from a CT scan that shows no bleed." The young woman took May's pulse and checked an IV that Josh noticed only when she touched it. "She's stable, and we'll be admitting her to ICU."

"That's it?" Three sentences didn't seem to cover everything he needed to know. His mind swirled with unanswerable questions, like *When will she wake up* and *Please tell me she's not going to die.*

At that moment, Chris strode in, his face a mask of controlled fury. A vein in his forehead throbbed, and his always-mottled nose took on a purplish hue. He looked like a more plausible candidate for stroke than May.

Josh let out a heavy breath and leaned forward, reaching through the bed rail to touch his mother. Her skin was reassuringly warm. He needed to get his head on straight so he could deal with all of this.

"Don't worry, we've got the perp under arrest." Chris spat the words with more venom than Josh had ever seen in the man.

"What. Happened." He forced the words out past tight vocal cords, and clenched his hands. *Mother of God, pray for us…*

"Opal McBride—"

Chris kept talking, but Josh couldn't make sense of the words. *Opal?* Opal would never hit May. She didn't have it in her. She wouldn't even strike his mother in retaliation for his stupidity yesterday. He dragged his attention back to Chris's report.

"—when the patrol officer answered the distress call." His partner apparently felt the need to explain, and added, "From the alarm system."

Josh held a hand up. "Start over. You arrested Opal?"

Chris shot him an odd look. "Yeah. She was in your mom's shop, crouched over her on the floor, in possession of a gun that had been fired. Damn straight we arrested her."

A new wave of nausea rolled over Josh. *A gun?* His mind flashed to the confrontation in Jubilee, and how fearless Opal had been in the presence of Widow Reese's shotgun and Obadiah Finley's hunting rifle. He dragged in a lungful of air that smelled like unwashed bodies, blood, and antiseptic.

"Wh…what did she say?"

"McBride?" Chris snorted. "That she didn't do it, that the gun wasn't hers. What else do you think she'd say? Cop killer who's turned on little old ladies, prob'ly because they don't fight back."

Josh snapped upright and the room took a dizzying turn before it settled. He opened his mouth to deny what Chris had said—Opal would never harm May—but the seed of doubt had been sown.

What if she had? What if he, Josh, hadn't done enough to protect his mother? Was his judgment that clouded, that flawed, to allow him to miss signs of clever manipulation on Opal's part? He certainly had a history of bad judgment when it came to women.

The words died on his tongue.

A flock of nursing personnel bustled into the room, unplugging equipment and hooking it up to portable versions of the same, moving the IV fluid to a stand they'd fitted into a hole at the head of the bed, unlocking wheels, preparing to transport May to the ICU.

Josh stood, a kaleidoscope of images flickering through his mind like an old-time movie…

Opal, tenderly placing flowers at her grandmother's grave.

Opal, taking on the entire Louisville Metro Police force to keep her job.

Opal, at home in the mountains—and making do with Cherokee Park.

Opal's tears over her lost baby.

Opal, holding the secret of what happened with Tommy all these years.

Then again, maybe she'd spun the story and somehow tagged him as a soft touch. The notion was jarring, not only because he didn't like viewing himself in that light, but also, if he was honest, because it didn't quite fit.

Just like nothing about the reality of Opal had fit his preconceived notions back when they'd met. There was only one way to ferret out the truth.

"I'll talk to Opal after I know Mom's settled and there's nothing more I can do here."

Chris sent him another inscrutable look. He held Josh's gaze for a long, considering moment. Then shrugged. "Whatever, man. It's open and shut." He followed Josh to the elevator, unusually silent. Just before the doors opened, he said, "Something's not right here." He poked a beefy forefinger into Josh's chest. "And I think it has to do with you." Reaching into a pocket, he withdrew a stick of gum, unwrapped it, and stuck it in his mouth, all the while boring a hole into Josh's skull with his scrutiny. "Maybe it's you and me that need to talk."

The elevator dinged, saving Josh from having to reply. He pushed past his partner and sent him a dagger look as the doors slid closed. The consequences of befriending Opal suddenly loomed as a monumental problem. He'd been so enchanted by her spirit that he'd gone along with the notion that they were just two people who liked each other. Between his mother and Opal, he might not be able to keep a clear head. He should declare his conflict of interest and stay out of any investigation.

Never mind the dynamic of unequal power. It was a good thing they hadn't had sex—never mind that he wouldn't have allowed that to happen, as much as he might want it. His head began to throb with the roiling mess of thoughts and emotions. He thrust a hand through his hair and wondered if he could get some ibuprofen somewhere in the hospital.

Two hours later, he left his mother, still unconscious, still stable, in Jenn's care. His father was on the next plane back to Louisville, but wouldn't be in for hours. He bought some pain reliever in the gift shop on his way out, and drove through McDonald's on his way to Metro Corrections. His running shorts drew another round of sidelong looks, but he was too wound up to care.

They brought Opal to the only interrogation room available, one with one-way glass. He stood when she entered and took in the handcuffs, the scuff marks on the knees of her jeans, her hair, which had come loose from its braid and hung in tangles. She looked smaller, more vulnerable. *Just like Mom*. He shoved the comparison away.

"Josh! How's May?" Her voice was as stark as the fear on her face.

"What the hell happened?"

"I told them—" Opal's expression was earnest. Open.

"The truth?"

She recoiled as though he had slapped her. "Yes." Confusion rolled across her face. "Why are you asking me these questions? Don't you believe me?"

"I'm a cop, Opal." For a split second, Josh wished he weren't, that he was just an ordinary joe. That he could take her in his arms and derive comfort from her solid, reassuring presence. That he could in turn reassure her. But he wasn't, and he couldn't, so he hardened his heart. "I'm trained to *dis*trust and verify."

"Please…" She glanced at the floor, then lifted her gaze to meet his. "Just tell me how May is. Please."

"Why? Are you afraid the charge will be murder instead of assault?" The words spewed forth like sewage and hung in the air between them. Shame snaked through him, and his neck heated.

Surprise flooded her face. The light in her eyes dimmed, reminding him of a candle being snuffed out. She shuttered her features and took a step backward. It was then that he noticed she had instinctively leaned into him, anticipating his embrace. A hank of hair slid over her nose, bisecting her face and making her look forlorn. Lost.

"No, Detective. I don't care about the charges." She glared at him, subverting any sense of helplessness he had attributed to her, and lifted her hands to move the hair out of her face. It slid back and she gave up. "I care about *May*."

His face felt wooden, his lips stiff as he answered. "Unconscious, but stable. No bleed—yet. She's in ICU."

Her expression fell. Her lips trembled, but she firmed them and looked him in the eye. "You have to catch her."

Josh had lost any control he'd had over this interview, probably right when Opal walked through the door. He rubbed his head, the ache duller but still throbbing in spite of the pills he'd swallowed half an hour ago. "Catch who?"

She shot him a look that said *you moron*. "Viper." She pronounced the syllables separately and slowly, as though he wouldn't understand her English.

"Viper." His mind felt like sludge. "I'm not making the connection here."

"You had the stupid alarm system put in, Josh!" She flushed and glanced away. When she brought her gaze back to him, the freckles on her nose had blended into the dusky tone of her skin. "Viper showed up today with a gun. I shouted at May to hit the panic button and go lock herself in the office. She didn't. I mean, she must have hit the panic button because the phone started ringing and then the sirens started, but she came toward us instead of seeking shelter."

A haunted expression filled her eyes. "I tackled Viper and we fought over the gun. It went off, the sirens got closer, and she jumped up and ran off. I couldn't find May..." Opal clasped her hands together to stop their trembling. "Then...I saw her on the floor. I thought she'd been shot, but I couldn't find any blood. So I stabilized her neck in case she woke up before the cops got there."

Josh ran a hand around his nape, which had tightened as Opal spoke. May had agreed to the minimum security of door alarms to deter burglars and the panic buttons, one around her neck and one in the office, but she'd drawn the line at cameras. Even discreet ones placed where no one would notice. *I don't distrust my customers*, she'd said. *That's not the point*, he'd countered. It had been about Viper and her ilk all along.

Now it came down to Opal's word versus the evidence. A replay of the situation with Tommy. And he was too distressed to dissect the evidence, much less evaluate it through the lens of her words.

She lifted her head, a picture of dignity even in handcuffs. Her voice low and resigned, she said, "We're done. Do your job, Detective." Her mask slipped a bit as she added, "Please...keep me informed about May."

He let her go, hearing the unspoken meaning of her words loud and clear. *We're done.* Not the interview. Her. Him. Them. Done. No second chance, not even once the debacle over Thomas Finley's death had been exposed. Pain ripped into his heart, and he lifted his hand to cover that region of his chest.

As he followed her out, Chris emerged from the observation room and blocked his way.

A weight lodged in Josh's gut like a stone. *No.* He had a wild hope that Chris had missed his conversation with Opal, but the stormy expression on his partner's face killed that notion.

"Seems like you and Miss Opal have a history." He gave Josh a look of disgust as he popped the gum he still chewed. "I think it's time we had a little discussion." He wheeled and stalked off, leaving

Josh to contemplate his own annihilation, both personal and professional.

His head moved beyond throbbing to pounding.

He'd gladly give up his career in exchange for his mom's full recovery, and now that Chris knew about Opal, losing his career was a distinct possibility.

Then he realized that without Opal at his side—now a given, thanks to his impulsive accusation—the problems with his job paled. Losing her hurt far worse than Lisa's abandonment at the altar, an insight he didn't want to examine too closely.

His heart was so bruised he didn't know where to turn.

As Father Barney would say, 'twas a fine mess he'd made.

Chapter Thirty-Six

OPAL WALKED BACK to her cell in shock, barely noticing when the corrections officer removed the handcuffs and closed the door. Apparently she rated segregation because of her record, which she actually didn't mind, as the events of the last few hours had drained her. The idea of dealing with other detainees sapped the little energy she retained. She sank down onto the cold concrete slab that doubled as chair and bed.

Josh didn't believe her.

The trust she'd built in him, in his integrity, had been shattered with his words. *Are you afraid you'll be charged with murder?* Her breath caught again, just as it had when he uttered the damning statement.

She'd never been afraid of that. Been there, done that. She knew what to expect of the justice system and prison. Nothing new there. Even the crushing of her dreams didn't matter if May didn't recover. Why couldn't Josh see that? Opal squelched the temptation to indulge in self-pity.

Instead, she tried to figure out what she could have done differently, to get that big detective to listen to her. It had been clear from the first moment he stuck his head in the cruiser that he viewed her with contempt. He'd ignored her repeated pleas for news about May. Rather, he'd badgered her. *Where'd you get the gun? You know you're going back to prison for that, don't you. Why'd you assault her? Robbery?*

She'd told him the same thing she just told Josh, but he had sneered at her. *Who's gonna believe the word of a con? A murderer?* He'd slammed the door, and she'd craned her neck to watch the EMTs load May into the ambulance and drive off. Until she knew that May was on the mend, the empty place in her gut would remain.

Hours passed. A meal tray arrived. The odors made her nauseous, and she was relieved when they took it away, untouched. Then the electronic lock clicked and the door swung open. A different CO beckoned her to follow.

Opal stood and extended her hands for the cuffs, uneasy at the disruption in the isolation she had expected to continue until morning, when arraignment would happen. However, she could hardly decline this summons.

They retraced the earlier route, and she was deposited in an interrogation room much like the one where she'd seen Josh. Anxiety bit at the edges of her composure. At least she'd re-braided her hair, so it no longer hung in her face. Looking less bedraggled didn't translate to feeling braver, but she would cling to the never-let-them-see-you-sweat school of thought anyway.

A few minutes later the door opened, and the big detective entered, followed by Josh, who had showered and changed into slacks and a button-down shirt, open at the throat. With a sense of utter disconnect, she recognized Father Barnabas trailing both of them.

She wondered if Josh had come as friend or foe, but dismissed his presence as irrelevant either way. Of the three, Father Barnabas was the only man who would meet her eyes. Shame rolled through her at the knowledge that the priest was going to witness her at her worst. Heat flooded her face, and she fought the urge to hang her head.

"Och, Miss Opal McBride, 'tis a fine mess you're in." He greeted her with cheery compassion, as if she'd been hauled in for jaywalking instead of assault with intent to kill.

Tears sprang to her eyes at his blunt kindness. She managed a nod in his direction, wanting nothing more than to throw herself at him and weep.

"This meeting is subject to the same Miranda rights that I read to you earlier." The gruff detective lowered himself into a chair. "You want an attorney?"

She didn't know if the lawyers here were any better or less overworked than the loser she'd drawn the first time around, but she nodded. "I do." Shooting a wary glance at Josh, she added, "I won't get a court-appointed one until tomorrow, though."

Josh cleared his throat. "I've called our family lawyer for you. He'll be here in about ten minutes."

Opal stared at him. Had she heard him right? "I can't afford him."

A muscle jumped in his jaw. "It's on my dime." He ducked his head so she couldn't see his expression, but a flush darkened the skin of his cheeks.

She knew him well enough to recognize embarrassment in his body language. It confused her. After their last encounter, Opal couldn't fathom why he had showed up again, or why he was offering resources.

"*Now* you're going to stick up for me?" She couldn't stop the words. "A little late, aren't you?"

The big guy made an abrupt motion, indicating the chairs. "Everybody sit. McBride, Detective Boone is on administrative leave until Internal Affairs sorts this out."

Opal's legs gave way and she sat in the nearest chair. "I don't understand." The words came out as little more than a whisper. Was there going to be no end to the damage she caused this family?

Father Barnabas took the chair next to her and rested a hand on her shoulder. "Have faith, Opal." He patted her twice, then removed his hand at the big detective's glower. "Sorry, Detective Hasselback," he said, with no repentance in his tone.

Hasselback. Josh's partner. Opal remembered him from her first day at Beans & Leaves. The pieces began to settle into place. He was the one who'd answered the phone the other night when she'd left the message. No wonder he had been so angry at the shop, so unwilling to listen.

Josh settled across from her. She lifted her gaze to his, ready for a heavy dose of censure. But he just looked miserable.

A lump the size of Mount Rushmore lodged in her throat. Terrified of the answer, she asked, "How's May?"

"There's some kind of scale they use to determine the depth of a coma. Her numbers show she's moving toward regaining consciousness." Josh rotated his head and rubbed his neck as he spoke. "They hope to move her out of ICU tomorrow."

Tension flowed out of Opal, and she slumped in relief. "Thank God." Her words were heartfelt, and Father Barnabas chuckled.

Hasselback spoke. "Detective Boone says you've been employed at Stitches in Time for several months."

Opal straightened. "Yes." She refrained from adding that she would have told him that this morning if he would have listened.

A knock sounded, and a man in a suit entered. Josh stood and shook his hand. "Thanks for coming, Ray." He turned to Opal. "This is your new client, Opal McBride."

"My pleasure," Ray said, and extended his hand across the table.

"Sir." Opal shook his hand awkwardly, her left hand dangling uselessly from the handcuffs. A spurt of nervousness made her mouth dry.

Detective Hasselback swiveled and skewered Josh with a glare. "Why'd you hide this from all of us?"

Ray whatever-his-last-name-was flicked a finger at Josh. "No comment."

Josh looked like he'd been ready to engage in a verbal war, but closed his mouth. He dipped his head and stared at the table.

Hasselback sighed. "Well then, McBride, tell me your version of what happened today."

This time she couldn't help letting a little attitude slip through. "I told you, at the shop. But since you've got such a short memory, I'll repeat it." She smiled sweetly—totally phony, and they both knew it—then recounted the events. Again. Clearly. Crisply. Ray didn't interrupt her.

Josh shifted and looked at Hasselback. "For the record, that's exactly what she told me, but you know that, because you were on the other side of the one-way."

Hasselback flattened his lips, which emphasized his jowls and made him look even more like a bulldog. "Yes, but you know I needed to get her statement with her lawyer present." The two detectives exchanged a tension-filled look. He shrugged. "If Mrs. Boone corroborates this information, and if we can track down this Viper character—or match the prints on the gun with a name—then McBride is off the hook for assault."

Hope flickered in Opal's heart.

"But I can't do anything about the consequences of her arrest in regard to parole." The big detective didn't sound particularly remorseful, a lot like Father Barnabas hadn't a few minutes earlier.

"I'll work on that." Ray faced Opal. "You should be out on bail tomorrow."

She knew hope was written all over her face now.

Hasselback shoved his bulk out of his chair. "I've got all I need for now. Y'all can stay and consult." He lumbered out of the room without a backward glance.

Josh's gaze followed him, then returned to Opal. "I owe you an apology."

For the first time since he'd entered the room, he let her see his eyes. Dark with regret, shame also lurked in their depths. "I'm sorry I didn't believe you from the first. I know better, and I have no excuse. *Mea culpa.*" He placed his right hand over his heart. "Mea maxima culpa."

Opal didn't know any Latin, but it was easy to figure out what he meant. Emotion churned in her gut. Josh clearly meant the words with every cell of his body, yet the wound of his betrayal still cut deep. Part of her wanted to make him hurt as badly as she did, but at a deeper level, she knew he'd struck out at her in the very human reaction of trying to assign blame in the face of catastrophe.

Heck, she'd done it herself for a few months after she'd gotten to prison. There had been plenty of folks to blame. The county for its heavy-handed social services that destroyed her life with Granny McBride. Sheriff Beuhly's legally sanctioned lynching. And Tommy, of course, especially once time and education had opened her eyes to the reality of his abuse.

But over time Opal had come to understand—and accept—her own part in the tragedy that stole Skye's life and her freedom. Inadvertent as it had been, she had robbed Tommy of life.

She had stopped viewing herself as a victim long ago. To the marrow of her bones, Opal knew if she refused Josh's apology, she would again don that label, this time of her own volition.

The idea made her shudder with revulsion.

Besides, the burden of May's injury went far beyond any payback Opal could bring herself to heap upon Josh.

He started to extend a hand to her but caught himself. "I'm sorry. I'll do anything in my power to make it up to you."

Opal longed to reach across the table and touch him, longed to comfort him Longed for him to comfort her, and for this breach of trust between them to be healed.

So she let the resentment flow away. Her throat tight, she said, "Accepted."

Relief flooded his face and washed a layer of tension away.

Father Barnabas nodded, but remained silent. Ray stood and addressed Josh. "Remember, no contact with May until Detective Hasselback interviews her."

Josh's face tightened. "I know."

"And once Miss McBride is released, it would be best if any contact the two of you have is witnessed by someone, until the IA investigation is over."

Josh glanced at her, his expression now guarded, like he wasn't sure how she felt about resuming contact with him, and nodded his understanding to Ray. The lawyer stood and headed out, leaving Josh, Father Barnabas, and Opal.

The sound of the door closing echoed in the stark room.

Father Barnabas broke the silence, his lilting voice gentle. "Josh told me much of what he witnessed in Jubilee. I would be honored to offer the blessing of the church to you, a healing rite that is more effective than what we as mere mortals are able to do on our own or for each other."

Opal blinked. "Um, I don't understand."

"My dear, the Jews have a tradition that goes back many millennia. Every seven years, their tradition calls for blanket forgiveness of debt and rancor. But each fiftieth year is a year of jubilee."

"I thought the name meant joy…"

"It does. Jubilee is a time of celebration when people receive their property back, and slaves go free." He waited for her to absorb his words.

"So…you're offering a prayer that frees me?" The idea held great appeal for her, whether she ever made it out from behind bars or not. Touched at his concern and willingness to pray for her, she asked, "Is there any catch? Like, I'm not Catholic. Do you get in trouble for doing this?"

Father Barnabas threw his head back and laughed. Even Josh cracked a smile. Opal relaxed a little.

"No, I never get in trouble for praying for anyone." He sobered. "But I would like you to recognize the extent of the prayer. If you lay out the guilt you carry over not being able to do better for Granny McBride—"

She shot a look at Josh. Had he told Father Barnabas everything? Josh met her gaze with calm reassurance, and made a *listen to him* motion with his head.

"—for not being able to save Skye—"

Her gaze flew to Josh again. He had. Even Skye's name. Hope bubbled up, overflowing in her heart, even though she didn't fully understand what was going on.

"—and for harming Tommy—"

Opal interrupted. "For not being able to protect May."

Father Barnabas smiled, a gentle curve of his lips. "Yes, that too. For all these transgressions that you've carried as your responsibility, and for all that you've charged yourself guilty of."

She nodded, her heart swelling.

He lifted his hands and placed them on her head, murmuring a prayer that included words like *absolved* and *forgiven* and *peace*.

Opal was too overcome with emotion to catch all of them, but she suddenly, inexplicably felt a thousand pounds lighter. Even the handcuffs encircling her wrists and the concrete separating her from sunshine and fresh air couldn't contain her sense of freedom. Tears coursed down her face, but she made no move to wipe them away.

Father Barnabas removed his hands after a long moment. "Go in peace, Opal McBride." He stood. "Do you have more to say, Josh?"

Josh nodded. He leaned across the table and wiped her face with a delicate touch that felt every bit the benediction that Father Barnabas had just bestowed. "I'm sorry I was an ass yesterday, Opal. If you'll forgive me, I'd…" He cleared his throat. "Let me start over. Yesterday was me being stupid and selfish. I don't handle surprises well." He rubbed his thumb across her lips, and her traitorous body sparked in response to his touch.

Her eyes drifted closed. "It doesn't matter, Josh. Let it go. I have." The memories of more passionate touches warmed her blood even as she quashed them. No use in torturing herself with dreams beyond her reach.

"Look at me, sweetheart."

The endearment surprised her, and she opened her eyes to find him regarding her with gentleness. "I didn't realize how much you mean to me until"—his voice broke and his eyes clouded—"until you walked out on me today."

A click of the door brought the jailer in. "Sir, regulations—"

"Yeah." Josh dropped his hand and sat. A wave of frustration crossed his face before he replaced it with cautious hope.

The guard sent him a pointed look, then withdrew.

"Even a few hours without you in my life, at my side…" He shook his head as though the remainder of the thought didn't bear contemplating. Then he lifted his gaze and captured hers. "What I'm trying to say is, will you marry me?"

Opal blinked. Father Barnabas and the drab concrete walls faded into the background, Josh's earnest and vulnerable expression commanding all her attention. *Marriage?*

"You don't have to answer now. And the timing is up to you." Suddenly he looked uncertain. "That is, if you'll have me."

"Oh, Josh…" Her heart filled with tenderness even as sadness rolled through her. "You can't mean that."

He placed his hands on the table, palms up. "Yes, I do mean it." His eyes darkened with intensity. Unguarded and open, he laid himself open to her scrutiny.

She shook her head before he finished speaking, cut to her core with the vulnerability he refused to hide. Opal's mind flashed to the hours they had spent talking over the past number of weeks, their deepening friendship cultivating a sense within her of no longer being alone. His attention had flattered and confused her, but never had she imagined this eventuality. Never. She scrambled to wrap her mind around his about-face, but the tsunami of events and emotions over the past day and a half had dulled her thinking. She finally settled on the only common factor that tied it all together.

"You're reacting out of guilt over your mom, Josh." When he made to deny it, she put up a hand. "Your job is on the line too. You're too unsettled to even think about decisions like this, much less make them, or act on them." Her heart felt physically heavy in her chest as she stated what should be obvious to him. "Besides, I'm the root cause of all your ills right now." Opal clamped her lips over the next words. The ones that said *You're crazy.* Instead, with a mixture of longing and regret, she said, "I'm not the woman you need for a wife."

Before he could mount a defense or a debate, she stood. She turned to Father Barnabas, who regarded both of them with an expression that saw beneath the surface, and said, "Thank you, from the bottom of my heart."

Opal didn't want to face Josh, but he'd gone out of his way and paid from his own pocket to help her even as he saw to May's care. She met his gaze and flinched at the devastation in his eyes. He looked as bereft as she felt.

"Thank you." Her throat closed over her pledge to pay him back over time, which he would likely refuse anyway, and she strode to the door.

The corrections officer grasped her arm in the oh-so-familiar grip of authority, and Opal fought to drive away the memory of Josh's first touch, that day when he'd thrown her out of May's shop.

He had been right.

May should never have hired her. Her boss, the kindest woman she'd known since Granny McBride, would be home, happily fixing supper or bouncing Caleb on her knee instead of hovering between life and death.

But Opal couldn't regret meeting May, or the joy she'd found in the Boone family.

Including Josh.

Father Barnabas's blessing floated into her mind as she followed the guard's lead back to her cell. Granny McBride's voice came right behind it. Between the priest's assurance of forgiveness and Granny's pithy *Don't waste time cryin' over spilt milk, girlie,* Opal blinked back self-pitying tears and replaced them with a watery smile.

As the officer removed her shackles and deposited her in the cell, Opal's aching heart returned to Josh's much warmer touches from the recent past, then to his proposal.

Tommy had never asked. He'd just assumed they'd go to the courthouse on her sixteenth birthday and say their vows in front of the justice of the peace.

If a girl only got one proper proposal of marriage in her life, this one had to be at the top of the pack in terms of oddness. She allowed herself to dream—just for a moment—of an earnest child, chin in hand and bent on an answer.

Tell me about how Daddy proposed, Mommy! She pictured a boy with Josh's dark hair and her green eyes, mostly so she wouldn't dwell on Skye's memory while within these walls.

A hiccupping half laugh, half sob caught her by surprise, and she buried her face in drawn-up knees. *Well, honey, Mommy was in jail and Daddy was out of a job, and our lives had just fallen apart. He asked me in front of a priest, with a guard on the other side of the door…*

Opal gave way to tears, because she knew without a doubt that her answer would have been, *Yes, a thousand times yes.*

If only…

If only Josh had said he loved her.

Chapter Thirty-Seven

"Any change?" Josh eased himself in the door of May's room, his voice pitched low. There was no way he could honor Ray's caution for no contact with his mom, not until she was out of the woods, anyway. Sitting at the bedside of an unconscious witness wouldn't jeopardize Opal's case. Besides, with Ray at Opal's back, Josh doubted Chris even needed his mother's statement.

His heart felt bruised. He couldn't remember leaving Metro Corrections or the ten-minute drive to the hospital, a telling indication of his level of stress. Apparently he had done okay on autopilot, as he'd arrived in one piece and without a citation for running stop lights.

Jenn looked up, her features drawn and hair tangled from napping in the recliner next to the hospital bed. She unlaced her fingers from their mother's hand and tugged her shirt into place as she sat up. Dark smudges rested beneath her eyes.

"She's stable, but hasn't woken up yet. Dad will land between eleven and midnight." She yawned.

"Go on home. I'll take the next shift." He refrained from telling her she looked like shit, mostly because she would return the sentiment in spades, and then badger him about Opal. He shoved the image of Opal turning her back on him for the second time in one day, this time choosing incarceration over him. That prompted memories of his almost-wedding day to burble like bad sushi.

The weight of his failure to stand up for Opal either yesterday or today was what made bile rise, though. Now he'd lost her because of his cowardice and stupidity.

No wonder. Why would she entertain marriage to such a man? Viewing himself in that unflattering light made him squirm, prompting a vision of another soul-baring visit to Father Barney's confessional. Not that absolution would repair the emptiness in his heart.

"Do you need to grab something to eat or a cup of coffee before I go?" Jenn stood, an automatic stretch taking over as soon as she was upright.

Josh shook his head. He didn't think he could keep anything down. Not until his mother turned the corner, and even then, trying to force food past the boulder of guilt in his chest loomed as an impossible feat.

Jenn picked up her purse and slung it over her shoulder, then impulsively put her arms around him and squeezed. Her hug warmed him a little, but didn't touch the gaping hole that Opal's rejection had left. He returned the embrace, then set his sister away from him.

"Get. Caleb needs you." Josh turned her toward the door. She slipped free of his hands and reversed direction, leaning over to give May a kiss. Then she left, taking care to latch the door with a barely audible click.

Josh nudged the recliner away from the bedside and replaced it with a chair. He sat, then reached through the side rails to grasp May's hand, reassured by the warmth of her skin despite the utter stillness of her features. Her chest rose and fell, but that was her only movement. He rested his forehead on the rail, listening to the hypnotic beep of the heart monitor.

Long moments passed as Josh tried to dredge up a prayer, but mere words could not express the depth of his emotions. He'd given passing thought to the eventual deaths of his parents, but it had always been a vague abstraction, even when he'd been so intent on keeping Opal out of May's life.

But this…this silent shell in place of the vibrant, lively person he loved terrified him. It dwarfed Opal's rebuff, as final—and gentle—as it had been. Even the ignominy of being under investigation by Internal Affairs and on administrative leave didn't take up much real estate in his emotional landscape, although it added to its general bleakness.

Mom, you have to pull through. He closed his eyes, too drained to think anymore. The room took on the quality of a cocoon. An oasis in the swirling, unsettling events of the day. He may have dozed. An undetermined amount of time later, the swish of the door opening brought him out of his stupor. He rotated his head and peered though gritty and raw eyes, expecting to see a nurse.

Instead, Chris's bulk filled the doorway.

Josh dropped his head into the hand not entwined with May's. "I thought we were done." Chris's livid interrogation of the afternoon still stung, and his appearance in May's room was like sandpaper on Josh's already wounded psyche.

Chris let the door fall shut, and the room closed in on Josh.

"Is she any better?" His partner's voice carried concern underlaid with belligerence.

"No." Josh lifted his head and glared at Chris. "Your part here is finished. I'll let you know when Mom's able to talk to you." He bit back words of anger, knowing he'd betrayed Chris at least as badly as the man had hurt him. Maybe worse.

"I don't think so." Chris shook his head, looking like a bear shaking water from his fur. "It's time you and me cleared the air."

This time Josh heard the pain beneath the man's bluster. It was an arrow to his heart. His shoulders slumped in defeat. His throat constricted as he placed his mom's hand on the sheet. "Let's take this out into the hall."

A glance at the array of machines gave him logical reassurance that he could step away from her bedside, and he forced himself to ignore the irrational sense that if he left her alone, her life force would fail.

He motioned for Chris to precede him. He wasn't taking any chances on her overhearing what was likely to be a blistering conversation. One of the nurses had mentioned that hearing was the last sense lost and the first recovered when a patient was unconscious. Much of their exchange would center around Opal, and he respected the women's relationship too much to allow anyone to sully it in his mother's presence.

He made sure the door was latched, then moved a few feet toward the quiet end of the hall. "Say your piece then, Chris, and get it over with." He shoved his hands into his pockets and faced his partner.

"Why didn't you tell *me*?" Bewilderment showed in his Chris's eyes, and he splayed his hands in palms-out entreaty.

Josh's gut twisted. He swallowed past the sudden lump in his throat. He hadn't meant to damage their friendship, but he had.

"How could I?" Josh let his partner see his own vulnerability, suddenly tired of trying to save face. "We're cops. We arrest people like Opal." He strove to find the words to explain the tangle of conflicting emotions and obligations his life had become. "She's... She's just not what we…what I thought." He shoved a hand through his hair.

"Did she hoodwink you, man?" Chris raised a beefy hand and pointed at Josh. "'Cause you seem pretty bewitched."

"No." Josh's anger flared at the implications. "IA is going to do the digging here. You don't have to. Not your job."

"Not my job, but you're my buddy. My partner." His already florid face went a shade deeper. He dropped his arm to his side. "I deserve the truth."

Silence hung between them. Josh's neck heated in a flush that crept past his jaw and warmed his cheeks. He forced the tension out of his shoulders.

"No, she didn't hoodwink me. We went through everything this afternoon. My trips to Jubilee, the state police investigation. She didn't want anything to do with it. I'm the one who pushed." He held his hands out in a mirror of Chris's earlier gesture. "In terms of IA, there's nothing to tell. We met after she got off work a number of times, went to late-night diners. We walked. Talked."

"You banging her?" Chris jutted his chin out, his eyes glittering and dangerous.

Josh's temper flashed. "None of your damn business." The words came out in a near snarl and he curled his hands into fists. "Don't you *ever* speak about Opal like that."

Chris sneered. "Why not? It's not like she's pure as the driven snow."

Fury propelled Josh toward Chris, his fist darting out with a punishing jab. Chris blocked the punch, and Josh grabbed the front of his shirt instead, backing him into the wall with a muffled thud.

"She's a better person than you know." Josh's breath heaved in and out of his lungs like bellows. "The legal eagles will sort out their part. You've got no place as judge or jury." He sent his partner a deep-six look, his heart hollow at the knowledge that Opal wasn't going to be part of his life. But that didn't dampen his need to come to her defense. The awareness of his loss sharpened it.

A nurse hurried down the hall from the centralized station, alarm on her face and her body language determined.

The prospect of further confrontation made Josh's stomach churn. Disgusted with himself and at Chris, and pissed off over the whole situation, he added, "None of us can claim holier-than-thou status." He forced himself to release his grip and step back.

The nurse slowed. "Do I need to call security, gentlemen?"

"No, ma'am." Josh slipped his hands into his pockets, a truly stupid move if Chris decided to throw a punch of his own.

Chris's gaze flicked toward the nurse and he relaxed his posture. She watched them for a moment longer, then retreated with a look of warning. Chris returned his focus to Josh as he shrugged his shirt straight. His lips went flat before he spoke. "Yeah, well, everybody's gonna want to know. You want me on your side or not?"

Josh wondered if it mattered anymore. His reputation was already in shreds, even though IA would clear him. He uncurled his fingers one by one. Though their friendship had taken a body blow today, he recognized the olive branch Chris was offering via his inimitable gruffness.

He inhaled. On the exhale he said, "Yes, I want you on my side. No, I'm not"—he couldn't use the crude terminology that came so easily to Chris—"having sex with Opal." A muscle began to tic in his cheek.

Chris scowled as if assessing Josh's veracity, then gave him an abrupt nod. "Talk to you tomorrow, then." He pivoted and strode down the hall, leaving Josh frustrated and oddly reassured.

He returned to his mother's bedside, hating how helpless he felt and knowing he'd lost Opal through his own blind fear. His defense of her dignity had come far too late. *Mea culpa.*

It seemed he said that a lot where Opal was concerned.

Chapter Thirty-Eight

Opal stood in front of the door to May's room. She'd come straight to the hospital after Ray had arranged for her release. Finding the hospitals had been easy, but with several packed into a few square blocks, it had taken her three stops to get directions to the one she wanted. Overwhelmed by the sheer size of the building, the maze once she entered nearly sent her back out the door. But her need to know May's condition lent strength to her resolve.

Voices murmured inside, and she strained to differentiate them, but they were too low. Gathering her courage, she pressed a hand to the door and lifted the latch with the other.

The first person she saw was Jacob. He lay in a recliner, asleep in his pilot uniform, which was surprisingly unwrinkled for having been slept in. Embarrassment flashed through Opal, because she hadn't taken the two or three hours it would have taken for her to get to her apartment, shower, change, and return. *Her* clothes were rumpled, and though she'd been in segregation, carried the unique odor of incarceration. Concern for May overrode her hesitation, though, and she slipped partway into the room.

Josh stood with his back to the door, leaning over May. The rumble of his baritone provided a soothing counterpoint to his mother's melodious soprano. Opal's heart soared. *May is awake!* Relief flooded her. Light-headedness followed on its heels, and she tightened her fingers on the door, needing it to steady her.

Opal took in a shaky breath and began to ease back into the hallway. During the long hours of the night, she had decided to cut ties with the Boone family. She ignored the stab of pain it gave her, but for their sakes, she needed to be out of their lives.

She'd gotten the door an inch from closed when someone snatched it out of her grip from the other side. Shock rooted her in place, and she lifted her gaze. *Josh.*

Opal couldn't read his state of mind, just that his eyes were shuttered. Even so, she could see pain lurking in their depths. More than anything, she wanted to lift her hand to his cheek and offer comfort. Her heart, already shattered, broke a little more.

"Mom will want to see you." Simple words, a wealth of emotion in his voice.

And you? Do you want to see me? Opal turned, letting the strands of hair that had worked free of its braid hide her face. "I c-can't."

Josh stopped her with a hand on her arm.

"Yes, you can." His touch was gentle, as tender as it had been last night, in spite of the words she'd thrown at him before leaving.

She turned to face him and searched his eyes. "Please tell her I love her"—her voice trembled and she pressed her lips together to keep from weeping—"and that you're all better off without me."

Josh's expression softened. "No, we're not. I, especially, am not better off without you." He drew her a step closer, close enough that he could pull her into his embrace. "I need you. I thought I'd lost you last night, and I'll do anything to get you to reconsider."

The temptation to lean into his arms and to rest her head on his shoulders nearly brought Opal to her knees. Instead, she pressed her palms to his chest, greedy for the comfort of his heartbeat, yet knowing she had to let him go. For his own good. Even if it was the hardest thing she ever had to do.

She shook her head.

"Who's out there, Josh?" May's voice floated through the air, and Opal heard a rustle from the recliner.

Her stomach clenched.

Jacob appeared behind Josh. "It's Opal!" His eyes lit up and he opened the door. "Come in, come in."

Trapped, Opal straightened, though Josh didn't let her break free from his touch.

"May." Her vocal cords threatened to strangle the word. A nudge from Josh propelled her across the floor. When she got to the bed, tears made her vision waver.

"I'm fine, dear, thanks to you." May opened her arms and Opal fell into them, knowing it was going to be so much harder to leave now, but desperate for the love May offered without reservation. "There, there, don't cry."

"No, it's all my fault you got hurt." Opal broke into noisy sobs, vaguely aware of someone patting her on the back.

"For heaven's sake! You saved both of us with your courage, although the risk you took nearly gave me a heart attack. I told Chris how brave you were when he stopped in this morning, how you tackled that woman and took the gun away."

"Opal." Josh cleared his throat. "Could I speak with you, please?"

She disentangled herself from May's hug and stood, swiping her tears away with the back of her hands.

"Before we get into all that, I need to say something." His gaze warmed. "I had a lot of time to think last night. Not only was I an idiot"—his eyes flicked to his parents and back to Opal, a slight lift of his lips letting her know he'd chosen a tamer word than he'd used the first time he'd apologized—"but I left out the most important part."

He took her hands in his. Her heart gave a little skip of… Of what? Anxiety? Anticipation? The thrill that his touch always elicited in her?

"I love you, Opal McBride."

The air whooshed out of her lungs, and for the third time in ten minutes, her knees threatened to give way.

Love. Marriage. All that she'd believed herself unworthy of a few months ago. Children, and a family of her own, with the right man.

And the right man was standing in front of her, his eyes full of love, full of tenderness.

"Why?" Her mind stuttered to a standstill. Was it out of gratitude because she'd stopped Viper? Or did he really mean it?

Josh shook his head, his expression baffled, yet at peace. "Because you are who you are. Because you make me feel alive. Because I like *you*, and because I like who I am when I'm with you."

He tugged her into his embrace again and rested his cheek on her head. "Please say yes this time, Opal."

She listened to the steady thump of his heart, calmed by his nearness and knowing what his next words were going to be.

"Will you marry me?"

The words were whisper soft, meant for her ears only.

Yes. Yes, a thousand times yes, if only he'd say he loves me.

He'd said it, with his parents as witness.

"We'll work through all the rest, Opal. Together. It'll be okay. You don't have to be afraid anymore, and you don't have to go it alone." He went silent, waiting for her answer.

Yes. Yes, a thousand times yes, if only…

She lifted her gaze to meet his again. Could she trust this man to keep his word? To stand by her? Did she want to stand by him for the rest of her life?

His gaze searched hers, and searched her soul. He asked the question again, this time silently, with his eyes.

An image of her future without Josh flashed through her mind. She would succeed on her own, but the loss of his companionship tarnished the shine of any achievements she might accomplish. Quick on the thought's heels, a related insight followed.

If she rebuffed his proposal this time, she risked losing much of the peace that Father Barnabas's blessing had conferred. She had agreed to forgive herself, but suddenly understood that meant she shouldn't settle for the little she'd been allowed over the years. Forgiving herself carried a responsibility to reach higher, to stretch farther. To accept the gifts of love and family Josh offered.

Yes. Yes, a thousand times yes.

Her lips curled into a smile of their own volition. "Yes, Joshua Braddock Boone." Then louder, "Yes."

His face lit with joy. He tunneled one hand into her hair, but Opal beat him to the kiss, lifting herself up on her toes to meet his lips.

She didn't know the details beyond the moment, but she knew she'd come home.

Epilogue

A FRESH WAVE of pressure gathered in Opal's back, then cascaded around to her belly. She took a deep breath and let it out, and Josh leaned over to give her a quick kiss before he dug into his assigned task of rubbing her lower back.

"You're doing great, Opal." Josh's murmured encouragement helped her stay focused, and she squeezed his free hand as the contraction gathered strength.

"Are you sure you don't want an epidural, dear?" May's concerned face swam into view as the contraction eased.

"Nope." Opal had been in labor for several hours, and had spent much of her time absorbing as many details as she could. It would be a long time before she attained her goal of becoming a nurse midwife, but she considered this a great opportunity for on-the-job training. She grinned at May. "I want to experience the baby's birth. As completely as I can."

She didn't mention to her beloved mother-in-law that she needed to do this naturally—if possible—as a tribute to Skye. Josh understood Opal's thinking, which she couldn't even articulate clearly to him, much less anyone else.

Another contraction began, much sooner than the last, and as it bore down on her, much stronger. The nurse checked her and announced the birth was imminent, and left to alert the nurse midwife.

Opal's concentration narrowed to the work of bringing her child into the world. Josh supported her back as she pushed, and May leaned in with a damp cloth for her brow. The midwife arrived, and coached her through the final, intense stages. Then, with one more mighty push, she felt the baby's head slip out.

She looked in the mirror. "Hair. Lots." It was impossible to tell what color yet, and the infant made a face as its nose and mouth got suctioned.

"Once more, Opal." The midwife applied gentle pressure as Opal pushed with the last contraction, and suddenly her belly deflated.

"It's a boy!" The baby let loose a surprisingly deep cry as the midwife stood and placed him on Opal's chest.

"Oh!" Her eyes swam with tears. "Hello there, Jamieson. It's your mommy." She glanced up at Josh. "And your daddy."

He touched his son's cheek, and the baby immediately turned toward his hand, mouth open, seeking a nipple. They both burst into laughter and then May was there too, tears trickling down her face.

Unfettered joy warmed Opal. Her heart swelled, thinking of the past year and a half. She'd been blessed with all that she'd believed to be lost to her.

Family. May and Jacob had become surrogate parents and she loved them with all her heart. Jenn and Charlie, the siblings she never had. Caleb, a grounding force to remind her of the simplicity in life when she forgot. And Josh, her friend, her champion, her lover.

Faith. Father Barney, as she'd finally become accustomed to calling him, was a constant, full of blunt advice when appropriate and compassion when needed—and unshakable faith, always. He'd married them nearly a year ago, and would baptize Jamieson as soon as Opal was out of the hospital. A beacon for her, Father Barney had introduced her to a God of mercy rather than condemnation. As a result, Opal had been able to view Sheriff Beuhly, Obadiah, and even Tommy with similar clemency. God's justice would prevail. Meanwhile, it wasn't her place to judge. Great peace of mind had been her reward.

Friendship. Josh and Chris Hasselback had repaired their friendship, and Opal had discovered that the man's gruff exterior masked a heart of gold. Even so, she was grateful to be on his good side. The two men had combined forces to find Viper, who was back in prison, and along with Warden Phipps, had crippled Shaniqua's influence in the gang. Best, Opal had begun to explore the gift of friendships with other women, May and Jenn leading the way—and had discovered they had far more in common than not, in spite of her unconventional history.

Freedom. Sheriff Beuhly was mired in a legal battle over his illegal suppression of evidence and threats to Widow Reese. The case had taken time to build and would come to trial in a few months. Meanwhile, based on the evidence Trooper Nelson had amassed, the governor was set to pardon Opal. Soon, she hoped. She wanted to raise her son with a clean record.

She reached up and pulled Josh down for a kiss. The flash of a camera startled her, and she broke the kiss to peer at May.

"Your first family portrait," her mother-in-law said, holding her camera aloft.

Josh squeezed Opal's hand. "The first of many."

Opal rested her head on the pillow and smiled at her husband. Jamieson rooted for her breast, and she shifted her gown to accommodate him. He latched on and sucked with such vigor that she jumped.

A wave of gratitude washed through her for all she'd been given.

She stroked Jamieson's head. Her personal jubilee would continue to bear the fruit of a life well lived, a life full of hope. A life filled with love, fierce and tender, and above all, healing.

Opal tugged Josh close, lifting her face so she could kiss him again. "The first of many," she said, not caring whether she was agreeing with the proliferation of photographs or children.

Or maybe, simply happy moments.

Of those, she had no doubt.

On Writing This Book

Opal's Jubilee was inspired by pardons granted by then-Governor Ernie Fletcher of Kentucky on his last day of office in 2007. The controversial move granted clemency, pardons, or early parole reviews to twenty-one women who had been convicted of murder or attempted murder after experiencing years of domestic abuse.

To the best of my knowledge, none of the women have returned to prison.

Acknowledgments

I would like to express deep gratitude to:

Critique partners Caroline Fyffe, Sandy Loyd, Angie Ballard, and Lisa Tapp. Thank you for your generous gift of time and your wise advice as this book took shape.

Pam Berehulke, whose editorial guidance (and friendship) is irreplaceable.

Members of Louisville Romance Writers and the 2013 Golden Heart finalists (known as the Lucky 13s, or Luckies): Your support is vital on this sometimes daunting journey.

Staff and volunteers of the greater Louisville area's Center for Women and Families who, along with tireless advocates everywhere, provide education, resources, and support for all caught in the cycle of abuse. The training I received as a volunteer advocate found its home in the writing of *Hijacked*, *Unholy Bonds*, and *Opal's Jubilee*.

Priests and religious leaders who exhibit Father Barnabas's humor, candor, and compassion. The Opals of the world need you.

On a personal level, gratitude (and more) to:
My family, for your unwavering love and support.
My husband, for everything.
I love you.

About the Author

Leslie Lynch gives voice to characters who struggle to find healing for their brokenness—and discover unconventional solutions to life's unexpected twists.

Leslie lives near Louisville, Kentucky, with her husband and her adult children's cats. While not engaged in wrestling the beautiful and prolific greenery of their yard into submission, she flies as a volunteer for the Civil Air Patrol, loves the exuberant creativity and color of quilting and pottery…and, of course, writes.

You can find her at:

Website: www.leslielynch.com
Facebook: Leslie Lynch Writes
Twitter: @Leslie_Lynch_